REPLAY

A SPORTS ROMANCE NOVEL

AMY DAWS

REPLAY

CHAPTER 1

Tilly

"HOW'S THAT GOWN FITTING?" AN AMERICAN ACCENT CALLS through the thick curtain of my dressing room.

"Erm...I'm still naked," I reply as I pull the dress off the hanger.

"Sorry, I'm just really excited," the person that I can now identify as Leslie Clarke answers back. "You're Freya's sister-in-law, which means you're a VIP and have to look gorgeous for this charity gala on Friday."

I cringe and try to shake away my guilt over Freya's friend's generosity. "You really didn't have to go to all this trouble. I could have just popped over to Primark and found something cheap and easy," I add as I struggle to slip the dress on.

"Blasphemy!" Leslie squeals back. "Sloan! Tilly Logan is speaking blasphemy in our shop."

Sloan Harris' voice cuts through the fabric curtain next, also another American. "Your brother is excited to show you off to his football friends, so you need to feel gorgeous."

1

My nose twitches with nerves because this event will be my first proper night out since arriving in London three weeks ago. I'm here indefinitely helping my brother, Mac, and his wife, Freya, because Freya was restricted to bed rest with her pregnancy midway through her second trimester. It's an ordeal as she's right in the middle of selling her trendy line of pet clothing to a major department store and can't exactly delay the negotiations.

Thankfully, I have a master's in business retail and a fair bit of experience from my time working in London over five years ago. I was a buyer at Fortnum and Mason and climbing the corporate ladder before…well…before I decided to move back home to Scotland. But now I'm back and here to help Freya in any way she needs me. And that apparently includes taking her place at a football charity gala this Friday. Therefore, I needed a dress, and Freya's best mates who own this fabulous high-end boutique in east London were all too willing to whisk me away for a makeover.

"Just pretend you're Cinderella, and we're your fairy godmothers!" Leslie adds excitedly, pulling me out of my inner musings.

My nose wrinkles at that remark. I actually hate the whole concept of a fairy godmother. The fairy tale should have been Cinderella freeing herself, making her own damn dress, and walking her arse to the ball all on her own.

Perhaps that's the Scottish in me. We tend to solve our own problems and find our own way. Though if a friend in need asked me for help, I'd drop everything in a heartbeat. Hence, why I moved here from Scotland to help out my brother and his wife.

Sloan's voice interrupts my thoughts. "Even with all the celebrities we've styled in here, there is still nothing better than styling a friend of the family."

"It helps when that friend of the family is six feet tall with the body of a model." Leslie laughs. "Come on, Tilly. We're dying out here!"

"I'm coming!" I push back the curtain and find a brunette and a redhead gawking at me. Though Leslie's hair is that lush auburn colour. Far more gorgeous than my shade of red.

"Good God, we're geniuses," Leslie states with her lips parted.

"You're a genius…I only helped a little," Sloan volleys back, and the two high-five each other.

"Is it good?" I ask nervously. "I can't believe you guys don't have mirrors in your changing rooms."

"Because we want you to see yourself in the best lighting." Leslie grabs my hand and escorts me over to a round pedestal centred between three-way mirrors. "Reality is ninety percent lighting and ten percent camera angles."

"Is that a good thing?" I inquire, stepping up onto the platform. My eyes shift to the mirror and I gasp in astonishment.

If this is some kind of trick lighting, then *God bless it* because I look dead brilliant.

The dress is a long, metallic mermaid gown that hugs every inch of my body. I usually don't love silver as it can sometimes wash out my fair complexion and make my strawberry blond hair look redder than it is, but this gown is way too gorgeous to give a shit about that. And it magically manages to accentuate my very minimal curves, which is a feat in and of itself. I've always been the tall and gangly type. My granddad used to call me Spider when I was wee because I was all arms and legs. I've filled out a bit in my hips now that I've hit my thirties, but am still flat-chested compared to the two beautiful women beside me. I used to sleep with a Scottish lad in my early twenties who called my tits "empire biscuits" because he said they were only good for a nibble.

He was a cunt.

Most of the men from my past were cunts. I wasn't exactly making the best life choices back then.

Freya's best friend, Allie, appears on the other side of me, staring at my reflection in the mirror as she clutches the cutest baby I've ever seen to her hip. She voices the third American accent I've heard today. "Sloan, Leslie…you've outdone yourselves. Tilly, you look hot to trot."

"Is *that* a good thing?" I repeat with a laugh.

"Very good," Leslie confirms.

I shake my head in astonishment. Mac and Freya's friends always say exactly what's on their minds. I've met them all a handful of times for various events. The first time was a couple of years ago when they came up to Scotland with Mac for our village Highland Games. It was a joint bachelor/bachelorette trip for Allie, who was marrying Mac's teammate and best friend, Roan DeWalt. As I glance at the adorable baby on her hip, it's clear those two have been busy since I last saw them.

Allie retracts a piece of her long golden hair that her son, Neo, is doing his best to stick in his mouth. "Tilly, are you good with this gown? Satisfied?"

I nod at my reflection in amazement. "I'm more than okay with this. Cinderella or not, this is the most beautiful dress I've ever worn."

"Perfect!" Allie waves little Neo's hand in triumph. "Now Sloan, Leslie…go back to work. We have some footballers coming in for fittings soon, and Freya 2.0 needs the pedestal."

A woman at a nearby sewing machine rolls her eyes and shakes her head. Allie winces. "Sorry, Elodie. I forgot we promised no more Freya 2.0 references. You're doing a great job, and you're a valuable member of our team."

"I've been here for two years so I should hope so," she mumbles without looking up from her work.

Allie shoots me a sheepish look and guides me back towards the dressing rooms. "Elodie is amazing, but we miss Freya around here. How is the pet line deal going? I haven't talked to her in a few days."

"We're getting things sorted," I reply, tucking my hair behind my ears. "The contract Harrods sent us had some issues, though. I'm meeting with them on behalf of Freya next week in hopes we can sort it out."

"Issues?" Allie's brow furrows with concern.

I wave my hand. "Yeah, just some terminology that's not perfectly clear with what Freya had in mind. I've seen contracts like this before, but businesses all sort of have their own language, so I just need some clarity."

Allie nods thoughtfully. "You know what? I know someone who will probably be at the event on Friday and is a whiz with contracts! I could introduce you!"

"Oh, I don't think that's necessary. It's just big businesses trying to have their cake and eat it too. I'm just trying to ensure Freya gets the best deal possible."

"No, really. This is his specialty. Plus, he's helped my Harris cousins out of several jams and even me with well…a crazy thing in my past that happened with Roan. Anyways…he's *amazing,* and I'm sure he'll be there, so I'll make sure you two bump into each other just in case."

"Okay." I exhale heavily as the itch to refuse any sort of help niggles my insides. I don't like help. I like figuring things out on my own. However, this is Freya's best friend, and I can't mess this deal up, so maybe a second opinion isn't the worst idea.

After I undress quickly, they bag my gown up as I run upstairs to Freya's workshop and collect the pieces she wanted me to grab today. By the time I come downstairs, they have the dress at the counter, so I pull out my wallet to hand them my credit card.

"Your money is no good here," Sloan says with a knowing smirk. "You're basically family."

"I am?" I ask in confusion.

Sloan shrugs. "Pretty much. I mean, I'm married to the oldest Harris brother, Gareth, whose brother, Booker, plays football with Roan, and Roan is Allie's husband, and Allie is a Harris and Freya's best friend, and Roan is Mac's best friend, and you're Mac's sister, which just means—"

My eyes see spots.

"The more you fight it, the harder we smother you." Allie peeks her head around my shoulder with a coy smile. "Seriously, I was overwhelmed by it when I first came to town and was assaulted by this horde, but you get the hang of it eventually."

Sloan hits me with a cheeky smile, so I reluctantly take the bag from her hands. "Well, thank you. This is extremely generous."

"That's the ticket!" Sloan exclaims. "And thank you for helping our Freya. She's pretty much everybody's favourite."

I nod and smile. "I feel the same way."

With the dress hanging in the back of my car, I drive the short distance from Shoreditch to Freya and Mac's new house in Brick Lane. I roll my windows down and let in the August breeze as I take in the different neighbourhoods. It's different on the East End. It has a more artsy, cultural feel to it with little outdoor markets, vintage shops, art galleries, and street art all over which I could stare at for hours.

Freya and Mac have settled well here, too. Freya has her big deal coming from Harrods. Mac has a dream job as a developer for a video game company which confirms that deep down my brother is still just a boy trapped in a man's body. And they have this wonderfully tight-knit pseudo-family who is overbearingly sweet and growing their families as well.

They're certainly a night and day difference from the crowd I hung out with in West London over five years ago. I fell in with the twenty-something social climbers who worked in retail and shared tiny studio flats behind all the high streets. We worked nine to five and then met up at pubs and wine bars and drank late into the night while discussing who was up for the next big promotion.

On the weekends, we'd hit the nightclub scene and party into the wee hours of the morning. It's quite impressive I could work my way up at Fortnum and Mason with what little sleep I had. But work hard and play harder was the culture, so partying was how we blew off steam.

Regardless, I must admit I'm pleased to be back in London and having much less wild and crazy experiences. This way of life feels much safer.

I find a parking spot in front of Mac and Freya's brick home that's tucked discreetly away on a cobblestone side street. Freya is obsessed with horses, so the adorable little mews house where horses used to live is perfect. When she found out that little fun fact, they had to buy the property straight away. It's quite idyllic overall, though. It's three bedrooms and two and a half bathrooms with the perfect mix of restored old beams and exposed brick with contemporary touches. Plus, they have their own private garden with a lush cherry blossom tree out back. I didn't exactly love my flat and job back in Dundonald, so it was all too easy to put in my notice to help out for as long as they need me.

Furthermore, I'm looking at this situation as a test run to see if I can handle London better now than I did in the past. I hardly recognise the person I was five years ago, and that's certainly for the better. If I can remain the new and improved Tilly, then perhaps I can soon call London my home again as well. A proper night out with my brother will be a great test for me.

I grab my dress from the back seat before quietly letting myself in through the red front door. Freya was taking one of her cat naps when I left, so I don't want to disturb her or her insane felines, Hercules and Jasper. Jasper has warmed up to me nicely, but Hercules isn't budging no matter how many treats I try to sneak him.

I make my way up the floating staircase in their entryway to the guest bedroom upstairs. The master suite is on the main level to the right of the stairs with their living room area to the left and their kitchen and dining through that. This home has a cosy layout peppered with bright, eclectic furniture from all different decades. Completely Freya's style. Unique and one of a kind.

On the second level of the home is my room, a second loo, and a wee nursey that's already starting to fill up with baby items. I inhale a cleansing breath as I walk by, feeling surprisingly fulfilled by being here and helping them through all of this. The past few years I've been so engrossed in myself that it's nice to shift my focus. And if I happen to figure out what I'm going to do with my life in the process, well, it's a win-win situation.

CHAPTER 2

Santino

"**S**ANTINO MATE, I NEED YOUR RSVP FOR FRIDAY NIGHT'S gala."

I tear my gaze away from the contract on my desk that I'm reviewing to see Tanner Harris standing in my doorway. He's a welcome sight on this dismal Monday morning. I point to his get-up and reply, "I still can't get used to this."

"Used to what?" Tanner asks, running a hand over his inked arm with a quizzical scowl.

"You in a coach's kit." My gaze lowers to the white Bethnal Green, F.C. trainer vest and black Adidas tiro trousers. It was just over a year ago that Tanner was helping us win the FA Cup as our star striker. Now he's retired, along with one of our best midfielders, Maclay Logan.

My, how things have changed for our newly promoted Premier League team. This is usually what happens to clubs like ours, though. We move from Championship up to Premier League, get a few notable wins under our belts, and then suddenly, bigger, more established clubs start poaching our players. This means I'm now chained to my desk poring over contracts of new potential football recruits that Tanner's father, Vaughn Harris, the club manager, has sent me. I've been the staff lawyer for this club for nearly ten years now, and we've never needed so many new recruits all at once.

Tanner eyes me salaciously. "Are you missing the sight of my muscular thighs, Santino? Or is it my ink-covered abs you're yearning to get a peek of again, you saucy minx? I'm sure you could Google me to find some old photos to tide you over."

"Christ, no." I wince and push back from my desk as memories of Tanner's chequered past flash through my mind. "One nice thing about you being married and on the coaching staff is the fact that I no longer have to help cover up your sexual escapades as London's dirtiest footballer."

"I wouldn't say I was the dirtiest, would you?" he asks, scratching his beard thoughtfully. "My brothers have had plenty of bad press. And I don't even hold a candle to DeWalt's mess." His face twists in disgust. "Although the fact that his whole debacle involved my cousin, Allie, is something I try really hard to forget."

I hold my hand up to stop him. "You'll be in my office all day if you plan to go over all the headlines you four footy-playing brothers have garnered. I'm grateful you lot are all married and settled down finally. Covering up sex tape scandals and negotiating a fake dating arrangement were two duties I was not educated on in law school."

Tanner smiles proudly. "Well, we turned those ladies into our wives, so I'd say you drew up very favourable agreements for us."

"Which you never properly thanked me for," I reply with a sneer.

"Didn't you receive my handwritten letters? I was certain I dropped them in the post." Tanner shoots me a wink.

"How are Belle and Baby Joey, and what did you name your new one again?"

"Alexandra. We call her Alex. She's all of one now, so you really should know her name, old chap."

I hold my hands up defensively. "I'm sorry. I need a family cheat sheet when it comes to all the Harris Brothers offspring. Both you and

Camden have two each now, right? And Gareth has two. Plus, Booker is still trying to control those wild twin boys of his."

"A useless cause," Tanner huffs. "They're completely unhinged."

My shoulders shake with silent laughter. "Your sister still just has the one, though, right? Rocky is an easy one to remember."

"She's our little star, yes. And cousin Allie and Roan's little one is six months old now. Honestly, you're right. We're all breeding like it's the end of the world. I'll stop taking the piss because I'm not sure I can remember everyone's names now that I think about it."

I smile knowingly. "You're all quite happy, though, yes?"

Tanner's chest puffs out with pride. "More than we probably deserve."

I shake my head because the past few years have been a whirlwind of weddings and babies with this Harris Family that I've become close with. And chequered pasts aside, happiness could not have fallen on a worthier family. They had a tough childhood growing up without a mother, so seeing them all manage their football careers and find their partners in life is inspiring. Now two have even retired since I've been around. Christ, I'm getting old.

However, a lawyer's career is certainly longer than a footballer. I count myself lucky every day that Vaughn hired me fresh out of law school and has kept me around for nearly a decade now. I'm thirty-six-years-old and can't imagine working for any other club.

"Tanner," a familiar deep voice barks from outside my office. "Did you schedule those extra training sessions with the new defender coming from America next week?"

The patriarch of the family, Vaughn Harris, appears in the doorway beside his son. Vaughn is a former footballer too, so he's tall and broad-shouldered like his sons. However, Tanner's sleeved tattoos and blond hair tied up in a bun are a stark difference from Vaughn's trim grey hair. He's aged quite a bit the past few years and keeps talking about retirement. But he's a workaholic like me, so I'm expecting we'll have to force him out.

"Yes, I scheduled Roan with us so we have someone to attack, and I'm putting Booker in the net as well." Tanner turns to face his father and adds, "I've read the stats on Zander Williams but haven't seen the tapes yet. You think he'll be ready in time?"

"I'm hoping so," Vaughn replies and then offers a quick nod to me. "Finney getting injured in our friendly match last week really buggered up plans for our first match in a couple of weeks. He's doing physio with Indie, but she's not sure he'll be ready. It'll be quick for Williams, but if he passes his medical exam okay and gets the extra training, I think he can be decent enough for a backup."

"I just sent Williams his final contract," I offer to relax Vaughn a bit. He's been stressed about how down to the wire this player's deal has become. "He had a last-minute change, so we had to make some adjustments. It'd be a lot easier if he had an agent we could work with."

"I know," Vaughn grumbles, running his hand through his short hair, looking stressed. "God, I hate recruiting. It's more exhausting than watching my grandchildren without a nanny."

Tanner laughs. "You can blame Booker's demonic twins for that."

"Hush now. Teddy and Oli are just spirited. They take after you and Cam, you know." Vaughn glances at his watch. "Christ, I've got a call I need to be on. Tanner, make sure that training gets sorted. And Santino, let me know if there are any more issues with Williams."

"Will do." I wave him off as he jogs down the hallway towards his office that overlooks the pitch.

"Christ, he's bossy. It's like my childhood all over again." Tanner shudders and then turns his focus back to me. "So, are you responding yes to the charity dinner Friday?"

I push my styled hair back into place and rack my brain for the details of this event. "Remind me again what this is for?"

"It's a black-tie fundraiser for the *Shirt Off My Back* nonprofit I started a few years ago—it provides clothing to the homeless for job interviews and work programs."

"Ah, of course. I did all the paperwork for that. It's kind of ironic to have a black-tie event for a clothing nonprofit, isn't it?"

Tanner nods begrudgingly. "Yes, but the tossers like you who come to black-tie events write the fattest checks. Even Mac Logan donated a tidy sum from his grandfather's estate that he inherited."

The mention of Mac's name shifts my thoughts. "How is Mac by the way? Roan said something about his wife, Freya, being put on bed rest?"

"Yes, she was. My Belle is her doctor though and she's quite certain they're going to be alright if she takes it easy."

I nod thoughtfully. "So, will Freya be able to come to the event then?" If so, I will be steering very clear of the two of them. Mac doesn't hate me as much as he used to after I helped him out with a contract issue a couple of years back. But, considering I tried to date his wife back before she was his wife, it's just best to always give those two a wide berth.

"No, Mac's bringing his sister, Tilly, actually," Tanner replies casually, and I swear I hear a record scratch in my mind as the hairs on the back of my neck stand at attention.

"H-he's bringing Tilly?" I stutter several octaves higher than normal. Licking my lips, I try to act distracted and gather some papers on my desk just to keep my hands busy and hope like fuck Tanner doesn't notice my reaction.

"He is. Apparently, she's helping out with Freya's cat clothes or dog clothes or whatever it is she sells or makes…bloody hell, I'm knackered. There are just too many people connected to our family to keep up."

I clear my throat and begin to loosen my tie, feeling very warm all of a sudden. "So, you're saying Tilly is back here in London? Just for a visit?"

"For the foreseeable future, I suspect. At least until that baby arrives. She's apparently whip-smart in the retail industry so she's helping Freya with negotiations on a contract of some sort. I don't know much about it. Roan was saying a lot of words about it this past Sunday, but Vi was making Swedish pancakes, so I was mostly just focused on making sure I got my fair share. Bloody love Vi's Swedish pancakes."

Tanner continues rattling on about food, clearly having forgotten the fact that I don't just have history with Mac's wife, I have history with his sister, Tilly. History that I can't seem to forget no matter how hard I try.

Before I can think better of it, I hear myself replying, "I'll be there."

"At the event? Excellent! You're always very free with your riches." Tanner pulls up his clipboard and scribbles my name down. "And your plus one?"

"No plus one." I wince as a flash of my latest ex, Bria's, sad face crosses my mind. "Just me."

Tanner's face falls. "Oh, bloody hell, the two-month chump strikes again?" I growl with annoyance at the American nickname our scout in the states dubbed me with a few years ago. It's been picked up around the changing room with the players and I bloody hate it. "Come on now, what was wrong with Bria? She too pretty? Too successful? Oh… did she cook with too much garlic?"

"Sod off," I grumble. "I'm Italian, so garlic is basically a food group. We just weren't right for each other."

"Booker owes me ten quid," Tanner replies with a laugh as he refers to his younger brother, our goalkeeper. "I don't know why he thought Bria would be different for you. Hopeless romantic, that one. The team should have started a tally on how many birds you've dated in the past few years. I've never seen a bloke serial date as much as you. It's like you're on a mission to find every single female in London."

I shake my head at that grim take on my dating status. Bria was the closest I've come to someone I could actually see being with long term. She was smart, loved to travel, and enjoyed cooking. She ticked all the boxes I thought I'd want in a partner. But…there was no spark. My Italian nonno once told me that la famiglia is everything. They are your every day, always. And if I am with a woman who I care about, I should tend to her the same way I attend to my basil plant on my balcony…with love, care, and plenty of water. If I am with a woman who I don't want in my every day, always…I must stop watering that plant and let it go. Unfortunately, Bria wanted a sprinkler system installed.

I shoot Tanner a dubious look. "I have to admit that picking up random birds at nightclubs with you Harris Brothers was a lot more fun."

Tanner laughs. "We had some top nights. However, I can't say I truly miss them. Going to bed at eight o'clock with Belle has more perks than I'd ever imagined. Seriously Santino, if you find a woman who'll be your small spoon, you better not toss her after your two-month test run. Spooning is life." Tanner waggles his eyebrows playfully before turning on his heel and calling over his shoulder, "See you later."

As soon as he's gone, I immediately exhale the tension I hadn't realised I was holding in my shoulders. Just the mention of Tilly's name has thrust me back to moments of the past. Moments that I've tried for years now to forget. Christ, what's it been…four, five years?

Tilly and I met at a nightclub in Soho just after Mac signed on with Bethnal Green. I was out partying with the team as I often did back then, and Mac's sister showed up to meet him, and well… let's just say she didn't leave that night with her brother.

I swallow the knot in my throat as flashes of our multiple late-night trysts play on repeat in my mind. God, she was beautiful. And wild and outspoken. And her Scottish pride was the sexiest fucking thing I'd ever seen in my life. The best part was, she wanted nothing serious. We were both out for a good time, so it was the perfect situation.

That is until everything changed.

And I still can't forget her final words to me.

"You're not some knight in shining armour. You're just a whore meister with a guilty conscience." I've carried the weight of them with me ever since. I think it played a large part in why I eventually quit having casual sex. That and the fact that every single mate of mine was getting married and having babies. When the infamous Tanner Harris became more settled than me, it was time to take a hard look in the mirror at myself.

However, I have not had the Harris luck. I have been stuck in these endless cycles of monogamous dating that never seem to work out. But no matter how many women I've tried to connect with, no one seems to fit. No one seems to match that idea I have in my head for a partner who could be my every day, always. I am determined to succeed at this the same way I did with my career.

However, when the past reappears, that means something, right? Tilly Logan isn't just the cliché *"one that got away"*. She's the one who literally ran away. When she moved from London back to Scotland, she left me with a million unanswered questions.

Maybe if I got some answers, I could move on with my life and stop being a two-month chump. And maybe if she's back in London, things will be different for her now, too? Things are certainly different for me. More than I ever imagined possible.

CHAPTER 3

Tilly

"**J**ESUS CHRIST, IS THERE A REASON OUR ENTIRE LIVING ROOM is covered in pet shite?" My brother's Scottish accent is thick with his displeasure as he loosens the black tie around his neck.

Freya and I look up from our work to stare at my big brother, standing in front of their ancient fireplace. His large frame looks like he's about to burst out of the black suit that he wears to work every day now. Quite different than his football kit he wore only a year ago.

I close my laptop and glance down at our mess of pet clothing spread out on nearly every square inch of their sitting room. "There is a method to our madness, Mac," I state defensively.

Freya adjusts her position on the sofa where she's lying with her feet propped up on a pillow. "Don't make a fuss. Tilly and I are doing important work here. We'll be done in a tick."

"You're not supposed to be working," Mac growls and pulls his tie off over his head, messing up his red hair that's a few shades darker than mine. He tosses it onto the nearest armchair currently covered in plus-sized cat pajamas. *That tie is lost forever now.*

"I'm on modified bed rest, not full bed rest!" Freya tuts, her Cornish accent getting thicker with her own displeasure at her husband butting in where she clearly doesn't want him. "It's as if you have amnesia and forgot what the doctor said!"

I have to bite my lip to hide my amusement. Mac told me Freya starts to sound like Hagrid when she gets upset, so I'm just waiting for her to drop a hard *Harry Potter* at the end of her sentences. She rubs her five-month pregnant belly protectively and narrows her eyes up at her husband.

My brother crosses his arms, clearly in no way deterred. "If it were up to me, you'd put a pause on this entire business until that wee bairn is out safe and sound."

"Mac! That's what I'm here for!" I exclaim, once again coming to the defence of my poor sister-in-law. Good God, being married to my brother has to be awful for her.

"The doctor said I could still work as long as I kept my feet up. Where are my feet right now?" Freya wiggles her toes.

"I think you missed the part of her instructions that said *bed* rest. Not *sofa* rest."

"I think you missed the part of her instructions that said *modified*. I think a sofa falls safely under that category."

"I think we best call the doctor and get clearer instructions." Mac digs into his pocket and retrieves his mobile.

"You are not calling Belle Harris at this hour!" Freya says firmly. "Just because she's married to one of your former teammates doesn't mean we can bother her after hours."

"Tanner and Belle are our mates, Freya. Christ, we've been to their house several times. Belle took you on as a patient as a personal favour to a *friend*! I'm phoning her."

"Mac," Freya growls, her chin jutting out defiantly.

"Cookie," Mac volleys back, his voice low with warning despite his adorable pet name for her.

My head bounces back and forth as the two stare at each other in stony silence for a full sixty seconds. "Should I go up to my room and give you guys a wee bit of privacy?"

"No," they both reply in unison.

My brother turns his glacial gaze on me. "You've been living here three weeks and are supposed to be helping, not making matters worse."

"I am helping!" I exclaim defensively. "I am Freya's business eyes, ears, and body which means she didn't lift a finger today, I promise you."

"She's been an excellent lady-in-waiting," Freya coos with a pleased smirk.

I turn a quizzical look at my sister-in-law. "I thought we were calling me your intern?"

"Heavens no! You've got your master's in business for goodness' sake. You're more qualified to do this job than I am. Calling you an intern is an insult. I think I was just a bit peckish when I said that the other day."

"What about puppet? You had a really passionate Pinocchio rant on Tuesday," I ask, embracing Freya's idea of unconventional business titles fully because…well…why not?

Freya's nose wrinkles. "I don't fancy myself a puppet master. I want you to have some say in my business decisions or who knows where my pregnant, hormonal thoughts will take us."

"And you weren't keen on me being the Watson to your Sherlock, right?"

"No! We're strong, virile women in business. We need strong *female* names to really embrace our prowess in the corporate world of fashionable pet wear, right?"

"Right." I bite my lip thoughtfully. "And we were a definite no on calling me your bodyguard."

"Yes." Freya waves me off. "You're very tall and statuesque but quite thin, damn you. And I'm short and round, so honestly, I can't say who would win between the two of us in a proper mugging."

"What the hell are you two going on about?" Mac growls, rudely interrupting our conversation. "You sound properly mental!"

I pin Mac with a punishing glower. "We're trying to come up with my official title now that I'm fully employed at *Perfectly Sized Pets,* thank you very much. If you don't have anything useful to add to the conversation, you can be on your way. There's a roast and potatoes in the oven that I put together!" I exclaim while thrusting my fist in the air. "With Freya's guidance, of course, because I'm a crap cook."

"You did wonderfully today!" she coos.

"Thanks, Freya."

Mac's jaw tics with agitation as he shakes his head and stomps off towards the kitchen. "Ever since you've arrived, I feel like a third wheel in my own house."

Freya and I both cover our mouths as we try to conceal our giggles. Thank goodness I love my brother's wife because if not, it would have been a lot more painful to help them out in their current situation.

But how can you not love Freya? She's a quirky, fiery redhead, much like myself. She has freckles for days, and she managed to magically tame my stubborn Scot of a brother. Honestly, I've never seen Mac argue with someone the way he argues with her. They're like an old married couple who should have their own sitcom. But even when they're having a go at each other, he looks at her like she's his complete and total world. It's hard to watch because it's so incredibly intimate, yet I struggle to look away because it feels meaningful.

Regardless, I'm committed to being Freya's puppet, bodyguard, and baby-watching-Watson until the contract with Harrods is signed, sealed, and delivered with terms that will satisfy Freya to take a year for maternity leave. I'll do absolutely anything, including chopping potatoes for a roast so that wee nephew of mine stays safe and sound inside her.

They just found out they were having a boy last week, and Freya told me Mac wept like a baby during the scan. Stubborn tattoo'd Scot on the outside, soft as a cuddly teddy bear on the inside...that's my brother.

Freya exhales heavily, pulling me out of my musings. "I suppose we should clean up and eat since it's well after six. We have another episode of *Bridgerton* to consume after dinner!"

I growl out my frustration. "Why are we only watching one

episode at a time again? Netflix has groomed us to be binge-watchers, so this is complete torture."

"I know, but I burned through all fourteen seasons of *Heartland* at an embarrassingly fast rate. Taking our time means prolonging our enjoyment. I don't want to finish all of Netflix during this bed rest. That would be horrifying."

I lift my brows as an idea hits me. "But maybe since Mac and I will be gone to the charity gala tomorrow night, we should watch two episodes tonight. I mean, we've earned it today, don't you think?"

"Very well then." Freya giggles. "I just can't say no to you!"

Laughing, I rise from the sofa to begin tidying up our piles of options into a particular order so we can pick up where we left off tomorrow.

"Tilly should be Smarty Spice," Mac bellows out from the kitchen around a mouth full of food.

Freya frowns toward the door. "Sorry?"

After a short pause, Mac shouts back more clearly. "Tilly could be Smarty Spice and Freya, you can be Stylish Spice. It makes the most sense based on both of your talents, and well…you two fancy the Spice Girls, right? Aren't they kind of all about girl power?"

Freya's and my face light up.

"That's perfect, darling!" Freya exclaims jovially. "Alexa, play 'Wannabe' by the Spice Girls."

I squeal excitedly as the song plays over the sound system, then hear Mac chastise, "Freya, you'd better be sofa-dancing, or I will be calling Belle whether you like it or not."

"Oh, I am, darling," she says, rocking her pointer fingers up and down by her face. "I'm practicing my mummy-to-be dance moves. I'll leave the sexy gyrating to the single lady in the room."

I hear Mac grumble something along the lines of "barf", which makes me laugh out loud as I dance my computer up to my room, still reveling in the fact I'm going to have my first proper night out in London very soon.

I feel like Daphne Bridgerton at her coming out event. If only the queen could be there, touch my chin with her gloved hand, and say,

"Flawless, my dear", then I'd feel like maybe…just maybe…everything might finally be turning around for me.

As I turn to leave my room, I nearly trip over a box I shoved off to the side that arrived earlier today. I'd planned to leave this particular package at my parents' in Dundonald, but they must have thought I'd forgotten it, so they sent it in the post.

I kneel to look inside because it's been years since I've cracked this open. It's chock-full of scrapbooks featuring small photos I took of various street art that I'd seen during my time in London. Large murals, small bits of graffiti, even silly sayings scrawled onto toilet cubicle doors. If it intrigued me, I snapped a photo and scrapbooked it. I even made a tradition of matting and framing my favourite piece every single year. I've created quite a collection over time, but I haven't taken any new photos in years.

As I glance through the framed pieces, I can't help but notice that it's like looking at a roadmap of my life. They start off with colourful, carefree pieces that I captured in my university days and shift to anxious, grittier, and more troubled art. These are dated in the years following school, when I'd started working in the real world and feeling like a proper grown-up for the first time. It's interesting to see what drew my eye in those days.

As I thumb through loose photos at the bottom of the box, I stumble upon a small print that I never framed, and it makes me smile. It's a dingy alleyway featuring a white stucco building. In the centre of the dirty wall is a painted-on window with blue shutters and a giant orange cat peering out. It's the spitting image of Hercules, judgmental eyes and all. I decide instantly I should definitely give this to Freya.

Smiling, I close the box and shove it into my wardrobe. There is no sense in rehashing memories from the past when I have a new, bright future to focus on.

CHAPTER 4

Santino

MY MOBILE CHIMES WITH A NOTIFICATION AS THE CAB DROPS me off at tonight's charity location. I pause outside of The Shard when I see the text from Shawn, the American scout we hired this season to find us some cheaper talent to replenish our roster.

"What is this about?" I murmur to myself and open the message while stepping back to allow a couple to move past me. I scan it quickly to see it's more revisions to the new contract I sent Zander Williams. The defender was due to arrive this weekend, so I can't imagine what is going on now. I'll have to deal with this tomorrow with upper management, but I should probably loop Vaughn in on this development since he seemed a bit desperate to get Zander on the pitch. I begin to forward it off to Vaughn but pause when I recall he's on grandbaby duty tonight.

Normally, the man lives, breathes, and dies football. However, he's changed since becoming a grandfather. Balance and delegating are now his two favourite words, and it's been interesting watching this shift in him as he acquires more grandchildren. I don't have a father figure of my own to know how that goes, but he seems happier than ever before, so he must be doing something right.

Nevertheless, he's got enough chaos on his hands tonight with all those Harris offspring terrorizing his home out in Chigwell, so this message can keep until morning.

I slide my mobile into my pocket and give my name to the security crew standing by the main entrance. "Seventy-second floor," one man says as another opens the door for me to enter.

I make my way up to the event, adjusting my black tuxedo in the mirrored panels inside the lift. This tux has seen quite a few football events in the past few years, I think as I smooth my dark hair off to the side. Award galas, investor parties, press events. Although I have to say, the charities are always the easiest ones for me to say yes to.

Growing up, we didn't have a lot. My mother came from a close-knit family of Italians who all moved to the UK before I was born. My uncle had opened a small Italian supermarket in the Cotswolds with his British bride, and my grandparents later joined the business and grew it into a deli and bakery. They all still work there to this day and are very content with that life path, even if they barely make ends meet some years.

As a young boy, I wanted more. I remember watching football on the telly and wishing I could be a star who travelled the world playing a game for money. However, as I grew up, I didn't have the talent to make it on the pitch. When I was fourteen, my junior coach told me that devastating bit of information. When I began to argue with him about his assessment, he told me I'd make a better lawyer than a footballer. Clearly, his words made an impact.

As I walk into the event space sprawling with formally dressed couples and round banquet tables covered in white, my eyes are instantly pulled to the floor-to-ceiling windows on the right featuring a stunning view of River Thames. I've lived in London since I moved here for university, and views like this still manage to take my breath away.

Suddenly, my breath is being sucked out by another sight altogether. Tilly Logan is standing on the far side of the room, propped up against the window with the city lights twinkling behind her like she's a bloody mirage.

Fuck me.

I thought I was prepared to see her tonight. Hell, I even wondered if I might have trouble recognising her after all these years. What a foolish thought that was because she doesn't exactly blend into a crowd. And tonight, she sparkles like a chandelier.

My heart races as I drink in her tall, slim frame standing next to her brother, who's only a few inches above her since she's in heels. If I wasn't six foot four myself, I would have been intimidated the moment I met this statuesque woman five years ago. Not just because of her height but her overall presence. She has this way of just…sucking you in. And not in a temptress sort of way. More like a warm fire you want to stand close to for heat. The first night we ran into each other, I realised quickly that all the women wanted to be mates with her. And all the men wanted to fuck her.

Including me.

Right now.

"Fuck," I growl to myself and tear my gaze from her to see who else she's standing with. A huge chunk of the Harris horde, it would seem—mostly the Harris Brothers' wives.

I spot Booker's wife, Poppy, easily with her short blond hair, then Belle, the curvy brunette who is Tanner's wife, and Camden's wife, Indie, with curly red hair and iconic, black-framed glasses. I know Indie a bit better than the others as she's one of our football club's doctors. We just recently hired another doctor after Camden and Indie had their second child because Indie didn't want to travel with the team anymore. Most clubs would have let Indie go if she couldn't commit to the grueling pace of a football club.

Bethnal Green is not like most clubs.

"You're late, you tosser!" Tanner bellows from beside me as he slaps my shoulder.

"Late meeting," I mumble, clearing my throat and attempting to erase the indecent images of Tilly in my bed trying to make a replay in my mind. "I need a drink."

"Allow me to lead the way." Tanner ushers me over to where Roan and Booker are currently standing with drinks in hand.

A brilliant striker for our club, Roan came to us from South Africa. I was worried when Tanner retired because those two had great chemistry as our two top goal scorers. But he's adapted well to the new recruits.

Booker is the youngest of the Harris family and our starting goalkeeper. The boy never ages, I swear. He's tall and broad-chested with dark hair, and the eternal face of a teenager even though the father of twin boys is pushing thirty. I could easily see him being a dominating force between the posts in his forties.

Tanner grabs his younger brother's drink and holds it to his nose.

"Vodka or water?" He tips the glass to his lips, and I watch Booker's nose wrinkle as his bearded brother takes a sip. "Good man. Can't have you being buggered for tomorrow's friendly match against Shepperton."

He offers the glass back to Booker, who shakes his head. "All yours now."

Tanner scoffs as he holds the glass out. "We're brothers! What cooties do you think I have that you don't?"

Booker points at Tanner's long dirty-blond beard. "One never knows what you could have living in that Dumbledore situation of yours."

"Alright, you can't have a go at me tonight. This is my charity event, and I'm your coach now."

"Please." Booker laughs. "The goalie coach offers me a lot more direction than you ever do."

"Try going from playing with him on the pitch to having to take his commands," Roan grumbles in his South African accent as he shakes his head. "I'm still pissed at him for abandoning me as my fellow striker. Now I'm forced to play with these new recruits."

"It's what's best for the team, DeWalt," Tanner coos. "You would know this if you had the superior coaching gifts that I come by naturally."

"Or if I started to choose pancakes over training like you did,"

Roan teases. We all fight back a laugh as Tanner's eyes turn to murderous slits.

"Tanner on a power trip already?" a deep voice echoes from behind us, and I turn to see the eldest, Gareth Harris, standing behind me. He shakes my hand in a silent hello but turns his gaze backwards to the last of the Harris Brothers coming in behind him. "Camden, I think it's time to remind Tanner you're clearly the more athletic twin since he's retired at only thirty-two."

"You didn't make it much longer," Tanner volleys back to Gareth.

Gareth shakes his head with zero amusement on his face. "I went out after the World Cup win. What could be better than that?"

"I went out on our FA Cup win. That's nothing to sneeze at. And let's not forget I was on the pitch with you at that World Cup win, you big, grumpy bastard."

"Just admit it," Camden interjects. Tanner turns a fierce glare to his twin, who looks like a clean-cut Ken doll compared to Tanner's man bun, bearded look. "I'm a better striker than you, even with my dodgy knee."

Tanner smiles knowingly. "Sure, Cam. You're a better striker, but only because you didn't have the extra weight to carry around that I did."

"What weight? You and I have the same build…when you're in training, that is." Camden pokes his brother's belly, and I brace myself for Tanner's reply.

"I've seen you in the changing room, and I know I'm a lot heavier between the legs, bruv." Tanner winks, causing the group to erupt into deep, throaty laughter as Camden attempts to nut punch his brother in a tuxedo.

This is why I spent so many of my years partying with the Harris Brothers. As clients, they brought me more trouble than I could handle, but as mates, they're always entertaining. When they first informed me they had a bacon sandwich rule when it came to women—the rule being whoever licked it first claimed it—I just knew these idiots would bring fun into my life. And even though they're all wife'd up and have children now, they're still wild, fun, boyish footballers at heart.

We order drinks and catch up at the bar as I do my best to avoid looking over at Tilly. I'm not sure how easy it will be for us to talk if her brother remains close to her all night. Mac gave me the clear to get in touch with Tilly a couple of years ago, and the fact that I didn't follow through isn't something I want to particularly discuss with him.

Glancing over, I see Tilly completely at ease, and she appears to be having a genuinely good time. Mac gave me the impression Tilly was rather closed off since everything that happened, but seeing her now, that doesn't seem to be the case at all.

I didn't realise it was possible, but I think she looks better than she did five years ago. Brighter, healthier. More colour in her cheeks. She definitely has more curves, too. And they fucking suit her.

Tilly

You know that feeling when the wind changes from warm to cool, and it means a storm is coming? That's the exact sensation I get when I spot Santino Rossi walk into the conference hall tonight.

"Fucking hell," I murmur quietly as I try to carefully wipe my clammy palms off on my gown. How could I not expect him to be here? This place is crawling with footballers. And where there's footballers, Santino Rossi is never far behind.

Back when we met five years ago, my mates at the time were constantly chasing footballers. I never much cared for the athletes because I grew up watching my brother kill himself daily for training. Eating nothing but chicken and rice. No alcohol. Blah. Boring!

But when my friends found out my brother signed with Bethnal Green, they saw that as their ticket into all the good parties in London, so I could not avoid them.

Thankfully, Santino isn't a footballer—even though he looked like one. He's ridiculously tall, dark, and handsome. He even sweeps his inky black hair off to the side like so many players do. And I know from previous experiences with this man that he sports some serious muscles beneath that fitted black tuxedo he's wearing.

My memories of Santino are a wee bit fuzzy since we didn't exactly see each other in the daylight much. It was usually well past midnight when I'd phone him for a random booty call. And when I showed up, he'd always make me do this stupid sobriety test before we could get naked. I can't say I was ever stone-cold sober when we shagged, but he'd give me a firm no if I was completely pissed.

Our arrangement lasted for a few months, probably because we had these ironclad rules:

1. No exclusivity
2. No dates
3. No overnights
4. No personal questions
5. No drinking…well, once I got there at least.

It worked for us. He was a good-time guy, and I was a good-time girl. Neither of us had any interest in being serious. In fact, I remember him adamantly telling me the night we met that he was not a commitment kind of guy and never would be. He even went so far as to say he'd never have any children. It seemed a bit odd, but I didn't pry because…I wasn't looking for anything serious anyways.

The only thing that mattered was the incredible sex. It was like a mind-altering, euphoric, magic carpet ride type of shagging.

Until I buggered it all up.

I take a long sip of my drink to quell the anxiety I feel creeping up. I was having such a nice time visiting with Mac's friends, I actually forgot I was just having water. Now I'm noticing it with great detail.

Sloan and Allie have been reintroducing me to the entire Harris family. The men abandoned their wives ages ago to go talk football, but I've enjoyed chatting with the ladies. The Harris twins' wives, Belle and Indie, have been best friends since med school, and I find myself watching their interactions with envy. I lost touch with so many of my friends throughout the years, and between moving to London and moving back home, I miss having a good friend. Even a pal to come along with me when I walk through all the outdoor markets on the weekends would be nice. I try to give Freya and Mac some privacy, but it gets lonely and boring. I wonder if this Harris family can adopt me the way they've seemed to adopt Freya and Mac.

My eyes return to the bar, and I nearly growl into my drink. Why did Santino have to show up and distract me?

Mac notices my change in demeanor, and his eyes follow mine to where Santino stands at the bar with the Harris brothers. He turns his back on all the ladies talking near us. His voice is low and ominous when he leans in and asks, "Is it alright he's here?"

My spine straightens defensively. "Why would I care?" I take another drink.

"Because you look like you've just seen a ghost," Mac replies knowingly. "I still don't know exactly what the hell went on between you two, but I trusted you when you told me he wasn't the one who put you in your position five years ago."

"Mac," I warn, narrowing my eyes at him. "We're not discussing that."

"I know, I know," he grumbles and takes a drink. "I still would like to beat the piss out of him. He's got the kind of face that could just do with a nice smashing." Mac eyes me cautiously. "All you have to do is say the word, and I'll punt him out of here faster than a football."

I roll my eyes. "You're not punting anyone. You can barely bend your arms in that suit."

Mac's cheeks turn red as he smooths his hand over his lapel. "It's a wee bit tighter than the last time I wore it."

"Last time you wore it, you were probably drinking protein shakes and running five miles a day on the pitch."

Mac's nose wrinkles. "Bloody desk job is making me soft."

"You're soft because you're happy," I reply with a small smile, trying to change the subject.

Mac smiles back. "Aye."

He glances down at his mobile to reread the last text from Freya just five minutes ago. He's been texting her most of the night like a sweet, overprotective husband. Freya all but forced him to go out tonight. She said she needed some time to talk to their two cats, Hercules and Jasper, about the baby on the way.

God, she's weird. *I love her.*

Mac diverts his attention back to me. "Sorry if I've been a bit of a grumpy bear since you arrived. I've just been stressed about Freya and the bairn. You know I love the shite out of you for helping us out like this, don't you?"

"You didn't love the shite out of me before?"

Mac's brows furrow. "Of course I did, but…well…you've been different since—"

"Don't," I cut him off, my lips thinning nervously. "Don't bring it up. It's in the past, aye?" I plaster on a smile that I don't altogether feel, but I want my brother to let this train of thought go. Now.

Mac stares back at me, taking in every feature on my face and making me feel like he sees right through me. He gets a soft look in his eye that I swear to Christ, all Scottish men in my life have. It's the kind that says, *I'm tough as an ox on the outside but soft as a lily on the inside, and I've got too many feelings to know what to do with myself.*

His nostrils flare before he nods firmly. "Aye. I won't bring it up again." He wraps his arm around my shoulders, and the smell of his whiskey permeates my nose. "It's been good to see you like this, Tilly—a bit like the old Tilly, when you were wee."

"I'm the new Tilly," I correct with an elbow to his ribs to get his alcohol scent away from me. "New and improved and having a great time tonight, so thanks for bringing me out."

Glancing over, I see no sign of Santino at the bar anymore, so I shake my glass at Mac. "Going to get a refill."

"I can get it."

"That's okay." I wave him off. "I can take care of myself."

"So you keep telling me." Mac gets a proud look in his eye just like our dad does, but his attention is diverted to Roan and Booker, who have just entered our space.

I make my way to the bar and set my glass down as I wait for the bartender to finish with the couple he's currently serving. Drumming my fingers on the lacquered wood, I try to remember the last thing I said to Santino. I think it was quite cruel. But at that time in my life, I needed to be on my own. I didn't need a man meddling and trying to take over when I had heavy stuff to sort out.

"Hiya, Trouble," a familiar posh British accent utters from beside me, and my thoughts are instantly assaulted with a memory.

"You look like trouble," Santino Rossi says, a flash of wickedness in his dark, soulful eyes.

"You look like you like trouble." I take another shot before grabbing his tie and pulling his lips to mine.

I press a thumb into my palm to calm my nerves before turning to face the man whose face I can never forget, no matter how hard I try.

"Hello, Sonny," I reply with a lift of my brows as I take in Santino leaning at the end of the bar, looking like he's posing for a James Bond movie poster.

He laughs at my use of the nickname I gave him the first night we met as he strides toward my place at the bar. My eyes drink in his tall, broad frame because I'd hoped my memories of how attractive he was were exaggerated. I was drinking a lot of alcohol back then, and most of the places I saw Santino were dark nightclubs or low-lit bedrooms.

Unfortunately, he's even hotter than I remembered.

Damn him.

Why is it that men get older and hotter while women continue to fight signs of aging with expensive creams and horrid things like Spanx? Life is so unfair.

He sidles up next to me at the bar, and I struggle to meet his gaze, feeling strangely exposed in the bright conference hall lighting.

"You'll be pleased to learn that I've read all of the *Godfather* books since we met," he says, towering over me and reminding me of the fact that he is one of the very few men in my life who manage to make me feel small.

"You actually read the books?" I lift my eyes to meet his with genuine interest. "Most men would have opted for the films."

"Well, you wouldn't shut up about them, so I had to see what all the fuss was about." His dark eyes dance with mirth.

I purse my lips, trying to stop the butterflies in my belly. "And did you relate to your namesake, Santino 'Sonny' Corleone?"

His lips pull back into a smile, revealing his perfect white teeth that are a stunning contrast to his olive-skinned complexion. "My Italian mother isn't the *Godfather* fanatic you are, so I can't say he's my namesake." Santino presses his lips together to hide his amusement. "Though we do have one very *big* thing in common."

I cover my mouth to conceal my giggle because I know exactly what he's referring to. Santino "Sonny" Corleone was the eldest brother in *The Godfather*. He was known for being bad-tempered, violent…

…and *very* well endowed.

I face forward and school my features to appear uninterested. "I can't say I remember that particular fact about you."

Santino laughs softly, causing his arm to brush against me. He turns to look over his shoulder behind us. "Is your brother going to kick my arse if I stand too close to you?"

I follow his gaze to see Mac watching us with narrowed eyes. "You're safe…for now."

Santino turns his gaze back to me, and a tender look sweeps across his face. "How the bloody hell are you, Tilly Logan?"

I inhale deeply because it's a loaded question, considering our history. "I'm not bad, Santino Rossi."

"You look...*well*." He says the last word like it pains him as his eyes drift down my body.

As my nipples harden beneath the fabric of my dress, I inwardly chastise myself because I shouldn't be having these types of reactions around a man like Santino. Not anymore. I clear my throat to try to break this spell of sexual tension and nudge him with my elbow. "You look older."

When he laughs, I do my best not to giggle. Again. God, how does this man shove me back into being a young, flirty twenty-something in a matter of seconds? Do I really need to remind myself who I am now?

Our attention is diverted as the cute bartender I chatted with earlier approaches. He sweeps my glass up into his hand and leans across the bar towards me. "Same as before, gorgeous?"

"Yes, Anthony." I give him a knowing look, and he winks back at me.

When I turn my eyes back to Santino, he's frowning as he watches the bartender retreat. "Friend of yours?"

The set to his jaw seems almost territorial, so I tilt my head and reply coolly, "Oh yes, Anthony and I go way back."

Santino's dark brows lift. "He seems like a nice bloke."

"Yet something tells me you wouldn't be friends with him." I narrow my eyes up at him, grateful for this shift in conversation because I need to remind myself of the type of man Santino was when we knew each other years ago.

My response causes Santino to straighten from his propped position. He turns to face me. "And what is that supposed to mean?"

"Oh please, Sonny. It's been a few years, but I remember what you were like when I lived in London. A party boy looking for connections in business and in bed. You only spoke to women whose knickers you wanted to get into and men who could elevate your status. You like that elitist, social-climbing London crowd."

Santino makes a strange noise in his throat and turns to look out at the crowd. "Is that your impression of this lot? Even the Harris family?"

"God no," I reply, my head jerking back. "No, they're lovely and warm. But they hardly live in London."

"Sorry?"

"They're on the Eastend," I respond, feeling my cheeks heat with my brazen cheekiness that now feels like it's backfiring on me. "It's a completely different culture."

"And those in different parts of town?"

"Different breed." I shrug knowingly. "I bet you still live in Mayfair, don't you?"

"No."

"Covent Garden then."

"Wrong."

"Grosvenor Square?"

"It's nice there, but no. I moved into a flat in Bethnal Green just a few years ago. It's a nice, quiet neighbourhood. And very convenient being closer to the club." Santino takes a sip of his tumbler of amber liquid, and I find myself watching his thick neck as he swallows.

"Here you are, love," Anthony interjects, and I nearly jump out of my skin as he catches me gawking at Santino's Adam's apple. *Jesus Christ, Tilly...get your head on straight.*

"Cheers," I reply, taking my glass of clear liquid with a lime wedge. Turning, I press my back to the bar to watch the partygoers and hopefully keep my eyes off Santino's throat. "So...you're still working for Mac's former club then?" I ask, trying to change the subject.

"I am," he confirms, thankfully letting go of our earlier conversation. "The job is a bit slow now that there are less Harris Brothers playing." He laughs at his own joke just like he always did. "They kept me busy—a rambunctious lot, in case you didn't know."

"I'm getting that impression. They're all very sweet, but they don't seem to understand boundaries. Tanner asked me earlier if Freya had designed any knickers for cats. Bit strange since we'd only been talking all of nine seconds."

Santino laughs knowingly as he adjusts his bow tie. "So, you're here to save the day with Freya's business endeavors?"

"Aye…just helping her out." I shrug. "She's done all the hard work. I'm just here to help her finish it all up."

"That's very generous of you." He clears his throat. "Will you stay in London then after they have the baby?"

"Not sure," I say with a frown. "Depends how everything turns out, I guess."

He nods thoughtfully. "Did you enjoy living back in Dundonald?"

"Christ, no," I reply quickly and take a nervous sip. "I mean, I didn't mind seeing my family on a regular basis, but I hated my job there. And unless I wanted to drive to Glasgow every day, there wasn't much opportunity for anything better. Plus, my friends there are all married and having bairns, so it just never felt like a good fit. Things have changed too much for me, I guess."

I turn to find Santino's deep, soulful eyes on me, and the intensity of them causes me to inhale sharply. He always had the most direct gaze I'd ever encountered. The rest of the world just magically disappears when he stares at me like he is right now.

"Things have changed around here as well," he says softly, his voice guttural and full of something I'm not sure I want to decipher.

A heaviness descends between us. As he exhales, the cool wind of his breath hits my bare shoulder and travels all the way down my body, causing a ripple of liquid heat between my legs. This moment right here feels dangerous and full of wicked possibility.

It's high time for me to go.

"It was nice bumping into you, Sonny." I move to walk away, but Santino steps out to stop me.

His hand gently touches my forearm, and the contact feels like a thousand pins and needles erupting all over my flesh. "So that's it then?" he asks, his face full of question.

"What else did you expect?" Licking my lips, I try to ignore the jitters vibrating in my nervous system as I force myself to look up at him. I'm trying to come off cool and confident, but his square jaw is peppered with dark, freshly shaved stubble, and I have a horrifying urge to feel it slide across my breasts.

His eyes search mine. "I thought maybe you and I could catch up. Have dinner or something?"

"No dates, remember?" I respond jokingly, feeling desperate to get away from him and the incessant flashbacks in my stupid head. "That was rule number two, wasn't it?"

Santino jerks back as if I've just slapped him. "Tilly, that's not at all what I meant."

"You didn't hope this could be a wee reunion for the two of us?" Lifting my brows, I hit him with a forced smile. "There was no moment when you thought we could get drunk and be each other's late-night booty calls again?"

"Christ, no," he exclaims, his eyes filling with horror.

Even though I didn't want him to want me in the first place, his rejection wounds me. *I* want not to want him, and the fact he causes my body to inwardly convulse right now is really fucking inconvenient. I swallow nervously and try to think of something to say, but my bravado is faltering.

He must see my discomfort because he steps closer and says softly, "I just thought we could catch up as two old friends."

"We weren't truly friends, though, were we?" I reply crisply, my eyes darting over to my brother who looks like he's going to come tearing over here any second. "We were party mates at best. Let's not make it more than it was."

A deep grumble comes from Santino's chest, and I swear he visibly grows as he glowers down at me. "I was trying to be a friend at the end."

Chills rush down my body as memories of my past try to trickle in with his words. But these are memories I want nothing to do with anymore. They are memories I've blocked out. And for good reason.

I inhale a cleansing breath and step closer to him, my eyes narrowed with determination. "You may think you were, Santino, but that wasn't what I needed back then. Which is why it's best if we keep the past in the past and steer clear of each other while I'm here."

He blinks back at me in confusion as his eyes rove over my entire face, inspecting it for some sort of clue. When his gaze dips to my lips, I feel my chin rise ever so slightly like our mouths are two magnets pulling towards each other. Flutters erupt in my belly that I haven't felt in ages, and all of it, every single tiny tickle, pisses me off.

I'm stronger than this.

His voice is low when he replies, "Take care, Trouble."

Santino pulls back, and I take the opportunity to quickly walk away as fast as this dress will allow me. Even if Santino thinks he was trying to be a friend in my past, that doesn't mean he's someone I can trust with my present.

The auction portion of the evening begins, and I feel complete and utter relief when I see that our table is far, far away from Santino. I need space. *And perhaps a cold shower.* What the hell was that back at the bar? Sexual tension? A quarrel? Both? Either way, I need to stay firm in my decision to stay far, far away from him. Getting mixed up with Santino and everything he represents as one of London's premier manwhores isn't at all what I need in life.

I do my best to ignore all thoughts of Santino and focus on the announcer as he lists off the auction items up for bid. Looking around this lot, it's obvious this group has a lot of money because the bidding ratchets up to a price point that has my jaw nearly hitting the floor. Santino fits right in, I'm sure.

Mac and I didn't grow up wealthy by any means, but his career as a footballer definitely changed his financial status. Thankfully, he didn't turn into an insufferable arsehole like so many other footballers I see out there and start buying ridiculous cars and private jets. In fact, the craziest thing Mac did after his first big break was pay off my parents' home. He also paid the rent on my flat back in Dundonald when I moved home five years ago. I didn't want him to because the Scottish pride runs deep in me as well, but I wasn't exactly in a position to argue, and I bloody love the bastard for not taking no for an answer.

My finances are a bit more stable now, thanks in large part to the inheritance I received from my grandad, Fergus. Before he passed, he sold off the bed and breakfast property he owned, leaving him with a tidy sum to pass on to all of us. Although, in all honesty, I think I would have rather had the bed and breakfast than the money. I have fond memories of being there with my grandparents when I was wee. Life was so much simpler then.

But Granddad's money made it easy for me to leave my job in Dundonald to help out Freya and Mac, so it's kind of special that he's still an important part of our lives, even from the grave.

By ten o'clock, the auction wraps up, the lights dim, and a live band begins playing, ratcheting everyone up to full-blown party mode. I turn to Mac with a sheepish smile. "Would you hate me if I took the car home and made you get a taxi?"

Mac's eyes widen. "Freya said we can't come home until midnight!"

"Freya said *you* can't come home until midnight. I wasn't included in that late curfew." I laugh as I recall the argument they had about how many whiskeys Mac needed to drink tonight to ensure he was having a good time. Only Freya Cooke-Logan would be the type of pregnant wife to force her husband to let off some steam.

In fairness, I think she did it because he's driving her mental with all the fussing he's doing over her state.

"You don't want to dance and have a laugh?" Mac asks curiously. "You used to love this sort of scene."

"That was before, Mac."

"Aye, that's right. New and improved Tilly!" he says in a high-pitched voice that I think is supposed to be me but sounds more like Mrs. Doubtfire. He laughs and a tender look sweeps across his face. "I'm just taking the piss. You know I'm fucking proud of you, don't you?"

"Yes, because you've told me roughly twelve times tonight."

"Well, I am…you just…you've got life by the baw sack." He holds his hand up like he's gripping a small ball. "The world is your oyster!"

"Thanks, Macky." I force a smile and hold out my hand. "Now… keys?"

His eyes blink slowly, and I can tell the whiskeys are having the desired effect as he digs in his pocket and produces his valet card. "Give my Cookie a kiss for me."

"I'm not going to do that."

"Just on the shoulder." He eyes me wickedly. "That's my favourite spot to kiss her."

"Not happening."

He sighs heavily. "Are you sure I can't come home yet? I miss her."

"Not long now, you dope." I ruffle his shaggy red hair before turning to walk away from the table. "See you later."

Just as I'm rounding the corner for the loos, Allie's voice calls out excitedly. "Here she is!" I turn around to find Freya's friend walking toward me in a stunning black gown and dragging a reluctant Santino behind her. "Tilly! This is who I wanted to introduce you to!"

"Oh?" My eyes go wide as I watch Santino stop behind her, looking like a reluctant child being forced to go shopping for clothes.

"Santino Rossi is the club lawyer for Bethnal Green, and he's brilliant. I mean, you should see some of the scraps he's got the Harris family out of. You might not be able to tell this by looking at us, but we are all a hot mess express. Well, reformed hot messes hopefully! Anyways, he's a contract wizard, and he's reviewed all the guys' sponsorship deals, so I think he could help you out with the issues you and Freya are having with the Harrods contract."

I force a smile. "That's really sweet, but I was going to find a contract lawyer on Monday."

"Santino is your man!" she exclaims like she has the golden ticket. "And he's pretty much family, so you know he'll have Freya's best interest at heart."

Allie looks up at Santino with wide, innocent eyes. He forces a polite smile and replies through clenched teeth, "I'd be happy to take a look."

"I couldn't ask that of you," I rush back, feeling horrified after how I just blew him off earlier.

His lips thin. "It would be no problem."

"It's too much."

"Nonsense!" Allie peals, clearly feeling the effects of whatever she's been drinking tonight as well. "Why don't you two have a coffee on Monday and look over the papers? He'll get you all sorted, I'm sure of it." With a pause, Allie's head snaps back and forth between us as she recognises the tension in the room for the first time. "I'm sorry, but do you two know each other?"

Santino inhales deeply. "We met some years ago."

I swallow nervously and nod my confirmation.

"Awesome! That makes it even easier. So happy to reconnect you two. Take good care of her, Santino."

Allie marches off, leaving Santino and I standing in awkward silence. Finally, he says, "Look, if you can't handle meeting with me in person, I'll just send a courier to pick up the contracts. I can make notes and send it back to you."

"Can't handle meeting you in person?" I repeat his words, annoyed by his assessment of me. "What is that supposed to mean?"

Santino blinks back at me. "Didn't you just say a mere hour ago that you wanted nothing to do with me?"

"I didn't say that. I just…didn't want to…" My voice trails off as I find myself at a loss for words.

Santino licks his lips with frustration when he realises I'm not going to finish that thought. "I'll text my number to Allie, and she can get it to you."

"I still have your number," I snap, refusing to let Santino think I'm too weak to handle this. "If it hasn't changed, I mean."

"It hasn't." His body vibrates with frustration as he stares down at me. "Call me if you like then. Have your brother run interference if you think you need it. Makes no difference to me."

He turns on his heel to leave, and I hear myself call out, "Sonny—"

"Don't," Santino says, exhaling through his nostrils and turning his head just slightly. "Just don't."

My chest rises and falls in rapid succession as I watch him leave. What the hell just happened? Why is he so angry? What did I even do to warrant such behaviour? Is this how he acts when he's rejected? *Get over yourself, lad.*

I scamper off to the loo, fired up from that insane exchange. I take a moment to calm myself in front of the mirror because I need to get a grip before I drive back to Brick Lane.

Once I've collected myself, I walk towards the lifts just as a set of doors begins to close. "Can you hold that?" I call out, hoping the passenger inside has time to stop it. The sooner I get out of here, the better.

A masculine hand slams into the doors to push it open, and I nearly trip when I see Santino standing inside.

He hits me with a flat look as he gestures for me to get in. When the doors close, leaving the two of us encased in this small mirrored space where there's nowhere to hide, it suddenly feels very warm.

This is not my night.

CHAPTER 5

Santino

"**H**EADING OUT ALREADY?" TILLY'S VOICE CROAKS, WAVERING slightly at the end as she stands behind me in the lift.

I exhale slowly, trying to calm my temper. Is it actually anger I'm feeling? No, no, that would be too easy. It's more than that. Deeper.

It's hurt.

Tilly Logan managed to fucking wound me in a way no woman ever has before.

"Yes," I clip, staring up at the floor numbers as they tick downward at a snail's pace.

Don't engage, Santino. Don't engage. It's not worth it. Just wait for the lift ride to be over so you can both get the hell out of here.

"Didn't like the band?"

"Band was fine."

"Early meeting tomorrow morning?"

"Nope." *Just leave me alone, Tilly. You don't want me to drop truth on you right now.*

A few seconds of silence before, "Then why leave so early?"

"Why are you leaving early?" I snap, unable to hide the annoyance in my voice. I glance over my shoulder and add icily, "You're usually up for a good party."

"The same could be said for you," she retorts, her eyes narrowed in challenge.

I bark out a laugh. "It's funny how things change, isn't it?"

Suddenly, the lift stalls, and the lights go black leaving only the red emergency bulb illuminating the small space.

"What the fuck?" Tilly shrills, and we both look over at the lift panel to see that we've stopped. "What's happened?"

"I don't know." Stepping up to the keypad, I press the emergency call button.

"Oiy, can I help you?" A voice crackles through the small speaker.

"Yes, our lift just stopped, and the emergency light came on," I reply crisply.

"Yes, we can see that. Our repairman will head up right now to see what all the fuss is about."

"Fuck," Tilly mutters and then steps forward. "Can we get out and walk down?"

"You want to walk down fifty floors in that?" I point at her dress and shoes, my irritation ratcheting up to a whole new level as I realise she would rather hoof it down a million flights of stairs than be stuck in this lift with me.

"You're stuck between two floors, Miss, so that won't be possible. No worries, though. We'll do our very best to get you out as soon as possible."

"Oh my God," Tilly groans when the speaker shuts off. Turning, she runs her hands through her long hair. "This is awful."

"Calm down," I grumble, not able to control the disdain in my voice as I watch her shift nervously in the small space. "I won't be bothering you."

"Would you just stop," she snaps back at me, her expression matching the fiery red emergency light perfectly. "Not everything is about you."

"You made that abundantly clear tonight. Cheers for that." I lean against the side of the lift and cross my arms over my chest.

"If we're going to be stuck in this lift together, the least you could do is stop being an arsehole," she seethes, glaring at me.

"I'm being the arsehole?" I bark back, pointing at my chest.

"Yes. I'm sorry for wounding your precious pride tonight but get the hell over it." She continues to run a hand through her hair nervously as she eyes me with disgust.

"My pride?" I push myself off the wall, my jaw clenched with frustration. "This has nothing to do with my pride."

"Then what the hell is your problem?"

"Oh, I'm so glad you asked, Tilly." I walk up so we're only a foot apart, my body bowing over hers as I prepare to unload every fucking thought that ran through my mind during that entire bloody auction. "See, I have this girl from my past, gorgeous girl…fiery and fun and full of fucking life from what I remember. We had some really good times together. Sure, they were limited to some basic rules, but all good. Then tonight, I run into her after five years, and she brushes me off like I'm diseased. And that's confusing to me, because my last interactions with her were me being rather generous I thought…some might even say a gentleman." I throw my hands in the air wildly, waving them around as I try to make my point with a dramatic flair I can only hope will get through her thick skull. "As it turns out, she just thought I was nothing more than a manwhore with no morals and was just in it for some saviour bullshit that, frankly, hadn't even entered my mind back then. So she pushed me away like I was a sleazy arsehole, and I guess you could say it's been eating away at me for half a decade or so. And it turns out that five years later, nothing's changed! She still looks at me like I'm scum, so I guess you could say it'll keep eating at me for the foreseeable future. So no, it's not pride. It's genuine fucking confusion." I'm left winded after letting every single thought I've had all night out as I stare at the only woman who has haunted my thoughts for the past five years. Why the fuck do I care so damn much?

"Stop," she barks, her nose twitching with agitation.

"You have loads of nerve coming back here after five years and treating me as no more than a casual fuck after I offered—"

"Don't," she cuts me off. "Don't bring it up. The past is the past, and I don't want to rehash it." She starts pacing in the lift. Wringing her hands together nervously, she looks like a caged animal. "You don't know everything. I'm different. I've changed."

"So you say," I growl back, hating the fact my eyes linger on her body as she moves back and forth. Why does she have to look so damn beautiful? "I see the same wild girl you've always been. Impulsive, opinionated, no regard for other people's feelings…"

She turns and hits me with wide, enraged eyes. "Don't act like you know me. You don't know anything!"

"Well then, please do enlighten me." I cross my arms and wait for a revelation that will make sense of that moment we shared earlier when we went from two people staring at each other with carnal, fucking attraction to her metaphorically tossing a glass of wine in my face.

"I'm sober, you fucking eejit." She pins me with a menacing glower. "For some time now. I haven't had a proper drink since well… since London."

I blink rapidly, completely pummeled by that very unexpected response. "But…at the bar tonight."

"*Anthony* and I had a chat when I first arrived that I'd like to get alcohol-free drinks all night that looked like cocktails because telling people I'm sober isn't exactly a fun party trick."

My mind reels with this new information. "I had no idea."

"It's not something I broadcast." She crosses her arms over her chest. "But it was necessary after I moved out of London."

"I see," I reply dumbly because I'm not sure what else to say.

"That lifestyle I was living here all those years ago was not good. I was out of control, and you were right there to witness me at my worst."

A heaviness settles in my chest that I might have played any part in what happened to her. I wanted to help her in the end, but she wouldn't let me.

However, it was too little too late at that point. I'm a terrible fucking person.

"I'm sorry." The words are the only thing I can think to say.

Tilly looks up at me, her brows furrowed. "What are you sorry for?"

"I'm sorry I let that happen to you back then. I'm sorry I didn't try to do more. Be a better friend." The familiar guilt starts to build in the pit of my stomach, wishing still I could have done more.

"What?" she snaps, stepping towards me. "You didn't let that happen to me. You weren't even with me the night everything went sideways. I let it happen. I made the choice. You just had front row tickets to the show."

"But I should have tried."

"And you would have got a Glasgow Kiss of a headbutt from me if you would have." She steps back and curls into herself. "No one could get through to me back then. I was making bad choice after bad choice, and I wouldn't have changed because you wanted me to." She exhales heavily and blinks back her emotions. I have to fist my hands to my side to resist the urge to touch her right now as she adds, "I needed to be scared straight back then so I could finally see what I was doing to myself."

With a nod, I process what she's just said, hating she likely associates me as one of her many bad choices. "And you want nothing to do with me because of that?" Damn me for still being intrigued by this woman even after she rejected me.

"Aye," she replies, her chin quivering slightly as she avoids eye contact. "I don't want to reacquaint myself with any of my old habits from my time in London. I'm sorry, but that definitely includes you."

My nostrils flare at that very curt label of what we had together. I know it was just sex, but if I'm being honest, it clearly was turning into more for me. Or I wouldn't have offered what I offered to her that night in her flat. I just never got a chance to tell her all of that.

Now it's too late. Her mind is made up.

Silence descends between the two of us, and suddenly, the lift jolts and restarts its descent. We both look at each other, and then our eyes dart away because our bubble has been popped as reality crashes back around us.

My mind is reeling as I escort Tilly to the valet stand and wait for the driver to return with her car. She hit me with a lot of new information, and looking back at everything I said to her tonight, I feel like a complete arse.

When I open the door and watch her slide into the driver's seat, I can't stop my thoughts from spilling out. "I'm happy for your change, Tilly. I really am. You are incredibly strong, and you always have been, so it doesn't surprise me in the least that you're tackling this."

"Thank you." Her brows knit together as she lifts her eyes to mine. "I'm sorry if I was rude earlier. You didn't deserve that."

I shake my head. "I'm sorry too."

She offers me a soft smile and moves to close the door, but I stop her for one more second, dipping my head down to meet her eyes.

"But before you drive away, I need you to know you're not the only one who's changed."

"Okay?" she says it like a question as her eyes dip to my mouth.

My voice is low and controlled when I add, "Maybe I'll be able to show you more of that in the future."

Her lips part in surprise as I step back and close the door, turning on my heel to walk away from Tilly Logan. But something deep in my gut tells me I'm not walking away for good. And frankly, if Tilly knew everything about me, then there's no saying what she'd think of the person I am today.

CHAPTER 6

Santino

I TOSS AND TURN IN BED FOR A FULL HOUR WITH TILLY LOGAN AT the top of my mind. How could I be thinking of anything else? Her confession in the lift shocked me, and I still can't believe how wrong I was for thinking she was the same party girl I remembered her to be.

Five years ago, she would outdrink me at the clubs. I've never been a huge drinker. My nonno and nonna would always serve wine with dinner, but it was merely for food pairing, never to get drunk. I guess that act took away the allure of alcohol for me, so more often than not, I find myself sipping the same drink for hours at an event, just holding it to feel social.

Tilly was always on a mission, though. She and that group of friends she ran with all seemed to be in competition with one another to be the hottest, the drunkest, or the wildest. I'd usually seek Tilly out earlier in the evening to get her away from that lot before things got truly out of hand.

Now, to think of her sober and doing it on her own…it really shows me just how far she's come from when she lived here before.

Five Years Ago

Santino: You dead?

Trouble: No, why?

Santino: I haven't heard from you in three weeks.

Trouble: Don't you have other girls to warm your bed?

Santino: You know I have a thing for the Scottish lassies. Are you free tonight? I could come to yours.

Trouble: No, I'm sick.

Santino: Really? Are you hungover?

Trouble: No personal questions, remember? Rule number four.

Santino: How could I forget?

When Tilly doesn't reply after my last text, I pause and debate what to do next. It's been three months of us hooking up casually, and while I know we have our hard and fast rules like no personal questions, the fact that I haven't heard from her in three weeks makes me worry that she really could be feeling poorly.

I wouldn't worry about her if I didn't know her mates to all be selfish fucking twats who only care about themselves. And she's so damn stubborn, I bet she hasn't even told her brother who lives here in London now. The club's been travelling a lot the past few weeks, so knowing Tilly, she wouldn't want to bother him while he's in the middle of his first season here.

"Fuck it," I growl, standing up from my desk. "Rules were made to be broken."

In a flash, I'm at Tilly's building in Soho with soup and sweets in hand. My nonna always said that food heals the soul, and since I didn't want to waste more time making homemade pasta, store-bought chicken noodle and Cadburys are the best I could come up with.

As I knock on the door and wait for her to answer, I can't help but feel nervous. This is the first time I've ever done something like this for a woman. As the lawyer for a football club, I've adapted to the footballer way of life. Casual sex, partying, zero strings. I know at thirty-one that probably makes me pathetic, but being in a relationship is just not something I want out of life. Not after knowing my past and where I come from.

Tilly Logan didn't want commitment either, so we've been each other's booty call for the past few months now. We even came up with our own set of rules to keep things completely casual. I know I'm breaking some rules by allowing myself to care about her right now, but it doesn't mean anything. It just means I want her to get well.

"Hiya, Trouble," I say as the door opens, and my face falls instantly when I see her appearance.

Don't get me wrong, she's still beautiful. She's always beautiful.

But she does not look okay.

She's dressed in grey sweats, and her strawberry blond hair is tied up into a knot on top of her head. She's wearing glasses that I didn't even know she had, and her face is blotchy, eyes swollen.

"Have you been crying?" I ask, my voice uncertain as the shock of her appearance settles over me.

"What are you doing here, Sonny?" Her voice is hoarse as she swipes at her damp cheeks, her adorable nose twitching.

"Christ, you have been crying. What's wrong?" I force my way in the door and drop the food on the floor so I can take her in my arms.

Cuddling breaks our rules too, but I've never seen Tilly cry, and a crying woman doesn't sit well with me.

Pressing her face into my chest, she shakes her head. "You shouldn't be here."

"Why?" I inquire, noticing all the packed boxes around us.

"We have rules for a reason."

"I know but...fuck...what's going on?" Cupping her face, I force

her to look at me, hating the troubled look in her eyes. "You don't look like you have a cold."

Her chin wobbles as I slide a tear off her face. "That's because I don't."

"Then what is it?" An ominous feeling overcomes me that it could be some sort of serious health ailment. "Christ, are you dying? Is it cancer or something?"

"No," she scoffs, shoving me away from her. "God, Sonny!"

"What?" I snap. "Just tell me what the bloody hell is the matter then!"

"I'm pregnant, you cunt!"

Pins and needles erupt over my scalp as that reality hits me at full speed. "But we—" I begin to say that we always use condoms, but she cuts me off.

"It's not yours."

That reply is like a fist to the gut. It's not mine. Tilly is pregnant, but it's not mine. We're not exclusive...this I know...but fuck, I guess I just thought if she was with me nearly every weekend, who the hell else would she have time to shag? Clearly someone! Someone with stronger sperm than me. Someone who probably didn't wear a condom like I did every single fucking time without fail.

"We had rules," I growl, my anger coming from some dark and scary place. "We weren't exclusive, but we promised to be safe."

"I know," she cries, her voice garbled as she presses her jumper-covered hands to her cheeks. "I didn't—"

"Didn't what? Didn't care if the arsehole wore a condom? You always cared with me. And if you didn't care, I sure as bloody hell did!" I boom, my voice rising in anger and causing her to full-on cry.

"Santino, stop."

"Why?"

"Because you don't know everything."

"What don't I know?" I roar, uncertain where this anger is coming from but struggling to fight it.

"I don't...I can't..." She exhales heavily and crumples to the floor in front of me.

Christ, I'm a fucking monster. Rushing over, I lower myself down beside her, wrapping my arms around her balled-up figure. "Tilly, I'm sorry. I didn't mean it. I'm just…I don't know what I am. I'm an arsehole. This isn't what you need right now."

She looks up at me, her blue eyes red-rimmed and swimming with something more than just horror. "I don't remember it."

"Don't remember what?" I rub her back soothingly.

"That night…with that man…when I slept with him. I don't remember any of it."

My body stiffens with her admission as a thousand horrid scenarios play through my mind. Scenarios that would involve me fucking murdering the bastard who did this to her. "What are you saying exactly?" I ask slowly, trying to control my rage.

Tilly trembles in my arms, and I reach over to grab a blanket off the sofa. Wrapping it around her, I rub my hands up and down her arms over and over to calm her down. She needs to tell me what happened. I need to know. I have to know.

Finally, she says, "I was out with Honey and Valerie. We were at a pub. It was late…I was drinking a lot. And well, Honey had Molly."

"Who's Molly?"

"A drug, you idiot."

"Oh."

"Anyways, I wasn't going to take it, but I don't know…peer pressure sounds so stupid to blame it on. I'm twenty-seven years old. I'm not a teenager. But fuck, they made me feel ridiculous for not taking it, and so I just took it to shut them up. I didn't think it would be that strong. But then, Jesus, then everything got blurry. And I remember talking to a guy. I remember snogging him in the loo. Then it all just…goes black. Next thing I know, I'm waking up at three in the morning in some stranger's flat, and well…there was evidence we shagged…between my legs. I looked everywhere for a condom. I dug through that fucker's disgusting bins and everything. No sign. It's his, I know it is."

She begins sobbing, and I shush her, pulling her into my arms and rocking her back and forth. "So, who is he?"

"That's the worst part. I went back to his flat, and he was gone and

so was his stuff. It was just an Air BnB, I guess. He doesn't even live here, and I can't get his name from the hosts because of confidentiality bullshit. They said they'd give him my information, but he's never contacted me. I'm sure he wants nothing to do with this situation. I know I sure as hell don't."

"Fucking arsehole."

"Fucking cunt!" she adds.

I look around the flat again. "Why all the boxes?"

"I'm moving back to Scotland to live with my parents."

"What?" I pull back to pin her with a glower. "Why on earth are you doing that?"

"Because I'm knocked up, you eejit! I don't have the first idea what to do with a child. And my parents do. I have to move back home. I can't afford anything else, so I have no other choice."

"Your brother is here," I state stupidly.

"You know as well as I do that a footballer's schedule is mental." She exhales heavily and tosses the blanket off herself. "I hate leaving London, but I have to. This lifestyle isn't healthy. I'm a fucking mess."

Guilt niggles in my belly. The lifestyle she's talking about is the partying, the drinking. The occasional drug use. I've noticed Tilly's been a bit wild since the moment we met, and I have to admit, I wanted to cut her off at times. Stop her from drinking. But she's not my girlfriend, and well, we didn't talk about that kind of stuff. I'd never shag her if she was completely pissed and took great pains to ensure her sobriety when we were intimate. This fucking sicko that fucked her when she wasn't even coherent and now wants nothing to do with her deserves to be castrated.

A dark memory threatens to impede my thoughts, but I push it away before it can grow wings. My voice is deep and ominous when I say, "What if the baby is mine?"

"What?" she replies with a laugh, standing up to begin pacing the small flat. "Don't be stupid."

"It could be mine," I respond stubbornly, standing up to tower over her.

"You and I never go without a condom."

I shrug like she said nothing I cared about. "Condoms aren't one hundred percent."

"The timing aligns with this bloke."

"You slept with me three weeks ago."

"My period is only a week late, Santino. The timing isn't there. It's not yours. Calm the fuck down. You're in the clear."

I take a deep, cleansing breath, feeling a heavy sense of responsibility come over me. My mother was a teen mum, and I don't even know who my father is, so I guess it's safe to say that men who abandon their children don't sit well with me.

"What if I didn't want to be in the clear?" I ask, digging my heels in.

"What?"

"What if I claim this baby no matter what?"

"Santino! You've lost your fucking mind! You're a fucking man-whore if I ever saw one."

"So, what. I can change," I snap, annoyed at her dismissal of me. "I can be there for you and this baby. We can be together."

"Until you see the wee one and decide it's more work than it's worth and fuck off like all the other arseholes I've screwed. No, thank you."

"Tilly, I'm being serious."

"I don't even know what I'm doing with this situation yet!" she screams, turning on her heel to eye me harshly. "I'm a modern woman, Santino. I have choices! I don't just need you to marry me to make this a legitimate bairn. Maybe I won't even keep it!"

I swallow the knot in my throat and nod slowly. "Okay then. I'll support whatever you decide."

She shakes her head in disgust. "This has nothing to do with you. And don't look at me like that. Like you're some pompous do-gooder who's doing a charitable act. God, this is why you were only good for sex. You're a fucking pretentious arsehole who doesn't know the first thing about real problems."

"You don't know me, Tilly. You don't know my past or where I've come from." I stop that train of thought. "Just...let me be there for you through this."

"No," she snaps, walking over to the door and opening it for me to leave. "I don't trust this. I don't trust your intentions. I don't understand why you give a flying fuck about this baby. I just want you to leave."

"Don't be so fucking stubborn," I roar, walking over to stand in front of her again. "Why can't you believe that I might be coming from a genuine place here?"

"Because it doesn't matter! I don't need you. I got myself into this mess, so I can get myself sorted."

"But I can help...seriously, Tilly."

She shakes her head adamantly and eyes me with disdain. "I don't need a saviour. You're not some knight in shining armour. You're just a whore meister with a guilty conscience."

And with those parting words, Tilly Logan slams the door in my face and leaves London...and me...for good.

CHAPTER 7

Tilly

"**I**'M HAVING A COFFEE WITH SANTINO IN TWO DAYS," I say, dropping down onto the table in front of where Freya is currently resting on the sofa with her feet propped.

Her eyes go wide. "The man whose name we shall not speaketh?" Quickly closing her laptop, she sets it off to the side to give me her full attention.

I roll my eyes. "We can speaketh his name. I need to speaketh his name. I have to figure out how I'm going to handle this because he's going to look over the Harrods contracts, and well…as much as I hate to say it, we need him."

Freya rubs her lips together with a sheepish look. "I knew Santino was who Allie wanted to help us out, but I told her it was all up to you."

"A warning would have been nice!" I run my hand through my hair in exasperation. "I can't believe I didn't assume he was going to be there last night. God, I'm dense."

"You're not dense. You looked so lovely last night, and you were

56

so excited to go and have a proper evening out. You've been cooped up in this house with boring old pregnant me for far too long."

"You're anything but boring," I reply with a laugh as I think about the conversation she had with her food the other night. Something about grapes being millennials and raisins being baby boomers, and they're a family and deserve to live together in harmony. God, she's wonderful. I fix her with a withering stare. "But now you have to help me figure out things with Santino."

"I've been waiting for this moment my entire life." Freya reaches out to grab an imaginary bowl of popcorn, tossing some pieces into her mouth. "Tell me everything before your brother wakes up. What all happened between you two?"

I exhale heavily. "I'm not going to get into the past. But I will say… that attraction we had before. *It's still very much alive.*" My body shivers as I think of how stifling that lift ride was. The two of us, both angry, both misunderstood, both glowing red and breathing the same hot air.

"Of course the attraction is still there." She shrugs like it's the most obvious statement. "I dated him once, so I know how hot he is."

My nose wrinkles. "God, I clean forgot that fun fact."

Freya waves me off. "Only for forty minutes before your brother stormed in and practically carried me out of there like a caveman." She grins like she wasn't at all displeased by that scene. "I will say that Santino gets a bad rap. Allie actually told me the footballers at the club have been calling him the two-month chump. He exclusively dates women for a couple of months, and sadly, it just never seems to work out. But it's not for lack of trying."

"Two months?" I ask curiously. "Exclusive? That doesn't at all sound like the guy I used to know. Sounds a bit clinical and contrived."

Freya shrugs. "I think he's changed a lot. Even when we were on our date, he seemed very genuine and asked lots of thoughtful questions. I didn't at all get the impression he was looking for an easy shag."

"Interesting." My brows furrow as I try to consider that idea. "When we met, he was this sleazy suit-wearing, dark, dangerous and… extremely naughty in bed type of lad. God, the first night we met, we nearly shagged in the women's loo at some nightclub."

"Oh my God, that's hot." Freya squeals, bouncing slightly in her seated position.

"Not really," I reply with my lip curled. "It was stupid. I'm pretty sure we stopped because a security guard threatened to throw us out. And I was so stupid because I actually liked all that excitement. I was so out of control that I looked for anything to push my limits."

"Crikey," Freya responds flatly, her eyes fixated off into the distance. "A shag in a car wash is the most exciting thing I've ever done."

"Oh my God." I bark out a laugh and then lower my voice so we don't wake Mac. "Please tell me that wasn't with my brother."

Freya gets a sheepish look on her face. "I'm afraid it couldn't have been with anyone else since he's been my only shag."

"What does that—no way! You were a virgin when you met my brother?"

"Don't say it like that!"

"I'm not saying it like anything! I'm just…I'm shocked."

"Well, it shouldn't surprise you that a plump, Cornish, cat-loving seamstress doesn't exactly score big with the blokes."

"Did you guys wait until marriage? Do I want to know? God, I don't think I do. Tell me quickly," I rush out, desperate for this juicy nugget and trying my hardest to forget it's my brother we're talking about.

"We didn't wait." She rolls her eyes. "I'm not a prude. I'm just inexperienced. And your brother was my best mate, so it felt right."

My heart sighs at that sweet, innocent comment. Freya and Mac's love story is such a joy to watch…even if their life path is far different from mine.

"So, are you considering a replay with Santino?" Freya waggles her eyebrows.

"No," I reply quickly and then repeat for good measure, "No! I can't get swept up in him again. The last time we were together, I lost all my good sense. I can't allow myself to go down that path again. That's why I need to talk to you. How do I stop this ridiculous pull I feel to him? Like seriously, when I saw him at the bar, I was like a moth to a flame even though I knew I didn't want anything to do with him."

"Bleddy hell, that is a predicament." Freya rubs her lips together thoughtfully. "Maybe if you look rubbish when you see him? Like sweats and a messy bun. No mascara. If you don't feel sexy, then you won't be thinking about sex."

I nod slowly, my nose wiggling at that idea. "Actually, that's not a bad thought."

"Oh! And punch him in the shoulder like he's one of the bros. I always see Mac and the other footballers do that." Her face falls. "But don't swat him on his rear. They do that too, and I fear that could send him mixed messages."

"Duly noted." I laugh and shake my head. "I think I can do this."

"Of course you can." Freya smiles victoriously. "Crikey! Am I your love coach now?"

I pull a face. "Maybe anti-love coach?"

Freya's smile falters. "That doesn't sound very nice."

"I know, but I can't be repeating old habits if I want to get my life back. And Santino definitely falls under the category of old habits."

Freya exhales heavily. "You know what they say about old habits."

"What?"

She pins me with a serious look and deadpans, "They die hard… and that's not in reference to his willy."

CHAPTER 8

Santino

Sitting at an outdoor table outside a coffee shop in Bethnal Green with an espresso in hand, I try to calm my nerves before the arrival of Tilly Logan. The woman is a force of nature. Any time she comes near me, I lose all sense of control, both mentally and physically. The other night bloody well proved that.

Fucking hell.

Friday night at the charity was a disaster. I shouldn't have lost it on her in the lift, and I shouldn't have accused her of being the same person she was before. I should have known better. She just looked so bloody good. Everything incredible about us came rushing back in full force, and I desperately wanted it to be like old times.

Then she basically told me to get stuffed, and I couldn't help but feel angry.

Going into that evening, I fully admit I wanted to see what we could be like after a few years apart. I wanted to show her I've changed, and…I don't know…see how she's doing after everything that happened. The last time I saw her, her face was tear-stained, and she was moving away to have some stranger's baby. It killed me to have her slam that door in my face.

I wince at that thought because I'm trying to forget about the fact that I ever had real feelings for Tilly. They weren't something I ever expressed to her, so it's not like it's a well-known fact. And she clearly didn't give a toss about me then…or now.

Get your shit together, Santino. This is a business meeting today. Nothing more.

"I'm gonna make him an offer he can't refuse," a strange voice utters from behind me. When I turn around, my eyes widen when I see it's Tilly. Her face is pinched in a peculiar way, with her chin jutting up to the sky as she attempts a really horrible *Godfather* impression.

Forcing a smile, I stand to greet her. "Hiya, Tilly."

"Tilly?" she barks and whacks me on the shoulder. "I'm Don Corleone! Or even Michael Corleone says some version of that line in one of those movies, I think."

"How could I forget?" I touch the spot on my arm that she hit with more force than I thought her slender arms capable. My eyes take in her appearance because she looks like she's just crawled out of bed. "Did you forget about our meeting this morning?"

"No." Her hands instantly stab into her messy knot of pale red locks on top of her head. "Just keeping it business casual." She tugs nervously on her loose T-shirt hanging over a pair of cropped leggings. Her face is bare and fresh, and she looks even younger than when I first met her.

"Can I get you a drink inside?" I gesture to the coffee shop entrance.

"No, I've got it. Be back in a moment." She jogs past me and darts inside, looking a little flustered.

I'm not one to judge appearances, but you'd think she'd have treated this business meeting like an actual business meeting and dressed for the occasion. Slipping off my suit coat, I drape it onto the back of my chair, then unbutton my shirt cuffs to roll up my sleeves. If she's wearing pajamas, I'm not going to sit here and sweat my arse off in this blazing August heat.

She returns with an iced coffee and pauses by the table as she takes in my more casual look. There's a slight twitch to her nose as she drops onto the seat across from me with a forced smile. "Thanks for meeting with me today."

"It's no problem." I close out a text from my mum, then set my mobile face down on the table to give her my full attention. "My schedule is pretty flexible at the club."

"Well, Freya and I both really appreciate this help."

She opens her mouth to say more, but my mobile pings with another text notification. "Sorry, I thought I silenced that."

"It's okay…you can answer it if you need to."

I turn it over to see who it's from. "It's just my mum. She's been texting me location options for our annual trip all morning."

"Annual trip?" Tilly asks, her eyes widened.

"It's something we started doing a few years ago. Just me, her, and wherever an airplane can take us. She prefers spas and mud bath sort of locations. I like hiking and architectural ruins with lots of history that she says bores the life out of her. It's a treat. This year, it's her pick, so she's going a little nutty."

"That's a pretty cool thing to do with your mum." Tilly's face looks stunned and a little bewildered. "Can't say I do anything interesting with my mum except on the rare occasion when she lets me dry the dishes instead of wash."

I laugh at that comment, and then a heaviness creeps up in my belly. "Can I first start off by saying I'm sorry again for Friday night? I shouldn't have gone mental on you in the lift like that. It was unfair and—"

"There's nothing to apologise for." Tilly shakes her head, and her nose twitches. "I can understand why you were confused."

"I know, but still. I had no right." I hit her with a stern look to show her this is not up for discussion. When I'm wrong, I say I'm wrong.

"Let's just forget about it." She wraps her pink lips around her straw and takes a long sip before her eyes widen. "How was the friendly match on Saturday? I heard everyone talking about it at the charity event."

"Decent." Sitting back, I appreciate the change in topic. "I don't go to all the matches, but I oversaw the contract negotiations on a couple of the new recruits. I was curious how they looked, so I sat in the suite and watched."

She nods thoughtfully. "And did they look good?"

"I'd say so, yes. I'm no football coach or anything, though. Just a genuine fan with a vested interest in the club. And I love the atmosphere at Tower Park. There are far worse ways to spend a Saturday in Bethnal Green."

"You know, I never got to see Mac play there before I moved back to Dundonald," she replies, catching my eyes on her and then looking away quickly. "I saw him play for Rangers, of course, and that was amazing, but he always spoke so fondly of Tower Park. He said the energy was like nothing he'd ever experienced in all the clubs he played for. I should have made it a priority to visit the stadium when I lived here. It's one of my biggest regrets." I notice a dark look sweep across her face, but she quickly masks it with a polite smile.

"You should have seen a match when three of the four Harris Brothers all played together," I say, changing the subject because I can tell she's worried she shared too much. "Whenever one of the twins would score, Booker would always run out of the goalie net all the way across the pitch to celebrate with Tanner and Camden. Vaughn used to get so angry, telling Booker to save his legs, but deep down, you could tell he was chuffed. They are a fun family to watch on the pitch."

Tilly gets a curious look on her face. "Allie calls you family, so you must be quite close with the Harrises."

"I guess you could say I'm close with Vaughn." I pause briefly as I think about the quiet, contented bond we've formed throughout the years. It's mostly work-related, but there's a comfort between us. An unspoken trust. And he may not know this, but I've always admired how fiercely protective he is of his children. Losing his wife when all five of his kids were so young couldn't have been easy. And I've gathered from Gareth that they all went through some very dark years. But you'd never know that by looking at them now. "I used to be closer to the brothers when we were younger, as you may recall. But now things have changed. The Harris family are all single-handedly working to repopulate London, it seems."

Tilly smiles and manages to look carefree for a moment. Our eyes hold each other briefly, and suddenly, her face falls as she points nervously to the coffee shop. "This coffee is amazing, and those Danishes inside look braw."

"They taste as they look. I come here quite a bit and have to work out twice as hard as a result." I drag my finger around the edge of my coffee mug to give me something to focus on besides Tilly's stunning blue eyes. "The owner is a huge Bethnal Green fan, too."

"That's nice. I feel like I still have a lot of spots to see on this side of town. I usually try to stay in the house on weekdays in case Freya needs something. But on the weekends when Mac isn't working, I'm out as much as possible so the two of them can have some alone time. I've found some great places already. It's crazy how many things you notice when you walk around on your own rather than in a group that insists on going to the same spots over and over." She bites her lip nervously, and I find myself frowning at the thought of Tilly eating by herself.

"Have you not reconnected with your old mates that you used to run around with? What were their names? Wasn't there a girl named Jam or Maple?"

"Honey," Tilly corrects, and her face spreads into a genuine smile as she attempts to cover her giggle.

I can't help but laugh myself because watching her try not to laugh is a beautiful sight. A sight that I wish I didn't enjoy so much.

She finally composes herself and swipes haphazardly at the tears in her eyes. "Her name was Honey, and she was a cunt."

"Ouch," I exclaim with my brows lifted in amusement. "That's a bit harsh, isn't it?"

Tilly shakes her head. "No, it's the truth. Honey was a cunt then, and I'm sure she's a cunt now. I have no interest in reconnecting with any of those girls. They're all a bag of cunts."

My brows furrow, but I won't argue. "I never thought much about them either. They always seemed…"

"Like selfish, footballer WAG wannabe bitches who would toss their friend out of a moving car to get to a party quicker?"

I wince at that description. "That's probably pretty accurate."

She nods slowly and curls up into herself. "Which was a lot like me back then too."

My jaw tightens. "I never pegged you that way."

"I was awful." She hits me with a knowing look.

"You weren't awful," I argue, sitting back in my seat and eyeing her with sympathy. "In fact, I remember you only talking to me because I *wasn't* a footballer."

She rolls her big, blue eyes that look even bluer without any makeup on. "That doesn't exactly make me noble."

"I suppose not." I clench my fists to stop from remembering our past because it's clearly not something she thinks fondly of. "Still, it was obvious you were different than your friends."

"Well, I wasn't a gem. And I'm not saying it so you can argue with me. I'm saying it because it's the truth. I was on a very self-destructive path back then, and it's why I had to make a big change in my life."

I eye her thoughtfully for a moment, taking in the beautiful colour on her cheeks. Whatever changes she's made have certainly made her ten times more beautiful. I pause, trying to form the right words, and ask cautiously, "Can I ask if…well…did you go to a treatment facility?"

Her eyes widen at my direct question, but she straightens in her chair and answers it like the strong woman she is. "I didn't go to a facility, no. Actually, I didn't even do Alcoholics Anonymous or anything like that. After I…well…had the…"

"Miscarriage?" I offer, a heaviness in my chest as I say the word she seems unable to say. I'd heard about Tilly's loss a couple of months after she'd moved away. Mac was telling Roan in the team tunnel at Tower Park, and the acoustics carried the conversation around the corner right to my ears. It was as if I was meant to hear it. I hated that the news didn't come from her, but we weren't speaking at the time, so I can't say I blamed her for not ringing me.

Wincing, she takes a quick drink of her coffee, avoiding my eyes like the plague. "Anyways, afterwards, I told my parents and my grand-dad that I was planning to stay off the booze for good. I asked them to be there for me and hold me accountable. That was pretty much all it took."

"That's impressive," I reply, but in my mind, I'm thinking that if any woman could do it, it's Tilly.

"I don't like to tell people because it sounds like I'm simplifying a very real disease. But for me, it was just different. I think you can *not* be an alcoholic and still not have a good relationship with alcohol. It's just so ingrained in our culture that we have to drink to have fun or to fit in. Which means that people find it bizarre when you want to just quit. And after a while, I became addicted to feeling healthier. It was nice going to work without a headache. I also took up running, which gave me the sort of buzz I was maybe missing."

"I can understand all of that."

My eyes lower to her body to appreciate the muscles I know weren't there five years ago. She's stunning, even if she did show up today looking like she's fresh out of bed. She's sitting here, speaking of a very personal issue with no wavering in her voice and no insecurity in her posture. She's confident in her decision. She's happy.

I shoot her a cheeky smile. "So, has it been a full five years sober?"

"Not fully," she says with a half-smile. "I've had a wee nip of wine with my folks on occasion mostly because it was a safe space, and I wanted to see if I could handle it. Which I could." She smirks victori-ously, yet her face falls slightly when she adds, "And I had a whiskey with my granddad before he passed."

I note the pain in her voice. "I was sorry to hear about your grandfather."

"Thanks." She exhales softly. "I heard you helped Mac get trans-ferred to Scotland when granddad was sick."

I shrug. "That's sort of my job."

"But it wasn't your job to put a buy-back clause in his contract so he could come back to his team here in Bethnal Green eventually, was it?" Her eyes narrow on me in challenge, and my body reacts instinctually to that familiar look.

I clear my throat. "I knew Mac was acting emotionally, and I just wanted him to have options when he was ready."

She gets a tender look in her eyes. "That was really kind of you."

"It's just my job."

She blinks back at me curiously with a twitch to her nose. "I wouldn't have expected you to do something like that five years ago."

I pin Tilly with a look. "I told you on Friday…you're not the only one who's changed."

We both go quiet for a moment as we finally absorb what each other has said. Honestly, this is what I wanted to achieve on Friday night. Just simple respect and consideration that life has not stood still since she's been away. It's important to me she knows that…even though I'm not exactly sure why yet.

The mood is fizzled when Tilly suddenly states, "God, I'm awful. Moaning on about things of the past when I swore I wouldn't. And you have a proper job to get back to, so we really should get down to business."

She digs into her bag to retrieve a manila envelope and slides it across the table. I do my best to focus on the papers in front of me as Tilly narrates the issues she's flagged with tabs in the contract. I don't have a lot of experience in retail contracts, but I've done enough endorsement deals for our players and various name brands to see what Harrods is trying to get away with.

"There are definitely some rights in here that Freya will want to keep hold of, and it looks as though they are trying to claim them with their tricky wording. It's good you were dubious of this because I'd definitely make some revisions to this contract."

"That's what I've been trying to get them to do over the past few weeks," she says, her eyes severe as she looks down at the contract. "I tell them the terms I want amended, and they come back with a new contract that still doesn't get everything quite right. It's maddening."

"I could draw up a new contract for you if you like. I mean, they're the ones buying Freya's product, so the contract really should come from her camp with her terms."

"Would you be able to do that?" Tilly asks, chewing her plump lower lip nervously. "I'm meeting with them on Friday is the only problem. That doesn't give you much time."

"It's no problem. I can get it done before then."

"Sonny, that would be brilliant." She pauses, and a nervous flush fills her cheeks. "I mean…Santino."

"It's fine," I reply with a wave of my hand. "And I'll even come along to the meeting with you. I am not saying this to sound arrogant or act like I don't think you can handle it, but any business that comes to a meeting with a lawyer present adds a level of credibility, so maybe they'll quit fucking you about."

Her lips thin, but she nods. "I hate to say it, but I'm sure you're right."

"Why don't we plan to meet again on Wednesday to go over the revisions and make sure they're right before I print the final copy for Friday?"

"That would be great."

I close the envelope and press my hand over it. "We can do dinner so that you don't have to leave Freya home alone again."

"Dinner?" Her eyes widen. "I don't think that's necessary."

"You said you wanted to see a bit more of this side of town, right?"

"Aye."

"Well, I know a great Indian spot that is truly a legend around here. People even come from the pompous west side to enjoy it."

She levels me with a glare. "Very funny."

I lean across the table, invading some of her personal space to whisper loudly, "I'm not trying to be funny."

She backs up to press firmly into her chair as she processes my request more seriously. "I just don't think dinner is a good idea, Santino."

"Why not?" I ask, unrelenting.

"You know why." Her eyes spark with something resembling attraction, which only inspires me more.

I eye her warily. "I know you have been in London for nearly a month and only get out of that house on the weekends. I know that you haven't reacquainted with your old mates because they are…as you so poetically said earlier…a bag of cunts. Most of Freya's friends are married and having babies, which is very similar to my friends. Which leads me to the certainty that you could use a mate to see the city with, and why the bloody hell not make that pal me?"

Her face heats as our eyes connect, and just when I think she's going to reject me and tell me to get stuffed all over again, she nods. "Okay. Indian sounds great."

"Great." I rise and grab my suit coat off the back of my chair.

"On one condition." Tilly's eyes squint in the morning sun up at me.

"Name it." I smile cockily.

She hits me with an amused look. "I've got to get permission from my brother first."

CHAPTER 9

Tilly

"**N**O. FUCK NO. NOT IN A MILLION YEARS. YOU'VE ALL LOST your goddamn bloody minds." Freya and I stare up at my brother, who's, once again, standing in front of their fireplace looking like he's going to pop out of his suit from all the agitation.

"Mac," Freya says in a warning tone.

"Don't you Mac me, woman. I am not, under any circumstances, letting my wee sister go out with that bawbag!"

"It's not a date!" I exclaim defensively. "We're just friends…ish. Business colleagues more. We're looking over the new contract, and it'll be completely platonic."

"I don't give a flying fucktank. You're not going out with him. I know you told me he wasn't the one to put you in that position five years ago, but I still don't trust the bastard. If he wasn't guilty, then why the fuck didn't he call you a couple of years ago like he said he was going to?"

I exhale heavily. Mac mentioned to me after our grandfather passed that Santino wanted to talk to me, but only with Mac's blessing.

Well, amazingly enough, Mac gave him the all-clear, but Santino never called.

I don't know why.

I don't want to know why.

I don't want to know what he was going to say because it wouldn't have changed my situation at the time anyways. At that point in my sobriety, I was still being very careful with my choices. Mac was trying to get me to open up to him more, but I just wasn't interested. I knew I needed to stay the course. And the fact he thought Santino, of all people, might be able to say something to get me to open up is laughable at best. Especially because he clearly still can't stand the man.

However, dinner with him tomorrow now feels like a challenge I want to accept. I'm ready to push my limits, and trying friendship out with Santino feels like an exciting new test for myself.

"Giving me some cryptic bullshit about how he had something to tell me but not until he told you. Fuck that shite!" Mac grumbles in frustration. "I don't like a man who has secrets, Tilly. I have no secrets. Hell, I'll even tell you that my baw sack has changed since I quit playing football. It's got saggier. I'm considering wearing a jockstrap to work for the support. That's how un-secretive I am!"

"I never needed to know that." I cringe at the unpleasant fact my brother just assaulted me with.

"Well, now you know," he barks.

I sigh heavily. "I told you before, and I'll tell you again. I don't care what Santino wanted to tell me. I have no feelings for him, Mac. He's seriously just like the one person I know from my time here in London who isn't the absolute worst type of human, and I'd like to be able to give you guys a weeknight away from Smarty Spice."

Freya smiles at me like a cat that got the cream.

"And I don't like the way my wife is smiling at you." Mac thrusts an accusing finger at Freya. "She's looking like you two have a secret. Cookie, you and I have no secrets. I shouldn't have to remind you that we are man and wife."

"Fine…you want to know my secret?" Freya tuts, her brows lifted with great amusement.

"Aye," Mac booms, nodding his head in preparation.

"I'm Team Santino."

Mac's eyes go wide. "You're what?"

Freya shrugs, undeterred by my fuming brother. "I'm Team Santino, and I don't care who knows it."

"Freya!" I exclaim with accusing eyes. "You're supposed to be my anti-love coach. How can you be Team Santino?"

She smiles sweetly. "I think you two make a nice pair, and you deserve this."

"This isn't a fucking set of ponies we're mating! This is my sister. And Santino is a sleazy lawyer bawbag—"

"Who saved your football career by making it possible for you to come back to Bethnal Green after things didn't go well in Glasgow." Freya stares him down like she's daring him to tell her it isn't true.

Mac jerks his head back and begins pacing in front of the fireplace. "Don't remind me."

"Mac, there was a reason Tilly wouldn't let you pummel him all those years ago when you found out about that money he sent her in Dundonald. And there's a reason she wants to go out to dinner with him."

"As friends," I add firmly, flinching at the mention of money because I sooo do not want to go down that path. Clearly, my beloved sister-in-law needs a stern reminder. "And the past is in the past."

She winks playfully at me. "Take care, love. Mummy has Daddy on the ropes." She swerves her eyes back to Mac. "Your sister is a strong, independent woman with a master's degree and more brains than both of us put together. Now you need to stop being an odious protective big brother and let her make her own choices here. She's doing a lot for us right now, and I could cry just thinking about how helpful she's been to me these past few weeks. She left her life back in Dundonald to be here for us, so we're going to let her have a life while she's here. End of discussion."

Mac's shoulders rise and fall as he heaves big breaths and opens his mouth to speak but then smartly closes it. Finally, he turns to me.

"You tell him that if he puts one fucking finger on you, he's getting a Glasgow Kiss from me, alright?"

"You bet, Macky." I smile at my big brother, who's been reduced to rubble by a couple of women.

When he storms off into the kitchen, Freya looks at me. "What is a Glasgow Kiss again?"

"A headbutt."

Freya's face twists up. "That doesn't sound very nice."

"It's not supposed to be." I giggle.

"Well, we best watch another episode of *Bridgerton* to get you fully *in the mood* for your date." She shoots me a cheeky wink that I shake my head at.

"It's not a date."

"Okay, wee sister."

And just like that...I have a big sister whether I like it or not.

CHAPTER 10

Santino

Getting the text from Tilly that Mac gave her the all-clear for our "business meeting" was a surprise, to say the least. I half expected to have to enlist Tanner or Roan to talk to Mac on my behalf. That stubborn Scot doesn't forgive easily.

However, Tilly is much like her brother in that regard—strong, determined, and loves to march to the beat of her own drum. But as I pull up in front of Mac and Freya's home in Brick Lane, I hope that her accepting my invitation tonight means she wants this night to happen for more reasons than to just piss off her brother.

Because I have high hopes for this evening.

That coffee with Tilly felt like old times but brighter, clearer, and more honest. Years ago, I was perfectly fine to know a woman's body and not her mind. Now, I want it all, especially from the very different Tilly Logan.

So, that's my goal for tonight. To see if that spark we once shared is still there. To see if perhaps there could be more to our story than the original version now that Tilly and I aren't holding back from each other. Her sobriety in no way deters me. In fact, I think it's highly attractive. We'll finally get to know each other how we should have in the beginning, with no barriers of alcohol or arbitrary rules coming between us.

I knock on the door and cringe when Mac's large frame appears. His red hair is soaked in sweat as he stands with boxing gloves on and zero smiles for me.

"Santino," he says through clenched teeth.

"Hiya, Mac, good to see you again." I hold my hand out to shake his, but he just stares me down, refusing to even fist bump me.

"Mac, stop being a grumpy bear," a familiar Cornish accent calls out from inside. "And take off those ridiculous boxing gloves. You've been done working out for twenty minutes."

Mac steps back to let me inside. Upon entering, I look left to see Freya sacked out on the sofa with her feet up on the coffee table and a big orange cat on her lap.

"Hello, Freya. Congratulations on the baby on the way." I point stupidly to her pronounced pregnant belly.

"Thanks, Santino. So nice to see you again," she replies cheerily while petting the cat.

When Mac grumbles from beside me, I look over, expecting him to say something, but he doesn't. He just mutters his annoyance and begrudgingly removes his gloves.

I turn my attention back to Freya. "How long until the due date again?"

"Oh, baby should come before Christmas, God willing. We have a scan next week to see if I can get off this bed rest anytime soon." She beams happily at Mac, who I can feel still glowering at me. "Tilly has been a godsend. And thank you for helping us with this contract. You and Tilly seem to have everything under control, so I'm focusing on my primary job as a human incubator."

"As you should," I reply with a forced smile. "And Tilly is very on top of everything. I think the revisions I made for both of you this week should be beneficial for Friday's meeting."

"And I hear you're going to that meeting with her? That's so thoughtful of you. Mac, isn't that thoughtful of Santino?"

Mac tucks his gloves under his arms and grumbles again, although this time it sounded more like a growl.

"Mac," Freya snaps his name, and he turns his scowl to her. "Thoughtful, right?"

"Aye, sure." He turns his narrowed eyes at me. "As long as he's thoughtful with *everything*."

I swallow the knot in my throat and nod slowly. "You don't have to worry about that, Mac."

"I best not."

Suddenly, our attention is diverted to the staircase as we hear Tilly descend. My eyes can't help but drink in her ripped black jeans, chunky boots, and a white-and-black-striped tank top that flows down her narrow body in a casual yet somehow sexy way. I told her to dress comfortably because of my plans for later, but I didn't anticipate her "comfortable" look to still be so sexy.

"That's what you're wearing?" Mac barks, eyeing his sister up and down. "You said this was a business meeting."

"It is." Tilly shrugs her shoulders and glances nervously over at me. "What are you, the fashion police?"

"You look great!" Freya calls out, effectively silencing her husband.

Mac opens his mouth, but Tilly steps between us and grabs my arm to pull me towards the door. "See you both later. Enjoy your evening alone."

"I still don't know why you couldn't have had the meeting here. We have a perfectly good kitchen table that holds papers nicely. It's strong...made of oak." Mac stands in the doorway and watches us walk out to my car. He points a finger at my Audi. "That's what you drive?"

"Yes?"

"Figures," he huffs.

My brows puzzle as Tilly yells, "Bye!" and slams herself in my car, ignoring her brother completely.

I hurry around to the driver's side, feeling Mac's eyes on me the entire time. As I pull away, I glance over at Tilly. "You sure your brother is okay with this?"

"Too late to turn back now, Sonny. Just drive." Her voice wavers at the end like she's nervous.

"You doing okay there?"

"Yep," she quips as she peeks at me out of the corner of her eye. "You?"

"I'm better now that your brother isn't growling at me anymore." I glance back, halfway expecting Mac to be tailing me. My eyes notice Tilly frowning thoughtfully. "Something on your mind there, Trouble?"

"Yes."

"Care to share?"

"I think we should have rules," she blurts out as she teases the frayed edge of a hole in her jeans.

"Rules for what?"

"Rules for this 'business meeting.'" I can't help but fight back a laugh at the weird tone she uses to say business meeting.

"Why don't we just call this a couple of friends going to eat food?" I suggest, my body resisting this idea because I want this time to be different. I want her to just be herself and let her guard down a bit with me. However, if Tilly wants rules, maybe it's because she's nervous.

I like that I make Tilly nervous.

"Considering we've both seen each other naked, we need rules," Tilly rushes out, and I nearly choke on my own shock.

I glance over to see her chewing nervously on her lower lip as I ask, "What did you have in mind?"

"Rule number one…"

I press my lips together because she's adorably flustered right now but clearly has given this some thought.

"No talking about the past. Only the present or future. But the fact that we have history is off the table now. Okay?"

"Okay..." I reply slowly, wishing I could pull this car over to take a walk down memory lane right bloody now.

"Number two," she continues. "No flirting or over-friendly compliments. And no chivalry. Don't open doors for me or be a gentleman. Just treat me like one of the guys."

My hands tighten around the steering wheel because just having Tilly in my car, invading my nose with her familiar honeysuckle scent that she had five years ago, will make that rule an almost definite impossibility. "I'll do my best."

"Please do," she quips. "Also, we pay for our own food."

"I can't give you that one," I argue, staring at the road. "This is a business meeting, so I'll pay."

"You said you're not charging me for your services, though."

"So?"

"So, at the very least then, I should buy your dinner."

"What happened to paying for our own food?" I ask, holding back a teasing smile.

"I don't care. I'm buying dinner. End of discussion." Hearing her resigned tone, I can't help but feel like I've already won.

"Anything else you want to add to this list?"

"Nothing I can think of for now. Do you have anything you want to add?"

I exhale heavily. I could think of many things I want to add, but I'm almost certain she wouldn't agree with them.

Tilly

Santino takes me to Dishoom in Shoreditch. It's a vibrant, trendy little place that has a line around the building. However, Santino bypasses everyone, and a man by the name of Keenil immediately ushers us to a cosy little two-seater right by the window. When I ask Santino how we got seated so quickly, he waves me off, saying the owner is a big football fan.

"Drinks?" the waitress asks, her pen and paper in hand.

"I'll have a chai tea, please."

"Make that two," Santino adds.

I frown. "You don't have to do that."

"Do what?"

"Drink tea. You can have a drink. I won't start convulsing at the table."

"I love the chai tea here. Truly."

The waitress takes off, not the least bit interested, and I exhale slowly. Santino ordering a non-alcoholic drink feels dangerously chivalrous, and that was one of the rules I did not want him to break tonight. I don't need a reason to be attracted to him.

But if I'm being honest, the gesture is really sweet.

Throughout dinner, I find myself stress-eating naan and talking incessantly about Freya's pet clothing selections for Harrods and how she continues to gain followers on Instagram. I think I even tell a long-winded story about how her cat Hercules won't let me try any of the clothes on him because he hates me and hisses anytime I go near him. Then I share how her cat Jasper and I get on well and he sleeps on the spare pillow on my bed every night now, and oh my God, I sound like a crazy fucking single cat lady. Who fucking cares about Freya and Mac's stupid cats right now? What is wrong with me?

I take a long drink of tea to calm my mind because I know what's wrong with me. I'm talking a lot because I'm nervous. And I'm nervous because Santino looks stupidly hot tonight.

Don't get me wrong, he's always been sinfully attractive in his tailored suits and slicked-back business hairstyle. But tonight, he's casual sexy in a pair of soft, faded jeans and trainers plus a sort of expensive-looking jumper that I'm sure cost more than my entire outfit. And his black hair is soft without a spot of gel in sight. Its natural waves continually flop over his forehead, reminding me of the times we were intimate. He would be on top of me, driving deep inside, his hair a mess from my fingers raking through it. The vivid memories of how he made me feel when we were tangled up cause a warmth to spread within me. *Stop it, Tilly. Stop it right now. This is not a walk down memory lane. This is not a date. This is a business meeting.*

In fact, he told me to dress comfortably, which means he wanted to be sure I didn't show up in a sexy little black dress and heels. That means Santino doesn't want a walk down memory lane either.

So this is good.

I can just…relax and be myself tonight.

I become a bit less twitchy as we go over the new contract he drew up. It's perfect in every way, and I find myself truly grateful for Allie forcing him on me because if Harrods can agree to this, then it'll be full steam ahead after our meeting on Friday.

When we order coffee and dessert, I find my curiosity about how Santino has changed knocking too hard in my head to ignore. Biting the bullet, I ask, "So, tell me about this two-month chump nickname I hear you have?"

Santino's dark brows lift as he holds his cup of coffee to his lips. "Sorry?"

I fight back a smile. "I hear you're some kind of monogamous heartbreaker nowadays."

Santino shakes his head and rolls his eyes. "Who told you that?"

"Freya via Allie, Allie via Roan, I think?"

"One thing you need to know about the Harris family and all their friends and cousins is that there's no such thing as a secret. Not that my dating life has anything to hide, but when there's any bit of gossip offered to someone, everyone will hear about it. And I mean everyone."

Giggling, I stab my fork into a sweet Modawk dumpling stuffed with nutmeg and saffron. "So, what does it mean exactly?"

"Pretty much what it sounds like." He sighs heavily. "I can't seem to make a relationship stick for very long. Some end after a few weeks, some after a couple of months."

My brows furrow because Santino seems so different and mature now. Going on annual trips with his mother, volunteering to help out Freya and me. This definitely isn't the same sleazy nightclub lad I met five years ago, but maybe deep down, he's still a womanizing arsehole who can't commit. "What's the problem you think?" I inquire, even though I probably already know the answer.

He shrugs. "Lack of connection, lack of interest, lack of...good sex." His dark eyes narrow on me, and I feel a flutter in my belly that really needs to go away.

"Sounds...lacking. How many have there been?" I swallow the knot in my throat because I hate that I keep asking more questions. I never cared who he slept with even when we were sleeping with each other, so why do I give a toss now?

"God, I've lost count." He reaches across the table and snags a dumpling off my plate. "At first, I was letting the Harris wives set me up, then I tried to find someone on my own. It's not for lack of trying, I'll tell you that."

"What inspired this sudden change of heart for you?" I ask, watching his square, whiskered jaw as he chews his sweet treat. "Last I knew, you were running away screaming from commitment."

"Careful now." He winks. "Don't want to break one of our non-date rules."

I roll my eyes. "Are you avoiding the question?"

He gets a serious look in his eye. "No, but I don't think you're going to like the answer."

My stomach falls. "Tell me anyways."

He sits back in his seat and exhales heavily, a dark look fleeting across his face that he instantly masks. "Part of it was just that I was too old to be going out to clubs with footballers and hooking up with girls who were all trying to shag a Harris Brother. Honestly, it's pathetic when I look back on it. I should have had my own life by then." His face grows serious when he adds, "But the real reason had a lot more to do with everything that happened to you."

"Me?" My skin prickles with anxiety.

He nods slowly, his eyes becoming grave. "There are things about my past that made what happened to you affect me on a deep, dark level."

"What kinds of things?" I ask, my body leaning into him with curiosity.

His face goes hard, and he shakes his head firmly. "It's not important, but it is…strangely connected. After you left, I realised that all the things I had been avoiding for my own fucked-up reasons suddenly weren't all that scary."

I blink back at him, my mind reeling with that cryptic information. What is he referring to? What about my situation could have possibly triggered something in him? I open my mouth to ask questions, to pry, to challenge and get the full story…but I can't. Asking deep questions like that would not only break the rules, it would smash them to pieces.

I bite my lip and force my very gentle reply, "Well, I guess there's one good thing that came out of my situation. Now you're the perfect single man."

"Hardly." His shoulders shake with silent laughter. "Actually, if you want the truth of it, after you left, I think I got worse for a bit."

"That sounds much more on-brand for Santino Rossi."

"Yeah…it was a phase. Then the Harris Brothers all started getting married, one on top of the other, and I finally started believing that if they could have it, so could I."

He shrugs like what he said is no big deal when I know it's a very big deal. Santino was anti-relationship from the moment I met him. He made that very clear…which, at the time, was part of the appeal. It's fascinating to see how different he is now.

Silence descends on us as emotion creeps up in the depths of my eyes. "Can I ask you a question?" I hear my heart speaking even though my mind wants it to shut the bloody hell up.

"Always," he replies, his face taking on a severe look.

"What was it you wanted to talk to me about a couple of years ago…when you asked for Mac's blessing?" My face flames with heat that I pray to fuck he can't see.

He flinches, and his eyes instantly cast downward. "It's not important now."

"It must have been somewhat important for you to approach my brother," I volley back, wondering if it had anything to do with things from his past that he alluded to.

He looks up at me with narrowed eyes. "I feel like this is more than breaking your rules."

"You didn't want rules to begin with." I stare him down with blatant challenge as my inner voice screams at me for being weak.

He sighs heavily as his eyes rove over my face, taking in every feature in a way that makes me feel naked. "You know, I don't care what you said in the lift. I still blame myself for what happened to you."

My lips part. "Why?"

His face bends in sympathy. "Even with our stupid rules we had in the past, I could see you weren't right. I could see you were struggling."

I shake my head slowly. "It had nothing to do with you."

"I know but—"

"But nothing," I cut him off. "I made my own choices that night. Choices that had consequences, and well…it doesn't matter now. Things turned out as they were meant to, and now I'm here, eating dumplings."

He smiles slowly. "With an old friend."

I narrow my eyes at him. "Business colleague."

When he laughs, the sound sends a flurry through my lower belly. "You're going to be my friend, Tilly Logan."

"Whatever you say, Sonny," I grumble and then take another sip of my coffee "And don't think I didn't realise you just deftly avoided my question."

He rolls his eyes. "Sober or not, you're still nothing but trouble, Tilly Logan."

And I have a sinking feeling that Santino Rossi might like trouble.

CHAPTER 11

Tilly

MIRACULOUSLY, SANTINO LET ME PAY FOR DINNER, AND WHEN we're back in his car, I realise we're not heading home towards Brick Lane. "Where are we going?"

"I have a surprise for you."

"Oh?"

"It's why I told you to dress comfortably." He shoots me a wink as he rounds a corner. "That's my building right there," he says casually.

I glance over at a large, four-level brick and glass structure. It stands out amongst the other more dated buildings. "Is that where we're going?" I ask, my pulse quickening as images of us stumbling through his old flat as we ditch our clothes piece by piece fill my mind.

"No," he replies with a laugh. "We're just passing it on the way."

"Oh." I exhale heavily and do my best to get my mind out of the gutter.

Moments later, he pulls up to a fenced-in parking garage. An older man comes out of a brick security booth and approaches the vehicle. Santino rolls the window down. "Hiya, Sedgwick."

"Good evening, Mr. Rossi." Sedgwick dips his head to make eye contact with me. "Hello, Miss."

"Um, hi?" I croak, my eyes zeroing in on his jacket that says Tower Park Grounds Crew on the left breast pocket.

"Are we all clear?" Santino asks.

"You sure are. Roger kicked the lights on for you a bit ago, so they should be nice and warmed up."

"Brilliant. You guys are amazing."

Sedgwick hits Santino with a serious look. "Well, we appreciated you working on our union contracts pro bono, so this is the least we can do." Sedgwick dips his head and gives me a kind smile. "You must be a special young lady to warrant this kind of an evening."

"I'm not even sure what's going on yet," I reply with a nervous chuckle.

"You will soon enough," Sedgwick says cheerily and taps the car before heading to the remote gate panel to open it for us.

"I'm not that keen on surprises, Sonny," I say nervously, and my mind goes wild with what we could be doing at Tower Park late at night.

Santino pats my leg. "It's really not that big of a deal, I promise you. Sedgwick is a good friend of Tanner's and was more than happy to do this."

His hand lingers on my leg for a moment, his fingers brushing the bare skin peeking out through one of the holes in my jeans. My entire body erupts in goosebumps, and arousal pulses between my legs. I swallow nervously as I stare at his large, masculine hand alongside my pale skin.

He notices my eyes watching his touch, and he quickly pulls his hand away, placing it back on the wheel. "Sorry."

"It's fine," I rush out. *Jesus, it was more than fine, and I need to get control of myself right now.*

He turns to me with a hopeful look on his face like my reply was an opening. "It is fine?"

"I mean, it's not fine!" I blurt out, my head snapping forward and my face flaming with humiliation. "But it's fine. I mean…don't let it happen again." The last bit comes out a bit too harsh, and I cringe.

He huffs out a laugh and pulls through the gates to park right by a small side door with a dim yellow light overhead. We hop out of the car, and I frown at him. "We're at Tower Park right now, right?"

"We are." He winks.

"Why?" I ask as he pulls out a key to unlock the door.

"You said you never got to see Tower Park before so I thought I'd give you a little tour." My lips part in shock, but my attention is diverted as he opens the door to a long, dimly lit hallway. "You're far too young and beautiful to live with regrets. Follow me."

He glances at my hand like he wants to hold it, so I quickly stuff it into my pocket to take that option away. I barely made it through his touch in the car, so there's no way I'll survive an intimate hand hold.

We make our way down the dingy concrete hallway, and Santino has to duck past low-hanging light fixtures, pointing them out to me as well.

"Was this hallway built for trolls?" My voice echoes loudly in the space.

He huffs. "No, just goblins and hobbits. Trolls have the north entrance." He laughs at his own joke, and I roll my eyes, fighting back my own smile.

"Just around here," Santino says, stepping back and lightly placing his hand on the small of my back to guide me around the corner, making my body hum to his touch once more. "This is the home team entrance."

My eyes squint against the onslaught of stadium lights pouring in through the long, white tunnel. The electric green pitch shimmers off in the distance. "Oh, my God."

I walk quickly and hear Santino behind me as we emerge out of the tunnel and onto the beautiful grounds of Tower Park Football Stadium. I shield my eyes, allowing them to adjust to the light as I stand at the edge and stare out at the lush green grass.

"Can I walk out there?" I ask, turning back to find Santino watching me with great interest.

"Of course," he replies with a laugh. "I didn't bring you down here just to look at it."

I stick my tongue out childishly and make my way towards the middle of the pitch where there's a sack of footballs in the centre circle. The grass is spongey beneath my flat boots and I do a turn to take in the bright, stadium lights illuminating the grass and the stands. One whole side of the stadium spells out TOWER PARK on old wooden, white painted chairs. The other side looks like it has several suites and offices glassed off at the top. It feels big and important. Magical and overpowering.

The last time I was on a pitch like this was in Glasgow with my brother and grandfather. My grandfather was very ill back in Dundonald, and Mac took a transfer to play for Rangers as a sort of dying wish to him. After the game, we were able to come down onto the pitch, and I'll never ever forget the look on my granddad's face.

Pride.

Pure, unencumbered, bubbling over with red-rimmed eyes pride.

I remember watching them embrace and feeling pangs of envy for not doing more with my life to make our grandfather proud before he died. Then I remembered hating myself for having such a horrible emotion during such an important end of life moment for him. I was so twisted up in my own head that I didn't truly take in the stadium atmosphere like I should have.

This moment right here at Tower Park…it feels like a second chance.

Santino walks slowly toward me, his hands shoved in his denim pockets like this is just another day at the office for him. "Pretty great, right?"

I nod and feel a tight knot forming in my throat. "Is it weird that I want to cry?"

His face falls with concern. "Depends on why you want to cry, I guess."

I inhale deeply and try to compose myself, my eyes burning with unshed tears. "It's just overwhelming."

"What is?"

"Life," I reply honestly, my chin quivering as I gaze at him through watery eyes. "I missed so much of it when I was drinking all the time. And then I became so hyper-focused on getting sober that I missed out on that span of time as well. It wasn't until my mum called and told me Freya almost lost the baby," my voice cracks as the memory of a call that still haunts my dreams plays on repeat in my mind. "She called and told me they were at the hospital and it was this strange sense of déjà vu that scared me so much, it woke me up."

I run a trembling hand through my hair, staring up at the bright lights that are blurry from my tears. "I had so much tunnel-vision on my own journey that I was missing out on everyone else's. My family. People who loved me and supported me through my darkest days. They were all dealing with their own personal horrors, and I was so self-absorbed my own brother didn't feel like he could call and tell me about the most terrifying moment of his life."

Memories of my own past flood in my mind as tears stream freely down my face. I swipe them away, trying to collect myself because this is not the time nor the place to be having a crisis of conscience.

"Helping them now...this is my chance to make up for lost time." I clear my throat and steel myself to look brave and unbothered. "Which is why these past few weeks, being back here in London...it feels like the first time I've allowed myself to really live, not just survive." I do a slow spin, pointing at the grand space all around me. "And it's overwhelming because everything is so clear and so present, and I can see it all so vividly. It makes me feel sad for everything I missed out on before."

Santino's face bends with sympathy. "You're here now, though, right?" he asks softly.

"I guess," I shrug, still hating myself for the choices of my past.

He walks towards me. "You are here, Tilly. You're here, and you're doing great. You're helping out your brother and Freya. You're doing an incredible job with Freya's business. Now is what matters, remember? Isn't that one of your rules? No talking about the past. That includes self-loathing past choices, okay?"

My chin quivers as Santino reaches out to rub my shoulder. It's a comforting, gentle caress that makes me realise it's been ages since I've been vulnerable like this in front of anyone. Even my brother and parents don't see me like this. I always told them just enough so they wouldn't worry, but I never truly revealed all that I experienced.

I couldn't. I was too ashamed.

"Come here," Santino says, grabbing my arm and pulling me close.

"I'm fine," I reply, sniffing loudly and trying to force my tears to retreat.

"Of course, you're fine," he states firmly and before I know what's happening, he wraps his arms around me in a tight hug.

My hands flop down by my sides as I mentally resist his embrace. But as soon as his familiar scent invades my nose, tiny flickers of memories come pouring into my mind. Moments in Santino's flat, my flat, moments where he would look at me from across a crowded pub and all I wanted to do was leave with him and never look back.

We were just sex on the surface, but the fact that I have recollections of the connection we shared, that pull…it makes me grateful. Like I didn't completely black out my entire history.

He cups the back of my head and sifts his fingers through my hair. It feels so good and so comforting that the tears I was trying to hold back begin to slip out as my head lowers into that perfect space on his shoulder. I cinch my arms around his waist and hold on as I allow myself to savour this moment. It's been a long time since I've had a man hold me. A very long time. And the fact that it's Santino Rossi of all people is a surprise for so many reasons.

Santino wasn't the hugging and comforting type of bloke. When he touched me in the past, it was for both of our pleasures. This feels strangely selfless, which isn't a side to him I'm used to seeing.

Finally, I collect myself and murmur into his chest, "You know this is breaking several of my rules."

Santino squeezes me tighter and growls in my ear. "Friends can hug."

My lips pull back into a reluctant smile as I mumble into his collarbone, "This feels like more than a hug."

"Friends give long, lingering hugs all the time." His chest shakes with silent laughter, and finally, he releases me, stepping back and staring down at me with a kind look of concern. He swipes his thumb along my tear-stained cheek. "You good?"

"Aye, sure," I brush him off, taking a step back and hitting him with a wobbly smile. "Nothing a stiff drink couldn't fix or a decade's worth of therapy."

He smiles proudly at me and then waggles his brows. "Want to kick a ball around?"

This question shocks me. "You know how to play football?"

"I was quite good at the local youth club, I'll have you know." He bends over and dumps out the bag of balls.

"You were?" I can't hide the disbelief on my face even if I tried.

He shoots me a roguish smile as he picks up a ball and tosses it between his two hands. "Well, my mum thought so."

I belly laugh at that comment. "God, I can only imagine."

"What about you?" He backs away from me and drops the ball onto his foot to do several kick ups. "You have a brother who played professionally, surely you learned something along the way."

"Oh, I know plenty, don't you worry." Suddenly, I dart towards him and give him a hard push before stealing the ball.

"Oh fuck," Santino huffs and turns to chase after me as I dribble my way down the pitch towards the net. "I wasn't ready!"

"Rookie mistake, Sonny. You should always be ready!" I laugh and then squeal when he swoops in and steals the ball back from me. "Shit!"

"Oh yes," Santino replies back, laughing more than I've ever seen him laugh in all the time I've known him. "My coach never thought I had what it took but my mum always believed in me."

My belly hurts from laughing and running as I grab at his jumper to try to steal the ball back from him.

"Oiy! Watch the hands, Logan!" he bellows.

"You have to play a little dirty sometimes, Rossi! Don't be such a delicate flower."

"I'm not delicate! I just follow the—"

Suddenly, our legs get tangled and before I know it, he's falling backwards and taking me down with him. I land with an *oof* on top of him and his hands somehow end up on my waist as mine press into his firm, very sculpted chest.

We're both smiling and laughing and breathing hard. Really hard. So hard that the motion is causing our bodies to move on top of each other in a way that feels completely…divine.

Santino's laughter dies as his gaze lowers to my lips. I stare back at his in response, and when I feel him lift his head off the grass and come closer to my mouth, I quickly roll onto my back and scramble back up on my feet.

"That was a cheap shot," I bark, feeling the flush of heat in my cheeks. *And between my legs.*

Santino props himself onto his elbows, his head shaking back and forth. "You were the one who fouled me."

"I didn't foul you! You were blocking the whole time! You would have got a yellow card for sure."

He growls, and then suddenly, he's back on his feet and chasing after the ball. I sprint after him, but maintain more personal space this time. No more rules can be broken tonight. Not on my watch.

CHAPTER 12

Santino

I STAND OUTSIDE HARRODS' CORPORATE OFFICE LATE FRIDAY afternoon fiddling with my tie as I wait for Tilly to arrive for our meeting. My mind has been wondering what she's going to be wearing or how she's going to act because, well, Tilly has been occupying most of my thoughts this past week. At least five times, I picked up my mobile to phone her, but I stopped myself because I don't want to scare her away. And if I told her everything that's been rushing through my mind for the past forty-eight hours, she would probably run away faster than I could catch her...even while she dribbles a football.

The truth of the matter is, that dinner Wednesday night was a game changer for me. Maybe it's her sobriety that's made her even more stunning, or maybe it's because she kicked my arse on the pitch just after she opened up her soul to me and left tears on my shirt, but I want her now more than ever before. And the fact that all I did for the past two days was wank off like a fucking teenager is embarrassing to say the least. I'm a thirty-six-year-old man. I should be better than this.

But no woman in my entire life has affected me the way Tilly has. And Christ, it's only been a week.

This feeling of wanting something I can't have doesn't sit well with me. But I have to play it smart with Tilly. This friendship thing is working between us, and I need to let her come to me, or she will put her walls up again like the stunning Scottish fortress I know she can be. So, for now, I just have to be patient for as long as it takes. And hope like fuck it doesn't take long.

My eyes look left because I can feel her coming before I see her. She looks like a tall, gorgeous business mogul walking the streets of West London like she owns this town. She's dressed in a crisp, sheer white blouse and black wide-leg trousers with heels. Her long strawberry blond hair is pinned back into a low bun, and her makeup is striking against her fair skin.

Fuck me, if I was on the other end of this business meeting, I'd give this woman anything she wants.

When her eyes connect with mine, she offers me a confident smile like she's completely unfazed by my presence. *Unlike me.*

"You're early," she says, approaching me at a quick pace and adjusting her handbag on her shoulder. "Have you been waiting long?"

"My previous meeting ended early." I clear my throat to get my shit together. "Sorry we couldn't ride together."

"Oh, it's fine," she replies with a wave of her hand as she tucks a stray lock behind her ear.

"Have everything you need?" I glance down at her like I need to double-check, but in all honesty, I just want another glimpse of her body.

"I believe so." She touches her twitching nose. "I printed off a few copies of the contract."

"So did I. Plus, I couriered it over to them yesterday, so they should be ready for us."

"Oh yes, you told me that." Her eyes lower to my suit, and she inhales sharply. "Shall we do this?"

I gesture towards the door. "I'll follow you."

We check in at the front counter and get visitor passes for the twentieth floor. When we step into the lift and end up crammed in behind at least ten other people, we both peer at each other from the corner of our eye. Her knowing smirk hits me right in the gut. The last time we were in a lift together, things got a little heated.

I wanted to fuck her then, even when I was angry with her.

And bloody hell, I want to fuck her now.

Basically, I want to fuck her always.

I truly have lost my mind.

The receptionist ushers us to a traditionally furnished, glassed-off conference room with a long maple table and at least a dozen wheelie chairs. Tilly and I sit at one end and await the executive's arrival.

"Are you nervous?" I ask, watching her lay out several copies of the contract she most likely won't need while silently applauding her for being over-prepared.

"Not nervous, just ready to get this finalised." Her blue eyes flash to mine, and she looks pensive and unsure. "I thought we'd be past this point by now and going over the logistics with the factories. I don't like that we're behind schedule."

I reach out and touch her hand. "They're going to approve the contract today, I'm sure of it. Just show them who's boss."

She smiles softly and then glances down at my hand on hers. Suddenly, our attention is diverted as the doors open, and three people stride into the conference room to join us.

"Ah, hello, Ms. Logan, so good to see you again." A woman walks over to shake Tilly's hand.

"Hi, Mrs. Woodland. Nice to see you."

"How is our lovely Freya? Resting comfortably, I hope?"

"She is, thank you for asking. She and the baby on the way are doing quite well."

"Brilliant." She turns her gaze to me. "This must be…?"

"Mr. Santino Rossi, Perfectly Sized Pets' legal counsel," Tilly answers, turning to me with a nervous smile.

"Ah, yes." Mrs. Woodland eyes me up and down as she shakes my hand. "Didn't like our contract, I take it?"

"No, I thought it was great," I reply, pulling my hand back and unbuttoning my suit coat. "I just like my stationery better." I shoot her a wink, and it works like a charm as she erupts into a fit of overzealous giggles.

She introduces us to the rest of the team as they take their seats across from us. "We've reviewed your new contract in detail, and I believe we have an agreement, but we want to propose one more thing today."

Tilly's eyes widen as she looks at me with a mixture of excitement and anxiety. "What is it?"

"We'd like to hire you here at Harrods, Tilly, as the head executive for this new department." Mrs. Woodland pushes a manila envelope across the table. "I looked you up and spoke to your former employer at Fortnum and Mason, and we think you have what it takes to work here as a welcome asset to our team."

Tilly blinks silently back at Mrs. Woodland like she's just sprouted three heads, so she continues. "We want you to find new, fresh talent and establish business relationships with potential vendors for our growing pet department. Within the department, you can work on selling reports and ensure there are no chargebacks once production begins for Freya's line and any other future pet products we may procure down the road. And we want to be sure we get the right product into the stores so it doesn't just sell, but it sells well. You'd work here at our corporate office and be on the cusp of this new venture for our luxury department store. After dealing with your tenacity these past few weeks, we think you will be perfect for this position."

Tilly remains frozen for an extraordinarily long time beside me, so I gently nudge her with my elbow. "Tilly."

"Yes?"

"Did you hear them?"

"I think so." She blinks rapidly.

I clear my throat and offer Mrs. Woodland a polite smile. "Sorry, one question: Can you confirm if Freya's contract is contingent on Tilly accepting this offer?"

"Heavens no!" Mrs. Woodland exclaims. "We've already signed your contract, Mr. Rossi." She slides a second manila envelope over to me, and I open it to see for my own eyes. My verbiage and my stationery are all on full display with all their perfect signatures. "We just need Freya's signature on that, and we're all set to move forward."

"That is good news." I glance over at Tilly, who still seems a bit shaken by the earlier offer. "Could you possibly give my client the room for a moment to consult with counsel?"

Mrs. Woodland smiles at me. "We don't need an answer today. The position wouldn't begin for at least another four to six weeks. We do understand your personal situation with helping out your sister-in-law while she's on bed rest, though, so if that timeline needs to be pushed back, we have some work-from-home options we can discuss as well. Give it a think and consult with whomever you like." She eyes me up and down and then turns her focus back to Tilly. "This could work out excellently for both Harrods and Freya. A true partnership with Tilly having both parties' best interests at heart."

"It does sound mutually beneficial," I offer since Tilly still hasn't snapped out of her shock while her nose twitches nervously.

Mrs. Woodland shoots me a wink as she and her colleagues leave the room. As soon as they're out of eyesight, I grab Tilly's chair and swivel her to face me. "Tilly, what's the matter? You just got a job offer that sounds like a brilliant opportunity for you."

"I need to talk to Freya," she rushes out, her blue eyes wide and wary.

"About what?"

"What if she wants this job?" Tilly's face gazes back at me in horror. "I mean, how awful…she's on bed rest while I'm here taking credit for all her hard work."

My brow furrows. "No one thinks you're taking credit for her work. They're offering you this job because of their interactions with you for the past month, not Freya. Plus, didn't you say that Freya is the creative designer? Isn't that where she thrives?"

"Yes."

"They're not offering you a creative position. And Freya will still be in charge of her line at Harrods with this signed contract. It's actually you that will be out of a job once this all gets going, so this is a win-win situation. And frankly, I venture a guess that Harrods pays a lot better than Freya."

I slide the folder over to her, and she looks at it like it might burn her. "Christ, this is a big decision."

"You have time to think it over," I reply quickly, holding back a laugh because she's adorably flustered. "But for now, you should celebrate. They saw something in you after just a month of working with you." I press my lips together to stop myself from saying that I saw the same in one week. "You're exactly where you're meant to be, and I think this is a sign of more good things to come."

Tilly finally allows a smile to spread across her face. "Thank you, Santino." Leaning in, she throws her arms around my neck, hugging me fiercely. "You've been such a tremendous help."

I squeeze her back, laughing into her neck. "I didn't do anything. This was all you."

She pulls back, her eyes flicking back and forth between mine. "I still can't believe this."

"Believe it." I smile as I tuck a loose tendril behind her ear, relishing in the feel of her in my arms. "Whether you accept this position or not, we should celebrate because the contract is signed."

She licks her lips and smiles at me for a moment. It's heart-stopping, and it takes everything in me not to grab her face and kiss her right here, right now.

Then suddenly, her face falls, and I see doubt creeping back in. "We better not."

"Why not?" I ask, refusing to go down without a fight.

Turning, she begins picking up her spare contracts and stuffing them into her bag. "Well, there's not much to celebrate with when you're sober."

"Bollocks," I scoff, my hand landing on her thigh. "We can grab a couple of fizzy drinks at the corner shop, then go sit in a park somewhere."

She freezes and glances down at my hand with a look of discomfort, so I quickly remove it, feeling strangely rejected all over again.

"It's not a good idea, Sonny."

My jaw tightens as I take in her refusal at full throttle. "If you say so." Exhaling heavily, I hand her the contract.

With a nervous swallow, she takes the folder. "Thanks."

And that is now my third rejection from the ever-evasive Tilly Logan, who I just can't seem to walk away from.

CHAPTER 13

Tilly

OVER THE WEEKEND, I'M RIDDLED WITH ANXIETY. THE OFFER from Harrods is ridiculous. It's more money than I ever dreamed of making even back when I was working my way up at Fortnum and Mason. And when I told Freya and Mac, they were both over the moon excited for me. Freya all but told me she would not let me meet my nephew if I didn't accept the job. And Mac did that proud Scottish father smile his son will feel in full force for his whole life. I even called to tell my parents the good news, and they didn't seem at all surprised that I most likely won't be coming back to Dundonald after Freya has the baby.

"You're too smart for the likes of this wee place, Till," my dad said, sounding like he was getting choked up.

"Now I can see both my kids in one place when we come to visit," my mum cooed soothingly. "And I'll be visiting a lot once that baby is born!"

They always know exactly what to say to make me feel special. Yet still…I can't shake this anxiety.

And I think I know why.

"Heading out?" Freya chirps from her sofa throne as I try to quietly sneak out the front door on Sunday at noon.

I pause and turn, glancing around for any sign of Mac.

"He went out to pick me up some wine gums." Freya touches her belly fondly. "The baby demanded it."

I laugh, then walk over to sit beside her. "I'm going over to Santino's."

"I knew it!" she squeals excitedly, her round cheeks pulling back as she smiles. "You saucy minx. You two are having The Sex, aren't you?"

"No!" I exclaim defensively, feeling a hum begin inside me just at the mention of sleeping with Santino. "No, this is purely a friendship thing. I just feel like a shite because Friday after our meeting, he wanted to celebrate the contract and my job offer, and I kind of rejected him."

"Why did you reject him?"

"Because he's bloody perfect!" I nearly shout because I'm so fucking sick of being confused by him.

"He's got a lot of nerve!" Freya tuts in solidarity. "Doesn't he know we women only want men who are damaged so that we can project our insecurities on them and feel superior in our less awful fuckedupness?"

"Right!" I reply with a huff. "And I don't need a distraction like him in my life because I'm here for you. And the baby!" I smile at Freya's belly that I swear gets bigger by the day. "This is my do-over with you and Mac. I'm here to be the sister I should have been over the past decade or so."

"Tilly." Freya says my name in a chastising tone that gives me an instant sneak peek of what she'll sound like as a mother. "You do not owe us anything more than your love and affection."

"What?" I ask with a confused laugh.

"When you offered to come here and help us out, it wasn't so you could chain yourself to my leg and pay your dues. You're not punching a clock, and we're not going to accuse you of not caring the minute you don't log forty hours!"

"I know that."

She clutches her belly firmly, her nostrils flaring with determination. "Then don't use me as an excuse for your fear."

I inhale sharply at her very pointed words. She must take pity on my shock because she reaches forward to touch my leg soothingly. "I just want you to see that we are doing quite well here. And we love having you here. I have greatly enjoyed the experience of living with a sister, but none of that should come at the expense of your own happiness. You're quite capable of having it all, Smarty Spice."

She shoots me a very Freya-like wink, and I expel a soft laugh. "All that may be true, but I'm not sure Santino is the man to take that gamble with. A leopard doesn't truly change his spots."

"If you say so." Freya huffs and hits me with a knowing look. "Although, you somehow managed to change yours, didn't you?"

I groan exhaustedly. "It's not the same thing."

"It's not that different, Smarty Spice! It's not unheard of for people to change. You're sober now, so the idea that Santino might not be the Lord Voldemort manwhore we all took him to be could be a faint possibility."

I bite my lip as I ponder that thought for a moment and then quickly shake it away. "Well, it doesn't matter anyways because we're just friends. And I'm only going over there for a quick chat because he did a lot for us with this deal and I don't want to be a total cunt. Just a quick apology, then I'm out of there."

"If you say so," Freya replies with a sneaky smile. "Where should I tell your brother you ran off to?"

I swallow nervously. "Just tell him I went out to the markets. I'll probably shop on my way back, so it won't be a complete lie."

Freya nods excitedly. "I've got your back, sis."

I drive my car over to the building I remember Santino pointing out the other night after dinner. I could text him and tell him I'm coming over but after being such a prat, I think this warrants a bit of an un-expected gesture.

That is…if he's home in the middle of a Sunday. I mean, it's just venturing on one o'clock. If he has a date for the night, surely it wouldn't start until later, right? Unless he had someone sleepover last night. And she's still there now? Oh my God, that would be humiliating.

My hands tighten around the wheel, and I wonder if I should turn back now and save myself all the trouble. But then I remember how thoughtful he was to draw up that contract and how thrilled Freya was to sign it and scan it over to them right away. Santino didn't have to help us, but he did, which means I didn't have to be such an arse to him when he simply wanted to celebrate.

I find Santino's building with ease. The enormous floor-to-ceiling windows make everyone inside look like they're in a fishbowl. I stand at the entrance, searching for his buzzer, and then see P beside his name.

"Of course he's in the penthouse," I grumble and lift my finger to press it.

"A little help please," a young female calls out as she attempts to push a buggy out the door.

"Oh, of course." I rush over to hold the door open as she scoots her way out with a giggling baby cooing from within.

"Cheers for that. After lugging this thing down two levels, I'm spent."

I laugh and watch her walk away, looking the picture of a flustered new mummy. Funnily enough, I could never see myself with kids. Or pregnant, for that matter. I just never inherited that maternal instinct so many women have. Being the cool aunt is a vibe I feel much more capable of handling. And very soon, Freya and Mac will be giving me that title.

I realise I'm still standing there with the door open, so I bypass the buzzer and make my way up the four levels to the top floor. I take the steps slowly, trying to mentally prepare myself to see Santino again.

The reason I was such a twat when he asked to celebrate was because all I wanted to do at that moment was kiss him right there in that boardroom. That would have been horribly awkward of me, not to mention highly unprofessional. But the way Santino was looking at me with pride and genuine happiness all over his face was overwhelming. That job offer—that moment in my career—felt like something I never thought possible. I was so struck with emotion that I got swept up in those feelings I have struggled to keep quiet. And those feelings were fixating on Santino's brooding pout that I can faintly remember the taste of.

But…Santino and I are just friends. I know that. He knows that. Which is why this visit will be just two mates toasting with a couple of platonic fizzy drinks.

When I reach the top floor, I can hear classic Italian music coming out of the flat with a large P on the door. I hesitate and consider tucking tail and leaving because the thought of Santino entertaining a guest hurts me on some deep, dark stupid level that I have no right to be offended by. Moreover, even if he does have a guest over, that doesn't mean I can't stop by to say thank you. I just need to say what I came to say and let him get on with his day. *No more running, Tilly.*

With a deep breath, I knock on the door and prepare myself for some beautiful woman to answer in a slip of a dress and freshly fucked hair because that would be just my luck. However, when the door swings open, I'm shocked to find an old, white-haired woman standing on the other side. She's wiping her hands off on a white apron splattered in red sauce, and she's staring at me like I'm interrupting a very important meeting.

"Oh, I'm sorry…I must have the wrong flat," I choke out, my voice drowned out over the loud instrumental melody. I feel a semblance of relief as I turn to leave, but before I do, my eyes catch sight of something behind her that causes me to nearly drop the glass bottles in my hands.

It's Santino.

In a kitchen.

Cutting up tomatoes?

He's wearing a pair of grey trousers and a white dress shirt with the sleeves rolled up his arms. There's a white apron tied around his waist, just like the woman currently glowering at me. When he casually glances over to see who's standing in the doorway, his face is the picture of shocked.

"Tilly?" his lips say, but I can hardly hear him over the loud music pumping through the sound system.

The woman beside me begins shouting over the music to Santino, but I can't understand her because she's speaking Italian. Santino yells back in the same language and grabs a towel off the counter to wipe off his hands before he turns down the music. As he strides over, he and the woman speak quickly to each other for what feels like ages as I stand there like a fool holding a couple of non-alcoholic drinks in hand while trying not to drool over the fact that Santino speaks Italian.

What the hell else is he hiding?

Finally, she waves him off, pointing aggressively towards the stove as she heads back towards the kitchen. Santino steps out into the hallway and closes the door behind him. "What are you doing here?"

"God, I'm so sorry. This was a horrible idea." I turn to leave, but he grabs me by the waist, spinning me around to look at him.

"Sorry, that came out wrong." His hands squeeze my hips for a moment before releasing me. "I mean…how are you here? How did you know where my flat was?"

"You pointed it out the other night, and the call button said you were the penthouse, so I…um…went up the stairs? Some woman with a pram needed help outside, so the door was open, and then I just let myself in. I should have buzzed, though. I didn't know you'd have company over."

I lift my hands to cover my face, which is highly awkward because I'm holding two bottles of orange fizzy drinks. Santino grabs my wrists to gently lower them. "It's fine, Tilly."

"Nope, it's not." I laugh nervously. "Whoever that woman was is clearly not happy to see a stranger at the door."

Santino's lips turn down as he fights back a smile. "Nonna doesn't smile at anyone. She says smiling causes wrinkles."

Suddenly, the door opens and a much younger woman with short, dark hair stands before us with her hands on her hips. "Who do we have here?" she asks in a very faint Italian accent.

Santino replies a bit begrudgingly, "Mamma, this is Tilly."

"Tilly?" she says, crossing her arms over her chest and eyeing me up and down. "È la tua ragazza?"

Santino clears his throat loudly and pins his mother with a look of silent warning. "No, Mamma. È un'amica."

Her brows drop as she inspects my face with rapt fascination. "Sei bella."

"I'm sorry?" I ask, not understanding a word of what the two of them are saying.

Santino spins his focus back to me with an uncomfortable look on his face. "My mother says you're beautiful." He closes his eyes like he's mortified. "Listen, now might not be the best time."

I nod in agreement and make a move to leave, but Santino's mother grips my arm and pulls me toward the doorway. "Now is a great time. We are making salsa di Pomodoro, and it's busywork. Come, you can help."

"Okay…" I shoot an apologetic look over my shoulder to a dejected Santino as his mother drags me into his flat.

My eyes instantly widen when I take in his place. We walk into his large eat-in kitchen that features glossy-white cabinets and black marble countertops. The appliances are all stainless steel, and the giant hood over the stove hosting two large pots indicates this is a chef's kitchen, which is not a feature I would have expected for Santino's place. But I suppose it shouldn't surprise me that he managed to bring the modern luxurious side of London to the Eastend. His flat matches his style—posh, expensive, and just a hint of arrogance.

Past the kitchen is a sunken living room with wraparound floor-to-ceiling windows that step out onto a balcony. Everything is bathed in natural light, and I can't help but be green with envy.

Santino's mother pulls me through the kitchen. "I'm Carlotta, and that is mia mamma at the stove. You can call her Nonna, everyone does. And this is Nonno." Nonno is a tall man with inky dark hair like Santino. He grunts his hello from his position at the high glass-top dining table where he's lining up several Mason jars. "Over there is my stepdaughter, Angela." Carlotta points towards the living room where a blonde who looks to be in her mid-twenties is sacked out on the white sectional sofa with her face buried in her mobile. She offers a less than enthusiastic wave as a man appears beside us. "And this is my husband, Bart."

Bart grins with a huge crust of bread in his mouth. He finishes his bite and replies around a full mouth, "Hiya. Nice to meet you. What was your name?"

"Tilly." I take his offered hand, noting his British accent. "Nice to meet you too."

"Hope you're ready to work." He winks and stuffs more bread into his mouth. "The perk to this type of business is that you get to eat loads as well."

Suddenly, Nonna grabs my hand and pulls me over to the stove. "You tall...this good job for you," she states, her Italian accent much heavier than her daughter's. She pushes the step stool away from the stove and grabs the thick wooden stick inside one of the giant pots of tomatoes. "You stir. You no need step. You big." She holds her hand up above her head, indicating tall, so I nod in agreement. "You stir, and little by little, tomatoes break, and then you add more tomatoes." She points at the tomatoes in the strainer on the counter. "These clean. Santino cut them, and they are ready. You wait until this boil before you add. Keep stirring. Stirring makes good."

"Angela, go out and pick some basil," Carlotta calls out to the living room. Angela sighs heavily before heaving herself off the sofa and walking out to the balcony where apparently Santino has plants? I feel like I'm in the middle of some elaborate prank, and any minute now, they're going to all start laughing at me.

Nonna points at the pantry cupboard. "When these jars all full of sauce, it looks nice in there. Full. That makes me happy," she says without cracking a smile. "You learn quick with me. I'm a good teacher." She grabs my hand and stirs more aggressively. "You must stir a lot or it sticks on bottom. Gira, gira, gira."

She leaves me to a job that I do not feel at all qualified for. What happens if the tomatoes stick to the bottom? Will it ruin the whole batch? When do I need to add more tomatoes? Do I have to do anything with that basil?

"Gira means stir," Santino's warm breath whispers against my neck as he appears out of nowhere behind me.

"I figured that one out," I huff back, waffling between amused and nervous because Santino's proximity has sent flutters in places I should not be feeling flutters right now. "Am I doing this right?"

Santino moves to lean on the counter next to me, watching me for a long moment. "You need to use more chest."

"What?" I frown up at him, trying not to get mesmerised by his disheveled appearance that I've quickly realised is my favourite look on him. His dress shirt sleeves are rolled up, revealing his muscular forearms that I noticed when we had coffee the other morning. His dark hair is soft and wavy off to the side, and his eyes are practically glittering with mirth.

"Your chest swivels, and your stirring matches it." He holds his hands up, pretending to hold a wooden stick to demonstrate.

I attempt the motion myself and feel ridiculous. "You've got to be taking the piss." I narrow my challenging eyes at him.

The corners of his mouth turn down as his shoulders shake with laughter. "God, yes, but it was worth it to see you attempt that."

"I'm being serious, though. Do you actually know what you're doing with this? I am not a cook. I've somehow survived my entire adult life on takeaway."

"You can't come from an Italian family and not know your way around the kitchen. They disown you for that." He crosses his arms over his chest and eyes me thoughtfully. "Sorry, but I'm still trying to comprehend the fact that you're here...in my flat...in front of my stove, making sauce with my family."

"I'm trying to comprehend the fact that you have a basil plant out there." I gesture towards the balcony. "This really is your flat, right? Does your mum live here, too?"

"I'm a grown man, Tilly. No, I do not live with my mother." He laughs and shakes his head. "I have a parsley plant out there too if you're truly that fascinated by green things."

"God, this is strange." I bite my lip nervously and glance down at my torn jeans and white tee. I'd have certainly worn something a bit more respectable had I known I was meeting Santino's family. I turn my focus back to my task and drag the wooden stick along the bottom of the pot. "I can make up some excuse to leave. I just couldn't think fast enough when your mum grabbed me. This is most definitely not what I intended today."

Santino's eyes move up and down my body with a heated look in his expression that I really don't want to notice right now. "What did you intend exactly?" He hits me with a direct gaze that feels as though he can read all the inappropriate thoughts I've been having about him the past few days.

I peer over my shoulder to see his family all working around the table and thankfully not paying any attention to us. While stirring, I reply quietly, "Well, I felt bad after our meeting Friday. You did a lot to help me out, and I don't know why I blew you off like that."

"You don't know why?" Narrowing his eyes, he watches me carefully.

"I mean…I know why." I inhale deeply, trying to force away the desire I feel every time this man is around me. I clear my throat and add, "But it doesn't matter because I know nothing will happen between us."

He pushes himself off the counter to join me by the stove and stir the second pot. It's an innocent enough motion, but his arm brushes against mine, and the sensation causes those flutters to rush through my belly again. "Are you sure nothing will happen?"

I swallow the knot in my throat and feign bravado. "Yes, I'm strong enough to resist your charms, or I wouldn't be here right now."

He turns to look at me, a smug grin spreading over his roguish face. "You think I'm charming?"

A growl vibrates in my throat. "*I* don't think you're charming. It's clear that *you* think you're charming. But I think you're just an arrogant pain in the arse."

He laughs softly, and his voice is warm and wicked when he replies, "I think you're merely stirring the pot, Tilly."

CHAPTER 14

Santino

WHEN MY FAMILY SHOWED UP AT MY FLAT TODAY WITH CRATES of tomatoes, jars, and salsa di Pomodoro supplies, I was in a sour mood. It doesn't help that every time Nonna walks in my flat, she tells me everything that is on her mind, good, bad, or otherwise…mostly bad.

"Your pants are too tight, this salad is too salty, you need more sunlight on your face, a white sofa is not a smart purchase. Good windows here."

It's a treat.

However, I always know where I stand with Nonna, so that's something to be respected.

Then my mother snapped at me for cutting the tomatoes wrong while Angela did nothing but moan about the fact that her boyfriend wasn't invited to help out today. And Bart, bloody hell, my stepfather is a kind man, but he does more eating than working, and it drives me absolutely mental to watch him riffle through my pantry like he owns it.

Nevertheless, this is my family. This is what they do. They show up a few times a year on Sundays to stock my shelves with whatever essentials they think I need. In today's case, it's sauce. So, we work for several hours, eat, and they leave me with a giant mess to clean up.

Normally, it's a process I enjoy. Nonna and Mum taught me how to cook at a very young age, so being in the kitchen is never a bother.

However, today, I was not in the mood to deal with everyone. I just wanted a quiet day alone to brood with my thoughts.

Then…Tilly showed up.

And fuck me if my mood hasn't cheered right the bloody hell up.

Which brings me to my next point. Why is the sight of Tilly dumping scoops of boiled tomatoes into the electric strainer with my nonna so fucking hot?

Wait…shit…that sounds wrong.

It's not my nonna that's hot. I mean, don't get me wrong, she's a lovely woman, but Tilly with my nonna…asking questions, following directions, doing whatever is asked of her without hesitation… it's causing me to feel things.

Things I've never felt before.

It's not love. Christ, that's insane.

It's just…chemistry. Pure, undeniable chemistry that I am struggling to gain control of. Has any woman ever rocked my control like this? I know the answer to that question.

Tilly and I work alongside each other for the next couple of hours, laughing and flirting as we strain and jar tomato sauce. When a large chunk splatters her nice, painfully tight tee, and both of us react like a couple of immature teenagers under the glowering eyes of Nonna, I realise that just being friends with Tilly is too hard. My patience is spent. The more I'm around her, the more I want her. And seeing her get out of her head and have some fun with me again is all the sign I need to know that we have the potential to be more.

Going back to our previous arrangement with rules and limits is out of the question. Too much has changed. And as nerve-wracking as it may be, I need to know that she feels the same way. Otherwise, we may need to stop whatever this is right fucking now before she truly becomes "the one who got away".

I can't help but notice my mother watching our interactions with great interest. She's clearly intrigued. Most likely because I haven't brought a girl around my family in well over a decade. The last time I brought a girl home was probably secondary school, and the reasons I haven't done it since then still weigh heavily on my mind.

Now, my mother's eyes twinkle as she sets the table for us to all eat dinner, taking care to put Tilly right beside me and sit herself directly across from Tilly. It's clear she likes Tilly, but I think she'd like any woman I brought around because it means there's hope for her son, whom she'd long feared was hopeless.

For years, my mother and I had a strained relationship because I resented her for reasons I didn't fully understand. And when I was a teenager, and she started a second family with Bart and Angela, I felt like they didn't want me around anymore.

However, our annual trips have done a world of good for our relationship. Spending that quality time with her has helped me understand that she thought she was doing what was best for me.

"So, you said you all run an Italian deli up in the Cotswolds?" Tilly asks as she passes a basket of bread past a distracted Angela over to Bart at the head of the table.

My mother nods proudly. "Yes, it's a supermarket and deli in Bourton-on-the-Water. We have high-quality Italian products, plus our bakery, deli counter, and kitchen with some tables for eating. We often have a line out the door."

"I do the baking," Nonna says from beside Mum, squinting her face as she scrapes the last bit of sauce off her plate with a wedge of bread. "Nonno, the cooking."

"Angela runs the till when she manages to stay off her mobile long enough," Bart adds, reaching over and grabbing her mobile out of her hands.

She scoffs. "I run the till brilliantly. The customers love me."

Nonno grumbles at the other head of the table, and Tilly seems to enjoy this interaction. "So, how long have you guys owned it then?" she asks before taking a sip of her fizzy drink.

"My brother, Antonio, started it with his wife, who's from there, nearly forty years ago. It was just a supermarket back then. A few years later, my parents decided to leave Venice and join him in the Cotswolds." Mum glances at Nonna, who looks stoic as she continues. "It was quite the journey for them, considering I was sixteen and pregnant with Santino. Then suddenly, there we were, picking out family recipes for a restaurant we were opening in a small, British village. It's hard to believe how quickly our lives changed back then."

Tilly blinks in fascination. "Wait, are you saying you had Santino at sixteen?"

I tense, unsure how my family will take this very direct question from a woman they've only just met. Frankly, a bold question from Tilly is exactly what I would expect from her, but it's not the way most people react when my mother decides to casually drop this little detail for shock factor. Most people avoid the question. Most people aren't Tilly.

The clattering of a fork hitting a plate turns our heads to find Nonna quickly recovering it. "My daughter—"

"Got pregnant very young, yes." My mother straightens and tilts her head to the side.

"I see," Tilly replies, a look of astonishment in her eyes as she gazes back at my mum for a long silent moment. "My parents had my older brother when they were both eighteen, but they'd finished secondary school by then, so it's not nearly the same. It's amazing that you all were able to start a new life in a new country, open a deli, and have a wee baby on board. What an accomplishment."

Nonna gazes back at Tilly with wide eyes while Nonno focuses on his empty plate. My mother responds slowly, "Everyone has their own journeys to take. Santino's journey was to become a lawyer." She raises her glass to me. "The first of our family to go to university… and then he added law school on top of that."

"Alla salute, Santino!" Nonno lifts his glass to me and winks.

Tilly smiles warmly and offers her glass to me as well. "An excellent journey indeed."

My mum's eyes fixate on Tilly's drink, pointedly noticing hers and mine are the only glasses at the table not filled with red wine. "And you, Tilly? What is your journey?"

Tilly straightens in her chair, and the two of them look at each other like they're in the middle of a standoff that I'm not sure is a good thing. She inhales sharply and replies with a professional edge to her voice, "I'm planning to accept an executive position that was just offered to me on Friday at Harrods. It's a dream job for someone like me with a master's in business retail, so I hope that it's the start of a new beginning for me."

"So, you've decided to accept?" I ask, unable to hide my pleased reaction over a more permanent placement of Tilly in London. "That's brilliant, Tilly."

"Thanks," she says, tucking her hair behind her ear. "It's a great opportunity. I'd be a fool to say no." Our eyes lock for a moment, and this new reality settles in over us.

My mother's voice interrupts. "Do you not enjoy wine, Tilly?"

"Mamma," I state through clenched teeth.

"It's okay," Tilly cuts me off and straightens her posture towards my mother. "It's a part of my journey, and you shared a great deal about yours to me." She touches the drink in front of her. "I don't drink alcohol because I make poor choices when I do."

My mother tilts her head, and it's impossible to miss her eyebrows rise in judgment. "I see."

Tilly offers a polite smile my mother doesn't deserve. "Thankfully, I've got a better handle on that now. So, I've learned it's better to indulge in something that won't get me in trouble." She turns her eyes to Nonna and adds, "Like this incredible food. Truly, I've never tasted anything this delicious. You've all outdone yourselves, and I appreciate you letting me be a wee part of creating it."

The entire table is stunned into a rare silence, and it's Nonno that breaks the awkwardness. "Too much pasta can give you this." He pats his belly proudly, and the table instantly relaxes at his successful attempt to lighten the mood.

After coffee and cake, my mother finally says, "My goodness, look at the time. We best be going. We have a long drive home."

Everyone stands up from the table and begins packing up the supplies they brought with them.

"You're not staying in the city?" Tilly asks, glancing over at me curiously.

"Nonno only sleeps in Nonno's bed," Angela drawls, and we all smile at that very evident truth.

I wink and nudge Tilly. "Nonno has a bad back."

"Sorry to leave you with the mess," my mother says, coming over and giving me two kisses on the cheek. She steps to the side and offers the same to Tilly. "Stay strong, bella ragazza. Though something tells me that won't be a problem for you." She bops her on the nose, and in a frenzy, everyone else says goodbye, my grandmother telling me to mop the floor as she leaves.

By the time I close my flat door, I feel like I could collapse from exhaustion. I stride back into the kitchen where Tilly is rinsing plates and loading them into the dishwasher. "You don't have to do that," I offer, moving to stand next to her.

"You need the help," she huffs with a laugh. "This place is a disaster."

I run my hand through my hair. "Yeah, it usually takes me a couple of hours to get it back to its original state after they invade."

"Many hands make light work." She winks at me, and just that tiny gesture causes my body to awaken all over again.

We make quick work of the mess, and as I finish wiping down the table, Tilly stands awkwardly beside it. "How often does your family all come to visit like this?"

I pause my action. "They come here a few times a year to stock my pantry. Nonna says we always make sauce on Sundays after a hard week because making sauce is how you clear your mind for the next week. She also says that no one can tell you how to make your sauce even while she's telling you how to make your sauce."

"I noticed that," Tilly replies with a laugh.

"She's a walking contradiction," I say with a huff. "She tells everyone everything on her mind. Thankfully, she's quite sharp, so she's usually right."

Tilly nods thoughtfully, chewing on her lip. "Did I upset your mother by prying about her being so young when she had you?"

I lift my brows. "Surprisingly, I think she was okay with it."

She cringes and tugs on her shirt that's still covered in tomato sauce. "I have that foot-in-mouth syndrome."

"I hadn't noticed." I wink at her.

She wrinkles her nose. "So you don't think she hates me?"

"No," I reply, feeling smug over the fact that she seems highly concerned with what my mother thinks of her. I toss the rag into the sink and lean against the kitchen table. "I think she was just thrilled to see me with a woman."

Tilly's eyes lift curiously. "Does she think you like men?"

I laugh and shake my head. "No."

"So, you just…don't bring your two-month chump women around your family?"

"No."

Tilly shifts nervously on her feet. "Well, sorry to get her hopes up with me."

I wave her off. "It's fine. I told her you and I were just friends."

"Oh." Tilly looks rejected.

I fucking love it.

She inhales sharply. "Where is your father in all of this?"

I stiffen at that question but then force myself to relax. "He has never been in the picture. It's always just been my grandparents, my uncle and his wife, and my mother. Until she met Bart when I was fifteen. He had Angela with his first wife."

"Are you close to Bart?" she asks, moving away from the head of the table to lean on the open space beside me.

"Not really," I reply with a shrug. "He's a nice enough bloke, but I was nearly out of the house when he entered the picture, so there wasn't much time for us to really connect."

"And your sister?"

"Is spoiled. But a good kid."

She smiles affectionately while staring at the ground. "You know, it was surprising to see this side to you."

"What side is that?"

She shrugs. "I don't know…like…human?"

"Do I give off extra-terrestrial vibes?"

"Aye, a bit. I mean, you're tall, dark, and handsome, and ridiculously fit. You have a gorgeous flat and a brilliant job. I've been desperately holding on to the idea you're still a sleazy manwhore who picks up a different woman every weekend."

I hit her with a deadpan look. "I told you I'm not that guy anymore."

"I know." Her brows furrow for a moment. "It became quite clear when I saw you with your family." Something in her voice and the fact that she hasn't started walking toward the door gives me hope.

I stand up off the table and position myself in front of her. "Any other questions?"

She jerks her head back, clearly not realising how many inquiries she's been thrusting my way during the past five minutes. "Sorry… foot in mouth again."

"It's okay," I reply, reaching out to take her hand in mine. "I like your mouth."

She gazes up at me nervously as I close the space between us. "I thought we were just friends."

"We are." I tilt my head and allow my eyes to drift lazily over her face.

She glances down at our joined hands. "Then what are you doing?"

"I figure if friends can have long lingering hugs, then friends can surely hold hands alone in a kitchen."

She nods slowly, and her tongue slips out to moisten her lips as I close the small space between us. She inhales deeply and lifts her eyes to meet mine. They're full of longing and attraction, all the fucking sensations I've been feeling since the moment I saw her at that charity event over a week ago now.

She exhales a shaky breath and lifts her lips towards mine.

I pause a fraction of an inch from her mouth and whisper, "Tilly?"

"Yes?" her breath stutters as she waits for contact.

"Are you about to kiss me?"

"That was the general thought," she huffs breathlessly.

I slide my nose along her cheek. "I like that thought."

"Then why are we talking?"

"Because…" I pull back and frown down at her. "I have some rules."

Her face contorts, and the mood is killed. "Rules?"

"Well, just one rule."

"What?" she asks, annoyance dripping in her tone.

I brace myself for her wrath. "We have to be exclusive."

"What?" She laughs, her face twisted in confusion.

I shake my head. "I told you I've changed."

She blinks back in confusion. "So, what are you asking for exactly? To have me be your next two-month ride?" She chokes out the phrase. "Look, I don't need to be another one of your two-monthers. I know you're Mr. Monogamous now, but how do you know that's what I want?"

"What do you want?"

"I don't know…"

"Yes, you do."

"No, I don't."

I step back, giving her some space. "Don't think about it, just say what you want. Get out of your head."

"I can't get out of my head because that's when mistakes happen." She crosses her arms over her chest and begins pacing in front of the table. "After everything I've shared with you the past week, you think a relationship with me is a good idea?"

"I think it's a better idea than kissing you and not knowing when I'll get to kiss you again." I eye her sternly because it's a truth that I hate. As resistant as Tilly has been towards me since she came back, I don't trust that she won't kiss and run. She's run before.

Tilly's steps falter because she knows what I'm saying is true.

I soften my tone. "I'm not looking for hookups anymore. And I'd rather have you and know you're mine than have you and worry that you could be someone else's."

Her eyes widen. "You can't be serious."

"I'm dead serious."

"Sonny."

"Trouble…"

She inhales deeply. "I'm not sure this is a good idea."

"Why?" I reach out and touch her hip, halting her motion. "Look at us, Tilly. Our attraction is still here. Stronger than ever. Our bodies are like two magnets, finding each other all day long. Do you know how hard it was not to grab you any time you came near me today? I would have just fucking done it if it wasn't for the fact that my nonna would have beat me over the head with her disgusting sauce stick." I comb my fingers through hers, enjoying the smile at the edge of her lips. "Trust this. Trust us. Believe that we've both changed. That we can handle more now because we've changed. Doesn't it sound exciting for us to get to know each other now? With clear intentions?"

"Jesus," she huffs nervously, and I can see her resolve weakening.

I cup her cheek and dip my lips towards hers. "Just say yes. Say you'll be mine."

"What are you, a bloody valentine?" she huffs with a hyenic laugh.

I smile, biting my lip as the urge to kiss her becomes so intense, I don't know if I'll be able to hold out much longer. Her scent, her body, her blue eyes…they've haunted me all week, and I want her to say yes to this. To giving us a chance.

"Come on, Trouble. Giving us a replay will be a challenge for us both, and I know you love a challenge."

CHAPTER 15

Tilly

"**Y**es."

Three little letters.

Very big results.

Results being Santino's lips crashing down on mine.

It takes me a few staggered breaths to realise what's happening. But as soon as I do, my hands grab onto his neck to meet the demanding pressure of his kiss. In one swift motion, our lips break as he grips my waist and hoists me up onto his dining table. We're eye level with one another now, and the wicked look in his dark eyes causes my heart rate to ratchet up to a whole new level.

He steps toward me and commands my lips again. I wrap my legs around him, relishing in the hardness of his body. Our tongues thrust greedily against each other as his hand grips my hair in a masterful hold that causes a swell of pressure between my legs.

Who knew making sauce would be such epic foreplay?

Not this Scottish lass. Not at all.

But watching Santino interact with his family, seeing this gentler side to him, a side where he pulled out the chair for his nonna and silently poured both of us fizzy drinks while everyone else drank red wine…he lost that dark and dangerous vibe to him that I was always scared of. He's somehow transformed into this sexy, domestic God-like creature that I instinctually crave.

Well, when we're not making out at least.

His hands rove over my body, and I lose myself to the sensation, my centre throbbing with an ache that has not been satisfied in quite some time. I arch into him, grab his hand, and place it on my breast. I need his touch; I need his roughness. Santino always had that perfect mix of commanding gentleness. And feeling him now, stone-cold sober with no haziness of alcohol or drugs…it's all even better than I remember. My body is a live wire ready to ignite at just the hard squeeze his fingers apply over my shirt-covered nipple.

Holy shit, I'm going to come.

Fuck.

No.

Not yet.

It's too soon.

This is all too soon.

"Santino." I pull my lips away from him and suck in a big gulp of air as my eyelids fight a heaviness.

"Yes?" he murmurs, trailing kisses down my neck. The whiskers from his jaw send tingles all over my body as he grabs my ear and bites gently. "What is it, Trouble? Where do you want me? I want to taste you everywhere."

Oh my God, I suck so much for what I'm about to say next.

"I, um…want to slow down." I tense in his arms, my body literally hating me right now.

He instantly pulls back and blinks in confusion, his dark eyes scanning mine with concern. "Shit. Are you okay? Is this not…? Did I misread…"

"You're fine," I expel on a breath of longing, touching my finger to his lips hungrily while wanting them all over my body. "I said yes. I want this. I want it very much."

"Good." He offers me a lopsided smile that makes him look more boyish than I've ever seen him.

"I just...I need to tell you something." I rub my forehead nervously, trying to figure out how I'm going to say this as I struggle to catch my breath.

His brows knit together as his gaze darts from my lips to my eyes. "You can tell me anything."

I swallow the knot in my throat as my nose begins to twitch like it has a mind of its own. "I...um..."

"Tilly." He says my name gently as his hands move from my hips to cup my face as he slides his thumbs soothingly along my cheeks and forces me to look at him. "Whatever it is, you can tell me."

I nod woodenly and feel tears burn the backs of my eyes as he looks at me with so much concern and compassion, it's difficult to accept. I don't feel like I deserve it. I'm a mess.

"I...haven't slept with anyone since...well..." I focus on his buttoned shirt, struggling to make eye contact as embarrassment heats my cheeks.

"Since when?" he asks curiously.

I inhale through my nose and force myself to be honest. "Since London."

He blinks back at me for a long second as he processes that. "Fuck," he finally replies. "Him?"

I nod, my chin wobbling at that realisation and then shaking that thought away as fast as I can.

"Why?" he inquires, confusion in his voice.

I shrug and sniff, running my hand through my hair nervously. "I don't know. Fear? Regret? Self-punishment?"

"Christ." Santino tilts his head as he looks at me with a new expression I can't quite decipher. God, please don't be pity. I can't take pity from him. Finally, he shakes off his stupor and leans in to press a chaste kiss to my forehead. "Tell me what you need."

I shake my head, trying to come off like this is no big deal but feeling like it's an enormous deal. An embarrassing, gigantic, idiotic issue.

"Look…I get it if this is a lot more than you bargained for. I should have told you before you asked me to…like…be yours and all that."

"Tilly…"

"No, it's fine. It's messy. I'm messy. I'm sure I still have stuff to work through with another therapist, so I think it's better if you and I just call it now before it gets too complicated."

Santino steps back, staring at me like I've just slapped him. "You want to call it?"

"I can't ask you to—"

He holds his hand up, cutting me off, his jaw muscle ticking angrily. "If you want to call it because you don't want me, then you call it for that reason. But don't call it because of some fucked-up shit you have in your head that you're too damaged for me. Because you're not."

"But I am," I exclaim, my heart breaking over the knowledge that I'm self-sabotaging this, something my therapist back in Scotland told me I'm very good at. "You've got your whole life together here, Santino. You have a basil plant on your balcony, for Christ's sake."

"Who cares? Maybe I want to share my basil plant with you."

"Well, I'm still a work in progress, and I don't need you fixing me with your fresh basil!"

"I'm not trying to fix you, Tilly," he snaps, desperation in his voice. "And we have to stop talking about basil, or I'm going to throw that bloody plant over the ledge."

I reach out to cup his cheek, hating his tortured eyes. "You tried to fix me all those years ago, and at the time, I didn't get it…but now I do. It's just you…you're a fixer. You're this saint wrapped up in a suit, and I don't want you to feel like you need to help me."

"I don't feel like that." Santino's voice takes on an aggressive edge I don't think I've ever heard from him. "You're not the only one with baggage, Tilly. Jesus Christ. My life is not perfect. Far from it."

I stare at him in wonder because I see nothing but a beautiful, perfect man in front of me, and I'm bringing in a truckload of baggage to drag him down. "You have an amazing career, a great flat, a lovely family. Meanwhile, I'm living with my brother. You have your shit together, Sonny. You can't deny that!"

"Everyone has their demons, Tilly." His tone is serious as a flash of pain crosses his face. "But it's not something I want to talk about right now. Bloody hell. What happened? Can we calm the fuck down for a moment?"

"Okay." I cross my arms over my chest nervously as we both go quiet. I hate that I had to stop things, but the idea of Santino taking me to his bed right now scares the shit out of me. It's been so long, and I barely remember the last time I had sex. What if I freak out in the middle of it?

Santino exhales heavily, breaking the tense silence. "Look, I know you and I have a past, but that doesn't mean we have to fall right back into where we left off. We can take things slow. Start fresh. Let's just see each other for a bit. Hell, people on their first dates don't unload years' worth of baggage on each other, right?"

I shrug helplessly. "I suppose not."

He nods slowly and steps into me. "So, let's treat this like our first date, okay?"

"Do you let all your first dates make sauce with your entire family?"

"You haven't met my zio yet." He steps between my legs, his hands skating up my thighs and making me regret everything I've just said. "We'll save that for the second date."

"If you get a second date," I reply coyly, resting my arms on his shoulders as I sift my fingers through his short, inky locks.

He presses his lips to mine and murmurs, "No turning back now, Trouble."

"Okay then." My body swirls with need over his pet name for me that brings back all sorts of erotic memories we've shared in the past.

"We'll take everything slow. No sex. No stripping off clothes. It'll be fun. Like we're teenagers again." He pulls back, a smirk teasing the edges of his lips as he plays with a lock of my hair. "Tonight, however…" He pauses, his gaze roving over my face with complete adoration. "Just let me kiss the fuck out of you."

My heart instantly lightens. I don't know how he managed to turn this fucked-up conversation around, but he did, and he did it well. "Very well then, Sonny."

He smiles victoriously and leans in to kiss me again. It's softer, gentler, but all fucking man.

I pull back, parting our lips with an audible pop. "Maybe we can add in a little dry humping?"

He presses his forehead to mine and growls. "You are too much trouble for your own good."

CHAPTER 16

Tilly

"**G**OOD MORNING!" FREYA CALLS OUT THE NEXT DAY AS I ENTER the kitchen to find her seated at the table with Hercules draped over her shoulder. Jasper is hot on my heels, and Hercules doesn't seem to like it. He stares at our sudden appearance with unmitigated irritation, like we've just interrupted a peaceful morning. "You were gone for ages yesterday," Freya says with a knowing tone to her voice.

I stride over to the kettle with a sheepish look on my face. "Did you need me here?"

"Oh, heavens no. Allie and I rewatched the first three episodes of *Bridgerton* in bed while Mac played a new video game he's been working on with Roan all afternoon. It was a lovely, lazy Sunday. Allie even painted my toes." She wiggles her feet under the table. "It's getting difficult to reach them."

"That sounds lovely." I fill one of Freya's kitty coffee mugs that she seems to have an endless supply of. This one features a cat wearing a raincoat with big bold letters spelling out "WAP" on the side.

Maybe not a great cup to have around once the bairn is old enough to understand.

I sit on the seat across from Freya and glance down to see that her breakfast appears to be celery and clotted cream. Definitely not a combo I've seen in my life, let alone for breakfast, but Freya's pregnancy cravings are as unique as her personality.

"Is Mac off to work already?" I ask, glancing toward the other side of the flat to see if there's any sign of his work bag in the hallway.

"Yes, he's gone and I'm bursting at the seams, literally." She points at her belly. "What happened yesterday?"

My eyes flare. "A lot more than I expected." I take a sip of my tea.

"Oh my God, you shagged him," she exclaims, slapping her hand on the table. Hercules jumps at the noise and shoots me a glower like it's my fault his mummy is excited.

"I didn't shag him." I run my hands through my hair nervously.

"You didn't?" She looks disappointed.

"We're…taking it slow, I think?"

Freya's brows pinch together. "Okay…but you've already had the sex before so what does that mean exactly?"

"Well, it's kind of weird because he asked me to be…" I cringe as I prepare myself to say the words. "Be exclusive."

"What?" Freya squeals at a high pitch, and like a shot, Hercules flies out of her arms and flops onto the floor, taking a swing at poor, unsuspecting Jasper before darting off. Jasper looks completely unaffected as he licks his paw and rubs his ear. "You're exclusive already? How did that happen?"

"I don't know." I grip my mug tightly. "I showed up at his house, and his whole family was there making sauce—his mum, his grandparents and step family. They pulled me in to help, and the day was just so nice and *normal*. And I guess I sort of felt like I was seeing Santino for the first time, you know? He has a basil plant on his balcony!"

"Shut up!" Freya cries out again, just as intrigued as I was by that fact. "What kind of single man grows plants on a balcony?"

I shrug. "Hot ones, I guess."

She nods knowingly. "Very hot."

"And when I made a move to kiss him—"

"You made the first move?" Freya squeals again. "Good God, this is reaching *Bridgerton* levels of hotness! You know, I think watching *Bridgerton* while pregnant was a bad idea. These pregnancy hormones are causing me to have the most sensual dreams of my entire life. I should have stuck to *Heartland*. Horses are much less sexually inspiring."

My nose wrinkles. "Well, I should hope so."

She sighs. "But...I do love ponies." She looks forlorn and then shakes away that thought. "Anyways, I'm so proud of you and your Scottish lady balls!"

I laugh and shake my head. "Well, he stopped me just before I was going to kiss him and said something like, *'I'd rather have you and know you're mine, then have you and want you to be mine'.*"

Her jaw drops. "I've just come."

"Right?" My voice goes embarrassingly high at the end.

"So, let me get this straight." Freya dunks her celery stalk into her dish of cream and points her finger at me. "You've been in London a month and you already have a boyfriend? If I wasn't married and up the duff, I would truly loathe you."

"He's not a boyfriend." I shake off that nerve-wracking thought. "It's just...I don't know. We're dating, I guess? It's going to be seriously complicated."

"Why is that?"

I chew my lip nervously. "Well, we're taking it slow because I haven't slept with anyone since..." my voice trails off because it's too hard to finish.

Freya's hand moves protectively to her belly. "Since the miscarriage?"

I cringe as she states the word I hate the most. I hate it for so many reasons, but mostly, I hate it because I think I caused it. And that haunts me every day of my life.

"Oh Tilly." Freya's voice goes soft as she takes in my inner struggle.

She reaches out to touch my hand, but I pull it back quickly. "Don't pity me, please. I hate pity. I'm good. I'm fine. I'm around you every day and not falling apart. I just…wasn't ready to jump in the sack with him after…"

"Five whole years," Freya states with wide eyes. "Makes sense. So, what did Santino say?"

"He said he was fine with it. He said taking it slow could be fun. We made out on his sofa for like an hour before I thought I should get home in case Mac was readying a search party."

Freya sighs wistfully. "This sounds wonderful."

I shrug. "I'm not getting my hopes up. I told Santino last night that I'm messy, and I will totally understand if he wants to cut and run."

Freya shakes her head sadly at me. "Give yourself more credit, Tilly. You've done so much for yourself, and now you're doing so much for me, and you're accepting a big new job today. You're far from messy. You're annoyingly lovely if you ask me."

"Thanks, Frey." I muster up a smile I don't altogether feel. "Hey, before we get to work selecting the final pet pieces for Harrods, would you mind if I haul that folding table stored in the hallway cubby up to my bedroom?"

"Not at all," Freya exclaims around a fresh bite of celery. "We're not using it for anything. What are you working on?"

"Well, I was thinking of unpacking my scrapbooking stuff. I came upon all these old photos I'd taken ages ago that never made it into a book, and I guess I'm suddenly feeling the itch to get them sorted."

"By all means!" Freya replies, her eyes wide and excited. "I'm still waiting for the photo you gave me of Hercules' twin to get back from the framers. I think it'll look great here in the kitchen, don't you?"

I laugh softly. "I told you that you didn't need to frame it. It's not a professional picture, just an old mobile shot."

"Nonsense! I love it!" Freya tuts. "It will have a place of pride in this room. It will feel like Hercules is always watching over us."

"With disdain," I add flatly while taking a sip of my tea.

She giggles and then eyes me curiously. "What on earth could be inspiring your creative juices, I wonder?"

I grumble at her, but she's saved by the bell when my mobile chirps beside me. I pull it up to see it's a text from Santino, and Freya waves me off with a giddy smile.

I take my mobile out the back door into the garden and open the text.

Santino: Good morning.

Tilly: Hello to you.

Santino: You thinking about me?

Tilly: You wish.

Santino: Well, I'm definitely thinking about you.

Tilly: Anyone ever tell you that you come on a little strong?

Santino: Nope. This is a first. There's a lot of things I do with you that I've never done with anyone else.

Tilly: Like?

Santino: It's probably a little too much information since we're taking things slow, so it's best to keep it mysterious.

I bite my lip at that response because knowing Santino, whatever it was is naughty. An ache throbs between my legs at just the thought of that. Jesus, this attraction is intense. Which is good. It's fun and exciting, and it makes me feel alive. And while I want to stand firm on taking things slow, I don't want to lose what I remember being so incredible about Santino.

His dirty mouth.

Tilly: Don't tease me like that, Sonny. I'm a big girl. I can take it.

Santino: Very well then. You'll be pleased to know that I had to jerk off last night after you left and your sexy lips were all I thought about as I did it.

Nothing could wipe the smug grin off my face right now. Biting my lip, I pull my mobile up to reply.

Tilly: I might have you beat.

Santino: Do tell…in graphic detail if we're being so candid this lovely Monday morning.

Tilly: Well, it was two times for me. Vibrator. It's the only thing that's seen me through my very long dry spell.

Santino: Christ, I'm going to need to jerk off before going to work.

Tilly: Sorry.

Santino: Don't be. Dinner Wednesday? I'm overrun with work right now so I can't do sooner.

Tilly: Wednesday should work.

Santino: Good. We need to talk about some stuff.

Tilly: Like?

Santino: Like telling your brother we're seeing each other.

Tilly: Pass.

Santino: Trouble...

Tilly: Can't we just enjoy ourselves for a little while first? He's literally a descendant from one of the earliest cavemen. He'll ruin everything. Let's just hold off for now.

Santino: How long are we talking?

Tilly: Not long...just until we...maybe...stop using battery-operated devices.

CHAPTER 17

Santino

THE NEXT FEW DAYS, I WIND UP HAVING TO WORK EXTRA HOURS on more ridiculous contract negotiations for Zander Williams. The kid is infuriating me. He was supposed to be here and playing for us already, but now he won't be able to start until the transfer window opens in January.

Normally, this is the kind of mess I would work on at all hours of the night, but the past couple of nights, I've been busy on the phone with Tilly. I actually can't even remember the last time I talked this much to a woman I wasn't sleeping with. This taking it slow business is more intriguing than I would have expected.

As I finish changing for our date tonight, Vaughn's name comes up on my mobile. "Hiya, Vaughn."

"Santino, where are you? You're not in your office."

"I'm home."

"Home? It's only six o'clock," he replies in a confused tone.

I flinch because I like to be the last one out of the office most evenings, but tonight, nothing was going to stop me from seeing Tilly. "Yeah, sorry. I have plans tonight."

"No need to be sorry, son, I just…well…you're usually always here."

I inhale deeply over the very bizarre fact that I'm choosing a woman over work. This is yet another first I'm doing with Tilly. "What did you need?"

"Where is the Zander Williams contract at? I know we missed the window, but I'm just curious if it's all falling apart or if we'll be able to get him in January?"

"The sporting director is trying to work with him still," I reply regretfully. "Apparently, his current club decided last minute they wanted to hold on to him until January, so I think that's the core issue. He's also now asked to negotiate housing into his contract, which means I need to talk to some property owners we work with to see what's available in January when he could start."

Vaughn harumphs. "Well, thankfully, Finney seems to be on the mend, so I think he'll be okay for our first match. Clearly, Zander is young and doesn't understand the basics of contract negotiations. But Shawn won't shut up about how brilliant he is as a sweeper. Says he plays like Gareth did when he first started out at United, and well, that's exactly the kind of player we need."

"I completely agree. I think if we can find him a flat, maybe this will be the last revision."

"My son-in-law, Hayden…Vi's husband…has a couple of buildings that might be great. Let's reach out to him first. It'll be nice to keep it in the family."

"My thoughts exactly."

"Okay…well…enjoy your plans."

We hang up just as the buzzer to my flat goes off, so I run over to hold the call button. "I'm on my way down." I grab my keys and fly down the four flights to find Tilly standing outside my flat. She turns to give me a full view of her, and I can't help but smile because she is a sight for sore eyes.

She's wearing a strapless black leather dress with a zip all the way up the front. She's made what would normally be a sinfully sexy dress more casual by slipping a soft white tee beneath it. I glance down to see she's wearing a pair of black Converse trainers, dutifully following my instructions for her to wear comfortable footwear, not that I really had to worry. Tilly's always had a little casual edge to her style.

In the past, I always noticed her friends would dress in skintight minidresses with high heels, leaving nothing to the imagination. Tilly would show off half as much skin and still manage to look ten times sexier. She'd often be wearing a dress as well, but she'd throw a leather jacket over the top or choose to wear leggings and combat boots instead of a short skirt. Whatever her style is called, it's a combination that I fully appreciate.

"Sei bellissima stasera," I growl, sliding my hands into her loose, straight locks as I press my lips to hers for a quick kiss. I drag the backs of my fingers down her pale cheek and add, "Beautiful."

She grips my arms, her eyes wide and challenging. "How did I never know you spoke Italian?"

"I'm a man of mystery." I dip my nose to the area below her ear, inhaling her intoxicating scent of honey and citrus. After spending the night making out with her a few days ago, I haven't been able to stop craving her scent. She arches into my touch, and the motion causes my cock to stir inside my jeans. Pulling back, I stare at her lips. "And no one said I spoke good Italian. I might have just told you that you look like a beetroot."

Her hands slide up the short sleeves of my shirt, her fingers biting into my biceps. "I love beetroots."

"Nobody loves beetroots." I laugh and tilt my head with a smug look. "Hai delle labbra così deliziose...Vorrei tanto baciarti."

Her jaw drops. "What did you just say?"

Smiling, I lean in and whisper against her lips, "I said your lips are so delicious...I would really like to kiss you."

Without pause, I fuse our mouths together and tease my tongue along her lush lips. She tastes minty, and that, coupled with her honey scent, has me deepening the kiss even further. Her hands move from my arms to my waist as she fists my T-shirt. When I thrust my tongue deep into her mouth, she inhales sharply, and her faint moan vibrates against my lips. Moving my hands down to her arse, I pull her into me so she can feel the effect she's having on me.

"Okay, Sonny Corleone, no need to get cheeky." She breaks our kiss, her face adorably flushed as she glances around nervously and finger combs her mussed locks. "We're in public, after all."

I shove my hands into my pockets. "It's been a long time."

"It's been a few days."

"Give or take five years." I wink playfully, causing her to roll her eyes.

"Don't act like you've been pining over me all this time." She shoves me playfully. "Now, where are you taking me tonight? We better not be playing football again because this dress wasn't meant for high kicks."

With a tilt of my head, I can't even be bothered to fight the smile on my face. "No football. But, are you completely famished, or can you hold out for a bit?"

"I'm okay, why?"

"I had an idea for tonight, but it would be better to do while we still have some daylight."

"Okay." She frowns up at me curiously.

I pull my mobile out of my pocket. "I found this app that tells you where the best street art is featured near us."

Tilly's head jerks back in shock. "You what?"

"I remember you always used to take photos of graffiti so I thought we could do our own little walking tour—"

"How on earth did you know I took photos?" she asks, looking a bit shaken.

I shrug my shoulders. "I don't know. There were times in the past when we'd be walking to my place or yours after being out, and we'd have to stop so you could do your thing."

"And you remember that?" She stares at me with an expression I can't quite place. It's either irritation or confusion, and there's a great deal of grey area between the two, so fuck knows what she's really thinking.

I nod. "I remember loads of things. But look, if you're not into that anymore, we can do something else. I mean, it's summertime in London, so…the options are endless." I glance down at my mobile to do a quick search.

"No," she says a bit forcibly as her hands close over mine. "I'd actually really love to do that."

The corner of my mouth lifts into a smile. "Okay then. Let's get a move on, Trouble."

The tour is perfect. It's an easy walk, allowing us lots of time to talk and reconnect. She tells me about signing the paperwork for her new Harrods job that won't begin for at least another month. I can tell she's excited about it because her voice rises up to a higher pitch whenever she mentions it. I complain about work because it's been a pig of a start to the new season. Last-minute contract changes are never an issue, and I feel responsible for not getting Zander squared away for Vaughn because I can tell he's eager to get him on the pitch. It feels nice to have someone to talk to about this stuff, even if Tilly doesn't fully understand my job. I've talked about work with the women I've dated, but most just nod and smile and seem bored. Tilly offers up challenging questions for me to look at my issues from different angles. It's refreshing.

And the artwork we're finding is interesting to say the least. Displays ranging from giant, multilevel murals to tiny little phone box scrawls that I wouldn't really classify as art, but Tilly seems enraptured by all of them, big and small. She takes several photos from different angles, inspecting the images for clarity before allowing us to move on to the next stop. Her blue eyes are wide and excited as she takes in the sights on this perfect summer night.

Tilly is the most striking art I've witnessed tonight. Her strawberry locks are glowing in the setting sun as she talks a mile a minute about past photos she's taken. She tells me how she used to send copies to her grandmother when she was still alive because she loved street art, but her grandfather, Fergus, hated them. He said they were criminals and nothing more, yet she kept sending them to him after her grandmother died, and he hung every photo up on the fridge…

albeit begrudgingly. She said while Fergus and Mac talked football, she and Fergus argued over what constituted art. She's completely in the moment with me tonight, and it's stunning to watch.

Since she's come back, I've noticed that she's often in her own head thinking a thousand different thoughts that she isn't sharing with the world. However, I've witnessed her truly letting go a few times to the point that her smile lights up her eyes. I saw it on the pitch at Tower Park, cooking with my nonna…and right now.

I'm sensing a theme.

"Where do Mac and Freya think you are tonight?" I ask as we begin walking to the pizza place I suggested for dinner.

"Catching up with an old friend." Tilly glances at me out of the corner of her eye. "Although Freya knows the truth."

I eye her curiously. "She does?"

Tilly shrugs. "It just…came out. I've really adapted nicely to the concept of a sister. She's loads easier to talk to than Mac."

"I see," I reply, feeling pleased that she's talking about me. "And you don't think she'll tell her husband?"

"She said it's my news to tell, not hers."

"Are we news?" I lace my fingers with hers and give it a hearty squeeze.

"I think it remains to be seen if we turn into official news, don't you?" She glances at me with an adorably pensive look.

"I'd say things are off to a very good start." I lift her hand and twirl her, not missing a step on our walk.

Tilly laughs. "You seem so secure in everything. I'm just not there yet. I think you and I have to get to know each other again. I mean… with our previous rules and all of that, this really is all new to us."

This remark makes my brows furrow. "We've spent hours on the phone over the past couple of days. You don't feel like that's us getting to know each other?"

"I do. I just…feel like I have to get used to the new you. If you would have told me five years ago you make sauce with your nonna, I would have been like…mind blown." She punctuates the comment with the hand gesture.

"Ouch." I stare forward, trying to ignore the hit to my apparent fragile ego.

"Sorry," she wraps her free hand around my arm. "There's no way you had a great past impression of me either."

I huff out a dry laugh. "I do actually."

She frowns up at me. "Seriously?"

"Yes." I pull my arm free to wrap around her shoulders. "You were challenging and outspoken, and you always knew exactly what you wanted, from a drink to a sexual position. You were motivated and brave and bold."

"I was drunk," she murmurs, shaking her head in disgust. "The booze made me brave."

"Bollocks," I scoff. "You were brave with my mother at dinner the other night. Asking her pointed questions about being a teen mother. Most people don't do that."

She puzzles up at me. "Isn't that a bad thing?"

"Not for me," I state defiantly. "I like your honesty. It's what I grew up with, so it feels right to me. And don't forget," I glance behind us to make sure no one is walking nearby as I lean in and whisper, "when we were shagging, you were never fully pissed. I made sure of that."

Tilly groans and covers her face. "Those stupid sobriety tests you used to make me do when I'd show up at your flat at all hours of the night were awful."

"Awfully brilliant." My shoulders shake as I fight back a laugh. "They were like free entertainment. I really was an arrogant arsehole back then."

"You were." She sighs heavily. "But you had some redeeming moments. I wish more men would have been like you."

My stomach twists because the more she puts me on a pedestal, the worse it will feel when I tell her about my past. That is, *if* I tell her about my past. I've spent the past few years hoping to meet a woman I would want to share this personal detail about myself with, but it's too soon to know if Tilly is that woman yet. She feels like she could be. This feels like the start of something ten times more real and honest than any of my past relationships. Maybe it's because we have history. Or maybe it's because Tilly is and always has been special.

Either way, I need to get my head on straight and keep taking things slow. Overwatering a plant can kill it just as easily as under-watering. And I may not deserve this second chance, but I'm going to do everything I can not to fuck it up.

CHAPTER 18

Tilly

"**O**KAY, NOW TOUCH THE HEEL OF YOUR LEFT FOOT TO THE tips of the toes on your right foot with those hands stretched outward," Santino commands from his seat on the sofa.

My face falls as I try to compute that insanely specific command. "Are you sure I did this when I was pissed?"

"Oh yes," he deadpans. "Every time."

I struggle to balance as I stand in the middle of his living room in front of the telly doing a ridiculous sobriety test even though I've not had a sip of alcohol all night. Neither has Santino, for that matter.

Dinner was lovely. We discussed light, silly things like the fact that Santino hates cats. Apparently, he has a literal fear of them because when he was young, he had a sleepover at a mate's house, and their black cat somehow got inside his sleeping bag. When Santino slipped inside, the wee bugger attacked the shit out of him, leaving his shins and calves covered in wounds.

I, of course, laughed my arse off at that.

Then I told him of my failed attempts to win over Hercules with small bits of deli meat. The arsehole will take my offering and scamper off to eat it in privacy, never to be heard from again. Why can't he be more like Jasper?

"Now you need to touch your nose with your left index finger while bending over to grip your right ankle with your right hand."

"These can't be scientific," I state, struggling to get into position. "I mean, what kind of research did you do for these types of—"

Suddenly, I begin to fall, and when my hand flies out to catch myself, I manage to whack it on the television console that causes a sharp stab of pain to radiate up my wrist. I land in a harumph onto Santino's furry rug, groaning loudly as I clutch my wrist tightly to combat the ache.

"Shit," Santino says, flying off the couch to crouch down beside me. He places a gentle hand on my hip. "Are you okay?"

"I'm fine," I groan and roll onto my back with a laugh, shaking out my hand. "Just uncoordinated."

"Did you break anything?" Santino's eyes drift over my hand as he inspects me.

"Just my pride," I mumble, feeling all kinds of stupid.

He smirks and kisses the inside of my wrist. "Did you know I could see your knickers when you bent over?" His eyes are now dark pools of wickedness.

"I thought it felt a wee bit breezy down there." I bite my lip as my libido awakens. *Not that she was ever truly sleeping this evening.*

"Do you need help standing?" he asks, the corners of his mouth turning down as he fights back a smile.

"I'd say no, but I think that might take some of the fun out of it." I giggle like a schoolgirl.

"Nothing but trouble," he murmurs, wrapping an arm behind my back and the other under my knees. He rises with ease, and I wrap my hands around his neck for stability, trying to ignore the butterflies going bananas in my belly. As a taller female, something's just really sexy about being with a man who can easily handle the size of me.

He brings me over to the sofa and plunks me down onto his lap, pressing my back against the armrest. "Do you feel dizzy?" He tucks a strand of hair behind my ear.

I close my eyes and bask in the attention. "Definitely."

"Are you drunk?" he questions with a laugh.

"Completely pissed." I open my eyes and hit him with a Cheshire cat grin.

His face grows serious as a muscle jumps in his jaw. "Then I suppose I won't be able to touch you tonight." He hums a noise of disapproval.

My brows furrow. "Where were you planning to touch me?"

His brows arch knowingly. "Oh, a couple of different places that didn't include your wrist."

I lick my lips, then drag a finger along his hard chest, resisting the urge to lean in and inhale his spicy, masculine cologne. "You know, scientifically, it would be really hard for me to be pissed without having had a drop of alcohol."

"That is a very valid point." He tsks, our breaths mingling, eyes hooded.

My voice is a whisper when I add, "So perhaps you can make an exception to your rule, just this once."

With a sexy half-smile, he leans forward and touches his lips to mine, kissing me sweetly for a moment with no tongue. It's gentle and innocent, and when his hand interlocks with mine, I feel a rush of intimacy I've never really experienced before.

When our lips break, he pulls back to look at me, and the hunger in his eyes causes me to inhale a shaky breath. His nostrils flare as his gaze dips to my lips, and when he angles and comes back for another kiss, it's deeper and more urgent this time. His tongue sweeps between my lips, thrusting inside with a commanding force. I release his hand to rake my fingers through his hair, need trembling all the way through my fingertips. His free hand glides along my ribs and down the outside of my leg, his thumb curling in towards my inner thigh. The sensation strikes a nerve that I feel squarely between my legs and as we continue kissing, my legs part, aching for his touch.

Slowly, his fingertips slide up my inner thigh at a tantalizingly slow pace. I moan into his lips, and he interprets that correctly as he slips past the hem of my short dress and brushes his knuckles over the top of my knickers. I inhale a sharp hiss of air, pressing my forehead to his and holding on to his neck for dear life.

"You want me to touch you here?" Santino asks, his voice deep and thick with arousal as he presses his index finger over the silk of my knickers. "Do you like how this feels?"

I nod, biting my lip and physically unable to kiss him because all I can think about is breathing.

"Tell me," he commands, his nose brushing mine.

"Touch me, Santino," I croak, my voice an achy whisper. "God, please. Touch me."

He glances down at where his hand is currently concealed beneath my dress and flattens two fingers over the fabric. He gently rubs side to side over my clit, causing a heady rush of pressure in my pelvis. My legs squeeze around his hand as I squirm and shift on his lap, my body practically coming undone from the incessant teasing.

"Please," I beg, aching for more contact, my eyes struggling to open. "Please, Sonny."

Suddenly, his finger slips past the strip of fabric, and when his bare skin touches my bare skin, it's as if my entire body is on fire.

"You're soaked for me, Tilly," he groans, running his finger along my slit as his lips and tongue tease the space below my ear. "Fucking dripping wet."

My head falls back as I release a deep moan and feel my pelvis thrust up into his hand. It's like my body has a mind of its own right now and is revolting against me for keeping it alone for so long. It's completely ignoring all common acts of modesty.

Santino inserts one long finger inside me, and I cry out loudly, my body tensing on top of him. I open my eyes to find him watching my face with greedy fascination as his groin hardens beneath my arse.

"So fucking tight," he rasps as he pumps inside me in slow, measured strokes. "Christ, you feel incredible."

My eyes roll into the back of my head when he inserts a second finger and strokes an area that feels very, very right. Too right. My

God. Not even my best vibrator with the suction attachment gets me going this fast. But the feel of Santino's hard, muscled body beneath me, the sensation of his warm breath on my neck, and the view of his muscled forearm contracting as he pumps inside me, stimulating that one particular spot over and over again…it's all causing me to lose control.

He must recognise the urgency in my body because he begins pumping in and out quicker now. "Fuck Tilly, are you going to come for me like this?" His voice is awestruck and full of wonder.

I gasp, my hand grabbing his between my legs as I begin aggressively riding him, pumping my hips up to meet his fingers thrust for thrust.

"Jesus," he replies, his voice gravelly. "I can't believe you're going to…"

"Santino," I cry out, curling into his chest as all the tension I've been holding inside my body for five long years unfurls in pulsating waves of pleasure around his fingers.

He remains frozen for a long while as he hugs me to his chest, our breaths heavy as I recover from that out-of-body experience I just had. I grip the taut muscles of his chest as reality begins to creep back into my consciousness. Good God, I just climaxed from being fingered.

Mortification begins to pinprick in my mind. What must Santino think of me? When he knew me before, I was wild and confident. Brave and bold, he said. Letting him comfort me after my first orgasm from just a couple of fingers is anything but bold.

Knowing I need to turn this situation around, I quickly slip off his lap and kneel between his legs. "Payback time," I say with a smile as I shimmy the hem of my dress back into place. Christ, my knickers are drenched.

"Tilly." Santino grips my arms to shift my focus from his very strained erection trapped inside his jeans to him. His eyes are hooded on me when he states, "I'm not done with you yet."

"You are for tonight," I respond boldly and move to unbutton his jeans. "It's my turn to call the shots."

When his erection bobs out of his jeans, I can't help but stare at it in wonder. I didn't remember it being this thick. Or this long. Did it grow in five years, or is my memory just that shit? That's the thing about my substance abuse back then. Everything is fuzzy, and it makes me constantly wonder what was real and what was fake. However, right now, I'm of sound mind and body, and I really want to feel the girth of Santino between my lips.

I wrap my fingers tightly around him, and his audible hiss of pleasure is all the reassurance I need. I tease the tip of his cock with my tongue before pulling him deep into my throat.

"Fuck," he growls, his hand reaching out to brush my hair off to one side. He wraps it around his fist and holds it back as I release him with an audible pop. "You really don't have to."

"I want to," I reply and then spread my lips around him again.

The noises he makes and the pleasure he's experiencing as I continue to suck him off are everything I need to feel in control of this situation again. Losing myself like that in front of him when we've just barely started whatever it is we're doing isn't wise. There's a reason I haven't been intimate with a man in five years. Staying in control is an important part of my life now.

I don't fully understand why I decided to have Santino be the first man I become intimate with after all these years. Maybe because he's familiar. Maybe because even when my life was total chaos, he was some small form of safety? But he's not my saviour. I saved myself. And I can't let him call all the shots as we reconnect or I risk losing that part of myself that I found in my sobriety.

"Tilly," Santino's gruff voice calls out as I lose myself in the act. "I'm close."

I peer up at him as I pump my mouth over his throbbing erection. His neck muscles are taut, and he's gripping my hair hard at the roots. The tightness is exhilarating. It's empowering to have a man out of control like this in front of me. So empowering that instead of releasing him and letting him go into a tissue, I suck harder, dragging my teeth along his shaft.

"Oh fuck!" he cries out, curling forward and releasing my hair to splay his hands out on his sofa.

In a few more seconds, his cock pulses between my lips, and a warm, salty liquid hits the back of my throat. He groans as he empties himself inside me, his hands moving to my shoulders as he jerks out his full release.

When he's done, I sit back on my heels and wipe the edges of my mouth. Without a word, Santino reaches forward and grabs me by the arms, hauling me up to straddle his lap. My dress rides up to my hips as he stares into my eyes with a look of complete adoration.

"Spend the night with me." It's a statement but there's question in his eyes.

I glance down at his chest. "I better not."

"Why?"

"You know why."

"I'm not asking for sex." He tilts his head and captures my eyes, trying to read me.

"It's not that." I run a hand through his hair, trying to think of an excuse. "It's my brother. He'll wonder where I am."

"Then let's tell him we're seeing each other. I'm not afraid of him."

"Neither am I," I reply firmly and then decide to hit Santino with honesty because deep down, I know he'll be okay with it. "But spending the night also isn't taking things slow."

He hums a noise in the back of his throat while affectionately rubbing his hands up and down my arms. "I understand. Whatever you're comfortable with is fine. You're in charge."

I smile boldly at him and prop my hands on my hips. "It's good you remembered because there was a moment there when you were barking orders at me that I thought you'd forgotten."

He laughs and pulls me into his chest, his voice deep and rumbly when he says, "Feel free to remind me like that any time."

CHAPTER 19

Santino

I's Saturday afternoon before I have plans to see Tilly again. She said her brother noticed how late she got home Wednesday night and asked her a lot of awkward questions that she somehow successfully dodged. When she texted me the next day, she said it'd be easier for us to see each other during the day on the weekends because he notices less when she's not out at night.

I'm not a huge fan of this sneaking around business because I don't need to give Mac any more reason to hate me, but I understand Tilly's desire to see how things go with us. Maybe we'll realise in a couple of weeks that the connection we had in our past is just that…a thing of the past.

However, watching her come on my hand Wednesday night was about the sexiest fucking thing I've ever done with a woman. There was something mind-blowingly erotic about the innocence of it all. No sex, no shedding of clothes, just a simple slip of a finger. And maybe it was hotter because she hadn't been touched in so long, but watching her come undone while she took control of her own pleasure…

fuck. And what she did afterwards to me…Christ, I get hard just thinking about it.

My mobile trills from its spot on the counter, and I see it's my mother calling. I swear it's like her brain is hardwired to know when I'm having indecent thoughts.

"Hello?" I answer, tucking my mobile against my ear as I reach in my fridge to grab the groceries to make Tilly dinner.

"What are you making her?" my mother's voice chirps loudly.

"Food," I reply curtly. I should never have told my mother I was cooking for her when she called a couple of days ago. She is like a dog with a bone.

"Tell me exactly. And what wine are you pairing with it?"

"No wine, Mamma. Remember?"

"Oh, that's right, she can't drink." Her tone is flat. "Gosh, no wine with dinner is a travesty."

"It's fine."

"And you don't drink because of her? Are you never going to drink again if you stay with this girl?"

I shrug. "It hasn't been a bother yet. And she can drink. She just chooses not to."

"Interesting."

"I can hear your judgment."

"I'm not judging," she responds defensively. "I'm just processing. Wine is like water to Italians."

"I know, but it's really not that big of a deal. I'm making us espressos."

"What did you make for dessert?"

I sigh heavily. "Are you really going to make me do this?"

"What?"

I stop fussing with the food. "You and Nonna taught me how to cook, now trust that I will cook her a brilliant dinner that won't make her vomit all over the table."

"This is not a joke." Her voice is softer when she adds, "You've never cooked for a woman before."

My brows furrow. "You don't know that."

"Well, have you?"

My nostrils flare. "No."

"Exactly." She tsks into the line. "This is important, and you making jokes isn't going to distract me. You were so moody last Sunday. Then she showed up, and it was like somebody turned a light on inside you. You said you dated her once before?"

"We weren't technically dating. Just…friends." I wince, hoping she doesn't pry further on that subject.

She harumphs. "Friends make good lovers."

"Okay, Mamma, I need to hang up. She's going to be here soon."

"Will you tell her?" she rushes out before I have a chance to say goodbye.

"Tell her what?"

"You know what I'm talking about, Santino. Don't play dumb."

My entire body goes still, my hands clenching into fists at the sudden change in topic. My voice is low when I reply, "Mum, it's too soon for that."

"I know, but that's all you and I have talked about on our trips. You want someone you don't have to hide from. This is the first one I've ever met so that has to mean something, doesn't it?"

Her voice becomes trembly at the end, and my resolve softens. "Please don't cry, Mamma."

"I'm not crying," she croaks, clearly crying. "I just want this for you, very badly. It took me ages to find Bart, and I don't want that life for you. You work so hard, and you've become so successful and made a wonderful life for yourself. You deserve someone to love the real you with no secrets."

I exhale heavily because this is the reason I haven't introduced my mum to the women I date. She gets her hopes up, and it stirs up feelings of the past, which is not helpful. "Thank you, Mamma. But right now, we're just having fun. I don't want to put pressure on this."

"Okay." She sniffles loudly. "Fun is good. You work too much."

"I know. I really do need to go now, okay?"

"Okay, ti amo, Santino."

"Ti amo, Mamma."

When we hang up, I stride over to turn the music on my sound system. I need to shake off that unexpectedly intense conversation with my mother because that's not where I want my head to be. Tonight needs to be about Tilly, not my fucked-up past.

A bit later, my buzzer goes off, and I let Tilly up, doing my best to pre-arrange the bits I want her to help me with. I know she doesn't like cooking, but it'll be fun pushing her out of her comfort zone. And food is like foreplay, so this should be the perfect starter for us.

When she knocks on the door, I open it to find her covered in rain. "Shit, I didn't even notice it was raining out." I glance over my shoulder at the dark clouds through my windows.

"It opened up on me just as I parked my car, and I, of course, didn't even think about bringing an umbrella."

"Come in." I clutch her hand and pull her towards me.

She kicks her flats off at the door and removes her oversized denim jacket. I hang it on the nearby hook to dry out and turn to take in the sight of her. She's wearing a loose pair of high-waisted jeans and a black off-the-shoulder crop top. She looks good enough to eat.

"You look like trouble." I step towards her to swipe away some raindrops from her cheeks. Her scent is even more alluring mixed with the rain, and I can't help but lower my head and taste her lips. Her silky tongue slips between my lips, and the friction causes my body to hum to life. My hands slide from her face to her waist, shaping the delicate exposed skin of her sides and teasing the edges of her top. I wonder what would happen if I reached up and unclasped her bra right here in the entry?

As if reading my mind, she pulls away from my lips, her breath shaky as she steadies herself on my arms. "Is that how you greet all your guests?"

My eyes dance on hers. "Only the ones I really like." She fails to hide her pleased smirk. "Are you hungry?"

"Starving."

I point towards my kitchen. "Good, you can help me cook."

She runs a hand through her damp hair, wearing a dubious look on her face. "That's not a good life choice, Sonny."

"Why?" I reply with a laugh.

She stares at all of the supplies and wrinkles her nose. "I told you…I'm a takeaway girl. Point me in the direction of a menu, and I'm loads of help."

I roll my eyes. "I'm just putting you in charge of the antipasto tray."

She winces. "That's like charcuterie, right?"

"More or less." I place my hands on her waist because I can't not touch her as I walk her over to the workstation I set up by the fridge. Standing behind her, I rest my chin on her shoulder and show her the items I picked up at the market. Cured meats, olives, mushrooms, a couple of different cheeses, plus a loaf of bread. "Most of it is already prepared. Just spread it out on this round board here. Think of it like decorating, but with food."

She smiles and grabs a knife out of the holder in front of her. "I'll try not to screw it up."

I kiss the space below her ear, and she curls into me. It feels so good, it's hard for me to step away, but I have the first course on the stove and it needs tending to. I move to my own work area and set about chopping up the fresh garlic to toss into the red sauce. "Oh, there are a couple of limonate in the fridge. You want to grab them? The bottle opener is in the drawer right in front of you."

She pauses her work and grabs two glass bottles. "You know you can drink alcohol around me, right?" she asks, prying the cap off the bottle and sliding it over to where I stand stirring the sauce on the stove. "It's been years since I've stopped drinking, and I told you I have had a drink since then and been fine. I'm not that fragile."

"I know, but you still don't choose to drink most of the time." I grab the bottle in front of me and take a cooling sip. "Plus, I don't mind."

"Do you really mean that?" She turns her attention back to the bread she was slicing.

"If I wanted to drink, I'd drink. But honestly, I enjoy being sober with you." I shoot her a wink, which seems to satisfy her as she pops a cube of cheese into her mouth.

She grabs her drink and slides closer to peer into the two pans I have on the stove. "So, what is on the menu for tonight?"

"First, antipasto." I point at her board. "Then the primo dish of red sauce and penne. Then I have a roasted chicken in the oven for the secondo with broccolini as the contorno. And finally, we'll end with the dolce...dessert. Although full confession, I picked that up at the store. There's a really good bakery around the corner that makes the best cannoli. Seriously, they are better than my nonna's, but if you ever tell her I said that, I'll have you murdered."

Her eyes widen as she takes a sip out of her glass bottle and heads back to her tray prepping. "Homicide seems a bit intense for a cannoli."

"Food is life or death in my family," I state with no hint of amusement. "Nonna actually hated one of our neighbours in Bourton because they put parsley in their minestrone." I pin Tilly with a grave look. "That's an unforgivable sin, in case you didn't know."

"I had no idea," she replies with wide eyes. "Good thing I never make minestrone."

This makes me genuinely laugh.

She pops a green olive into her mouth. "You can't eat like this by yourself every night. There's no way you can consume this much food and look the way you do."

I side-eye her while dropping the pasta into the boiling water. "You've noticed how I look, Tilly?"

She rolls her eyes and grabs a grape. "I mean, you haven't given me a proper show, but I can get a general idea just by the look of you." Her eyes drift down my body.

"So, you *have* been eyeing me up," I say, feeling smug.

"No," she volleys back, shooting daggers at me. "Your ego is surviving perfectly fine without my attentions."

I huff out a noise as I reach over and snag an olive off her board. "What kind of food does your family make?"

"Mmm," she replies as she swallows a sip of her lemonade. "My mother is a very proper meat and two vegetable type of cook. She would think a curry is something exotic."

I laugh again. "Are your parents disappointed you're not moving back to Scotland?"

"Aye, sure, but they were pleased about my job opportunity. Plus, I think they're going to be making a lot of visits to London once Freya and Mac have the baby."

I watch Tilly for a long moment as she works and hesitate asking her a question I'm sure she won't want to answer. But knowing she wouldn't hold back from asking me, I decide to just come out with it. "Is it hard for you to be around Freya?"

"Why would it be?" She frowns over at me, looking genuinely confused.

I swallow the knot in my throat. "Because she's pregnant, and you've lost a baby before."

When her hands still, I immediately regret going so deep so fast. We were laughing and flirting and having a great time, and I completely buggered this all up. "I'm sorry, you don't have to answer that."

"It's fine," she says quietly, turning her attention back to the food in front of her. "I guess I don't really think much about it because… well…it was connected to such a difficult time in my life that isn't a part of me anymore. So I try to just leave it in the past."

I nod slowly. "Doesn't mean it isn't still hard, right?"

She turns sad eyes to me. "I suppose so."

I remain quiet for a moment as she appears to be processing something. "Do you want to talk about it?"

She chews her lower lip and glances down. "I don't really talk about it to anyone ever. I made my family promise not to bring it up ever again, and they honoured that wish. Then I became so focused on staying sober that I guess the experience sort of got left behind."

My body aches because I hate the fact that she went through it alone. I know she had her family around her, but she didn't have a partner or the man that put her in that position to be with her. It reminds me of my mother being pregnant and alone with me.

"How far along were you?"

"Only nine weeks," she says with a sigh. "I'd just had a scan the week before. The whole experience feels like another lifetime. One moment, I'm debating my options and trying to decide if I was even going to keep the baby. The next, I was having a scan and hearing the heartbeat."

She clears her throat and begins to mindlessly tear pieces off a slice of bread. "No one can prepare you for that sound. Their heartbeats are really fast in the beginning, and it sounds like the thunder of a galloping horse so it's hard to believe it's even a real baby. But the effect it had on me was immediate…which was bizarre because I never fancied myself a mum. I just couldn't picture myself pregnant. Then, within seconds of hearing that sound, I knew I couldn't possibly…" Her voice breaks on the end before adding, "Then, just as I began to come around to the idea of being a mum, I lost it. It was over before it even began." She stops messing with the bread and wipes her hands on her jeans nervously. "Watching Freya's belly grow isn't a bother. I was never far enough along to even have that sensation." Tilly smiles a bit wobbly. "But the other night, Mac placed his hand on Freya's belly for a full hour waiting for a wee kick, and when it happened…"

Tilly's voice trails off as tears slip freely down her cheeks. I leave the food at the stove to pull her into my arms. She huffs out a self-deprecating laugh. "It's been years, Santino. I really don't need to be comforted."

"Why not?"

"Because I'm over it. I was just so happy for my brother."

I run my hand up and down her spine. "But is it something you ever truly get over?"

She doesn't answer that, just sags into my arms and lets me hold her as the weight of the moment settles around us. Most of the time, Tilly is tough and untouchable. But even five years ago, I remember these quiet moments when she opened up like a butterfly. The only problem was, no one could ever catch her.

She pulls back and smiles up at me through watery eyes. "I'm going to be an amazing aunt, I'll have you know. And aunts have it so much easier, right? We get to drop the wee ones off when we're done with them. Spoil them rotten and not be bothered with middle of the night feedings or sore nipples. It's brilliant, really."

I push her hair back from her face, swiping at the trail of leftover tears. "I think you're incredible."

"Why?" she huffs with a laugh, turning away from me and resisting my words.

"Because you've coped with a lot, and now you're here volunteering to be a caretaker for your pregnant sister-in-law…most wouldn't be able to handle it." She turns back to look at me, and I don't miss the slight twitch to her nose as she ponders what I've said.

"I love them." She lifts her eyebrows and shrugs. "And I like a challenge."

"This I already knew." I lean down to kiss her lips softly, loving how she wraps her arms around my waist and squeezes me like she needs a hug and a kiss all at once. When her stomach grumbles between the two of us, we break apart laughing. "We really need to get this dinner going."

"Yes, we do."

We manage not to burn anything, mostly because I keep Tilly away from the oven, and she sets the table beautifully. We take our time eating the antipasto, primo, and secondo. Tilly savours each course and asks questions about how I made everything even though I know she will never attempt it.

When I bring out the cannoli and make us espressos, apparently, it's Tilly's turn to ask me the tough questions.

"Have you ever been in love?" she inquires, clutching her espresso cup. She's seated right beside me, curled into her chair with her legs tucked under her chin.

"With cannoli? Every bloody day of my life." I take a bite, relishing in the light crunch of the pastry and the gooey sweet centre.

"Don't avoid the question." She pins me with a look. "You hit me with the deep questions before we'd even had starters."

I grimace and sit back in my chair, turning in my stool so my legs are spread around her chair. "I can't say that I have."

"Not even when you were young?" She sets her mug down and props her chin on her hand. "Teenage love can be silly, but it's still love."

I shrug. "No, not even then."

"How is that possible?" she asks me pointedly. "You told me you've been seriously dating women for a few years now. Are you saying none of them wormed their way into your dark Italian heart?"

"I don't know what to tell you. I never felt it."

"Did they feel it towards you?" Her brows knit together in curiosity.

"I don't know. One or two maybe." I ring the edge of my mug, avoiding her eyes.

She inhales sharply and touches my thigh. "They loved you, and you...what? Said nothing?"

"God, you won't let this go, will you?" I laugh and comb my fingers through hers, holding her hand on my lap. "If they said it and I didn't feel the same way, that was usually when I ended things. I didn't want to lead anyone on."

"Maybe you just weren't patient enough?"

"If it was the right person, I would have known." I squeeze her hand playfully and reach out to grab my mug. "The two-month chump label I have been stuck with is because I figured out that if I gave women two full months, I'd be able to walk away with certainty."

"Interesting," Tilly replies with a frown. "A bit clinical for love, I'd say."

"I have no regrets, so it must have worked."

She licks her lips, disbelief still painted all over her gorgeous face. "It's just strange because you have great examples of love in front of you. Your grandparents seem very stable. Your mum and Bart look like they get on well. I'm just trying to figure out why you wouldn't have fallen in love once by now?"

I exhale and then give her the only answer I can without unloading a lifetime's worth of baggage on her. "Perhaps it's because I never knew my own father so the thought of a man and a woman loving each other through anything just seemed like a load of bollocks."

Her lower lip juts out. "That's sad."

I shrug. "I resented my mother for a long time for not telling me who my father was. It felt deceitful and wrong and like she was hiding something from me. A part of who I was. I think it caused me to struggle to ever trust women."

"What caused you to open up your heart then?"

"Who says I've opened my heart?"

"Well, the laundry list of women you've been dating seems like change."

"Yes, but that doesn't necessarily mean I've fully given myself to anyone. I can connect with a woman but not fully trust in that connection enough to fall in love with them."

Her eyes bend with sympathy. "So why bother even trying?"

"Because I want it all," I reply firmly, tossing my arms out wide. "I used to just want to be successful in my career, but now I want more. I want what I didn't have as a child, and I want to get to the point I can be my true self with someone."

She smiles and sips her coffee thoughtfully. "This is fascinating."

"Not that fascinating." I laugh.

"It is." She hits me with wide, excited eyes. "I have a feeling, Santino Rossi, that when you fall in love, it's going to be fireworks."

She stares at me, and I stare back at her, trying to decide if she'll be the one who pushes me over the edge. It's too soon to tell. Is my immediate interest in Tilly just because of our shared history? Or is it because of the situation that happened to her before she left? If either of those two instances wouldn't have happened, would she have been the person I'd given my heart to? I just don't know.

I shake that nerve-wracking thought away and squeeze her leg. "What about you?"

"What about me?" She takes a small bite of the dolce.

"Have you ever been in love?"

Her brows lift as she chews. "Only a few times."

"Of course, you have." I grin and shake my head.

"What's that supposed to mean?" She pins me with a menacing look.

"You had heartbreaker written all over you when we first met. And you were very free with your feelings back then. Whatever you felt, you said."

She tsks knowingly. "I suppose that's true. Although, looking back, I'm not really sure I knew what love truly was. My experiences since then have changed me a bit."

"I can see that." I watch her thoughtfully for a long moment, amazed that she's here with me right now after all this time. Could we have been this open with each other five years ago? It's doubtful.

We end up talking for another hour over a second espresso, and as we finish cleaning up, she says, "You know what? I've been here three times now and still have never seen your bedroom."

My cock stirs in my trousers over the thought of her in my bedroom. "What happened to taking it slow?" I ask, brows lifted curiously.

She props her hands on her hips. "Getting a tour of the rest of your flat doesn't mean we're shagging, okay? Come on now, give me a tour of your splendors, Mr. Rossi."

"Very well, Ms. Logan." I hold my hands out dramatically. "This right here is the kitchen." She narrows her eyes at me, but I won't be deterred. "This is a stove." I touch it mockingly as her lips thin. "This here is called a *taaable*. Over there is a lamp."

"You are such an eejit." She darts for me, but I take off out of the kitchen, making a mad dash through the living room and around the corner to the hallway that leads to the bedrooms.

I call over my shoulder, "This is the guest room," and am shocked to see she's right behind me. She wraps her arms around my waist like she's trying to tackle me. "Fuck, you're faster than your brother, I expect. Not very strong, though."

"You are such an arsehole," she cries, trying and failing to sweep my legs and laughing the entire time. God, it's sexy.

I grab her by the wrist and toss her over my shoulder. Using my most pompous voice that I know she'll love, I smack her bottom and carry her into my room. "This is the master suite. It features sweeping views of Bethnal Green city lights, a real up-and-coming neighbourhood based on all the latest trends. Here we have a luxurious king bed with high thread count sheets, and a large en suite bathroom featuring a soaker tub and a walk-in tile shower, naturally."

I turn us sideways so I can see our reflection in the mirror. Her red hair is hanging and covering her face as she braces herself on my arse. She moves her hair out of the way to glower at me in the mirror. "Stick to the brooding Italian vibe, Santino. You're not even close to funny."

God, I love her like this. Cheeky mouth, challenging, and entirely at my mercy. "You don't think I'm funny?" I ask as I step into the tiled shower and put my hand on the water faucet. "Would you like to inspect the water pressure? That could be very funny."

"Don't you dare!" she exclaims, thumping her fists into my back to fight me. "I have my mobile in my pocket."

"No, you don't. It's on the table. But nice try, Trouble!"

When I turn the water on, she screams. It's fucking freezing. This was a bad life choice.

"Just give it a minute," I call out, wincing through the onslaught of cold water and her kicking and screaming. "It'll warm up in a tic."

"You are the biggest arsehole in the world!" she growls.

"Oh, come now, I'm sure my arsehole is of average size."

"Put me down!"

She squirms over top of me as the water finally begins to heat. I put her down, holding her by the waist so she doesn't make a run for it as her fist lands on my chest. She looks up at me through the streaming water, and I can't help but laugh. Eventually, her anger turns to amusement as well, as she swipes the water out of her eyes and grins up at me.

One moment, she's pissed, kicking and screaming. The next, our lips are locked, tongues thrusting, and hands groping every available square inch of each other's bodies over top of the really annoying and highly inconvenient wet clothing.

A guttural noise echoes from my chest when she begins rubbing her hand firmly over my cock that's currently really uncomfortable in these tight, wet trousers. The friction is mind-blowing, and I fear I might relieve myself too quickly, so I reach under her top and unclasp her bra. It's strapless, so with one quick tug, it drops instantly to the shower floor. When I look back at her through the water and see her pert nipples sticking out through the black fabric, I nearly come undone for a whole other reason.

"Fuck," I say, cupping her petite breasts and dipping my head to her left nipple. I bite it firmly through the fabric, sucking through the water as she cries out, clutching my head to her chest. I slip my other hand beneath the fabric and cup her bare breast, reveling in the sensation of her hard nipple against my palm and fingertips. My cock weeps against the seam of my trousers, but I'm determined to give Tilly what she gave me earlier this week.

I stand back up, my hands shaping over all of her curves and stopping at the button on her jeans. My voice is low and drenched with arousal when I murmur, "I want to taste you, Tilly."

She puffs a loud breath of air, gripping the glass shower door as she nods slowly, her lips parted, hair stuck to the sides of her face. God, she's fucking stunning.

"Lose this," she croaks. Grabbing the hem of my shirt, she pulls it over my head, and it flops in a soaked heap onto the tiled floor. Then I work on getting her jeans off while her hands skate greedily over my muscles. She's wearing a blue lace thong that I would normally admire, but right now, I'm craving the taste of her more than even that bloody cannoli I rambled on about earlier.

I press her back to the cool tile wall, hearing a loud hiss from her as I kneel and stare at her bare pussy dripping wet before me. I grip her leg and prop it on my shoulder before my mouth descends, taking a long, luxurious sweep of her centre.

"Santino," she cries loudly as her hand grips my wet hair, and I assault her sex with my tongue, water pounding on my back.

I grip her hips, pulling her into me, smothering my entire face with her essence as I devour her. Fuck, she tastes good and naughty, and the things I want to do with her are fucking endless. A lifetime with this pussy wouldn't be enough time.

I pull back and thrust two fingers inside her, staring up at her as she rides my hand, her hips thrusting into my touch just as they did the other night. God, she's horny and responsive and wet and tight. My cock threatens to spill inside my trousers because she feels so good. I dip my head and flick my tongue over her clit while pumping my fingers deep inside her.

"Oh my God," she says, her thighs tightening around my face. "I'm—"

She's coming. Fucking hell, I've never felt a woman come on me like this. Her sex pulses around my fingers wildly, her entire body clamping as she tenses and contracts over and over again.

When she's finished, I rise, keeping a firm hold on her hips as her legs seem ready to give out. She's trembling, so I move the hot water over her body as I lean in and give her a sloppy kiss. She kisses me back, but it's lazy and adorable. She's spent. She's gorgeous.

She's mine.

I trail a kiss to her ear and bite it gently before murmuring, "You know, my ego is going to be out of control if you keep coming this fast for me every time."

She huffs out a laugh, her eyes hooded as she recovers from the delirium. "Don't get too cocky. I'm out of practise."

I growl and bite her neck which wakes her right up. Her hand glides down my chest, smoothing over my abs. "Just as I remember. Rock-hard muscles."

"Just as I remember." I tweak her top-covered nipples. "Perfect tits."

With a cringe, she covers them up with her hands. "I have tiny biscuits for breasts."

I frown at that statement. "You say that like it's a bad thing." I reach down and pull her top up, taking a good long look at the breasts I had in my mouth mere moments ago. "Good cannoli nipples, too."

She bursts out laughing and shoves me. "I don't think that's a compliment."

I cage her against the shower wall and nudge my nose with hers playfully. "It is to me, and I'm the only man seeing your biscuits right now so what I say matters."

Her hand moves from my chest to my groin. "This is much bigger than a cannoli."

"Okay, now we're just embarrassing ourselves."

We both burst out laughing and kiss around smiles as she slips her hand inside my trousers and strokes me to completion. It doesn't take long for me either. Fucking hell, if foreplay with Tilly is this good, I can only imagine what sex will be like when we finally get there.

As we towel off, she glances at the clothes in a heap in my shower. "What am I going to wear home?"

"I'll find something for you." I wrap a towel around my waist and pad barefoot into my bedroom. Inside the walk-in closet, I retrieve a grey T-shirt and a pair of joggers that have always been a bit snug.

When I return to the loo, she's wrapping her hair in a towel and wiping at the makeup streaks running down her face. "I'm a mess," she says into the mirror.

"You're perfect." I move to stand behind her and gaze at our reflections. Her pale skin, my dark skin, her blue eyes, my black. We are opposites yet, I like what I'm looking at right now.

I retrieve a couple of cotton balls out of the drawer for her and sit on the counter as she scrubs at her face. "What are you doing next weekend?"

"I'm actually going to the big football game." She side-eyes me with a sneaky expression.

"Are you?" I tilt my head at the fact that she's kept this little secret from me.

"Mac and Freya were invited, and I guess they included me on that invitation. Apparently, it's a big rivalry match, and everyone is going?"

"Yeah, Camden Harris plays for Arsenal, and Booker Harris plays for Bethnal, so usually any time the brothers face-off, it becomes a family affair with all the kids at the match. However, since it's an evening game they don't usually bring all the little ones, which will make the suite a lot less chaotic."

"Are you saying you are going to be there?" She props a hand on her hip and hits me with big, doe eyes.

"Don't act like you didn't know."

"I didn't!"

"Your obsession with me is getting a little intense." I slide off the counter and turn to face her in the mirror, noticing her eyes trailing down my chest. "We might need to take a step back and re-evaluate our situation."

"Is that right?" she exclaims, splaying her hands out on the counter to glower at my reflection. "As I'm standing naked in your loo, you're saying this to me? No wonder those poor women could only stand two months with you and that monstrous ego."

I grab her around the waist and tickle her sides mercilessly, causing her towel to slip down off her bouncing breasts enough for me to have a really fucking lovely image to catalogue in my mind forever. Who needs shagging when you have naked Tilly to tease constantly?

She dries her hair and dresses in the clothes I gave her. I stare at her in fascination as I realise I can't decide if I like the image of her in a towel or my clothes better. When she thinks I'm not looking, I catch her pulling the shirt up to her nose and inhaling deeply. She gets a girlie smile on her face, and I know without a doubt, I definitely like her in my clothes better.

"Brunch tomorrow?" I ask, walking her to the door and really wishing she didn't have to leave.

"I suppose I could sneak away." She stands up on her tiptoes and kisses me. "This sneaking around business is actually kind of fun."

"Speak for yourself," I grumble, my hands wrapping around her waist and lowering to her arse. "What will your brother say when you show up in a strange man's clothes tonight?"

She licks her lips and slides her hands up my arms. "I'm sure he won't even notice. He's usually immersed in video games at this time of night." She kisses me again, and it's making it even harder for me to let her leave right now.

"You're sure you have to go?" Fuck me, I'm pouting now. I've completely lost my man card.

"I'm sure." She pulls away. "I'll see you tomorrow."

"Okay, Trouble. See you tomorrow."

CHAPTER 20

Tilly

Santino: I think we should tell Mac we're seeing each other before the match tomorrow.

Tilly: Pass, next question.

Santino: I'm being serious, Tilly. I'm not sure I'll be able to be around you and him at the same time.

Tilly: Why? Are you scared you won't be able to control yourself?

Santino: I'm scared you won't be able to control yourself. You made me meet you for lunch this week three times just so you could suck my face off in a dirty alley.

Tilly: Balls. We were always next to some beautiful street art because that app you found is amazing. And need I remind you that you were the one who turned it into a dirty groping session.

Santino: You were the one who stuffed your knickers in my suit pocket!

Tilly: That was supposed to be funny.

Santino: Oh sure. It was a real laugh getting a hard-on at work just thinking about them sitting there.

Tilly: See, you have no control.

Santino: I could make you lose control easily.

Tilly: You overestimate your charm, Rossi. I can resist you in the direst of circumstances.

Santino: Is that a fact?

Tilly: Yes, which is why we are not telling my brother yet because I can control myself.

Santino: This sounds like a challenge.

Tilly: Please don't try to give me your boxers. I'm afraid it doesn't have the same effect in reverse.

Santino: God, you really do have a cheeky mouth. I'm going to really enjoy fucking it after the match on Saturday.

Tilly: Don't go threatening me with a good time!

Santino: God, I cannot win with you.

Tilly: Best to just give up now.

Santino: Just you wait until Saturday. I'll figure something out to pay you back for that cheeky mouth.

CHAPTER 21

Tilly

T OWER PARK ON GAME DAY IS EVEN MORE INCREDIBLE THAN A private tour at night, which I never thought possible. The energy of the fans all decked out in green and white as they pour into the stadium and have food and drinks before they take their seats is electric. When I grew up, football was a religion at our house. My father and granddad would discuss Mac's career like Mac had no say in the matter while Mum and I worked to just be his cheerleaders and support system. A professional athlete's life isn't easy, and Mac has always been such a pleaser that oftentimes, he'd lose sight of what he wanted in his life just because he was so focused on making others proud of him.

That's why living with him this past month and a half and witnessing first-hand what he's like as a husband and soon-to-be father has been such a pleasure. He's definitely coming into his own and asserting himself more. Freya and I are currently riding on the back of a utility golf cart for our trip through Tower Park because even though

Freya's doctor cleared her for some light activity and walking, Mac still didn't think she should walk all the way up to the family suite.

My brother really is an adorable, stubborn ox.

If they have a daughter in the future, that poor girl will have no chance of a normal life.

The cart just barely fits on the lift to take us up to the upper level, and as we draw closer to the VIP suite, the noise of people inside is noticeable.

"Thanks for the ride, Sedgwick," Mac says, hopping off the cart and coming to the back to help Freya.

I slip out the other side and offer Sedgwick a nervous smile. "Thank you."

He winks knowingly and taps his nose, not saying a word about the fact that I was here with Santino just a couple of weeks ago. I wonder if Santino said something to him? Surely, he must have. Lord knows Mac would not have been happy to hear his sister was escorted around an empty football stadium at night by a man he loathes.

I hate the fact that Mac has hard feelings towards Santino. I've told him before that he had nothing to do with what happened to me five years ago. I know Mac believes me, but he also knows there's more to the story, so until I'm ready to tell Mac everything, I just don't see how I can change his mind.

And the truth is, I don't want to tell him. I'm horrified to think of the situation I put myself in. Telling Mac and my parents that I didn't even remember the name of the bloke that night is a disgrace that I cannot stomach. Ever. So, once I'd lost the pregnancy and changed my life around, I decided leaving the past in the past was best for everyone. Including me.

Which clearly worked because things are going great for me now. And Santino is part of that greatness. I'm not sure I've ever experienced such a mature, adult relationship…if that's even what we're doing. We don't have any official labels or anything, but I know we're exclusive, so does that make him my boyfriend? Have I ever cared more about a label with a man?

The answer is no. I have not.

Which is why the very last thing I want to do is rock the boat and tell my brother about us. He'll just ruin our momentum, and we're still sorting out what we are to each other.

I try to ignore the insecure sensation buzzing in my belly as I follow Mac and Freya into the suite packed with people. It's a decent-sized room that opens up to the pitch and several rows of stadium seats on a large balcony. Inside, there's a long buffet table of food and several high-top tables plus a small bar. The walls are papered with images of Bethnal Green players. I instantly spot Booker Harris in his bright neon green keeper gloves, and on the opposite wall is Mac's mate, Roan DeWalt, in a mid-kick position.

"Hey, guys!" Allie says, coming over and giving Freya a big hug. "Oh my God, Freya, it's so good to see you out and about!"

"It feels good to be out and about!" Freya cups her belly. "I've forgotten what it's like to put on real clothes." She tucks her hand to her mouth and whispers loudly, "However, I've become a real lover of the muumuus in my time at home."

"Well, you look great." Allie rubs Freya's belly affectionately. "I'm so happy you're able to get up and move a bit."

"We should find you a chair," Mac grumbles, looking around for a seat.

"Calm down, Mac. She's not been standing even a full minute." I pat his arm reassuringly and can't help but laugh at the worry in his eyes.

"We have another scan next week, and Belle said if all goes well, my restrictions might be lifted completely," Freya adds hopefully.

"But she's still going to take it easy," Mac harrumphs.

"And I'm not going anywhere regardless," I add, trying to give my brother some semblance of support. "I'm here until the baby is out."

"Thank goodness for that," Mac huffs, still clearly anxious that Freya's not yet in a chair.

Just then, Belle comes striding over with a warm smile. "How is my favourite patient doing?" she asks, pushing her dark hair back behind her shoulders. "Feel good to be up and moving?"

"Oh my goodness, yes," Freya exclaims, her round cheeks pulling back into a smile. "I'm chuffed to bits. But could you do a quick exam on Mac here? I think he's caught a case of overprotective-itis."

"Oh, he's been afflicted with that for years," I interject, punching my brother lightly on the shoulder. "It's like herpes, and I'm afraid it sticks with him."

Everyone laughs, and Freya takes pity on Mac and allows him to usher her over to a seat by the windows overlooking the pitch where she can prop her feet up.

"Where's Indie?" I ask Belle as we both glance out the window onto the pitch to watch the players warming up.

"She's down there with Tanner somewhere. Let's go out and have a look." I follow her out to the edge of the balcony, and we both scan the area down below. Finally, she points out towards the sideline. "There she is in those awful tan trousers and the green polo. Do you see her?"

Her curly red hair sticks out instantly. "Ah yes, there she is. Talk about an incredible seat to watch her husband play. Was Indie one of the team doctors at Bethnal before Camden left to play for Arsenal?"

"No, he was gone before Indie got the job. But she worked on him in other meaningful ways, if you know what I mean." She laughs and shakes her head. "Tell me that those players don't struggle to keep their willies in check while she examines their injuries. She's a total stunner." Belle points at the pitch and adds, "Oh look, there's Cam."

We both go quiet as we watch Cam in his Arsenal gear jog across the pitch towards Indie. She stops what she's doing and turns, placing her hands on her hips and shaking her head. He clearly is not discouraged as he reaches out and scoops her up into his arms, planting a very indecent kiss on her lips. She swats at him, and suddenly, Vaughn is beside them, pointing at the pitch and talking to his son with zero amusement on his face. Cam smiles playfully and rejoins his team for warmups.

"God, they are adorable. Two small kids at home and they still snog like teenagers in public. Though I can't judge, I'm busy checking out Tanner myself." She points towards the end of the pitch where Tanner is standing with Booker in his keeper kit. "He debated cutting his hair when he got the coaching position to look more professional, but I begged him not to. I have a thing for the man bun, caveman look."

I laugh at that. "To each their own."

"What's your type?" Belle asks, nudging my arm playfully, her dark eyes glittering with mischief. "Anybody caught your eye in London since you came back?"

My cheeks flame instantly. "Oh…no, not really. I do enjoy a classic tall, dark, and handsome type, though." I glance over my shoulder, wondering when Santino will get here. He texted me earlier this morning and told me to "get ready for his surprise". Whatever that means.

Belle's eyes widen. "Would you hate me if I introduced you to my brother, Ronald?"

"Your brother?" I repeat a bit distractedly.

"Yes! He's a single father and a corporate lawyer. He used to be completely under the thumb of my pompous, social-climbing father, but since he lost his wife a couple of years ago, he's so different. He's been coming around a lot more, a bit desperate for a taste of what normal life is that doesn't include staff, lavish parties, and constant arse kissing." She eyes me up and down with a big smile on her face. "You look like you'd be a nice dose of fun for him. He's the heir of a Lord if that's your thing?"

"It's not," I reply instantly, running a nervous hand through my hair.

"No bother, it's not something he brags about anymore, thank God." She turns around to look back into the suite. "I wonder where he is. He said he was on his way a while ago."

"I'm going to go get myself a drink," I state quickly, trying to figure out an excuse not to meet this brother of Belle's. "Need anything?"

"No, I'm fine, thanks. I'll find you later!" She gives me an enthusiastic thumbs-up, and I smile awkwardly while making my way towards the bar.

Glancing over, I see Mac and Freya are settled in their little corner with Sloan, Gareth, Leslie, and her husband Theo, plus Allie, and Booker's wife, Poppy, so I head straight for the bar for some much-needed space. Apparently, it isn't just Tanner who struggles with boundaries but his wife too. What should I have said, though? That I'm seeing someone and my brother doesn't know? That would have been a huge opening for questions I cannot answer. This is the trouble about being exclusive with someone in secret.

"Can I get a club soda with lime please?" I ask, splaying my hands out on the bar and feeling a chill run up my spine.

The bartender retreats just as a deep voice whispers in my ear, "Revenge is a dish best served cold."

The familiar smell of Santino's cologne wafts over me, and I can't fight the smile that spreads across my face. I turn to look at him, my eyes drinking in his pale grey suit. His dark hair is artfully mussed, and it's literally painful not to stand on my toes and kiss him. "Look at you quoting *Godfather* to me."

"The student surpasses the teacher." He has a wicked look in his eye that I don't like. "Plus, it's a very fitting quote for what I have in store for you today."

"Which is what exactly?" I glance over my shoulder to see if anyone is looking at us, but Santino doesn't seem the least bit concerned.

He hands me a small gift bag. "I have a little gift for you." His eyes dance with mirth.

"A gift is not very discreet."

"Don't worry. It's well concealed at the bottom." When his eyes drop to my lips, I feel my insides clench with need.

This dating in secret thing wasn't an issue for me until right this moment. I inhale a cleansing breath and turn my focus to the gift bag. "What's in here?"

He lifts his brows. "Just a little payback for your cheeky mouth yesterday."

I fight back a satisfied smirk. "I was just stating a fact that you clearly want me more than I want you. It's a bit sad, actually. I mean, you are four years my senior. I would think you'd have more control than this."

He growls and discreetly reaches over and pinches me on the side. I have to fight back a squeal just as my drink gets delivered to me.

The bartender points at Santino. "I'll have a whiskey on the rocks please."

My brows lift at his casual order of alcohol in front of me. Strangely, it makes me feel proud. Like he heard me say to him that I could handle him drinking around me, and he trusts my words. I appreciate that level of respect from a man. Growing up Scottish, overprotective men are an everyday occurrence. My granddad, my father, and especially my brother were all certain they knew what was best for me. It's a wonderful thing to have men that care so deeply, but it can be infantilizing at times.

So, to see Santino respect my words and take them to heart makes me feel seen in a very meaningful way. I shake away the butterflies in my belly and ask, "Do I open this now?"

"No," Santino barks, holding back a laugh that makes him look young and carefree. "You'll have to nip into the loo to open it. And... you'll definitely have to put it on in there. That's nonnegotiable."

My cheeks flame with heat. "What on—"

"Fancy seeing you here, Santino," my brother's voice cuts in gruffly from the other side of me.

Santino offers Mac a dazzling, unfazed smile. "Hiya, Mac. Nice to see you."

Mac grunts his displeasure, and his gaze lowers to the drink in my hand. He gets a curious expression on his face before addressing Santino again. "Can I help you with something?"

"No, I'm good. Just having a nice chat with your sister."

Mac growls and points at the bag in my hand. "What's that you got there, Tilly?"

"It's a jersey with your former number, and Logan scrawled on the back," Santino answers with ease. "I was in the gift shop storage room the other day and found some of your old gear in boxes so I thought your sister might like it. I have another box for you and the family sitting by the door for you to grab on your way out tonight."

Mac scowls at Santino. "You must be joking."

Santino's brows lift. "I'm not. There was even a baby piece in there. A onesie or something?"

"Shit," Mac barks, clearly as stunned by this entire exchange as I am. "That was rather thoughtful of you."

Santino shrugs. "Tilly just mentioned she hadn't been to Tower Park before so I wasn't sure if she had a kit. I should have known she'd have something to wear."

He glances at the Bethnal Green pullover I'm wearing, and I sense an opening. "Yes, but my top doesn't say Logan on the back, and I'd love to represent my retired brother." I flash a toothy smile to both of them. "I'll just pop into the loo and have a change."

I slink away from my brother and Santino, my heart beating wildly in my chest from that very uncomfortable exchange. Once inside the safety of the suite loo, I open the bag up to find a very nice white jersey with green trim and big block letters on the back that say Logan. He wasn't lying! Plus, it fits perfectly. As I smooth the hem over top of my wide-legged jeans and finger comb my loose hair in the mirror, my heart swells with pride. Not just because I'm wearing my brother's number today but because this was an extremely thoughtful gift from Santino. I'm not sure I've ever received such a sweet gift from a man.

Knowing this gift can't be all hearts and flowers, I glance into the bag again and dig beneath several layers of tissue paper before I find a small box and an envelope. I open it up to see a note from Santino:

You say you like a challenge...put these on and see how challenging this match gets when I have all the control.

Frowning, I open up the box, and my eyes widen when I see what's inside.

It's the knickers I stuffed into his suit pocket the other day, but there's something attached to the centre strip of fabric.

"It can't be," I whisper as I look down at the wee black device shaped like a very slim keyboard mouse. On the back, I spot a charging port and a simple on/off switch.

He's given me fucking vibrating knickers. What a cunt.

Cringing, I slide the switch to on, and a soft buzz alights in my hand, confirming my original assessment. Liquid heat instantly pools in my belly as I imagine Santino using this on me. I mean, I don't hate that idea. The thought of him pushing in this door right now and assaulting my sex with this wee thing is enough to have my entire body quivering with anticipation.

But giving it to me with my knickers doesn't sound like that's what he wants me to do right now. "He can't be serious."

As if on cue, my mobile pings inside my pocket, and I pull it out to see a text from Santino.

Santino: Yes, I gave you vibrating knickers, and yes, I have complete control over them through an app on my mobile. Leave the switch to on.

Tilly: You can't expect me to put these on now.

Santino: Oh, I absolutely do, Tilly. Unless of course, you'd rather I have a nice talk with Mac about my feelings for you? I think I've warmed him up nicely with the bag of old kits.

Tilly: You are such an eejit.

Santino: So, is that a yes to wearing them? I've been hard all day thinking about having your pleasure at the tips of my fingers. I have very nimble fingers if you recall.

I swallow nervously as an erotic thrill pulses in my veins. This is the Santino I was attracted to five years ago. Domineering, demanding, and discreetly kinky. Inhaling sharply, I type back my reply.

Tilly: I'll wear them with pride, Sonny.

Santino: Oh Trouble, this is going to be so much fun.

I slowly make my way out to the stadium seats on the balcony just as the football game begins, acutely aware of the foreign object between my thighs. It has a ridged nub on the front that grinds against my clit as I walk, causing my body to stir without even a tease of vibrations yet. *This is going to really test my strength.*

Santino's eyes follow me from his spot at the bar where he's standing with Gareth. I do my best to avoid that smug expression dancing in his eyes. I'm a Scottish lass through and through, and he's not going to get the best of me.

I find an open seat on the end of the back row next to Freya. Mac is on the other side of her, and Allie and Sloan are farther in from them. I casually glance through the glass wall behind me to see that Santino has moved from the bar to sit squarely behind Mac. His dark eyes are swimming with wicked revenge.

As the match starts, I do my best to focus on the players whizzing the football up and down the pitch. Normally, I can get sucked right into a match and scream louder than most spectators. But normally, I don't have a vibrator between my lower lips and Santino's dark eyes watching my every move.

The game is a bit dull at first with very little action in front of either goal. But at the thirteen-minute mark, Camden Harris has fast footwork that confuses his defender, leaving him wide open for a shot at close range. A hard kick to the bottom left corner is saved by a diving catch from Booker Harris, and the entire stadium is on their feet, erupting in a chant of *Harris! Harris! Harris!*

Everyone in the suite laughs and cheers loudly because it's a kind gesture to both brothers as they point to each other in a beautiful display of brotherly sportsmanship. Freya and I are clapping and smiling like loons when suddenly, the space between my legs alights with a sensation that has me nearly falling onto Belle sitting in front of me.

"Are you okay, Tilly?" Freya asks, her voice nearly drowned out by the cheers.

My lips thin as I give her a crisp nod and struggle to keep my breath steady. "I'm great! What a save from Booker!"

"I know, the baby of the family is such a star!" She waves her hands in the air excitedly, joining in the chants again as she high-fives Booker's wife, Poppy, sitting next to Belle.

When she directs her attention to the pitch along with everyone else, I feel the vibration move from the front of the device to the back, zigging and zagging, to and fro. What in the hell? Does this thing have a bloody sensor pad? *Fuck me, I'm in trouble.*

My thighs press together involuntarily as I catch the eye of Allie, who raises an eyebrow at my troubled expression. I wave her off with a grimace and pretend to have a coughing fit to cover up my erratic breath.

Glancing over my shoulder, I find Santino watching me with a hungry look in his eyes that makes me want to rip this thing out of my knickers and throw it in his face.

Though, the eejit would probably like that too much.

When everyone begins to take their seats again, I exhale with relief as the vibrating stops. However, my centre is still pulsating with need as I gingerly sit down and cringe with embarrassment at the sensation of my damp knickers.

Is it really weird that I want him to turn it on again?

I do my best to focus on the match, and the next exciting bit happens when poor defending of Arsenal's box allows for loads of passing between Bethnal Green offence. Finally, Roan DeWalt finds himself open and hammers it high up by the upper post, slipping well beyond the keeper's hands and safely into the net.

I don't even have a chance to cheer before the vibrator zings up to an even higher level than before. Everyone is around me losing their minds over an amazing goal kick, and all I can do is focus on the sensations pillaging my centre with so much ferocity, I'm white-knuckle gripping the armrests and trying to keep from moaning.

With great effort, I rise on shaky legs and hope not to draw any attention. I jam my hands into my pockets as my thoughts waffle between wanting to yank the vibrator out of its position to get some relief and feeling the urge to climb over the back of this chair and ride this out until I climax like a freak.

"Do you hear that?" I hear Freya ask Mac as she grips his ink-covered arm.

"Hear what?" Mac yells back, clapping loudly for his friend's score.

"There's a buzzing sound." She glances around. "Is it your mobile?"

Mac frowns, clearly annoyed that Freya is making him do this in the middle of an exciting match but he digs into his pocket to check anyways. "It's not me."

"Well, I didn't bring my mobile inside." Freya looks around curiously. "Check with Allie beside you."

"Cookie, I don't know why it even matters."

"Just ask her!"

He harumphs and turns away from Freya to ask Allie, who is bewildered by all the excitement.

Meanwhile, sweat beads across my forehead as I close my eyes and bite back the positively feral noises that want to rip free from my throat. Heat spreads through my body as I balance myself on the chair in front of me and have an out-of-body experience. I can feel myself nudging closer and closer to release while simultaneously pleading with my body not to do this here. *Don't do this, Tilly. You're stronger than this. You can fight this!*

Over the noise of the stadium, I gasp as the knickers ratchet up to an unbearable level, and my core hits a fever pitch that refuses to be ignored. My entire body begins to quake as I close my eyes and hold on for dear life as bursts of light flash across my darkened vision.

Seconds, minutes, or hours later…who knows how much time has passed…I open my eyes and see spots as I take in the pitch and all the fans recovering after a glorious goal.

Holy fuck, I just climaxed during a football match. I truly am Scottish.

Thankfully, the vibrating stops, and I let out a rushed breath as I wipe my damp hands on my sides. At this point, though, my centre has developed its own heartbeat as it continues to quiver and pulsate between my thighs. I thrust a hand through my hair, using the motion to shoot murderous eyes at Santino, who looks like he's really fucking enjoying himself.

The prick. The awful, horribly sexy, and painfully tantalizing prick. I hate him.

I glance around nervously, hoping no one saw what just happened and grateful to Freya's sweet innocent confusion for distracting anyone who may have been close enough to notice.

My God, I'm not going to make it through a full match of this.

Santino thankfully takes pity on me for the next twenty minutes and allows my body to regain control of itself. Unfortunately, my mind is anywhere but on football. All I can feel is the vibrator between my legs. My body is on full alert, bracing itself for the next onslaught. A light sheen of nervous sweat coats my skin, and my breasts feel heavy, my nipples rock hard as I imagine the piece between my legs being Santino's cock instead of this stupid toy.

If I gave him the look, I know without a doubt he would follow me into the loo and fuck me to completion over and over and over. It would feel so fucking incredible after…

Wait. No sex.

We're not doing that yet.

Stop thinking about sex, Tilly!

It's smart for us to take it slow. Fucking Santino in the loo would be old Tilly. And I am not old Tilly. I'm new and improved Tilly with maturity and control and sobriety.

Except right now, I'm drunk on arousal.

"I'm just going to go grab another drink," I state when it's the halfway mark of the game. I need some fresh air, or I'm going to crawl out of my skin at any moment.

"I'll get it," Mac barks, his tone gruff as he stands up to make his way past Freya.

I frown up at him. "I can manage, Mac."

"It's fine." He grabs my glass out of my cupholder and doesn't even cast me a simple glance. "You stay here with Freya."

"Mac okay?" I ask Freya, my gaze following my brother as he walks towards the bar looking tense.

"He's stressed about me, I expect." She sighs softly. "I think me being here is making him anxious. Would you mind too terribly much if we left now? You don't have to come home with us. I'm sure you could take a taxi or get a ride with Vi and Hayden. They live in Brick Lane as well. Or you could sneak off with Santino if you get a chance." She nudges me with her elbow.

"Oh, it's fine. I can take a taxi."

Suddenly, the area between my legs is blasted at a level I cannot even attempt to hide on my face.

"Are you alright, Smarty Spice?" Freya touches my arm with a worried look on her face. I delicately attempt to shrug her off because even if this is insanely naughty to be doing in a room full of people, the last thing I need is my bloody sister-in-law holding my hand while I orgasm again. *Kill me now!*

I nod and force a smile as I choke out, "Just a cramp in my thigh."

Freya's hand reaches down to touch my leg. "You should eat a banana!"

Nodding, I grab her hand in horror, squeezing it firmly to get it away from my vibrating pelvis. "Do they have bananas here?" I ask through clenched teeth.

"Doubtful." Freya looks crestfallen, but her eyes widen. "I hear that noise again! It's a faint buzzing. Do you hear it?"

I shake my head instantly, my hair curtaining around my face as I do.

"It sounds like a bee. I'm really allergic to bees. Do you think it could be a bee?" Freya looks around worriedly. "It's either that or the baseline to a Spice Girls song I suspect."

"I don't hear anything," I croak out, my groin involuntarily grinding into the sensation between my legs.

Freya tuts. "You know, I've never actually been diagnosed with a bee allergy, but I never got on with honey. I think they say you have a natural distaste for things you're allergic too, right?"

"I really don't know." My voice squeaks at the end and mercifully the vibrating stops just as Mac returns.

"Mac darling, would you be terribly upset if we left?" Freya asks as Mac hands me a fresh glass.

He frowns down at her. "Are you not feeling well? Should we talk to Belle?"

"I'm feeling wonderful, darling. Just thinking a good cuddle on the sofa with you sounds a lot better than this crowd. Plus, I think there's a bee circling the suite, and me and bees do not get on."

"Whatever you like, Cookie." Mac steps in to help Freya up. "Tilly, are you coming?"

"She's going to stay," Freya says quickly, patting Mac on the arm. "She can get a lift home with Vi or whoever."

Mac frowns down at me. "Are you sure?"

"I'm fine, Mac," I reply, waving him away. "I'm enjoying the match. This is my first Tower Park game, remember?"

"Aye, okay." Mac eyes me dubiously but then turns his attention back to Freya as they slowly make their way through the suite, saying goodbye to everyone as they go.

As soon as they're out of sight, I exhale heavily, my entire body feeling like it's going to burst into flames. That was intense. Maybe telling my brother I'm seeing Santino would have been easier than that mess of a football half. Santino definitely plays dirty.

Suddenly, a voice chimes from behind me. "Here she is!" I turn to find Belle with her arms wrapped around a man that looks like the clean-cut version of Henry Cavill. "Ronald, this is Tilly! Tilly, this is my brother, Ronald. Are those seats open?"

I barely croak out the word yes before she shuffles in past me, planting her brother squarely beside me. "Ronald, Tilly is from Dundonald! We went there a few years ago for their annual Highland Games."

"Is that right?" He offers me a weak smile, clearly uncomfortable by his sister's overeager matchmaking.

"Most people have never heard of Dundonald," I say because this is horribly awkward, and some silence needs to be filled.

"Yeah, I'm afraid I haven't." He takes a sip of his beer and glances down at the pitch. "Has it been a good match so far?"

I nod but then cringe because I can't even remember most of the game, so I offer a really generic, "Yeah, always."

Belle leans forward and smiles at the two of us. "You two look cute together."

Ronald scowls at his sister. "Belle."

"What?" she coos back with wide eyes. "I'm just stating a fact."

He drinks his beer again as Belle shoots a menacing glower at her brother. "It's best if you stick to medicine instead of matchmaking."

"Oh, Ron," Belle exclaims with a laugh. "Loosen up a bit!"

I stare straight ahead, wondering if it would be rude of me to leave right now. Suddenly, I feel Ronald's warmth press against my arm as he leans over and murmurs, "Sorry about my sister."

"Oh, it's fine." I wave him off.

He shakes his head, and I can feel him staring at me, so I turn to look at him. His dark-lashed eyes are sincere when he says, "It's not fine. It's awkward, and I'm sorry. She's just so very desperate to bring me into her world."

With a smile, I offer a complacent shrug. "Is that such a bad thing? This is certainly more my brother's world than mine, but I'm having a nice enough time."

He exhales heavily. "It's just too soon." When a pained look fleets across his face, I instantly recall the words Belle said earlier.

"He lost his wife…"

I rub my lips together thoughtfully before asking, "What was her name?"

"Rose." He says it almost reverently, and I feel a chill run up my spine.

"That's a pretty name," I offer with a soft smile.

He nods gratefully. "So is Tilly."

We have a nice, quiet moment of understanding when suddenly, the area between my legs erupts. My eyes widen and swerve to Santino, who's standing behind the glass with a glacial look in his eyes.

I shake my head angrily at him, and the fucking prick adjusts something on his mobile to increase the intensity.

With great effort, I mumble an excuse to extract myself from my location. I can't sit next to another person while my lady bits call for Scotland.

Ronald barely glances at me as I take a stumbling step towards the man responsible for my current state. I barely manage to bite a moan back as I struggle for air and make a beeline towards Santino.

He's a walking dead man.

CHAPTER 22

Santino

I KILL THE VIBRATING APP AS SOON AS I SEE TILLY EXTRACT HERSELF from that bloke looking at her like she's good enough to eat. I'll be the only one eating her, thank you very fucking much, mate. I motion for her to follow me out of the suite, and her eyes look positively lethal as we enter the empty hallway.

"What the fuck was that?" she hisses, her nostrils flaring with her temper.

"It's called a vibrating app, and you knew the game we were playing, so why act surprised now?" I snap, my body tense with a possessiveness I'm not used to feeling.

"It was a game earlier when you did it during the goals." She crosses her arms over her chest and juts her posture towards me. "Doing it to me in front of that man was just cruel."

"Cruel?" My body flushes with anger. "It was cruel the way you were staring at that prat. I thought we had a deal!"

"What deal?"

"You and I. We set up our terms before I even put my lips on your body. You and I were going to figure out what we are but exclusively."

"Sonny," she growls, stepping closer to me with rage in her eyes. Her voice is low and guttural as she says, "That guy was just talking to me. I wasn't staring at him in any certain way except to listen to what he was fucking saying!"

"Well, I didn't like it." My tone is acidic because I hate how foolish I feel right now. I hate how seeing her smile sweetly at him made me lose my fucking mind. More than all of that, I hate that I feel completely powerless with this woman. I crave her every fucking day, and we're still doing this stupid secretive song and dance.

Reaching out, I gently grip her shoulders, forcing her to look at me. "Look, Tilly. You're the one holding all the cards here. I asked you to be mine, you said yes. You wanted to take things slow, and I'm fine with that. I asked to tell your brother about us, you said no. I'm doing my fucking best not to push you at every turn, but I'm only so strong."

Her eyes swim with uncertainty. "What do you want from me?"

"I want more," I huff, my entire body aching to be wrapped around her. My voice softens when I repeat my words for no other reason than because it's true. "I want more."

She inhales and exhales slowly, her face warring with indecision that I fucking hate. How is she not secure in this? How has she not seen what we've had these past few weeks? I've never felt this way about a woman. Ever. She's the exception. She was the exception five years ago, and she's the exception now.

"Can we go back to my place now?" I beg because no matter how unsure she is, I can't leave her like this.

She nods woodenly, and I feel my body sag with relief because a dark part inside me feared she might bolt after my jealous fit. The vibrating knickers went from fun to punishing all in a blink because I turned into an insecure arse.

I lace my fingers in hers and pull her down the hall towards the steps because even if I was a prat, I need to feel her skin against mine. This whole evening was fucking painful. When I walked into the suite and saw her at the bar, it took every bit of my strength not to step up behind her and wrap my arms around her waist. But that wasn't what she wanted. Yes, I was punishing her with that vibrator, but only because I had a sick hope that if I'd showed her how badly she wants me, she'd finally drop her shield and tell me what we are. It's been weeks, and I still don't fucking know for sure.

All I know is that she wanted to play it safe tonight, so I tried. But watching her fight back her pleasure, her cheeks flushed, teeth sunken into her lip—she was a wet fucking dream for me.

Christ.

I need to be inside her.

I shake that thought away because we're waiting. We're waiting because when I go inside her, I need to know what we are. None of this uncertainty and secrecy. I fucking hate it.

God, I'm a mess. I've been reduced to an insecure, pouting idiot in my own bloody mind. I just need to taste her and remind myself how good we are, and my head will feel right again.

As soon as we're outside of the stadium and standing by my car, I press her up against the passenger door and grab her face. "What are you doing?" she asks, her brows knit together with confusion.

"I've been hard for the past hour, and I can't shake this feeling that I'm losing you."

Her eyes widen with genuine shock. "You're not losing me."

"Then please, vorrei tanto baciarti." I run my thumbs along her cheekbones. "Please let me fucking kiss you."

When she glances at my lips, that's all the reply I need as I slant my mouth and crush into hers. It's not a sweet, reacquainting kiss that dips our toes into the shallow end of our desires. It's a hard, plunging cannonball of devouring that sends shockwaves of longing all the way to the depths of my soul.

She moans against my lips and grabs my jacket, pulling me close so our chests rub together. I hungrily devour her in the middle of a parking lot, reminding myself of the fact she wants me just as much as I want her. I know this.

And I know she wasn't flirting tonight, so why the bloody hell did I get so upset?

Because Tilly is like a wild stallion that will bolt at the first sign of trouble. And if I want to keep moving forward with her, I need to allow her to set the pace, or I'll lose her completely.

Our tongues twine together, and I feel my cock thickening in my trousers. I'm not sure it ever went down from before, but now it's harder, angrier. Needier. If I inhale deeply enough, I can even smell the damp arousal between her legs, and knowing that gadget sits where I want to be causes my shaft to greedily press against her centre.

Christ, she tastes good. So fucking good. Her hips pump against mine, her leg wrapping around my hip as she grinds herself against me. I'm moments away from slipping my hand into her jeans and finger fucking her to climax when I hear a car horn blast in the distance.

"Fuck," I growl, pulling back and looking around nervously. Press usually linger outside the stadium after matches, and the last thing I need is someone taking creepy photos of this moment. "We need to go."

"Okay," she croaks.

I glance over and notice that her lips are raw from my assault. She looks like a wet fucking dream all over again. Nipples poking out through the thin fabric of her kit. Chest rising and falling with deep breaths. Her eyes dip to my groin, and I feel it thump with need.

A playful smirk teases the edge of her lips, and just like that, I know we're okay. That kiss was our version of makeup sex. And I'm okay with that. Tilly is beautiful and maddening and fun and surprising and that's how I know she's different. So as long as we keep moving forward. As long as she's not running from me, I can be patient.

For now.

CHAPTER 23

Tilly

IT'S WEDNESDAY NIGHT, AND I'M CURRENTLY UPSTAIRS IN MY bedroom getting ready for a date with Santino. Normally, I try not to go out on weeknights because my eejit of a brother asks endless questions about who I'm seeing and where I'm going. He seems to notice less when I pop out during the weekends. But this week, I find myself missing Santino. The words he said to me on Saturday night about feeling like he's losing me hurt me on a deep, dark level. It reminded me of the things my family said to me after I lost the pregnancy. My granddad, who's normally not an overly emotional man, once said to me that I was sitting right in front of him, and he still couldn't see me.

I hated those comments, but at that point in my life, I was focusing all my energy on my sobriety and getting my life back. I couldn't let anyone in because I had to stay in control of myself.

However, that was five long years ago. I'm not that old Tilly anymore. I'm new Tilly, and I want Santino to feel secure in what we are to each other. I'm mad at that fucking eejit. He's painfully perfect in so many ways but still challenges me and excites me. And the fact that he threw a wee fit at the football game because he was jealous actually turned me on in some sick way. What can I say? I like a spot of possessiveness in my man.

And that's what Santino is. My man. My...*boyfriend*. I haven't used that label with him yet because I was nervous to come out and say it. But he said he wanted more, so I want tonight to be a step forward for us. Then maybe I'll finally be brave enough to tell my stubborn Scot of a brother that I fancy a man he hates, and he can just bloody well get over it.

I make my way downstairs to head out for the night but pause when I hear Mac's voice coming from the kitchen. As I reach the bottom of the stairs, chills run over my entire body as I realise my brother is singing the lullaby that my granddad used to sing to us when we were wee.

I peer around the corner and spot Mac and Freya dancing in the kitchen. His arms are wrapped around her from behind, his hands splayed out on her belly as he sings softly into her ear.

The song is a Scottish lullaby called "Dream Angus". It's about the Celtic god of dreams who would go around passing out stories of love to everyone he met. The idea was that these wee dreams would help a bonnie bairn sleep soundly in her cradle because her heart would be full of love and contentment, and everyone sleeps soundly with love in their hearts.

Tears instantly fill my eyes because Mac sang this song at our granddad's funeral. I was nearly inconsolable at the time because I had so many regrets. Regrets for not being a better granddaughter. Regrets for not spending more time with him while he was still alive. Regrets for not opening up and sharing more with him. My granddad loved me fiercely, but I wished I would have been fearless enough to be honest with him.

I've been hyper-focused on my sobriety and personal control for so long now that I've not let myself be truly vulnerable. Not to my brother, my parents...not even Santino. I've been holding back for five long years, and it's exhausting.

Now, watching my brother hold his wife and sing a lullaby to their unborn baby…it makes my heart yearn for more. I deserve more. I've earned more. Which is why I realise now more than ever that I don't want regrets with Santino. And tonight, I need to tell him that.

Santino

Tilly's quiet at the restaurant tonight. Her mind is clearly working through something as I watch her little nose twitch away with worry. I fear she's still upset over what happened at the football match. I want to press her on it, but I know Tilly enough by now that she won't talk until she's ready. So, I give her the space to do it, hoping she'll share it with me eventually.

After dinner, we head back to my place, and all I want to do is curl up on the sofa with her until she has to go back to her brother's. Again. It's exhausting waiting for her to come to terms with what we are to each other, but she's worth being patient for.

When I get to my flat door, I push my key in and frown when I see it's already unlocked. "That's strange," I say, and my hand lifts to shift Tilly back behind the wall.

I slowly open the door to see why it's unlocked, and my eyes nearly bug out of my head at the sight of a curvy brunette having a glass of wine in my kitchen.

"Ciao, Santino!" My ex smiles brightly and sets her wine down as her heels clunk across the hardwood floor to where I'm standing in the doorway. She kisses me on both cheeks, her expensive perfume wafting all over me. "Where have you been?"

"Bria...I...um..."

Bria's eyes move past me. "Who is this?" she asks, pointing a manicured nail behind me.

"This is Tilly." I step off to the side to give her a full view.

Tilly shifts in front of me and crosses her arms over her chest. "Who are you?"

"I am an old family friend." Bria arches one perfect brow and slides an affectionate gaze back to me. "Santino and I grew up in the same neighbourhood in Bourton-on-the-Water and went to law school together."

"Did you now?" Tilly hits me with a sardonic look that I feel squarely in my nut sack. "Is that all?"

I feel my shoulders rising. "More or less."

Bria forces a smile that doesn't look all that genuine. "Santino, perhaps you and I can step out into the hallway to talk?"

I shake my head slowly. "Now's not a good time, Bria."

"How did you get in?" Tilly asks pointedly.

The corner of Bria's lip curls up into a half-smile as she reaches into her pocket and pulls out a key. "I've had this for ages."

"I had forgotten about that." I hold my hand out to Bria who stares at me curiously. "I should probably get that back."

She frowns at me. "Santino, ciccio."

I shake my head again, ignoring her pet name for me. "Sorry, Bria. But I really do think it's best if you go."

I grab the key from her hand, and she stares back at me like I have two heads before launching into a rant in fluent Italian. She scolds me for treating her this way after how long we've known each other and that I'll be done with this redhead in a month or two like all the others. I grimace and do my best to usher her to the door, feeling Tilly's heated gaze on us the entire time.

Finally, Tilly pushes me aside and presses her hand to the

doorframe. "Look, lass…I don't know what you're going on about right now, but my *boyfriend* asked you to leave."

Bria quirks a brow at Tilly and then me. "Boyfriend?"

"Aye," Tilly confirms, and I swear her Scottish accent gets thicker with her anger. "I don't know the translation in Italian, but I'll look it up and send it to you on a nice postcard of the two of us. Bye now." Tilly shuts the door in Bria's face and turns to me.

My eyes are wide as I say, "That was really—"

"You just give keys to these random women you date for your two little months?" Her tone is harsh as she crosses her arms in front of her.

"Are you jealous, Tilly Logan?" I can't help but smirk.

"Don't avoid the question," she snaps. "Why would she have your key if it was as casual as you said it always was with your women?"

"Bria was different."

"Different how?"

I exhale and rake my hand through my hair. "She's from Italy too. There were a lot of Italians in our neighbourhood, so our families became friends. We didn't try the dating thing until just this past year."

Tilly nods slowly and gazes back at me with a guarded look. "Did you love her?"

I huff out a noise. "You know I didn't."

"You've known her for ages, and she had a key to your flat." She brushes her red hair back and narrows her eyes at me.

"Because she watered my plants when I travelled with the team a few months ago."

"Your precious basil couldn't survive a weekend without you?" She rolls her eyes and glowers at me like a sullen teenager. It's really fucking sexy.

Because the truth is, I want Tilly to be jealous. I want her to feel the pain that I felt Saturday. It's the pain two people feel when they have strong feelings for each other but don't fucking own it yet.

I stalk towards her and feel a heaviness descend between us as I press my hands to the door around her head, caging her in so she can't run from this moment. "Did you mean what you said to her?"

"Don't change the subject," she hisses, her blue eyes wide on mine.

"Did you see how giant her breasts were? Hell, I would have fallen in love with her just for those. They looked like giant water balloons. How can someone that gorgeous go to law school? My God, I bet your mum is heartbroken you two haven't mended fences yet."

I stare affectionately down at her. "Are you done yet?"

"No." Tilly huffs, her lip jutting out into a pout. "She seems perfect."

"She's not you." I drop my hands to her hips and pull her towards me, dipping my lips to kiss her adorable twitching nose. "And in case you didn't know, sono pazzo di te."

Her hands slink up around my neck. "What does that mean?"

I move my lips to the shell of her ear and whisper, "I'm crazy about you."

She expels a little sigh and slides her fingers through my hair. "Probably because I'm not too posh to wear vibrating knickers at a football game."

My lips smile on her neck, and I pull back to hit her with a serious look. "I'm going to choose to ignore that snide remark about yourself because I really liked the fact that you called me your boyfriend earlier."

Her nose wrinkles adorably. "Well, she was trying to spray her scent all over you."

"So, you didn't mean it?" I tilt my head curiously, my body tensing in preparation because if there's one thing I know about Tilly, it's that I never know anything.

"Oh, I meant it." She stares at my chest, her fingers toying with my strands as her brows furrow. "I was going to talk to you about it tonight, but *Bria* stole my thunder."

Warmth radiates through my entire body. "Bria stole nothing." I press my forehead to hers. "I've been yours for quite some time now."

A small smile lights up her face as she inhales my words like she's trying to trap them in her chest. Her blue eyes pin me with a meaningful look. "Sorry it took me so long to get here."

"It's okay."

She rubs her lips together thoughtfully. "It's just that I've been on my own for so long that giving myself to someone like this feels scary. Like I could lose control."

"You're not going to lose control." I tilt her chin up, forcing her blue eyes to look into mine. "Giving yourself to someone just means you have support when you need it."

Her brows lift. "I do pretty good on my own, in case you didn't know."

"Oh, trust me, I know." I laugh and bite my lip to stop myself from kissing her sexy pout. "But maybe I need you?" The admission of that statement sends a wave of anxiety through my entire body.

She gives me a playful shove. "Clearly, you do need me to fight off gorgeous women in your flat."

"You're one to talk," I reply, squeezing her sides. As I hold her in my arms, I find myself needing to hear the words again. To make sure this is really real. "Is this it then? Are you my girlfriend, Tilly? Truly? Because if it was just to get Bria to leave, I need to know."

She sighs heavily. "Aye, sure if you want to get technical about it."

"Technical is a really sexy word." I smile broadly before picking her up and carrying her to my bedroom. She squeals in surprise as I technically lay her on my bed and technically prepare to adore her body for as long as she'll technically let me.

CHAPTER 24

Tilly

I AWAKEN THE NEXT MORNING SPREAD OUT ON SANTINO'S CHEST with his arms wrapped snuggly around me. The early morning light is pouring in through his half-shaded windows as I try to hide the smirk on my face as memories of our evening flood through my mind.

Did Santino blindfold me and use a feather tickler? Or was I just dreaming? I glance over at the bedside table and see the visual evidence.

Not a dream.

My smirk morphs into a full-blown smile now. No wonder I was spent by the end of the night and couldn't be bothered to get out of Santino's bed. The man is a freak, and never have I ever had so many orgasms from just his fingers and mouth.

And that fucking naughty tongue of his.

I fretted when Santino took me to bed because I thought with us having more official labels, he would expect to move to the next level in the bedroom as well. But as we stripped down, he could sense it right away when my mind whirled with fear and anxiety. When I told him I still wasn't ready and that I was sorry, that I really did want to be his girlfriend, but I needed more time, he covered my lips and said, *"I don't need to have sex with you to be with you. Just let me worship you."*

And worship me, he did.

My body squirms against the sheets as memories of the scarves he used to tie me to his bed drift through my mind. Once he had me secure, he stroked that tickler over every square inch of my body and then followed those paths with his sinfully sexy mouth.

And when he finally let me free to return the favour, it was only seconds into a very eager blow job that he flipped me around to straddle his face while his glistening cock was thrust back into mine.

He grabbed my hips and greedily ground me down onto his mouth, forcing me to ride his face like he was a starved man. His lips devoured my slick folds as he murmured naughty things like, "You taste so fucking good, and I'll never get enough of you." I matched his enthusiasm on him, sucking his cock so deep, I had tears in my eyes.

I don't recall ever doing this position with any other man in my life, but I guess the fact that we've been holding out on having sex meant it was time we got creative.

When he thrust three thick fingers up inside me and stroked my channel relentlessly, I came all over his face, screaming his name over and over again. Then he came without warning, spurting all over the sheets and even getting some in my hair. We were a mess of wild abandon, and it made our clean-up shower and sheet change all the more amusing.

I couldn't leave.

It was just too good of a night.

Santino looked like a cat that got the cream as I threw on one of his T-shirts and crawled into his bed with him. With clean sheets, lights out, and permanent smiles on our faces, we talked for hours until we finally succumbed to sleep.

I think I even woke up with that same smile, but now that I'm sitting here alone with my thoughts, Bria has crept up into my frontal lobe. Last night I was so overcome with making us official that I didn't fully have time to dissect who this woman was to Santino.

"Don't," Santino murmurs, his hands tightening around my body instinctively.

"Don't what?" I prop my head on his chest and gaze up at his gorgeous sleepy face, smiling at his crazy bed hair sticking out all over.

His eyes remain closed as he replies, "Don't go."

I laugh and glance over at his clock. "I've got an hour before my brother wakes up."

"In that case." He sits up and rolls us over on the bed so he's on top of me. His erection bulges through his boxers, pressing into my leg as he pins my wrists to the bed and devours my neck with his scruffy jaw. "Let's make the most of it."

He begins kissing his way down my chest, and my body rolls and heaves with desire. His chiseled back is on full display in the morning light, and I would love nothing more than to watch his muscles bend and snap beneath his skin as he devours me whole.

But…I have questions. And doubt. And confusion. And my little brain is like one of those annoying spinning tops that can't just relax and settle into the moment. When he reaches the top of my knickers, I finally find my voice. "Hold up, Sonny. Wait. We need to talk."

"Oh, Trouble," he growls, moving his lips away from my groin and giving my hard nipple a cheeky peck through his shirt. "I'll wait forever for you." He hits me with a lazy smile as he slides off me, his hand resting on my belly. "What's on your mind?"

I exhale heavily and begin toying with the hem of the sheet. "Bria."

I glance over to see his adorable sleepy smile has now been replaced with confusion. "Why the bloody hell are you thinking of her?"

"Because she had a key to your flat," I reply quickly.

He squeezes my side, a tender look sweeping across his face. "I told you that it was a minor oversight."

"There's got to be more to that story," I say, chewing my lips nervously. Santino is this rich, successful lawyer with a gorgeous flat, a loving, supportive family, and Bria was the perfect woman at his fingertips. What on earth went wrong there? And what on earth is he doing with me? "I want to know why it didn't work out."

He sighs and rolls onto his back, propping his arm behind his head. "It's not that great of a story."

"Indulge me." I turn on my side to watch him.

He groans and rubs his eyes, seemingly trying to wake up his brain a bit more. "I told you I'd known Bria since we were young, right?"

"Yes."

"Well, she was always interested in me. She made that very clear. But I never wanted to go there with her because I didn't want anything serious back then. And even when I changed my life around a bit, I avoided her because well…to be very candid…I thought she'd be the one. Our families were close, she understood my culture, and she was also a lawyer…so it just made a lot of sense. But at the time, I wasn't ready for that so I just stayed away from her. About six months ago, I ran into her when I was home visiting my family, and she hit me out of nowhere with an ultimatum. She told me I'd put her on ice for too long, and it was now or never."

Jealousy niggles at my belly, but I do my best to hide it and continue listening.

"So…we started dating," he continues with a shrug. "And it got serious rather quickly because we've known each other for ages. We were able to skip all that getting to know you stuff. I guess that's why I gave her a key because a level of trust was there already."

I exhale heavily, hating how much I hate this story. "So, what went wrong then?"

"Nothing specific. It just never felt right. I tried. Believe me, I tried. I wanted it to work because I feared if I couldn't make it work with Bria, I couldn't make it work with anyone. But after two months when she told me she loved me and I couldn't say it back, I knew that staying with her would be selfish and cruel. So I told her we needed some time apart."

I frown at that choice of wording. "So, did she think you two were just taking a break? Not fully over?"

"No," he replies quickly. "Maybe." He sighs and runs a hand through his hair. "I don't know."

I see the torment on his face, and it makes every nerve in my body feel insecure. Like he's with me but not really with me. I will be no different than all the other women he's dated. "Do you want to try again with her?"

His eyes snap to mine. "Why would you ask me that?"

I shrug nervously. "Because there's a lot of history there and family connections. Are you just passing the time with me?"

"Tilly." He says my name with so much force that I hold my breath for fear of what he'll say next. "I told you last night that I'm crazy about you. You and I haven't even been together a month, and I already feel a million times more for you than I ever did for Bria after knowing her most of my life. I am not passing the time with you."

He runs both hands through his hair, making it even more disheveled than before. "If she even so much as contacts me again, I will tell her it's inappropriate, okay?"

I rub my lips together and nod, trying to force his words into my hardened heart. It doesn't make sense. Why he cares about me…a recovering alcoholic who's living with her brother and forcing him to date her in secret because she is still trying to get her life together. But he's here. With me. Only time will tell if I'll make the cut past two months.

And as much as I hate to admit it, this relationship feels…important. Like there's a reason we've found each other again. I don't know why exactly, but I know that questioning it only makes me crazier. And Santino has had enough of my crazy for the past twenty-four hours.

I inhale sharply and reach out to sift my fingers through Santino's hair. "God, you're so into me."

He growls and nips at my finger. "That's what I've been trying to tell you."

"We better get busy then," I say with an all-business look. "I need to get home before my brother leaves for work, and you've got a situation down there that clearly needs tending to."

His body shakes with laughter as I slip under the covers to give him a proper Scottish goodbye.

Okay, I don't know for sure if a blow job is Scottish, but I suspect we give the best of them.

A bit later, I creep quietly into Mac and Freya's house. Mac is usually showering by this time, so if I hurry, I can get upstairs before he even knows I'm missing. Just as I hit the bottom step, Mac's voice calls out, "Tilly?"

"Christ!" I scream and see an orange furry ball bolt for the master bedroom. I turn on my heel to see Mac sitting in the living room on the sofa, dressed in his suit for work already. "Mac, my God. I didn't see you there."

"You were too busy trying to sneak in." He grips the arms of the sofa firmly, showing zero signs of amusement on his face. Very un-Mac-like.

My brows furrow. "I was just trying to be quiet because I assumed you'd still be sleeping."

"Where were you?" he asks, his eyes hitting mine with a severe look in them that I don't like.

I push back my wild hair that hasn't been brushed yet. "I stayed at a friend's flat."

"Which friend?" He tilts his head and eyes me harshly, which has my defences going right up.

"What's with the interview?" I ask, propping my hands on my hips because Mac isn't my father.

"Why are you avoiding the question?" he volleys back.

"Because I want to know why it's being asked," I reply firmly.

Mac's eyes narrow. "Tilly, I'm going to ask you a question, and I want you to be dead honest with me."

I exhale the pressure in my chest, certain I know where this is going and ready for it now more than ever. "Very well. Ask then."

"Are you drinking again?" he croaks, his voice raw with emotion that shocks me to my core.

"What?" I nearly gasp.

"Are you drinking? Be honest." His nostrils flare with determination.

"Mac."

"Just tell me," he snaps, his hand balling into a fist. "We can deal with this together."

I shake my head and rush over to the sofa to sit down beside him. I press my hands firmly on top of his and look him square in the eyes. "Mac, I promise you, I am not drinking again."

His jaw muscle jumps. "Are you doing drugs?"

"No!" I exclaim. Sitting back, I feel hurt as irritation runs through every inch of my body. "Mac, what on earth is going on here?"

"Something's not right with you, Tilly. I'm worried those awful friends you used to have are dragging you down. There's been a change in you lately."

"What kind of change?" I ask, my heart aching at this sense of distrust that my brother has in me.

"You're gone more often, for one."

"Am I not allowed to have a life of my own here?" I practically bark, sitting up straight and turning to face him. I've never once been drunk since I decided to quit drinking so for Mac to hit me like this out of nowhere is cruel and unfair. "I'm here for you and Freya and the baby, but even Freya's restrictions have been lifted somewhat so you can't say I'm even needed here as much as I was at first."

"Of course you're needed here," he states seriously, his voice guttural and raw. "I need you."

My lips part at his pained expression. "Mac."

"I mean it, Tilly. I don't want to lose you again. When you lived here in London while I was playing football, you were a fucking ghost."

My eyes well with tears as my big, strong brother who never shows an ounce of emotion admits his fears.

"You showed no interest in my matches even though I always reserved tickets for you. You'd show up at footballer events pissed out of your mind. Then you get pregnant and tell us fuck all about who the bastard was that did that to you. I'm not letting you go down that path again. I'll fucking lock you up and throw away the key to make you see sense if I have to."

"Mac," I growl, my voice garbled with unshed tears. "I've told you that I'm sorry for all of that."

"I know that," he huffs out angrily. "But fuck, Tilly. Cookie and I are having a baby, and I was just getting keen on the idea of you being a regular part of that wee one's life."

"That's what I want too!" I cry, pain slicing through my entire body.

"Then get your fucking shit together!" He stands up, buttoning his suit coat, then thrusts a finger at me. "Something is up with you. And if it's not alcohol or drugs, it's something else."

I exhale heavily, my body feeling like it's been punched with a thousand different memories of my past. Memories that I've tried my hardest to forget but roll through me, wreaking havoc on everything I thought I'd accomplished.

Shit, I've fucked up.

The most obvious fix to this situation is to tell Mac about Santino. But with the anger he's displaying at this moment, telling him will most certainly make a bad situation ten times worse. And I don't want that. Not at all. I want Mac to accept Santino and care for him like I do.

Goddammit, why didn't I just tell him from the start? Why did I have to be so stupidly guarded and secretive? Because I was scared? Because I didn't want to commit? Because I'm a fucking steel trap who hasn't let anyone in for five fucking years and obviously for good reason?

I hate myself right now. I'm hiding this relationship from Mac because I know to get him to accept Santino, I need to tell him the full story about the night I got pregnant. Because like it or not, that night and Santino are intrinsically connected in Mac's eyes. And Mac will never be able to forgive him until I'm brave enough to tell my brother the whole story.

That's why it's been easier to just be with Santino in private. It felt good to feel not broken. And it paid off because I've finally let someone in and allowed my heart to beat again.

However, this can't go on forever. Mac needs to know the truth because Santino deserves that. But to tell him now when he's already doubting my sincerity will complicate a very serious discussion. I need to handle this delicately for everyone's sake.

Steeling myself, I hit him with an excuse that I hope he'll accept. "I promise you, Mac, I'm not on drugs or drinking. I've just been distracted with the new job excitement and the idea of making my move to London permanent. I swear on my life that nothing bad is going on with me."

"I hope that's true." Mac stares down at me, his jaw taut with emotion that I hate as he turns to walk away. He pauses in the entryway and looks over his shoulder at me. "Freya and I have decided that we're going to call the bairn Fergie in honour of Granddad."

My chin wobbles, and tears sting my eyes. I swipe them away and croak, "That's so perfect, Mac."

"I thought you'd like it." He stomps heavily back over and leans down to press a kiss to my head. "I love you, Tilly."

I hold his hand on my shoulder. "I love you too, Macky."

And when he leaves, I feel an overwhelming urge to drink for the first time in years.

CHAPTER 25

Tilly

"THANKS FOR COMING WITH ME TO THIS SCAN," FREYA SAYS AS she rubs her belly over top of her medical gown in a small exam room at Chelsea and Westminster Hospital where Belle Harris is a foetal surgeon and occasional prenatal specialist to VIP patients like Freya.

"It's my pleasure," I reply, forcing a smile as I struggle to figure out what to text Santino about plans for this weekend.

"Mac was gutted he couldn't get away from work today, but they're presenting their new video game update to a big sponsor, so it really wasn't something he could miss."

"It's no problem." I blacken the screen on my mobile with a huff and put it away in my bag because I know nothing will sound right in a text.

"Who are you texting?" Freya asks curiously.

A guilty smile spreads across my face. "Santino."

Her brows waggle excitedly. "You guys have plans tomorrow? You usually like to go out to the markets on Saturdays, right?"

I shake my head. "No. I'm kind of…well…I'm not avoiding him, but I'm trying to back off for a moment."

"What? Why?" Freya gasps, her face crestfallen.

I hold my hands up defensively. "I'm not breaking it off. I'm just trying to kill time before I see him again."

"Whatever for?"

I sigh heavily. "You know why."

"Because Mac accused you of drinking again?"

She stares at me sadly, and I feel my eyes well with tears all over again. Every time I think of that pained look in Mac's eyes, my heart breaks. I hate this situation. I hate that I put myself in this situation by having a problem with alcohol at all.

I force a smile. "I wanted to tell him the truth about Santino and me right then, but you know my brother."

"He's a stubborn ox." She reaches over and holds my hand.

"I know," I reply with a self-deprecating laugh. "And so am I, which is why I'm waiting for things to calm down before I tell him."

Freya's eyes go wide. "Has it become serious between you two?"

I bite my lip and nod. "Starting to."

"Then your brother will understand."

"He will. I just think if I play it cool for a week or two and stop running off to snog Santino every spare moment, then he'll see I'm good, and we'll be in a better place before I tell him about us. I want him to like Santino, Freya. I *need* him to like him."

"Oh, Tilly." Freya says my name sweetly. "If I didn't know any better, I'd say you were in love."

My eyes go wide at that offhanded remark when suddenly Belle opens the door and comes striding in. "My favourite patient!" She smiles over at me. "Oh, hi Tilly! No Mac today?"

"I'm afraid not," Freya says with a sigh. "Work thing he couldn't get out of. He's gutted to miss this appointment. I think I heard him weeping in the shower this morning."

Belle's face falls. "We could have rescheduled."

"Heavens no!" Freya tuts. "You said this is the scan that might get me off bed rest completely, so I refuse to delay that wondrous act for a single moment."

Belle nods knowingly. "Well, let's get this show on the road then."

Freya gets situated with her gown up and the blanket over her lap as Belle spreads gel all over her belly before running the wand along her taut skin. The baby's very obvious shape comes into the frame, and he's wiggling all over the screen like he's doing an Irish jig.

"We might have a dancer here," Belle says, pointing at the screen and chasing the wee one around with her wand.

"Or a trick pony rider." Freya glances at me and winks. "I'm getting Tilly hooked on *Heartland* as soon as we finish *Bridgerton*."

Belle laughs and begins taking measurements and typing everything into the computer. After she's done, she offers Freya a warm smile. "Well, Freya, you're twenty-four weeks pregnant, the baby is hitting all his right growth markers, and that subchorionic hemorrhage that we saw a couple of months back is almost completely gone. There are only traces of it left, barely enough to measure."

"Oh my God!" Freya squeals excitedly.

"All that resting you've done has paid off," Belle replies, touching Freya's hand gently as Freya's eyes fill with tears.

She sobs a happy sound. "I'm fixing to burst I'm so happy!"

"You should be happy. Baby looks perfect."

"We're calling him Fergie," Freya offers, touching her belly affectionately as she sniffles. "Short for Fergus. That was his great-grandfather's name."

Belle smiles. "Fergie looks like a strong little guy, and I can't wait to meet him. But for now, I feel very comfortable taking you off bed rest completely."

"Thank good heavens for that!" Freya exclaims enthusiastically as Belle and I help her sit up on the exam table. "I'm just going to pop into the loo to change and call Mac with the good news!"

"Brilliant," Belle says, wiping the wand off with a smile. "And Freya, if you guys want to come in next week for another scan, I can set it up. That way you can show Mac the bleed is fully gone and hopefully ease his mind a bit?"

"Would you really do that?" Freya asks, sliding off the table.

"Of course! You're practically family."

"You are the sweetest pie I've ever tasted." Freya hugs Belle tightly and shuffles off to the attached bathroom to call Mac.

As Belle grabs her medical chart and prepares to leave, she pauses in front of me and gets a sneaky look on her face. "So, I'm sorry, but I have to ask. What did you think of Ronald? You left so quickly. Was he that horrible? He can be a pompous ass sometimes, but I really think he's changing."

"Oh God, no. He was nice!" I reassure, feeling horrible how that must have looked for her. "I mean, we didn't talk much, but for the small bit we did, he seemed great."

"Oh good." She exhales a sigh of relief and bites her lip nervously. "Should I maybe give him your number?"

I cringe and wrinkle my nose. "I'm afraid not."

"Why not?" she asks, her face the picture of confusion.

"I'm…seeing someone." Wow, saying that out loud is actually a lot freakier than I thought it would be. "It just got serious."

"Oh, really? Who?" Belle inquires, looking intrigued.

I bite my lip anxiously. "Santino Rossi."

"Oh my God!"

I hold my hands up. "Mac doesn't know yet."

"Protective big brother alert?" Belle asks knowingly.

"Protective, big, *Scottish* brother alert. He's on a whole other level."

Belle nods and smiles. "Well, I'm highly familiar with dating someone my family doesn't approve of. But as adults, your family is just there on the weekends, you know? The person you fall in love with is there every day. That's who you make your own family with…babies and all."

She begins rustling with her chart, having no idea that her comment has triggered a thought in me that I haven't truly considered until right this moment. "Belle, can I ask you a weird medical question?"

"You and anyone who ever runs into me at a party." She laughs and gives me her full attention. "Hit me."

I inhale deeply. "If a person has had a miscarriage before…what are the odds that they'll have a miscarriage again?"

Belle's brows knit. "How far along was the pregnancy?"

I swallow the lump in my throat. "Nine weeks?"

She nods knowingly. "First trimester miscarriages are very common, and the odds of another miscarriage are basically the same as if the patient had never miscarried."

I chew my lip. "Got it."

She tilts her head. "It was an intrauterine pregnancy, right?"

"What do you mean?"

"It wasn't in your tubes, was it?"

My face heats with embarrassment. "No. It wasn't."

She smiles reassuringly. "Then I think you'll be fine."

"I don't even know if I want to have kids," I rush out and shake my head, feeling really uncomfortable that I even had the nerve to ask this question. "I can't ever see myself as a mother."

"That's okay too," she offers helpfully. "But you know…you did have a baby inside you, so technically, you already are a mother."

My body stills at those very poignant words that hit me like a ton of bricks. "But I never even saw the baby. I just…started bleeding. Then they told me there was no heartbeat anymore, and it would pass on its own."

Belle nods sympathetically and reaches out to touch my leg. It's a gentle touch, but it feels meaningful. "You became a mother the moment you got that positive pregnancy test. Tell me you didn't change your life around for that baby before you ever even had a scan done."

I pause, knowing I can't dispute that fact.

"You were making decisions a mother would make."

"God," I croak, my chin trembling with unexpected emotion at her very logical words.

"Sorry." She laughs and pulls her hand back. "I wouldn't speak like this to all my patients, but since you're not my patient, I'm not afraid to tell you that I think you'd make an incredible mum."

When Freya emerges from the bathroom, my eyes are overrun with tears. "Oh Christ, what'd I miss?" She glances back and forth between Belle and me. "Are you guys talking about *Bridgerton* without me?"

CHAPTER 26

Santino

" I NEED YOU TO SIGN A NONDISCLOSURE AGREEMENT I'VE JUST emailed you." A woman by the name of Jane Williams says into the phone line at my office on a rather bleak Thursday evening.

It's nearly five, and I want to go home, but this woman demanded I call her in a rather peculiar email I received moments ago.

"Why do I need to sign anything?" I ask, confused at why the fuck Zander Williams' mother is asking me, the lawyer, to sign anything. It's nearly eleven at night on the East Coast where she's located in America. What the hell could be this important?

"Because I need to talk to someone, and I only trust a lawyer to actually follow the rules of an NDA. I'd rather not have to bother with suing someone who doesn't take this seriously."

I grip my tie curiously. "This is highly unlikely, and I'm not sure I'm comfortable with this."

"You will be grateful you did it once I tell you what I'm about to tell you."

Fuck me. This job is never-ending.

I sign the agreement in her official DocuSign site and send it back to her.

"Okay…got it. So, we're in agreement?" she confirms.

"We're in agreement," I droll, expecting her to tell me that her son has impregnated twenty women, and I'm going to have to clean up that mess once he starts with us in January.

"I need you to kill the contract you have with Zander Williams."

"Why?"

"Because Zander isn't just a random footballer from America. His father is Vaughn Harris."

I bark out a laugh, knowing full well the kind of entrapment situations footballers find themselves in all the time. Now, club managers usually don't have these sorts of issues, especially if the children are grown…but…

"Listen, mate, my name is Jane Williams, and I was best friends with Vaughn's wife, Vilma, since we were eighteen and were roommates at university. I was at the pub the night Vaughn met Vilma and swept her off her feet, I was at the Man U match he flew Vilma and a few of her friends out to on a private jet, and I was there at their wedding and her funeral. Make no mistake…this isn't a prank call."

The blood in my veins runs cold.

"I ran into Vaughn Harris six years after Vilma passed away, and he was just as miserable then as he was on the day he buried his wife. We were drunk, we were lonely, we were sad. We slept together, and a few weeks later, before I was due to move to America for work, I found out I was pregnant."

"Why on earth didn't you tell him? Or has he known this all along?" I ask, horrified equally by both thoughts.

"He has no idea, and I want to keep it that way."

"Why?" I inquire, my jaw permanently dropped at this point.

"The whys aren't your concern. But my son, Zander, cannot play for Vaughn's club. He doesn't know who his father is, but I can't be sure that playing alongside his half-brothers won't stir something up."

"Christ."

"Exactly. So…like I said…kill this contract. The Harris family needs no more headlines from what I see online."

I frown at that, feeling defensive about a family I've grown to see as my own. "They've all settled down over the past several years."

"You know as well as I do that this kind of news will blow all their lives up and the lives of those grandchildren they're all popping out."

I sigh heavily. "How the bloody hell did your son wind up being recruited by our club?"

"I don't know, but you have to fix this. You're the only one I can think of who can."

When we hang up, I feel the weight of the world resting on my shoulders. Why the fuck did I sign that bloody NDA? That was fucking stupid, is what that was. Vaughn Harris has a son he doesn't know about. A son who plays bloody football, of all things? And I can't even tell him? My God…what the hell do I do with this information?

I text Tilly and ask her if we can meet tonight because I need to unload this to someone. I need advice, I need a drink, I need…*her*. She blew me off all weekend, claiming she was busy with a factory emergency for Freya's pet line that Harrods is waiting on, and she had to sort it out. However, her texts have been vague and frankly, confusing as fuck.

Last I saw her, she spent the night in my flat and sucked me off before I demanded to return the favour…at rapid speed, I might add, all so she could get home before her brother woke up. Neither of us went without smiles that morning, so why has she been so hard to talk to this week? It's odd because I would have assumed that the change in our official status with each other would have propelled us forward, not backward. We've never gone this many days without seeing each other. And I'm finding I don't like it one bit.

My mobile buzzes, and her gorgeous face half-covered by a sheet in my bed lights up the screen. I swipe the call and growl into the line, "Where are you?"

She laughs awkwardly. "I'm at my brother's house."

"Why can't you be in my bed?" I murmur quietly as dirty thoughts invade my mind. "I've had a pig of a week and have been smelling your pillow like a proper freak every day."

There's a slight pause. "Well, I'm afraid you'll have to smell it for a bit longer."

My brows furrow as anxiety nips at me.

"I've been meaning to tell you this." She sighs heavily. "Mac thinks I'm drinking again."

"What?" I ask, annoyed that her brother thinks she would throw away everything she's worked so hard for these past several years. I run my fingers through my hair in frustration, hating that I can't be there for her when she obviously needs me.

"Yeah, I talked him off the ledge, but because I've been gone so much lately with you and acting a bit dodgy about where I've been, he thinks I'm hanging out with the wrong crowd again. God, it's like I'm twelve years old, and he's my dad."

"Well, then we just need to come clean and tell him what's going on," I state firmly. This is the easiest solution to the problem. To all the problems. I would be able to be there for her, and she'd be able to spend every night at my flat and in my arms. Then I could easily tell her brother where to stick it if he accuses her of this shit again.

"Not yet," she rushes out quickly. "Things between us are going so well, don't you think?"

"Up until the last week, yes. Which is even more reason we should tell him now," I say, getting up to pace my office.

"You have that backwards, Sonny. Mac is so worried about me that he will think you're causing me to make bad choices."

That remark stops me in my tracks. "But I'm not," I defend, loosening my tie and unbuttoning the top of my shirt.

"I know," she replies swiftly. "But we don't need to give him any more reason to dislike you."

"So, what's your plan here, Tilly?" I ask, raking my hand through my hair in frustration.

"Let's just keep playing it cool and give each other some space for a bit, and I'm sure he'll settle down."

"Space?" I snap into the line, my hand tightening on my mobile.

"Tilly, I don't want space. I already haven't seen you for a fucking week." My heart begins to hammer in my chest at the mere mention of us spending more time apart. Doesn't she want to see me as much as I'm dying to see her? Fuck, this is making me crazy.

"I'm only talking about a few more days! Mac has the attention span of a fruit fly. He'll forget about his worries very soon, and then we'll be game on again with no more secrets." She ends too happily for my liking. How can she be happy about any of this?

I shake my head, my entire body vibrating with anger. I've been patient. I've let her take the lead, and it was working. But I'm done with that shit now.

"No," I state through clenched teeth.

"What?"

"I'm saying no," my firm tone rattles through the line. I want Tilly Logan in my life, full stop, and nothing will stop me from making that fact very well-known, even if it means a tense conversation with her brother.

"Why?"

"Because, Tilly, I have feelings for you. Real fucking feelings and I don't want to go backwards. I'm not losing you again," I all but snarl, hoping she hears how serious I really am.

"You're not losing me! I have real fucking feelings too, Santino. More than I ever thought I'd have, but if we wait, it'll be better for us in the long run."

"No," I growl, hitting the top of my desk with my fist. I'm done letting her call the shots. This ends now. I can't hold back anymore. I refuse. "Sneaking around was fun at first, but the longer this has gone on, the more of an arse I feel like through all of this. We're fucking adults, Tilly. We're not feuding families in a Romeo and Juliet play. I'm telling Mac today, and you can't stop me." I grab my suit jacket and keys, making a beeline to the nearest exit.

"Santino—"

"I'm coming over. I'll see you in a bit."

CHAPTER 27

Tilly

T HE LINE GOES DEAD, AND I STAND FROZEN IN MY BEDROOM WITH
only the soft purr of Jasper on my bed to narrate the dread I feel
in the pit of my stomach. When I hear a bird chirp outside, my
shock wears off, and I whip myself into action.

First, I glance at myself in the mirror. Leggings and a ripped
T-shirt. Not my most fashionable look, but I don't really have time to
give a toss right now.

Next, I rush downstairs to see if Freya and Mac have returned
home from their scan yet. They haven't. Thank God. If Mac's going to
blow a gasket, I want to make sure that Freya is out of the line of fire
at the very least. And since there's no sign of Santino yet, maybe I can
catch him when he arrives and calm down the situation.

Pacing the house, I decide on a whim to panic clean while waiting for Santino to arrive. I waffle from straightening the furry throw
pillows to nervously peering out the window along with the judgmental eyes of Hercules that follow my every move.

"Oh, now you're not afraid of me?" I ask, glowering at the fat orange cat seated on the credenza in front of the window. "Now that I'm a total disaster and putting on a show for you, you're suddenly interested? Where's your popcorn?"

His whiskers flicker annoyingly.

I roll my eyes. "That's what I thought."

Santino's car finally pulls up just as I debate pulling the curtains down for a quick wash, so instead, I rush out to meet him at the curb.

"Now or never, Tilly," Santino growls, striding around his car and marching toward the front door.

"Let's go for a drive and talk about this like proper grown-ups first." I grab his arm and try to pull him back to the vehicle.

"You're the one acting like a child, not me," he booms, jerking his arm out of my grip. Dammit if I don't get a thrill of heat between my legs at his forceful tone.

He marches up the front steps and wrenches the door open. Hercules takes off at mach speed for the bedroom, clearly exceeding his daily rations for drama.

"Are you happy? You've upset Hercules."

"Where's Mac?" Santino seethes, turning his dark eyes on me.

"He's not here." I cross my arms nervously as I stand in front of the staircase.

Santino narrows his eyes at me. "Bollocks, you're acting nervous." He moves me out of his way and thumps up the stairs.

"He's not up here!" I call out after him, having trouble keeping up. Christ, he's fast in that sexy suit.

He reaches the landing and pauses at the nursery, doing a cursory glance like he's a copper sweeping a house for criminals. Then he opens the door to my room. He walks inside, taking in my display of photos up on the wall. He turns quizzical eyes on me. "He's really not here?"

"No." I step inside to close the door. "Do you feel like an eejit yet for marching in here like a psychopath?"

He blinks back at me, his dark eyes swimming with disappointment. "A bit."

I exhale heavily as I witness reasonable Santino returning to the universe. I step towards him and wrap my arms around his neck. "We will tell my brother, but right now, he and Freya are having scans done on the baby."

"Fine." He closes his eyes and wraps his arms around me, squeezing me in a big bear hug. He presses his nose into the area below my neck and inhales deeply like he's trying to reacquaint himself with my smell. His voice is soft and pained when he says, "This is real to me, Tilly. This isn't a game."

"This is real to me too," I reply defensively.

He pulls back and a nervousness sweeps across his face as he blinks back at me with a horrified look on his face. "Tilly?"

"What?" My entire body erupts in goosebumps because I'm terrified of what he's going to say next.

He inhales sharply and says, "Mi sono innamorato di te."

"What?" My brows furrow. "What did you just say? You want Indian takeaway again?"

His Adam's apple slides down his throat before he replies shakily, "I've fallen in love with you."

"What?" I gasp.

The muscle in his jaw jumps as he straightens and repeats softly, "I've fallen in love with you."

"I heard that part." I blink rapidly up at his stupidly beautiful face.

"What part didn't you hear?" he asks, confusion blanketing his face.

I shake my head from side to side, my entire body trembling. "I just…it's only been a few weeks." Is it okay for people to fall in love in a few weeks?

"I know," he says with a resounding sigh.

"You said you've never been in love before." I point an accusing finger at him, like this can't possibly be true.

"I know." A nervous grin teases the corners of his mouth as he watches me process this admission.

"So this is…"

"Real." He takes a step towards me, crowding me as his face grows serious again.

"Right." I turn and touch my temple, feeling a rush of adrenaline hit me out of nowhere as I begin to pace. "You just said you loved me."

"Yes."

I glance over at him. "I thought we were taking things slow?"

"I know." He winces.

I stop moving and prop my hands on my hips, a stinging happening in the backs of my eyes that I cannot seem to get a handle on. This is all happening really fast. Yet everything feels like it's going in slow motion as well. My chest swells with anxiety because there's been a feeling creeping up inside me for days, a feeling of comfort and giddiness. A feeling like there's a reason I came back to London and it wasn't just to help out Mac and Freya.

I've been ignoring these feelings because I'm not the type of person who free-falls into the great unknown. Especially not after everything I've worked for these past five years. I like to stay in control of myself. I like to stay in control of my emotions. And what I'm about to say feels very, very uncontrolled.

Finally, I nod firmly, answering with a shaky breath. "Okay then."

"Okay?" He looks confused.

"Well, I'm pretty much madly in love with you too, which is terrifying because I told myself when I came back to London that I'd focus entirely on me and my family, but then you came barreling back into my life with your stupid basil plant and messed that plan all up." I accentuate my point with a really elegant growl of frustration that truly punctuates the special moment.

Santino blinks back at me, his eyes dark and terrified in a way I've never seen before. "Did you just say you love me?"

"Yes!" I exclaim. "And I've never loved anyone the way I love you, so this is a lot of pressure right now, and I'm having a wee bit of a panic attack."

Suddenly, Santino closes the space between us and picks me up in his arms, so our faces are eye level. "Say it again."

"It was hard enough the first time." He growls his insistence as I sigh in defeat, my voice thick with emotion when I add, "I love you, you eejit." My entire body tingles with warmth over the intensity of that admission. "I didn't particularly love you marching in here and threatening to out our relationship to my brother without a second thought, but I love you, so I guess I'll get over that."

His lips are on mine now, attacking my words with hungry ferocity as he carries me over to the bed and lays down on top of me. His hard body is like the best weighted blanket money could ever buy as he kisses me fervently, his hands stroking my flushed cheeks and cupping the back of my neck to deepen the kiss.

My legs wrap around him, and I hug him to me, relishing this moment of innocence. Of passion. Intimacy is supposed to feel like this. Raw, vulnerable. An unpainted building, waiting for someone to splatter it with beautiful, original, untraditional art.

"Santino, I want you," I say, breaking our kiss and reaching between us to fumble with his trousers. "I want you to make love to me."

"Are you sure?" he asks, searching my eyes for confirmation. "We don't have to."

I cup his erection in my hand and nod firmly. "I'm sure."

In a flash, Santino lifts himself off me, and we both ditch our clothes in record time. His cock bobs towards me, long and strong and probably waiting for this moment for far longer than it wanted to.

When he pulls a condom out of his wallet, I take it from him, sliding it over his immense length with pleasure. I grip it and stare up at him with wide, wanting eyes. "I want to feel alive again. Loved and cherished. Not broken."

"You're not broken," he says, coming down over me and kissing my lips passionately. "And you are so cherished."

My heart, my belly, my mind, my everything are on overload. I need this. I need it now.

I scoot myself up to the head of the bed, and the mattress dips as he positions himself between my legs. Holding on to his back, I tell him in a shaky voice, "You'll probably need to go slow at first."

"Anything." He kisses me deeply, swirling his tongue with mine as his hand slips down between us. He swipes his fingers along my centre, growling into my lips as he notices how wet I am. "Always wet for me."

"Yes," I gasp as he pulls back to grind his shaft along my clit. "Are you ready?"

"Yes."

He positions his tip at my entrance and pushes in just a couple of inches. It's tight. Immensely tight. Tighter than I even realised a body that's had intercourse before could be. But as he presses in deeper, my arousal ratchets up, and the barrier feels less harsh and more needy. I find myself wrapping my legs tightly around him to pull him in quicker just to get the friction where I need it. I need it so, so bad.

When he's finally seated inside me, the pressure is so intense, my fingers dig into his shoulders. "Oh my God," I groan, my pelvis aching like it's developed its own heartbeat.

"Are you okay? Does it hurt?" He stares down at me, his hair flopping over his forehead in that perfect mussed way that drives me wild.

I nod fervently, wondering if one can become a reborn virgin in their thirties. "Just move, Santino. I need you to move."

He pulls back slowly and thrusts in one, two, three times, each time getting smoother and smoother and the pain dissipating more and more as my muscles stretch to allow the glorious stroking of a nerve inside me that hasn't been touched in ages.

When I was hesitant to have sex with Santino before, it's because I was scared. I was scared that the act could somehow trigger the memory of a strange man over top of me who I didn't want inside me. I was scared I could be like an amnesia victim who gets her entire memory triggered the moment a similar act occurs. It was stupid, but it was where my mind was at the time. I didn't want to remember that night. I wanted to forget everything about it, including what happened afterwards.

It wasn't that I never wanted to have sex again. I just knew before I did it, it would have to be with someone I trusted. Someone I cared about. The fact that it's with someone I love…it's an honour I didn't know I was even deserving of anymore.

Just as that thought crosses my mind, Santino rocks harder into me and whispers against my lips, "Ti amo."

I don't need a translation for that.

I love him, too. More than I ever thought my heart was capable of loving someone. After everything I experienced, giving myself to a man like this didn't feel possible. I didn't feel worthy. I felt ruined inside, like I let someone take a piece of me that I could never get back. But as Santino makes love to me, whispering words of Italian in my ear, against my breast, and across my lips, I finally start to believe that nothing inside me is gone. It's just been hiding in the dark, waiting for someone to pull it out.

CHAPTER 28

Santino

STAND IN TILLY'S ROOM, GAZING AT THE WALL OF PHOTOS SHE'S taken of various street art displays. They're framed and dated, lined up perfectly from the years she lived in London prior to meeting me. It's interesting to look back at what drew her eye then because they're all very dark and gritty, depicting portraits of pain and anger or high contrast designs that feel just...troubled.

Then the frames stop five years ago, and below those is a new one that I recognise from our tour a couple of weeks ago. It was a giant mural on Hanbury Street in Brick Lane of a stork carrying a baby wrapped in a blanket. There was a price tag hanging on a baby's toe that said FREE TO A GOOD HOME. It's bright and cheery but with a tiny bit of edge to it that's very Tilly today. Not Tilly of yesterday.

I point at it and glance over my shoulder. "Why did you pick this one?"

Tilly's eyes are not on my face as she lays under the covers with her hands propped behind her head. "I can't hear a word you say when you're standing here naked in my wee bedroom."

I roll my eyes. "You're such a bloke sometimes."

"You're such a lass sometimes." She giggles and it makes me want to kiss her.

I stalk over to the bed and slip under the covers, grabbing her body and pulling it against mine. The skin-on-skin contact is glorious. We've been intimate in a thousand different ways since we started seeing each other, but feeling her like this after we just made love… it's euphoric.

I release her body and point over at the photo again. "Tell me why you chose that one."

She moans her dissent but then rolls over to lay on my chest. Her finger traces circles around my nipple as she talks. "It made me think about my own situation."

"With the pregnancy?"

"Aye." When she pauses, I remain silent, waiting to hear what she wants to say without asking a question to hear what I want her to say. "I sometimes wonder what it would have been like if the baby lived. Would I have been a good mother? Would I have stayed in Dundonald? Would I have wanted to find a husband to give the baby a father?"

My body tenses at that last remark. "You didn't want me to help you back then, that's for sure."

She glances up at me, her head tilting curiously. "I still don't know why you offered what you did. I mean, to claim another man's child, no questions asked. And you came up with that decision in seconds. You were a young, successful bloke living your best life in London. What on earth would inspire you to give up your life like that?"

It feels as if an elephant is sitting on my chest with the last question. An elephant that I've been living with since I had a very unexpected conversation with my nonno at only twenty years old.

I swallow the knot in my throat and tuck a strand of hair behind Tilly's ear. "There's a reason for that…and it's something I've actually never told anybody."

Her brows furrow and she looks at me expectantly. When I open my mouth to bare my soul, suddenly, there's a loud slam from downstairs followed by clomping of someone's heavy footsteps on the stairs.

Tilly's eyes are full of terror. "Fuck, it's Mac!"

We both scramble off the bed, darting around her room to find the remnants of our clothes. Tilly slips on a robe as she grabs my trousers up off the floor. By the time we hear the steps outside the door, I only have my boxers on as I clutch the rest of my clothes to my chest. "What the fuck do I do?"

"Get in the wardrobe!" Tilly exclaims, shoving my trousers in my hand and pointing at the door in the corner. "If my brother sees you naked, he's going to castrate you. And he knows how because there was a farm next to grandmum's bed and breakfast, and well…let's just say Mac and I saw some horrifying things as kids."

"Really? You choose to tell me that sweet story of your childhood now?" I seethe as she nearly shoves me over a box, and I crash into the doorframe to catch myself.

There's a loud knock on the door as Mac's voice booms, "Tilly, are you alright? It sounds like you broke something."

"I'm fine!" she cries out, trying to shut the door on me before I'm out of the way.

"Ouch!" I hiss when the door hits my toe. I grab my foot and bounce on one leg, losing my balance as I stumble into the box again. As I begin to fall backwards over it, I reach out to grab onto Tilly's robe for support, taking her down with me and landing in a loud crash on the floor.

"Tilly!" Mac bellows, swinging the door open and catching the both of us in a very awkward position.

I'm halfway in the wardrobe in just my boxers with Tilly sprawled over the box between my legs, her face right in front of my cock and her robe…well…let's just say it's a full moon view for Mac.

"Christ, what the fuck am I looking at?" Mac hollers, averting his gaze as Tilly scrambles up off the box and adjusts her robe back to its rightful place. "If that was Santino Rossi in your bloody wardrobe, it's a good thing he's lying down because it'll be easier to bury him from down there!"

I hop up on my feet, trying my hardest to grab my shirt to cover myself. When Mac glances over to see we're both well…somewhat decent again, he comes tearing towards me, his eyes murderous slits as he reaches his hands out for my throat.

Suddenly, there's a loud hiss and a snarl before something grey and fuzzy leaps out from behind me in the closet and lands on Mac's face.

"Jasper!" Tilly screams as the cat attacks Mac, making some of the most horrifying noises I've ever heard in my life.

Mac expels a high-pitched scream that I think only dogs can hear as he tries to peel the animal off his face. The horrifying scene feels like it goes on for ages, and it must have because when he finally succeeds, the sight before me is not good.

CHAPTER 29

Tilly

THE TENSION ALL AROUND ME?

Heavy.

The emotions in the room?

Unstable.

The urge I have to giggle as I apply salve to the cat scratches all over my brother's face?

A very unfortunate problem.

"There, there, my precious boy. Everything is okay now," Freya coos, holding Jasper to her ample bosom and petting him gently.

Mac jerks his face away from the cotton ball I'm pressing to a gash above his eyebrow. He levels a glare at Freya. "I think you're meant to be consoling me…your husband."

"Oh hush…Jasper is clearly traumatised." Freya presses her lips to his ear, and a loud purr vibrates all around us.

"The wee bastard maimed me," Mac bellows, splaying his hands out on the dining room table where we're all huddled around. The scratches on his face actually get redder with his barely concealed rage.

"He's a rescue, Mac!" she tuts, turning herself away from him to protect Jasper. "You scared the life out of him with all that stomping and shouting."

Mac growls under his breath. "I wouldn't have lost my temper if this prat wasn't in my fucking wee sister's room butt-arse naked."

"I wasn't naked," Santino offers from a safe distance across the length of the table.

Mac opens his mouth, but I cut him off. "Mac," I state firmly, grabbing the finger he's directing towards Santino. "Santino is my boyfriend, and you're going to treat him with respect."

"Boyfriend." He huffs out a laugh, still not accepting the facts I told him as we helped him down the stairs in pursuit of a first aid kit. "For how long? He burns through women faster than kindling."

"Well, I'm expecting to be different because…I love him." The words feel sticky in my mouth but right all the same. I glance over nervously at Santino, and the smug expression on his face causes my heart to flutter in my chest.

Freya audibly gasps as her gaze snaps from me to Santino and back to me.

"Love?" Mac scoffs and crosses his arms over his chest, knocking away my hand holding the cotton ball to his cheek. "How could you possibly know you love him already?"

"I love her too," Santino says firmly and then turns his eyes to mine, holding them captive as he adds, "I think I've loved her for a very long time."

My lips part as I ponder the meaning of his words. He couldn't mean before, could he? Surely not five years ago. I was a mess then. Still a mess now but at least a sober mess.

"If you loved her, then you wouldn't have slagged off on her when she was pregnant," Mac seethes, waving his hand at Santino like he's an annoying fly.

"The baby wasn't his, Mac." I toss the cotton ball into his face and lean back on the table. "And you know that."

Mac's eyes narrow to slits. "That's about the only thing I do know."

He glowers over at Santino. "That and the fact this fucking bastard sent you money for an abortion."

"It wasn't money for an abortion!" I snap, hating that Mac has thought this all along about Santino. "He gave me money to hire a private investigator to try to track down the birth father."

"What?" Mac barks, his tone laced with confusion.

I exhale heavily, steeling myself to lay it all out there. Lay myself bare. I was vulnerable with Santino, and it paid off in the end. I can be vulnerable with my brother now.

"I was too ashamed to tell you the truth at the time, so I let you believe that's what the money was for." I turn sad eyes to Santino, who was only trying to eliminate any monetary barriers I had at the time, which was generous beyond comprehension.

"Who was the father?" Mac asks, his voice gruff.

I turn my eyes back to my brother who looks ill over this revelation. "I never found out. I did hire someone but he just kept hitting dead end after dead end. When I miscarried, I just decided to let it all go."

Mac shakes his head and presses his fists on top of the table. "I don't understand."

"I don't remember who got me pregnant, Mac!" I cry, hating the words coming out of my mouth but knowing I need to spell it all out for him. "I took some pills from a friend…who I thought was a friend…and next thing I know, I wake up in a stranger's flat with no memory of going home with him."

"Fuck off," Mac growls, his jaw clenching so hard, I think I hear his teeth grinding. "What friend?" He slides accusing eyes over to Santino.

"No one I speak to anymore," I snap, stepping between Mac and Santino's murderous stare off. "I hadn't even been around Santino for a few weeks, so you can quit staring at him like he let this happen to me. He wasn't even there. That's how I knew when I turned up pregnant, it was that stranger's baby."

"Fucking hell." Mac stares down at his hands, looking like he's going to cry.

"See?" I groan, horrified at this whole moment. "This is why I never wanted to tell you. That look…right there. Disappointment. Shame. Disgust. You feel all those things for me? Imagine how I feel knowing the situation I put myself in. Imagine me having to tell Mum or Dad…or worse even, Granddad. Imagine the dread in my mind when I moved back home on my own and had to tell them I was pregnant."

Mac's face softens.

"I was so ashamed, Mac. So fucking ashamed and I had no one to blame but myself."

Mac exhales heavily. "I'm sorry, Tilly."

"Don't be. It was my own doing." I cross my arms over my chest, feeling like I need to dig out that protective armour again if I'm going to survive this conversation. "But I need you to know that Santino is important to me. He's special. He was a friend to me all those years ago. The only real one I truly had." My voice catches in my throat as that realisation pummels me out of nowhere. "He offered to be with me even though we both knew there was no chance the baby was his. But I couldn't accept his kindness at the time. I didn't trust it, so I pushed him away."

My tear-filled eyes find Santino's, and I ache to be in his arms again. To thank him for showing me mercy at a moment when I didn't deserve it.

My voice is firm when I refocus on Mac. "But what I have with Santino now, Mac? I trust it. I trust it with my whole heart, and I am not pushing it away. I'm holding on to it with every fibre of my being, and I swear to Christ, if you screw this up for me…I will unleash the holy hells of terror on you, and that baby in your wife's belly will be the only one you ever get. Sorry, Frey."

"Don't be," she replies, her eyes wide as saucers as she looks to be nearly squeezing the life out of poor Jasper. "This is better than *Bridgerton.*"

Mac nods slowly, processing everything I just said in his slow caveman way. Finally, he turns grave eyes to Santino. "All that shite I've said to you the past few years. You never once corrected me. Why?"

The corner of Santino's mouth curves up into a sad smile. "Because I care about your sister."

Mac takes a deep breath, his head nodding for a long while before his chair scrapes loudly on the wood floor as he stands. He makes his way over to Santino, who stands quickly to be equal to my brother. Mac reaches a clawed-up hand towards my boyfriend and says, "I'm sorry I misjudged you."

Santino blinks back his shock, glancing over at me for a split second before taking Mac's offered hand. "It's okay."

"Thank you for being there for my sister." He places a hand on Santino's shoulder, and the two share a moment of peace that I never was sure I'd see.

My watery eyes slide over to a tearful Freya, who's full-on blubbering and using Jasper's fur to dab at her tears. "Sorry, bleddy pregnancy hormones."

I laugh and grab a napkin off the table, dabbing my twitchy nose. "What's my excuse then?"

Freya smiles and cracks a joke. "Maybe this pregnancy stuff is catching."

My eyes go wide, and I glance over at Santino, expecting to see him laughing along with all of us, but instead, I see a faint look of unease on his face that doesn't sit well with me.

CHAPTER 30

Santino

"**W**HAT AM I LOOKING AT RIGHT NOW?" TILLY'S VOICE ECHOES in the distance, tearing me out of a very relaxing moment. Mac and I peel the cucumber slices off our eyes to see Tilly and Freya standing in the doorway that leads out to their back garden. They're gaping at the two of us seated in the loungers beneath the cherry blossom tree like we've got two heads each.

"This is called a wee bit of self-care," Mac says with a flourish as he sits back and returns the cucumber slices to his eyes.

"We only popped to the shop ten minutes ago." Freya shifts a large salad in her hands and glances at Tilly. "Why have I come back to find my husband looking like Shrek?"

"It's a green tea face mask," I add helpfully, touching my jaw to find it's dried nicely in the heat. "My nonna makes it from scratch. They sell it at their market in Bourton. I brought some for everyone if you like. It's completely natural."

Tilly barks out a laugh. "Our second double date with these two, and you've already started a bromance with my brother?"

I shrug. "I have a thing for redheads."

Mac grumbles a warning tone under his mask, but he's a lot less intimidating covered in green muck.

"I think I liked it better when Mac hated you," Tilly says with a laugh.

Mac coyly lifts a cucumber off one eye. "I never hated him."

"You did too." I laugh heartily with a shake of my head.

"Okay, fine…but that's because you looked at my wee sister like you wanted to eat her."

My brows lift. "I still do that, mate."

"Yes, but now I've got the cucumbers." He taps his temple with his index finger and drops the vegetable back on his eye. "Plus, all my other mates are busy with football tonight. It's nice to have a fellow nine-to-five working stiff to grab a pint with on Fridays after a long week's work. So thanks for not being a complete twat, after all, Santino."

I turn a cheeky smile over to Tilly. "If that's not a glowing review, I don't know what is."

She lifts her hands. "By all means, let your freak flags fly."

My brows furrow. "There is nothing freaky about a proper facial regimen."

"Aye," Mac says, blindly holding his beer bottle in my direction. I grab mine up off the side table and clink our glasses.

"You two were supposed to be tending the barbecue." Freya shakes her head with exasperation and sets the salad on the table. "And those cucumbers were for our waters, Mac."

"The steaks are resting, Cookie." Mac sighs heavily. "Now come have a sit with me on this lounger and let Santino smear green shite on your face. It's surprisingly pleasant. Though Santino, if this doesn't come out of my beard, you and I are going to be in a very big fight."

An hour later, we all discover that getting the mask out of Mac's beard is a bit of a nightmare. But thankfully the girls' giggles and quick problem-solving involving a facial steamer fixes everything, and my newfound friendship with Tilly's brother seems to remain intact, which is really something.

If you'd have told me a couple of months ago that I'd be spending my Friday nights in Mac Logan's garden wearing a green tea face mask and having barbecues with him, Freya, and Tilly, I'd have told you that you were completely mental. Yet here we all sit, like proper grown-ups celebrating another end of a grueling workweek.

It's a welcome change of pace from the office, which was tense to say the least. Ever since that call from Zander Williams' mother, I've been avoiding Vaughn Harris like the plague. I know I can't tell him anything. I'm legally bound not to. But to kill a contract that's right in the middle of negotiations for an incoming footballer is well above my pay grade. He's supposed to be signing soon to come in a few months, which means I don't have much time to figure this out.

The biggest issue I see right now is the fact that I'm certain Vaughn Harris would want to know he has a son. I realise there are loads of monsters out there who couldn't give a toss about illegitimate offspring. *My own past is a prime example of that.* But that's not Vaughn. Sure, he made some mistakes as a single father after his wife died, but he's dedicated two decades of his life trying to make up for those missteps. And he's doing a wonderful job, from what I can tell.

However, this isn't my decision to make, so until I can get Jane Williams to phone me back to discuss this matter, it's best to avoid any interactions with the Harris family.

Thankfully, forgetting about work is monumentally easier with Tilly Logan in my life. She is the most welcome distraction of all time. Not having to hide our relationship these past couple of weeks has felt like a strange dream that I never want to wake up from.

The night of our intense talk with Mac and Freya, Freya insisted I stay for dinner. She said that Mac needed to see me and Tilly interact properly, or he'd never get used to the idea of us being together. It felt a bit weird because I'm used to Mac only making animal noises at me, but he turned out to be somewhat friendly. He offered me a beer and asked if I wanted to try out his new video game that he helped design.

It only got awkward when he brought up the subject of my underpants.

"So, you're a boxer's man." Mac takes a long sip of his beer and sets his controller down to look at me. "I would have bet money on you being a briefs bloke for sure."

I clear my throat and shift on the sofa, feeling Tilly's watchful eyes on us from the kitchen. "I like room to breathe."

Mac nods slowly. "Me too, lad. Me too." He claps my shoulder firmly and adds, "Remember that if you ever spend the night here. Got it?"

Which was code for, *I don't care if you're in love with my sister, if you shag her under my roof, I'll fucking kill you.*

But Tilly refused to go back to my place that night. She said she'd waited weeks to have me in her bed, so despite my protests, she dragged me upstairs while I nervously peered over my shoulder at Mac, who glowered at us the entire way up.

For the first twenty minutes in her bed, I was firm on the fact that we weren't having sex out of respect for Mac and Freya. *And because their bedroom was right below ours.*

But fuck me, Tilly can be very persuasive, so when she started nudging her arse into my cock and rolling back to show me how hard her nipples were…I knew I was done for.

Bloody hell, I'm weak.

And the image of Tilly muffling her cries of passion with her pillow as I took her from behind and rocked slowly inside her so I wouldn't creak the bed is an image still making me rock hard two full weeks later.

After that, we both agreed it was best to sleep over at my place. We really only separated when we had to work. She was with Freya during the day working on the final details for her Harrods deal, and I was doing my avoidance act at Bethnal Green F.C. When we meet back up at my place in the evenings, I can't get her naked fast enough.

It's safe to say we christened every surface of my flat. Tilly said we've been going at it more than the duke and duchess from *Bridgerton* on their honeymoon. I had no clue what that meant, but she said Freya would understand.

For the past couple of weeks, I find myself marveling over the fact that this is what being in love is like. Fuck me, I should have done this ages ago. And that spooning bit that Tanner mentioned isn't bad either. Tilly is my perfect little spoon. We even developed our own morning routine of showering together that will certainly never get old.

It even seems we're starting a new Friday evening tradition with Mac and Freya and a garden barbecue. Though the way Tilly looks in that tight green tee this evening made the thought of staying at my place very appealing. She must be enjoying my eyes on her because she keeps giving me these coy looks and I'm not sure I'll be able to wait until we're back at my place to strip her naked again. Perhaps we should nip upstairs to her room and be very, very quiet again. Maybe I'll use my tie to gag her so she's not too loud.

"You guys should come with us to the Cotswolds next weekend," Tilly exclaims, ripping me out of my dirty thoughts as she dishes out some sticky toffee pudding for dessert. The sun has just disappeared, and she looks like an angel as she glows under the string lights hung all over the garden. "We're doing an overnight trip. Santino is going to show me his family's shop, and we're going to take a drive in the country. Might be nice to get out of the city?"

"Oh, that sounds so lovely." Freya rubs her belly and looks at Mac regretfully. "But Belle told me even though things are looking good, she still doesn't recommend travel."

"Of course," Tilly replies quickly. "I should have assumed."

Freya glances down at her stomach. "I still can't believe I'm closing in on thirty weeks. I still can't believe how scary it all was and how good everything seems now."

Tilly smiles warmly as she passes out the dessert. "Well, you handled it brilliantly."

"It was a team effort." Freya raises her mocktail for a cheers. We all clink glasses as Freya clutches her belly. "Oof, little Fergie is definitely going to be a footballer. His kicks get more determined every day."

"Maybe you should go lie down," Mac says, his face marred with concern as he rubs her back. "I know you're off bed rest, but you've had a busy night, don't you think?"

Freya ruffles Mac's hair. "Very well, husband. Take me to bed… but don't forget the pudding."

Tilly sits beside me at the table as we watch Mac usher Freya inside. She scoops up a spoonful of dessert and points towards them with her spoon. "I can't believe how much she's showing and how far she still has to go."

"Is that uncommon?" I inquire, watching them disappear around the corner.

"Oh, I don't know, but she looks like she's fixing to burst already."

"Are you ready to be an aunt?" I ask, watching Tilly's dreamy look with fascination.

She smiles brightly. "I'm definitely ready. What about you?"

"What about me?"

"Do you want kids?" She takes another casual bite of her treat like she didn't just drop a very loaded question on me.

"Not particularly." A thickness forms in my throat. "Do you want kids?"

"I don't know for sure." Tilly's shoulders lift. "I think I'll wait to see how that wee one turns out before I decide. The Logan bloodline can be horribly stubborn." She giggles and tucks another bite of pudding into her mouth.

The sight is so lighthearted and sweet. The innocence of it all pokes at a very deep dark vortex in my soul. What if I can't give Tilly what she wants? What if me telling her who I am and where I come from ruins this hopeful innocence she has? She's come so far in her life, getting over her own pregnancy loss, getting sober, and now tackling a new job soon. She's doing so well and is so optimistic about life. Maybe me hitting her with my truth will send her spinning.

My spine straightens as a new reality settles in over me. I always thought that the moment I truly fell for someone, I'd want to tell her the truth about me and who I really am. I thought it would be cleansing and might bring my true heart forward. But what if I'm wrong? What if those thoughts were all selfish, delusional bullshit? What if it's like telling a woman you cheated on her just to relieve your own guilty conscience while crushing hers in the meantime?

I don't want to do that to Tilly. I love her. I love her so much, it's hard to breathe just thinking about it. Maybe living with this secret is more selfless than being open. At least then she won't look at me differently. Because who can truly ever love the child of a monster?

CHAPTER 31

Tilly

I REMEMBER A TRAIN RIDE WHEN I WAS A TEEN, AND I WAS SEATED directly across from a young couple. The two were whispering back and forth and laughing hysterically, his hands sliding up her leg, her hands teasing the inside of his jacket. They were like that for the entire two-hour journey. I remember wondering, how have they not run out of things to talk about? What is always so funny? Isn't it uncomfortable having her leg wedged up on his lap like that?

Santino and I…are now that couple.

The entire long train ride out to the Cotswolds, I cannot keep my hands off him. The smell of him, the feel of him, his husky voice whispering in my ear as we swap stories of our youth—it's so lovely I can't stop smiling. I may have babbled on a bit too long about my bed and breakfast memories with my grandparents, but Santino sat through it all with a smile on his face. I told him my grandmother used to pay me to make all the beds but then my grandfather would come in behind me and fix my shoddy work and demand half the payment for himself…which he later used to buy me ice cream.

I even told Santino a stupid story about being a flower girl for a wedding that was at the B&B because their own flower girl woke up vomiting. I was a big saviour until I ruined the entire ceremony by throwing a fit and ripping the flowers out of my hair.

I'm babbling for sure. And I'm babbling because this past week I find myself fantasising about things I've never fantasised about before. Like marriage and babies and happily ever afters. It's the most bizarre feeling because not too long ago, I didn't want kids. When I came back to London, I was all set to be Super Aunt Tilly, but now that I've fallen in love, everything has changed. And I'm old enough now to know that what I'm feeling with Santino is real and more important than anything I've ever experienced with past relationships.

It's all quite overwhelming when I think about it.

I exhale heavily and try to stop my mind from racing. It's far too soon to discuss such matters, and I think I freaked him out with the baby talk at Mac and Freya's last weekend. He's been a bit distracted this past week, and I'm not sure why. He said it was mostly work-related, and he was legally bound not to talk about it, but the truth is, there's still a lot I don't know about Santino. He's tried to share something from his past with me on more than one occasion, but we always seem to get distracted, or he changes the subject just as things get deep.

I'm hoping he sees this trip as a turning point for us. Maybe showing me where he grew up and meeting his family in a more official capacity will help him feel safe with me. Then perhaps, I can begin to fully unwrap the rest of the mysterious box that is Santino Rossi.

We arrive at a train station about eight miles away from Santino's village to find his grandfather waiting outside for us. He looks like a cute, proper granddad in a shirt, trousers, and white socks with sandals. Santino told me that we had to take the train today because if we didn't, Nonno wouldn't let him borrow his car to take a drive around the countryside like he wanted to. Apparently, Nonno is very posses-sive of his car. And when we walk out to the parking lot, I can see why.

"You like red?" Nonno asks, pointing at my hair and then to his Mini Cooper.

I take in the vintage box-shaped Mini Cooper that's easily de-cades-old, but you wouldn't be able to tell that by the paint job. The red is glossy and lush, a gorgeous contrast to the white roof and pipe design that rims the hood.

"I like that red better than this red." I point to his car and then to my hair.

"Both beautiful classics." Nonno kisses his fingertips and smiles proudly as he takes my small weekend bag and tosses it in the back seat.

"You washed it already, Nonno?" Santino asks, walking to the front of the vehicle to take it in.

Nonno scoffs. "You have lady friend…Cherry needs to look her best."

Santino laughs and walks over to open the passenger side door for me. "He named her Cherry, in case you didn't pick up on that. And he usually makes me wash her when I borrow it so he must re-ally like you."

I smirk over at Nonno. "Well, I am really charming."

"Cherry one…Cherry two," Nonno replies, pointing at the car, then to me before he slides into the driver's seat.

I beam proudly. "I think I just got a nickname from your grandfather."

"Just get in the car, Trouble," Santino growls and tweaks my arse as I slip into the tiny back seat. He hands me his backpack to sit be-side me and then folds himself into the front. I can't help but marvel at how two tall Italian men can even fit in this little rig because I have to sit with my legs off to the side on top of our bags back here. This must be why Santino told me to pack light. Had I known I would be wedged into a cute tin can today, I maybe wouldn't have chosen to wear a dress.

However, last time Santino's family saw me, I was wearing ripped jeans and had spilled sauce all over my white top. Meeting them in an official girlfriend capacity today means I wanted to look nice, which also means Freya helped dress me this morning. She found a floaty little spaghetti strap maxi dress in the back of my wardrobe that I hadn't worn in years. It's cream and a bit girlie, but I styled it with an oversized flannel and brown hiking boots to be more comfortable.

The journey is quiet as I sit in the back and try to quell the anxiety needling my belly. Last time I saw Santino's mother, we had a moment of frank honesty in front of everyone when I asked her about being a teen mother. I hope it didn't leave a sour taste in her mouth about me, but I couldn't help myself. I'm a curious person by nature, and when it comes to Santino, I want to know everything. He certainly knows everything about me. I've been more open with him than I have with most of my family. Hopefully this trip will deepen his trust in me, and we can schedule a little trip to Scotland next. My parents would be thrilled.

We pull into Bourton-on-the-Water, and I can't help but gaze wide-eyed at how beautiful it is. It's a quaint British village full of traditional stone houses that remind me of places we'd visit in the Highlands when I was wee. The village got its name because the entire town centres around a gently flowing river with several low arch-stoned bridges crossing in different places. Their high street runs parallel to the river and features several ornamental shops, restaurants, and artisan bakeries.

Nonno glances back at me. "Have you visited here before?"

"No, it's beautiful, though," I reply as he brakes for several ducks to cross the cobblestone street.

"Bourton-on-the-Water is the Venice of Cotswolds." Nonno points at a bridge where someone is rowing beneath. "It will never come close to our beautiful Italy, but it's home now."

I notice Santino stiffen in front of me, so I reach forward to touch his shoulder. He turns his head to look at me, forcing a smile that doesn't seem all that natural.

Moments later, we park in an alley beside a large brick building, and Santino holds my hand as we follow Nonno towards the street entrance of the deli. When Nonno rounds the corner out of sight, I pull Santino back and force him to look at me. "Are you alright?" I give his hand a hard squeeze.

"Of course," he responds, frowning. "Why wouldn't I be?"

I peer up at him, trying to see through those dark, masked eyes of his. "You seem off."

"Don't be silly." He pulls me close, wrapping his hands around my waist, offering me an easy smile. "I'm fine."

My head tilts. "Are you nervous for me to meet your family?"

He huffs out a laugh. "You've already met my family."

"I know, but not as your girlfriend." Insecurity niggles in my belly. "Do they know we're together now?"

"Yes, they know. Nonno washed the bloody car for you." His brows furrow with confusion. "Where's this coming from?"

My shoulders lift as I try to figure out why I'm losing my mind right now. "Just feeling nervous, I suppose."

"Don't be nervous." His hands tighten around my waist as his eyes fall to my lips. "You know I love you, right?"

A flutter of warmth runs through my entire body because those words from his lips still have not lost any impact. "You've mentioned that once or twice."

He goes quiet for a moment and then says, "And you're happy with me?" His face is full of uncertainty.

"Yes," I answer with a laugh because this is all so bizarre that we're both just messes of insecurity despite the fact that we've spent every spare minute together for the past few weeks. How could I not be happy with a man as perfect and wonderful as Santino? I splay my palms out on his chest, my fingers teasing the fabric of his dress shirt. "I'm so happy that I'm annoying myself."

"Good," he replies, hitting me with a smirk that sends flutters through my belly. "Because you're not annoying me one bit."

"My God, you're a charmer, aren't you?"

I lift my hand to run my fingers through his hair, and he sags into my caress with a smile. His jaw muscle jumps as he leans in and nudges my temple with his nose, inhaling deeply, which causes me to lift my lips to his. When our mouths connect, it's a soft, supple touch. His tongue strokes mine but not in the possessive, all-consuming way he's been kissing me all week. This kiss is more of a gentle awakening that still manages to make my nipples pebble beneath my lace bra.

"Santino!" We jerk apart like two teenagers who just got caught snogging…which…is pretty much exactly what's happening. It's his nonna standing at the front of the building, watching us with a very angry look on her face. "Vieni dentro velocemente!"

She turns and storms off, leaving Santino's mother behind as we make our way towards her, tails tucked firmly between our legs. His mother's eyes lock on me with a knowing smile. "It's really nice to see you again, Tilly."

"It's nice to be here," I reply, tucking my hair behind my ear.

Carlotta turns towards Santino. "Figlio mio." She pulls him down into a hug. "I'm so glad you're both here."

She stands between us and hooks her arms in ours, leading us around the corner towards the deli entrance. Just as we breach the threshold, several voices shout, "Happy Birthday!"

My jaw drops in confusion as I see Nonno, Bart, Angela, and a man and woman I haven't met standing there singing. Nonna appears again, now carrying a white-frosted cake covered in candles towards Santino.

"It's your birthday?" I ask, my eyes wide with horror as I glance at Santino, who does not look pleased.

"I told them I didn't want to celebrate." Santino shoots daggers at his mother, who's standing between us.

"He never wants to celebrate." Carlotta laughs, singing even louder, clearly not the least bit concerned by the mood radiating off her son. "But he is never home for his birthday so we shut down the whole shop in his honour."

Santino looks stunned as he glances around and confirms there are no customers in sight.

"Buon compleanno, Santino," Nonna says, holding the cake in front of him. "Esprimi un desiderio."

"You didn't have to do this." Santino sighs, his jaw taut as he begrudgingly leans forward and blows out the candles. "It's too much."

"Never too much," Nonno adds with a wink.

The party gets started and I'm quickly introduced to Santino's zio Antonio and his wife, Belinda, who are the official owners of the store. Belinda inherited this large, historic building when her parents died.

Today, Antonio and Belinda still live in the flat above the shop while Carlotta, Bart, and Angela are in Santino's childhood flat behind the shop with Nonno and Nonna one level below them. They all grew up within an arm's length of each other for Santino's entire life, and I find myself wildly fascinated with what that must have been like.

We return to the deli and have pasta, cake, espresso, biscotti, and a million other baked goods that Nonna keeps setting in front of me to sample. Nonno then gives me a tour of the supermarket and forces me to try all the cheeses and cured meats they have regularly shipped in from Italy. I'm so full from the fresh burrata that I fear Santino will have to roll me out of this adorable shop when we leave today.

However, my favourite part of all the sharing was when Carlotta showed me a photo album of her and Santino's annual trips the past several years. It's very nearly an album entirely dedicated to Santino. Images of him looking gorgeous on mountains, at restaurants, and in ancient cities. There's even a photo where he's getting a pedicure. It's adorable, and that green tea face mask makes a lot more sense now. Carlotta beams with pride over the memories she's made with her son, and I can tell she's happy to be sharing those memories with me today.

"Angela, why don't you help me clean up," Antonio says, standing up and adjusting his trousers.

Belinda jumps up to help as well. "Oh yes, look at the time. We'll have to open up for dinner soon." Angela rolls her eyes but still gets up to help, along with Bart.

"I can't believe you closed down the deli for this," Santino says, fiddling with one of the balloons in the middle of the long table we're seated around.

"You only turn thirty-seven once, love." Carlotta presses a kiss to her son's head before grabbing his coffee mug off the table. "And you never come here for your birthday, so we had to do something!"

"Why don't you like to celebrate your birthday?" I ask, nudging him with my elbow.

He shrugs his shoulders dismissively. "I'm too old for birthdays."

"Hush," Nonna says, waving him off as she stands up to grab a few dishes. "Your life is a blessing and deserves to be celebrated."

"I fully agree." I squeeze his hand encouragingly. He's been tense the entire time we've been here, but his eyes always soften when he looks at me. "Now, please tell me who that gorgeous child is in that photograph."

I point at a black and white photo on the wall behind Nonno, who turns and nods knowingly. "That è Santino."

"I knew it," I reply with a smile as I squint at the print of a little boy shirtless with a giant plate of spaghetti in front of him. His face is completely covered in sauce. "Those dark eyes are just as stunning on you then as they are now. How old are you there?"

"Four, I think," Santino answers, staring at the photograph with a thoughtful look in his eye. "I think it was my birthday then too."

"It was," Carlotta confirms as she rejoins us at the table. "He liked birthdays when he was young. He was a very spirited little child."

Nonno harumphs from across the table. "Got into trouble a lot."

"Did he?" I ask, my face beaming with this newfound knowledge. "Were you terribly naughty, Santino?"

Carlotta barks out a noise. "He was awful! He was grounded more than he was ever free."

I laugh, turning my attention to Nonno. "What was the naughtiest thing Santino ever did?"

"That's easy." Nonno's brows lift knowingly. "He stole my Cherry."

I have to clap my hand over my mouth to stop myself from snorting. "Santino!"

"I borrowed Cherry," Santino corrects, getting an adorably guilty look on his face. "And I washed her before I brought her back."

"At two o'clock in the morning," Nonno growls, his hands turning to fists on the table. "I was so angry, I couldn't speak English for a week."

My belly shakes with laughter. "What were you doing with Cherry? Were you with a girl?"

"No." Santino swallows nervously. "I used her for a street race… which I won."

Nonno and Nonna shake their heads and wave their hands, still as horrified by that episode today as they were however many years ago when it happened. They excuse themselves to help the others to prep, leaving me with Santino and his mother at the table.

Carlotta rests her chin on her fist and gazes affectionately at her son. "He wasn't all bad. Even as a naughty teenager, he had a very tender heart. It was actually hard to be too cross at him because he punished himself more than any of us ever could. It gutted him to disappoint the people he loved."

My lips turn down into a sad smile. "That's very sweet."

"This is very awkward for me," Santino grumbles, looking back and forth between the two of us. "I'm going to go talk to Nonno about *borrowing* Cherry again."

"No racing!" Carlotta laughs and watches Santino walk away before shifting her eyes to me. "It's really nice he brought you here."

"I still can't believe he didn't tell me it was his birthday."

Carlotta shakes her head. "He can be really private sometimes. And he's been weird about his birthday ever since…well…" She waves her hand. "It's my fault. It's always the mother's fault."

"Oh, but you two seem to get on brilliantly," I reply, touching her arm gently. "One of the first things he talked to me about was your annual trips."

"Really?"

"Yes!" I say excitedly. "He has lovely things to say about you. All of you, honestly."

Her lips pull back with a surprised smile. "That is really nice to hear." She leans in close and holds my hand in hers. "You're good for him, Tilly. I can tell. He's happy with you, and that's saying a lot for my son."

My heart swells. "Well, I'm very happy with him, too."

She stares over my shoulder at Santino. "On the outside, he's a bit hard around the edges, but that heart of his…when he opens it fully…it will be worth the wait, I promise you, darling. Just be patient with him."

A warm smile creeps across my face as the memory of him in my bedroom telling me that he'd fallen in love with me flashes through my mind. "I've actually seen his heart already. He didn't make me wait that long." I laugh and cover my cheeks.

"Is that true?" Carlotta's lips thin, and the look in her eyes is unmistakable.

Doubt.

The smile on my face fades as the doubt on her face turns into something else. Something I can't read. I'm about to ask her why she doesn't believe me when she looks over my shoulder and plasters on a grin.

"Are you ready?" Santino's deep voice interrupts, and I turn to see him standing behind me with a blanket and a basket in hand. He reaches out to pull me up out of the seat. "We need to get going if we want to catch the sunset."

I swallow the knot in my throat and nod woodenly, my mind whirling with confusion as Carlotta stands up to hug her son. "You will say goodbye before you head back to the city in the morning?" she asks, like she didn't just drop a bomb on my inner narrative. "And you're sure you want to stay at the hotel?"

"Yes, Mamma. We'll drop by in the morning."

Santino kisses her on the cheek and steps back so she can hug me. I can't tell if the trembling is coming from her or me, so I try to shake off the bizarre sensation coursing through my veins and tell myself I'm being silly right now. I plant a smile on my face and hope it looks genuine. The problem is that it was a lot easier just a few seconds ago.

CHAPTER 32

Tilly

O UR DRIVE IN THE MINI COOPER IS GORGEOUS. THE AUTUMN AIR is crisp, the October sun is warm, and the rolling English hills are stunning. With that said, it's hard to fully appreciate them because I'm busy trying to figure out if that doubt I saw on Carlotta's face was real or a figment of my imagination.

I'm in the passenger seat having a wee freak-out. Meanwhile, Santino is in the driver's seat of a classic car, looking like a sexy Italian god. He's wearing expensive sunglasses, and the wind is whipping through his dark hair like he's shooting a cologne advertisement.

I know he might be holding back from me, but as he caresses my hand on his lap, there is no doubt in my mind that he loves me. He must. I can't be that delusional.

But…he didn't tell me about his birthday…and I know there have been moments when he's wanted to share other things with me, but we've always been interrupted. I should have followed up by now, but we've been busy being happy, and I was just trying to live in the moment a bit.

Perhaps that's what this trip was all about. Maybe he's going to open up when we're alone this evening. Maybe he's going to bare his heart to me, and that peculiar expression his mother gave me will all make sense afterwards.

"There's a trail out here that I used to bike on as a child," he tells me, his voice warm as he lifts my hand up to his lips for a quick kiss.

"Bike or race?" I give his leg a cheeky squeeze and try to lighten my mood a bit.

He glances at me and lifts his brows behind his sunglasses. "Nonna forced me to bring more food, so if you're going to have a cheeky mouth, I could give you something to fill it with."

"No more food!" I shake my head in refusal. "I couldn't eat another bite if you forced me."

"Mmm," he says, a growly noise vibrating from his chest. "I'll have to think of something else to fill your mouth with." He laughs at his own joke and the smile on my face feels genuine again. We're good. Santino and I are in love. This is real.

A bit later, Santino parks near an old stone wall on the side of the road and grabs the basket and blanket. He takes my hand in his and walks us through a large field of poppies that are well past their bloom. The sun casts a lovely golden glow on everything as he points towards a wooden fence off in the distance. "Over there is a great view of Sherborne Park and a seventeenth-century estate that was restored when I was younger. We can sit there and watch the sunset if you like. The leaves are all changing now, so it should be nice."

"That sounds lovely," I reply as we make our way to a secluded space just beneath a large weeping willow.

Santino spreads the grey blanket out in the shade and sits with his back propped against the tree. When he opens his arms, I lower myself between his legs, my back laying against his front, his arms tight around me as his chin rests on my shoulder. The view of the old estate and the small lake nearby is gorgeous. We're content as we listen to the sound of farm animals in the distance and wind blowing through the willow branches.

Santino kisses my neck, his whiskers tickling my sensitive flesh as he pulls my flannel shirt off one shoulder. "You always smell so good," he murmurs, pressing his lips to my collarbone and biting at me like I'm a treat. "I want to just bottle you up and take you with me wherever I go."

I shift between his legs, my body reacting instantly to his touch. "What do you think you're doing?"

He pulls down the thin strap of my dress, causing goosebumps to ripple down my arm. "What do you think?"

"You want to do this here? Outside?" My body clenches at the thrill of that thought.

"I want to do it always." He drags his tongue up to the shell of my ear and whispers, "I want to taste every part of you right bloody now."

My body heaves at those naughty words, but I turn to look into his eyes before I give in to my urges. "Are you sure you don't want to talk instead?" I reach up and caress the back of his head, my fingers scraping gently along his scalp as I gaze into his eyes.

"I'm quite sure, yes." He stares hungrily at my mouth, his eyes pools of liquid heat before he gently cups my neck and fuses our lips together. He steals my breath as he plunges his tongue into my mouth in a deep, drugging kiss.

I get swept away for a moment as my body arches into his touch, aching for more. I always want more with this man. Never less. Finally, I break our kiss to say, "I'm still cross at you for not telling me it was your birthday. I would have got you a present."

"You're the only present I want, Trouble." His eyes are hooded and full of desire. "Let me make love to you."

It's a real, honest request, and at that moment, I feel like whatever doubt his mother may have had couldn't possibly be factual. This man is mine…body and soul. I know we haven't been together that terribly long, but our hearts have been connected for much, much longer.

This is real.

I nod, and in one quick move, he turns me around to straddle his lap. My arms wrap around his neck as our mouths connect again, tongues wet and wild against each other. His hands skate up under my long skirt, and his fingers wrap around my arse and tease the satin of my thong, sliding all the way down until he reaches my damp centre. I'm pretty much wet around him all the time, so it's no big surprise. He massages my clit over the thin fabric gently before moving to my backside again and applying expert pressure.

The act feels naughty and thrilling, not just because we're outside but because he's touching me in places he's never touched me before. I whimper against his lips as desire pools in my belly. My God, Santino is the only man who has ever known exactly how to make me come alive like this.

I ditch my flannel as he pulls down the straps of my dress so I can slip my arms out. My cream lace bra is now on full display for him and the animalistic noise he makes when he lowers the fabric to expose my hardened nipples nearly has me orgasming on the spot.

He cups my breasts firmly, massaging them in his large hands before dipping his head to suck one nipple into his mouth. I cry out when his teeth grip onto the tightened nub, and he growls his appreciation and moves over to the other. He sucks and laves so greedily that I feel myself shamelessly grinding against his lap. His erection is stone-hard through his denim, and the friction against the thin fabric of my knickers has me panting for more.

So much more.

To think I went without sex for five years seems inconceivable now. The past few weeks, I haven't gone a day without the touch of this man. The intimacy we've shared together has been something I didn't even know existed between two people. He's mine and I am his.

He slips his fingers through the side of my knickers and hums a deep noise. "Always so fucking wet for me, aren't you, Trouble?"

"Yes," I moan, riding his fingers without any shame. "Always for you."

"Let's get these off." Santino's voice is gruff against my neck as he tugs impatiently at my knickers. "I need to be inside you right fucking now."

I rise on wobbly legs, and he helps me slide them off over my boots and toss them to the side. I sit back down on his legs as we both frantically undo the buttons on his shirt. I need to feel his body against mine. Flesh against flesh.

Next are his jeans. I get them undone and reach inside his boxers to grab his hot, thick erection. I pump it and watch in fascination as his head falls back against the tree, his abs contracted, his large pecs rising and falling as the veins in his neck throb with need like the cock between my fingers. I rub my thumb over the dab of pre-come pooling at his tip, and he gasps a noise of undulating need.

Suddenly, his eyes snap to mine, and he grabs my arms and yanks me against his hard body. His lips cover mine as he positions his tip. In one quick motion, he pulls me down on top of him, pushing his cock up into my body.

Deep…so deep.

"Fuck," he groans, breaking our kiss to press his forehead against my bare chest. "I forgot a condom."

"It's fine," I gasp, my breath hot as I swivel over him, relishing the feel of his bare shaft inside me. I grab his face and force him to look at me. "I'm on the pill."

"Fuck, Tilly." His voice is husky as his hands grab my hips, rocking me slowly over top of him. His eyes are dark and tormented. "We should wait."

"Why?" I pant, pushing myself up to slide back down over him. "I love you like this."

"Fuck, you feel so good." His head falls back on the tree as he watches me ride him, his face full of desire and longing and even a bit awestruck. He drags his fingers from my cheek to my breast and says, "Sei il mio tutto amore mio." *You are my everything, my love.*

"I love you, too," I reply, only catching the last bit of what he said.

Suddenly, he grips my hips and thrusts upward, meeting my motions with more force than I could muster on my own. The effect is instant as he strokes my channel in that perfect spot that sends me into a surging frenzy of desire.

Within moments, my thighs begin to quiver as my release builds. I grab onto his shoulders and hold tight as he continues driving into me, kissing my neck hungrily as our breaths grow louder and louder, our noises now more animal than human. A pulsing sensation sweeps through my body as bolts of light explode behind my eyelids.

A hoarse cry rips from my throat as my climax takes over, and seconds later, Santino goes still, his grip punishing on my hips as he releases into me, his body convulsing as my sex milks his release drop by drop.

My head falls into his neck as his arms shelter me with warmth. His hand combs through my tangled hair as our chests slide against each other, our breaths fighting to regulate again. It's several moments before either of us can manage a coherent thought.

"We missed the sunset," he says, his voice gruff from our exertions.

"Your fault." I laugh and glance behind me to see the sun has disappeared behind the autumn landscape. I turn back to see him checking me out.

He cheekily fixes my bra so the cups are back in their rightful place. "I can't believe I'm about to say this, but I'm hungry."

We both laugh and clean ourselves up quickly because, like it or not, we are in a public place. Lord knows who could come upon us at any moment. The twilight is beautiful as we nibble on some fresh fruit, and for some bizarre reason, my mind drifts to something I've been meaning to talk to him about for the past few weeks.

"Listen, I know this is awkward because we haven't really spoken about it very much," I say, turning to sit crisscross so I'm facing Santino straight on. "But that money you sent me back in Dundonald for the private investigator? I want to pay you back."

"What?" Santino asks, popping a grape into his mouth and frowning at me. His hair is mussed from my hands, and he looks like sex on a stick leaning back on the tree with one leg propped.

"It's weighed heavily on me for a long time. I'm getting a really nice signing bonus at Harrods, so I'd like to just get that sorted." Waving him off, I dig into the basket for more fruit.

He stops eating and stares at me with a peculiar look on his face. "Tilly, I don't want your money. I don't need it."

"I know you don't need it," I reply firmly. "It's a pride thing for me. This has eaten away at me for ages, and now that we're together properly, I don't want this between us anymore."

"It was never between us." His nostrils flare. "I'd already forgotten about it."

"Well, I didn't." I blink at him, confused with why he's being so stubborn about this.

The muscle in his jaw tics. "Just donate it to a charity then."

"You donate it. It's your money," I exclaim, crossing my arms over my chest. "I have the check already written."

"I won't take it."

"Why not?"

"Because I won't." He slides his gaze from me and stares out at the view like the discussion is over.

I watch him curiously for a moment, that doubt from earlier creeping back in with a vengeance. "Why did you give it to me in the first place?"

"What do you mean?" he snaps, narrowing his eyes on me. "I was trying to help you."

"But it was above and beyond what any other bloke would do."

"So what?"

"So, I'm curious why. There must have been some sort of reason," I pry deeper, wanting to know every single part of him now more than ever.

"Why does there have to be a reason?" he growls, his anger bubbling to the surface.

I pause as I stare back at him. "Because there has to be a reason. Just like there has to be a reason you used to like celebrating birthdays as a child, but you don't anymore."

"Tilly." His jaw clenches as he glowers at me. "We don't need to discuss this. None of it matters."

That response only makes me more determined. "Look, I've tried to be patient and let you share with me when you're ready, but that's clearly not happening, so what am I supposed to do here?"

"Just leave it alone." His tone is harsh and final. "You don't need to know absolutely everything about me."

His words hit me with a deep, penetrable force that I did not see coming. I don't need to know everything about him? Which means there *is* something he's hiding from me. Something important or his mother wouldn't have looked at me the way she did earlier today.

"You're actually serious?" I clench my teeth with frustration, a chill running down my spine at his closed-off body language. It's so foreign to me, this entire exchange so unlike anything we've experienced together thus far.

"Of course, I'm serious." He shakes his head in disgust and that sets me off.

"Right." I toss a berry out into the grass and stand because I can't sit here and take this any longer. "So, these past several weeks, I've had to answer loads of difficult questions about my sobriety and my miscarriage and reveal parts of my pain and torment that I've not told anyone…even my brother"—I lean forward, my hands on my hips just like my mum when she has a go at my dad—"and you get to sit there and hide from me?"

"I'm not hiding from you." He stands up to face me. "I'm right in front of you."

"Then tell me what's going on because I can see in your face and your mother's face that you're not telling me something!" I toss my hands out to my sides. "If our love is real, you would share every part of yourself with me."

"Can you not just love me for who I am now?" he asks, his eyes flashing with a level of pain that I've never seen before.

I inhale a shaky breath because I see it now. He's different. Something in him is more guarded and withholding. He wasn't like this with me before. My voice is soft and unsure when I reply, "But you wanted to tell me something a few weeks ago. You said you did. Something you've never told anyone."

"Things changed." His eyes narrow with determination.

Fear and insecurity trickle into my belly. "Is it me? Do you not want me anymore?"

"Tilly, of course I want you. I fucking love you!" he growls. His temper boils over, causing the veins in his neck to swell angrily. "It's because I love you that I don't want to go there with you. You don't need to know this."

I swallow the painful knot in my throat, feeling like his words are shallow and meaningless. "So, because you love me, you get to decide what things to hide from me? What kind of love is that?"

He bends over to pick up the basket. "I think we should go."

"No!" I yank the basket out of his hand and toss it into the grass, forcing him to look at me. "I've cut myself open and bled for you, Sonny. You got to be the bandage that mended me. Now you won't let me even see your wound?"

"Just drop it." His jaw muscle tics angrily. "You don't know what you're asking."

"Santino, whatever it is, I can take it." I'm verging on desperation now, but it feels like he's slipping out of my fingers. "I'm a big girl. I've handled a lot in my life."

"And you don't need this on top of that," he barks, his voice deafening in the large wilderness. "Don't challenge me here. Not this time. You have to trust me on this."

"But you're not trusting me!" I cry, my eyes welling with tears at that painful realisation. The one thing I loved most about my relationship with Santino was feeling normal again. Feeling not broken and respected. Hell, even him having a beer with my brother the other night made me feel like he's one hundred percent confident in me and my strength. But this entire situation has thrust me right back to the mess of a person I was when I was taken advantage of by a complete stranger. And I'm not that girl anymore.

I step into his space, causing his body to bow over mine as emotion radiates between us. His eyes are slits as I stare up at him. "I don't need you to protect me or save me or fix me, Santino. I am your equal. I thought you knew that, but the way you're acting now reminds me of the man who stood on my doorstep and tried to save me five years ago. And if you don't trust me, then there's no need for us to be together."

He flinches like I've just slapped him, and the pain in his face hurts my heart, but I have to be strong. I have to demand respect because whatever he's giving me right now...isn't that.

Shock, disgust, pain, and resentment flash over his face like a film montage. So many emotions, I'm not sure what will come out of his mouth next. His voice is guttural when he replies, "So that's it then? You're going to cut and run just like before? Same old Tilly?"

Tears sting my eyes because his response confirms that he doesn't see me like I thought he did. And if I haven't earned his trust by now, I'll never earn it. And I've worked too hard, and I've come too far to let someone make me feel unworthy of their whole heart, only offering me the selective scraps that he deigns to throw my way.

I swipe away my errant tears and force myself to sound strong. "I didn't need a white knight five years ago, and I don't need one now."

"Well then." He laughs bitterly and bends over to pick up the basket. "We better be going. You don't want to miss the last train back to London."

He storms off, leaving me alone on that hill and wondering what on earth I've just done.

CHAPTER 33

Santino

"**W**HERE IS TILLY?" MY MOTHER ASKS AS I WALK INTO THE deli alone the next morning.

"She went home last night." I pass the keys off to Nonno behind the deli counter. "Can I get a ride to the train station now?"

He hits me with a very serious look before disappearing to go get his jacket in the storeroom.

My mother rushes around the counter to approach me. She whacks my arm. "What did you do?"

"Nothing," I grind out, my mind refusing to let my mother get in my head right now.

"Liar!" she exclaims, and the customers having a coffee at the tables behind me all look over.

"Would you calm down?" I hiss, my anger spiking hard in my veins but not because of Tilly. Because of my mother.

She exhales and nods. "I'm calm. Now, tell me what happened."

"It didn't work out." I shrug dismissively.

"What are you talking about?" Her face morphs into devastation. "I saw you two together hours ago. You're crazy about her. Vero amore. Real love!"

"It doesn't matter, Mamma," I grit through clenched teeth. "She went home. It's over. Just leave it be."

She presses her hands to her cheeks, shaking her head like a maniac. "It can't be over. Surely, you can apologise."

"Apologise for what?" Of course, my mother would assume this is all my fucking fault. I am the one with the fucked-up past, after all. Never mind the fact that Tilly found a reason to bolt before she even found out the whole truth. "For once, I didn't do anything."

"Then what didn't you do then?" she asks knowingly. She inhales sharply. "Did you tell her about—"

"No," I cut her off, not even wanting to think about those words. "Just forget it. It's over."

"Santino," she snaps, her tone acidic with barely concealed rage. "Tell me what happened, or I will get out the sauce stick and beat it out of you. I do not care that you are thirty-seven years old! What did you tell her?"

"I didn't tell her anything, and I won't tell her anything because she doesn't deserve that. She deserves something less fucked up than me." I sag against the counter, shaking my head in disgust.

My mother inhales a shaky breath. "But she loves you."

"She loves me because she doesn't know everything," I correct. "That's not real love."

"I know everything," she retorts, her voice cracking as tears well in her eyes. "I know everything more than anyone in this entire world. Do you think my love is not real?"

"No, but you're my mother."

"And who is Tilly?" She crosses her arms over her chest. "I saw a strong, determined girl who certainly knows her own mind. She loves you, Santino. That was very clear yesterday."

"It doesn't matter. I'm not doing this to her. I thought I could, and I can't. I just can't."

"What about you?" She pokes me in the chest. "Do you feel love?"

"Yes, I'm in love with her. I'm crazy about her," I bite back, hating that this conversation is cutting me open right in the middle of the deli.

"That's not what I was asking." She crosses her arms again and looks at me pointedly. "Do you love yourself?"

I scoff and roll my eyes, causing her to grab my chin and aggressively force me to look her in the eyes. "You are focusing on her reaction, but it is actually yours that I'm worried about."

"This isn't new information for me, Mamma." I jerk my face out of her hands and stand so she can't reach me anymore. "I've been living with this a long time."

"Not as long as me." She points at her chest. "And I promise you, what you're doing...it ends only one way...alone."

Nonno appears from the back, so I lean in to kiss her cheek. "I'm sorry, but I'm going back to London. I'll call you later."

Turning, I leave without looking back because I refuse to let my mother drag me down a path when all I'm trying to do is avoid thoughts of Tilly. I didn't think about her when I dropped her off at the train station last night, and I didn't think of her when I laid in that hotel room by myself. I'm not giving her any more of my time.

Thankfully, Nonno is silent during the car ride. It's clear he knows something is up, but he's respecting my brooding. I'm glad Nonno is the type that only speaks when he has something important to say. Something I should try to get better at, then maybe I wouldn't have found myself in this position.

When he pulls up to the train station, I reach into the back seat to grab my bag. I pull it forward, and he suddenly grips my arm, stopping me in my tracks.

"It is my fault," he huffs out, his brow furrowed.

"What is?"

"You and Cherry Two." He makes a breaking motion with his hands.

"How is it your fault?"

His lips shift off to the side as he exhales heavily through his nose. "I told you about your father. Maybe that was a big mistake."

A coldness settles over me at the direction this is going. "You told me because I was out of control and needed some direction in my life. And it worked. I wouldn't have gone to law school if it weren't for that conversation you and I had all those years ago."

He taps his chest, his jaw clenched with emotion. "It hurt me to tell you." His voice cracks as he makes a fist and pounds his heart. "It hurt your mother too. Maybe she was right, and you never should have known."

"Nonno, we don't have to talk about this. I'm not angry with you."

He holds his finger up to silence me. "Santino, la famiglia is your every day, always."

My eyes fall closed, and I nod. "I know this, Nonno."

"You've had many plants you water, but none you bring home to meet Cherry." He rubs his hand over the steering wheel like he's speaking about his most cherished possession…which might be partially true.

I exhale heavily. "I thought I could be honest with Tilly, but when it came down to it, I don't want her to know that about me. I don't want to hurt her."

"You're scared of hurting *your* heart, not hers." He points at my chest. "*You're* scared no one could love you. But look at me, Santino. Look into my eyes. Ti amerò per sempre."

My chest contracts with his words that I painfully repeat back to him. "I will love you forever too, Nonno."

"You have love." He sniffs and clears his throat, shaking away his emotion. "You remember that, and you can be brave and tell Cherry Two the truth. If she doesn't like it, it don't matter, because we are here." He shrugs like this is the easiest and most obvious solution in the world. But it's not. Nothing about this is easy.

The truth is, Tilly has a pattern of running when things begin to spiral out of her control. She ran when she got pregnant five years ago. She tried to pull away from me when Mac accused her of drinking again. Hell, she made us hide our relationship for weeks because she was so determined to have control. Now, she's run from me because I refuse to confess all my innermost secrets.

Well, this time, I'm not chasing her. I'm not breaking down her door to force her to talk to me. If this is how she deals with conflict, hiding our relationship in the beginning, then running away when things get too real…she was never going to be able to handle the heavy burden I carry. If she's the type to run now, she'll definitely be the type to run when she knows the truth. We're both better off this way.

CHAPTER 34

Tilly

“❝I WANT TO HOST A SURPRISE BABY SHOWER FOR FREYA AND MAC on Sunday. Do you think you could help me?” I ask Allie over the phone on Monday morning.

“Oh my God…I was just thinking of that! She wouldn’t let us plan anything once she was put on bed rest because Mac was so worried about the stress. But she’s doing so much better now!” Allie squeals so loudly in my ear I have to hold my mobile away from my face.

“She really is. I checked the Bethnal Green fixtures, and they have a home match on Saturday. I see that Arsenal plays Chelsea, so Camden should be in town too. After that, everyone is scattered for quite a while.”

“You’re so right,” Allie replies knowingly. “We have to do it this Sunday. And doing it now will make it more of a surprise for them, so it’s perfect.”

“I’m hoping you can help me with the guest list and a venue option? If it’s a lot of people, here won’t be big enough. Plus, it’ll kind of ruin the surprise if I start hanging streamers up.”

"My uncle Vaughn's house in Chigwell would be perfect!" she exclaims. "It's a mansion not too far out of London with tons of room for all the kids to play in the garden. Also! If I have Vaughn invite Mac and Freya to his weekly Sunday dinners, Mac won't be able to say no because well, Vaughn can be terrifying when he wants to be. I'm sure my uncle would be keen to help out! And if not, I'll sic his daughter, Vi, on him because no man in that family can say no to Vi."

"This sounds great, Allie! Okay, you get Vaughn sorted and send me the guest list. I'll handle everything else."

"This is going to be so much fun! A couple's shower with kids to truly terrorize Freya and Mac before their parental debut is just what the doctor ordered. Plus, the whole crew hasn't all been together in ages. What an amazing idea, Tilly!" she peals with a shrill laugh that has me smiling on my end.

Once we hang up, I immediately begin making a list of everything I'll need: decorations, game ideas, food and beverages—alcoholic and non-alcoholic for the mummy-to-be, kids, and me of course. Once that's complete, I pop into the nursery next door to my bedroom to take an inventory of everything Freya and Mac have bought already. I know once invites go out, everyone will want to know what to get them for presents. Since I can't exactly ask them to make a registry without spoiling the surprise, a proper snoop will have to do.

When I open the door to the nursery, I gasp at the transformation. Freya mentioned Mac had been busy in here, but I haven't been around enough to peek inside and see how it was coming along. It's positively stunning.

Freya said her inspiration was fresh farmhouse, and they pulled it off beautifully. A dark brown crib rests beneath the large west-facing window flanked with prints of horses and cows. A tall, rustic-looking wooden floor lamp by an antique rocking chair. The wall beside the chair features animal-print-covered shelves filled with old books my parents sent from our home. Bright bursts of colour are featured in the décor on the changing table, and I feel a knot form in my throat when I glance inside the crib and spot a baby vest folded neatly on top of the homemade quilt Freya's mum sent.

The moment my fingers touch the embroidered text of Jacob Fergus Logan across the front of the wee outfit, an unexpected sob bursts out of me, and I find myself gripping the crib for balance.

It's been two days since I left the Cotswolds, and I've managed to keep everything inside, not giving any ounce of time or energy to what happened there. I even checked into a hotel when I returned late Saturday night because I didn't want to go through the drama of telling Mac and Freya why I was home early.

I'm not ready to tell anyone what transpired between Santino and me when I've worked so hard to be this new, improved version of myself. To come slinking back home to my brother to say we're over after all that drama we went through is too humiliating to bear along with this heartbreak. I begged Mac to forgive Santino because I was madly in love with him, and now it's all just gone. In the blink of an eye.

I was so beside myself on that train ride home that an elderly man seated behind me asked if I wanted a hug. *A hug.* That nearly broke me. And to think that the stress of leaving Santino made me even consider digging into the hotel minibar I stayed at Saturday night just further confirms the fact that I was in way over my head. Falling for Santino and making myself vulnerable caused me to doubt everything I've been working for these past five years.

All so he could make a fool of me.

Looking back, I made a lot of mistakes with him. I let myself lose control, which is something I swore I would never do once I got sober. And him not trusting me was a trigger because I was vulnerable, and being vulnerable always leaves you open for attack. It's ridiculous because all along, I was working so hard to let my walls down for him when it was actually his walls that needed a swift boot in the arse.

And to use the excuse that he was protecting me? Fuck right off with that. I am my own person, and I decide what I can and cannot handle. His lack of understanding in that makes me wonder if anything he ever felt for me was real.

It was real for me.

It painfully still is.

My love for him is still so stupidly strong that I hate myself for not being able to turn it off like he so easily did. Perhaps that makes it obvious that his love wasn't real. No one who loves someone could just drop them off at the bloody train station to make the journey home alone. That is not love.

Regardless, I will get through this. I got myself sober on my own, I mourned the loss of a life I grew inside me on my own, so I can certainly get over a seven-week relationship with Santino Rossi.

"Tilly, tell your boyfriend to answer my texts!" Mac shouts from the lower level. His footsteps clomp up the stairs, and I quickly swipe my cheeks to hide any evidence of my tears. "The prat owes me ten quid from losing our bet Friday night."

Mac passes the open nursery door to head to my room but then pauses when he sees I'm in here, sitting in the rocking chair, holding wee Fergie's outfit in my hands.

I shoot him a sheepish smile. "This nursery is incredible, Mac."

He steps in and looks around, taking in the space with a twinkle in his eyes. "It's coming along. Freya's the brains. I'm just the brawn." He flexes his bicep and laughs. "What are you doing in here?"

I splay my hands out on the arms of the chair, rocking back and forth. "Just appreciating your efforts."

"Is that right?" His brows furrow as he watches me for a moment. "It looks to me like you're having a think over something." He leans on the changing table and crosses his arms. "Do you want to talk about it?"

I shake my head. "I'm fine. I'm just excited for you guys. Seeing all this set up makes it feel so real."

"Aye, sure." He rubs the back of his neck and gets an awkward look in his eyes. "Does it feel strange ever?"

"What?"

He shrugs and looks at the floor. "Thinking about the fact that you could have a wee five-year-old running around if things had turned out differently for you?"

My throat clamps up because I wasn't expecting that question. My miscarriage isn't something I'm comfortable discussing. Ever.

However, I suppose since opening up to Mac about everything that happened, perhaps pushing those boundaries would be good for me.

I exhale heavily and finally reply, "Not strange. Just…sad."

He nods thoughtfully. "You're sad still? Even though the arsehole who slept with you took advantage of you?"

My shoulders lift. "That wasn't the baby's fault." My chin wobbles, so I quickly look out the window and try to get control of myself.

Mac harumphs. "That bairn would have been lucky to have you, Tilly."

My eyes snap to his at the very surprising compliment from my brother. "That's a really nice thing to say, Mac." My voice is garbled with emotion that I can't even begin to hide.

"I'm known to be nice every once in a while. Every dog has his day, you know."

I croak out a laugh that relieves the pressure in my chest. "You're a very good dog."

He gets a tender look in his eye as he stares at me. "Your time will come, Tilly. I'm sure of it."

When he walks out, more tears fall because I fear now more than ever that my time will never come. And before Santino Rossi came back into my life, I was okay with that.

Now…I want more.

CHAPTER 35

Santino

Sunday: Lonely train ride home with a permanent scowl on my face. I hate everyone on this bloody train. And the fact that I was seated across from an elderly couple who held hands the entire journey feels like a giant, "Fuck off, Santino" from the universe.

Monday: I go to work early after sleeping like shit and stomping around in the middle of the night to hide anything relating to Tilly. I even throw away my bloody basil plant because I can't even stand to look at it anymore. All it does is remind me of her, and it can fuck right off.

Tuesday: Finally fall asleep only to wake in the middle of the night in a cold sweat after a horrid nightmare. The fact that I'm clutching Tilly's pillow and being painfully reminded of her sweet honey scent makes it impossible to go back to sleep. These sheets can fuck right off, too.

Wednesday: Continue ignoring calls from my mother. I know what she's going to say. Go find Tilly and apologise. Be open with her. Tell her your truth. The problem is, she doesn't need the truth. If she wouldn't stay with me without knowing this, then how can I ever expect her to stay with me after? Fuck off with that thought as well.

Thursday: I consider calling Tilly because I miss the sound of her voice but stop myself because she deserves better than me. The entire world deserves better than me. I drink my weight in whiskey.

Tilly

Monday: Baby shower prep. Happy thoughts only. Zero thoughts of Santino. Okay, one thought of Santino…and it's not a nice one. Cry myself to sleep.

Tuesday: I clean Freya and Mac's entire house and when I find a T-shirt of Santino's, I consider throwing it into the fireplace. Dodge Freya's questions about where Santino is by saying he's swamped at work. They have enough on their minds. They don't need to hear about my relationship drama. Spend the evening consoling a pint of ice cream and rewatching episodes of *Bridgerton* all while trying *not* to think about how much Santino is like the duke.

Wednesday: Baby shower invites all sent. Will hope and pray that no one will ask why Santino isn't at the party. Stop into Harrods to fill out employment paperwork. Hope by Monday morning, I'm back to my old self and ready to crush it at my new job. No thoughts of Santino. Okay, two thoughts…and they aren't nice.

Thursday: I miss him. Sleeping is impossible. I regret chucking that T-shirt of his in the bin. I consider drinking but know I won't give in to the pain like that. I want to call…desperately. But I can't. This is his mistake, and he has to be the one to fix this. Attempt to eat my weight in pasta instead.

Friday: Still no call from Santino. If he loved me, he would have rung me by now. Every single part of my body aches over that sad reality. Maybe it truly is over. Maybe it never should have started. Maybe I'm destined to be alone forever. *I love him.*

CHAPTER 36

Santino

"YOU'RE NOT SOME KNIGHT IN SHINING ARMOUR. YOU'RE JUST *a whore meister with a guilty conscience."*

Tilly's words from five years ago after I offered to be with her and her baby haunt me for the entire week. I hear them in the morning when I wake up. I think of them at night before I go to sleep. Even in my dreams, Tilly is there…screaming them at me over and over and calling me a monster. I even had a nightmare where every single woman I dated over the past few years showed up at my flat with Tilly and made sauce, and no matter how I told them to make it, they all ignored me, dumping in ridiculous ingredients like battery acid and cleaning products. My mind is a scary place.

Which is why I'm glad it's Friday. It's the end of quite possibly the longest week of my life. I'm tired, I'm grumpy, and I just want to go home. Even though I consider burning it to the ground at least every five minutes or so because every square inch of my flat smells like Tilly.

Christ, I'm a mess. I can't even sleep without her. When the fuck did that happen? I have been living on my own since I was twenty years old and one bad breakup has me tossing and turning? This isn't right.

It's best if I focus on more productive things, like work. Sadly, that's also a bit of a disaster because Zander Williams' mother has been dodging all of our scheduled calls, and I still don't know what I'm going to do about that whole situation.

I spoke to upper management about the status of Zander's contract, and they expect him to sign any day now. I tried to bring up some bullshit excuses for why I needed to look over the contract again, but they shook me off. They said he even approved the flat they selected for him in one of Hayden Clarke's properties. And unfortunately, I couldn't tell them that Hayden's wife, Vi Harris, is quite possibly Zander's half-sister so that might be awkward if they run into each other. *Christ, my whole life is fucked.*

I'm just getting ready to shut down my computer to drown my sorrows when Vaughn knocks on my office door. "Santino! I'm so glad I finally caught you. Where have you been the past few weeks?"

"Oh, I've been around," I rush out nervously like a guilty arsehole because I'm still avoiding him. "Well, not always in here. I was working in the conference rooms downstairs a bit."

"Conference rooms?" Vaughn frowns and crosses his arms over his chest. "Did you have a lot of meetings?"

"I did." I lie through my teeth because the truth is not an option. "How are you? How's the team doing?"

"Oh, they're doing okay, I suppose." Vaughn walks into my office and drops down onto one of the open seats in front of my desk. I'm nervous to be around him for fear of spilling the beans, but I have to say, seeing him again feels good. It's been hard staying away, and I respect the man too much to continue this farce for much longer.

He runs a hand through his grey hair and says, "The team's been a bit shaky early on. Losing to Arsenal was a big gut-check moment since that club's been struggling as well. I told the guys in the changing room that we need to look at this as a rebuilding year with all the players we've lost this season. I'm not coaching the team we are today. I'm coaching the team I know we can be someday. And if we keep working hard, we can hopefully keep our spot in the Premier League to show these arseholes that we belong here."

I nod and expel a soft laugh. "You are nowhere near retiring, are you?"

"Next season," he repeats the same line he's been telling all of us for years. "Tanner still needs me."

My brows lift. "Do you think Tanner will be your successor?"

"Christ, I don't know." He laughs at that. "He's actually a good coach when he's not fucking off. But you know none of that's up to me. It's up to the owners."

"Right." I click my pen thoughtfully, trying to picture Bethnal Green without Vaughn Harris. It's not a pleasant thought.

"Tell me about your life, Santino." He leans forward and slaps my desk. "I heard a little rumour about you." Vaughn taps his nose, and my eyes widen. "I heard that you're seeing Mac Logan's sister." His blue eyes crinkle with mischief, and I sag with relief that he's not referring to Zander Williams, but then the thought of Tilly turns my stomach to knots.

I rub the back of my neck. "Well...I was seeing her."

"Was?" Vaughn echoes. "Tanner just told me the news last week. What could have possibly happened in a week?"

"I wish I knew exactly." I run an exhausted hand through my hair, hating how even thinking about her hurts my insides.

Vaughn studies me for a long moment. "You don't look well."

"I'm fine." I tighten my tie, realising just now that I'm probably a bit of a mess after a long day. "It's just been a long week."

"How can I help?"

"Vaughn." With a laugh, I point at the door. "You have an entire bloody football club to manage out there. You don't need to come in here and be my therapist for the day. My work isn't suffering, I assure you."

"I'm not talking about work right now, Santino." Vaughn's face goes serious, giving me the same look he carries for a week after a loss. "We've been working together for nearly a decade now, and I've never seen you like this."

"Like what?"

"Devastated."

I blink back at him. "I'm not devastated."

"Son, you have dark circles under your eyes, and you look like you've lost weight. Hell, even your suit is a rumpled mess. I've never seen you in a wrinkled suit. You're completely gutted right now."

I glance down in horror as I realise I hadn't even looked at myself in the mirror before I came to work today. I don't even know if this suit was clean when I put it on. "I was running late."

"Bollocks," he scoffs, propping his elbows on his knees as he pins me with a hard glower. "Nearly every one of my children has botched up their relationships at some point. So, out with it, and let's see what can be done."

I rack my brain as I try to figure out how to tell my boss to kindly fuck off because any thoughts of Tilly Logan send me into an insomniac fit of despair. Instead, Jane Williams pops into my mind, so I decide to try another angle. "If someone had been hiding a secret from you…and they didn't tell you because they cared about you and were trying to protect you…that's okay, right? It's the decent, moral thing to do?"

Vaughn's brow furrows. "Are we talking about a child or an adult?"

"An adult, obviously." I swallow the lump in my throat.

Vaughn sits back and thinks for a moment. "Well, adults can make their own decisions in life. They've earned that right."

"Right…but let's say this person was legally bound not to share."

Vaughn frowns. "What does law have to do with love?"

My lips thin. "It's complicated."

"Well, uncomplicate it," Vaughn snaps, tapping his fist on his knee. His eyes go dark as he adds, "I lost the love of my life many years ago, Santino, and that was truly complicated. It changed me to my core. I was broken, hollow, angry. I wasn't right in the head. Nothing made sense without Vilma."

My chest contracts with those familiar words because I've been lost all week long without Tilly. Unsure what to do, what to eat, how to feel. Tilly Logan came storming back into my life, and I fell into a comfortable routine with her almost immediately like she was always meant to be here...*with me.*

Now she's out of my life, and *I miss her.* I miss the feel of her body against mine, and not just the sex. The sex was outstanding to be sure, but I miss touching her and watching her laugh when I tease her for being stubborn. I miss her calling me out for always laughing at my own jokes. I miss her twitching nose when she's overthinking something. I miss having her in my bed and watching her sleep. She looked so innocent in those moments. Untainted and untouched by life's horrors. Uncomplicated, just as she should be.

Christ, I'm in hell.

"What if what I'm doing is best for her, Vaughn?" I ask, no longer trying to make this conversation about Jane Williams because clearly, I'm not getting over Tilly anytime soon. "I don't want to drag Tilly down into my darkness. I want her to live a beautiful life, and selfishly, I want her to live it with me, but she has to trust that I know what's best for her in this particular situation."

Vaughn shakes his head sadly. "I used to think I knew what was best for Vilma." His nostrils flare as he sucks in a deep breath. "She was diagnosed with stage four cancer, and I forced her to do test after test, surgery after surgery. I made her see specialists and try different therapies. I made her do everything I thought was right and do you know what happened in the end? I ruined our love." His voice trembles at the end, and I can see the haunting pain and torment in his eyes.

It's like looking in a fucking mirror.

I swallow the painful knot in my throat. "But you were only trying to help. You loved her."

Vaughn flinches. "Santino mate, I was trying to help myself because I wasn't accepting reality. And trust me when I tell you that forcing your partner down a path that you think is right isn't what love is." He pins me with a serious look. "Love is sharing your joys and your sorrows. For better or worse."

My jaw clenches as I shake my head with disgust. "You don't know my sorrows. It's too much for me, let alone anyone else."

Vaughn leans forward. "Santino, my wife died of a cancer that wouldn't leave her body. If you have the ability to cut your cancer out and be free of it, you need to do that and trust that the love you and Tilly share will be strong enough to heal that wound."

His words have an immediate effect and they resonate so similarly to Tilly's last week. *"I've cut myself open and bled for you, Sonny. You got to be the bandage that mended me. Now you won't let me even see your wound?"*

My mother was right. I've been so concerned with Tilly's reaction; I've been ignoring the truth that I'm the one with the issue. I'm the one with the wound that I'm too scared to show anyone. I have to find the strength to forgive myself, or I'll never be able to be honest with Tilly. And I have to trust that Tilly won't do what I fear most and run away again.

My heart thunders in my chest as I finally reply, "Thank you, Vaughn. You've given me a lot to think about."

"Well, don't think too long." Vaughn taps my desk and stands. "Did you know Sunday dinner this weekend is being transformed into a baby shower?" He laughs and shrugs. "Either way, I expect to see you there."

CHAPTER 37

Tilly

Vaughn Harris' property is a beautiful, white-pillared house in the eastern suburbs of London. The grand staircase and marble flooring that greet you when you walk in are a bit intimidating, but after I followed Allie down the hall and turned left through the kitchen doors, I could tell nothing about this family was stuffy.

The warm, inviting space in the gourmet kitchen was meant for function, not fashion as the caterers have set up most of the food on the long kitchen island. Their eat-in kitchen is bigger than most people's formal dining rooms with a table that seats fourteen. The entire space opens up through several glass doors into the back garden with loads of patio furniture and everything you'd expect to see in a footballing family's house—goal posts, flags, and toys…loads and loads of outdoor toys for the children.

So…many…children.

"They're going to call the police," I gasp, my hand covering my mouth as I look at the madness spread out in Vaughn's garden. "Should we move everyone inside? Surely someone can hear this and is going to file a noise complaint." I turn wide eyes to Allie, who's holding a crying Neo on her hip.

She waves me off. "We do this all the time. It's fine!"

"You guys do this every Sunday?"

"It varies depending on schedules, but a lot of us make it every week. Be happy it's not raining!" She begins walking off to deal with an unhappy Neo.

Good God, I'd be sunk if it was raining. I shake my head in astonishment as I try to make sense of every person who has arrived at Vaughn's house this fine Sunday autumn afternoon. First, there was the oldest Harris brother, Gareth, and his wife, Sloan, from the boutique. They were a welcome sight because they arrived early and their tween daughter, Sophia, offered to help me with the decorations. Their toddler son, Milo, went tearing off up the grand staircase, and I haven't seen him since.

The next ones to show up were Booker, the goalkeeper and youngest Harris Brother, and his wife, Poppy, along with their twin boys, whose names escape me right now. Teddy and Oliver, I believe? Sweet names but those two little terrors have destroyed over half of the decorations Sophia and I have put up. Freya and Mac aren't due to arrive for another hour, and I fear nothing will be left if I don't find a cage to stick those two little demons in.

Deep breaths, Tilly. Deep breaths.

Camden, Indie, Tanner, and Belle all showed up together, each holding a child. I hadn't really thought about the adult to child ratio when I told Allie to invite whomever she thought Freya would want here, and now I'm sort of wondering why there are no nannies in sight. Aren't all these people loaded footballers and doctors? Where's the hired help?

When Vi Harris and her husband, Hayden, show up with just one child, I actually sag with relief. At least one Harris sibling isn't popping out children on an annual basis.

Added to the mix is Hayden's brother, Theo, and Leslie. They have their daughter, Marisa, in tow.

I should have ordered a bigger bouncy castle.

When my parents walk in the door, I nearly burst into tears because I've missed them terribly, and I need their help so fucking much.

"Tilly!" my mother, Jean, hugs me tightly, her warm embrace like a childhood memory all wrapped up in a touch. I was thrilled when they found a flight out yesterday to be here for the shower. They stayed in a hotel last night and are leaving late tonight, so it's a quick trip for them. They wanted a chance to see Freya before the baby was born, though, and plan to be back for a much longer visit after the birth.

She pulls back and touches my curled hair. "My God, you look stunning! And look at this beautiful blue dress. So feminine for you. Are you actually wearing heels?"

"Yeah, I guess," I reply with a laugh, sliding my hands over my hips. The dress is a piece from Kindred Spirits. A crushed velvet knee-length design with bell sleeves and a cinched satin waist. I playfully shove my mother's curious hands away and turn to my father, James, with a big smile. "Hiya, Dad."

"Hiya, wee lass." He pulls me close, cloaking me in the familiar scent of his Brute cologne. "What a fun party you have planned here for Macky and Freya."

"And I'm pretty sure they'll be surprised." I pull back and smile at the party already well underway. "Mac was cross at me for not coming with them to Sunday dinner here today because it's a sacred Harris tradition, but I told them I had loads of things to do before I start my new job tomorrow."

"Oh honey, we're so proud of you," my mother says, still stroking my hair affectionately.

My dad nudges me with his elbow. "Mum made us go shopping at Harrods before we came here. It's a very nice store, lass. A bit posh for my taste, but I'm sure you'll fit right in."

I giggle. "Thanks. They've been amazing with Freya's pet line deal. Everything is sorted and ready to go, and I'm just thrilled I was able to be useful for them."

"What's this I hear about a lad you're seeing?" Mum whispers coyly, her lips turning up into a sneaky smile. "Mac says he's the lawyer for the team and not the bawbag we all thought he was. I don't really remember knowing anything about a Santino Rossi, so can you explain what he's talking about?"

"Mum," I cut her off, shaking my head. "I'm sorry, but...Santino and I aren't a thing anymore."

Her face falls. "What?"

"And actually, Mac and Freya don't know yet, so if you could keep it quiet, I would really appreciate it. I just don't want to spoil their big day today."

"Do I need to have a talk to the lad?" My dad looks around, his eyes narrow slits. "Is he here?"

"No, Dad. He's not here. Relax. I don't need anyone to talk to him...it just...didn't work out." My throat hurts with that painful thought as I plaster on a smile for them.

My mother sighs. "Well, I'm just happy to hear you're finally dating again. If you found one, you can surely find another."

"Mum, I'm not searching for my soul mate. It was just a casual thing."

My parents both look crestfallen, but I don't have time to nurture their broken hearts over my broken heart, so I drag them over to where Vaughn and Freya's parents are seated at the proper grown-up table. Freya's parents left at five o'clock this morning to be here for the shower, so I know she's going to be thrilled to see them.

Finally, the time has come for Freya and Mac's arrival, so I hurry everybody inside from the back garden, telling them all to hush, much to the children's displeasure. Well, not all of them. Rocky and Sophia are actually holding my hands as we hear the front door open, and they decide we should crouch to brace for their entrance.

I frown when I hear no voices because Mac and Freya do nothing quietly. When the door to the kitchen opens, my heart lurches up into my throat because it's not my brother and his wife coming in.

It's Santino.

My legs turn to jelly as I take in the sight of him because I did not expect him to be here. He's dressed in a crisp black suit with no tie. He's left a few buttons open at the top of his white shirt, and his olive skin is on display, causing the spit in my mouth to dry up. His eyes almost instantly connect with mine, and we both freeze for a moment. I swear it feels like the entire universe is suspended in time as my heart thunders like tribal drums.

It feels like it's been seconds and years since I've seen him all at the same time. His face has a haunted look about it, and his suit doesn't hug him as tightly as it normally would.

Suddenly, I realise the entire room is staring at us, and our quiet moment is thwarted when Tanner bellows, "Get out of the way, Santino. Fuck!"

"Fuck!" one of the little toddlers repeats loudly, the sound echoing off the marble flooring.

Several voices begin chastising Tanner, and the kids all begin to giggle as they parrot the word their uncle just said. It's a chorus of fucks echoing down the hall with no matter of control whatsoever.

Suddenly, Mac and Freya emerge through the kitchen door with wide, confused eyes. About half of us notice and yell, "Surprise!" It goes silent for a moment, and another child says *fuck!* to fully punctuate the disaster of the moment.

I'm horrified.

"What's going on?" Freya asks, looking adorable in a long floral maternity dress as she grips Mac's arm and glances around curiously. "What's the surprise?"

I step forward, Sophia and Rocky still gripping my hands like steel traps, and now it seems we've gained a train of a few of the other girls...Marisa, Bex, and Joey. "We're throwing you guys a baby shower." I smile brightly, and my face falls when Freya begins blubbering.

"Don't cry!" I exclaim, glancing at my brother nervously, who... oh, for heaven's sake...he's crying too.

"I have to cry!" Freya proclaims, waving her hands in front of her red face. "I'm pregnant, and this is basically all I do now!"

"Fuck," Mac growls, dabbing at his own eyes. "I'm not pregnant. I'm just touched."

Everyone laughs at that, and guess what?
More fucks from the children.

Thank God this is a forgiving family.

The party begins mostly in the back garden, but people drift in and out for nibbles. The kids are all wild and at least partially contained in the bouncy castle while the adults enjoy the food and drink. I get the silly games going, doing my best to ignore Santino's presence, which is easy because he seems to be avoiding me also.

The best game I organised involves the guys putting balloons under their shirts and racing to see who can tie their shoes the fastest. Of course, the Harris Brothers one-up my game idea and add football into the mix. Now, not only do they have to tie their shoes with the balloon under their belly, but they have to dribble a football across the garden and do a header into the goal before dropping on their bellies and popping their balloons.

It's actually a little disturbing, and when I think about the fact that these are professional, highly-paid athletes running around with fake pregnant bellies while their father yells at them not to get injured, the entire scene takes on a life of its own. I end up nearly peeing myself from laughing so hard. Freya does pee herself. But it's fine. The mummies all say it's totally normal.

CHAPTER 38

Santino

WASN'T PREPARED FOR MANY THINGS TODAY. I WASN'T PREPARED
to stuff a balloon under my dress shirt. I wasn't prepared for Tanner
to challenge me to a goal post competition. I wasn't prepared to go
to a store and buy the first baby gift of my entire life. I got three cases
of diapers because everything online said that was a sensible gift idea.

And I wasn't prepared for how beautiful Tilly Logan would look
today.

She looks even more stunning than when I saw her at that charity gala over two months ago. I can't believe she can look so beautiful
and so unaffected when I've been a wreck for eight days straight now.

It's awful. My bed still smells like her because I refuse to change
my sheets. My flat is still covered in items she left behind, a tooth-
brush, some clothes, a few stray photographs she thought I'd like of
street art that I've yet to frame. I can't bring myself to box up any of
it. I would probably need to burn it all if I ever want to attempt to get
Tilly out of my mind.

But I don't want her out of my mind. I want her in my mind, in my arms, in my bed…and in my life.

As I watch her from across the grass, laughing with all the other women, part of my old doubt starts creeping in. Maybe she's better off without me. Maybe coming here was a mistake.

But then I recall playing football with her at Tower Park, and watching her appreciate random drawings on a phone box. I recall our morning showers together and how some days, we didn't even have sex in the shower because we were too busy talking. Now, she's right here in front of me, and all I can think is how much I miss her and want to touch her. The aching heaviness in my chest grows more intense the more I watch her.

God, I love her.

Vaughn's words resonated with me all weekend. And like it or not, my heart grew when I fell in love with her, and not being with her means that there's an emptiness inside me that I hate more than my demons. I have to talk to her.

Tilly goes inside for the tenth time, and I finally work up the nerve to talk to her. I see her walk out of the kitchen, and I hurry to follow her into the long entryway hallway that I came in.

"Tilly." My voice echoes in the cavernous expanse of Vaughn's home. "Can we talk?"

She hesitates by the staircase, her back turned to me, her shoulders raised. "I was just going to grab something in my car."

Suddenly, Booker's twins come tearing through the kitchen doorway, running into me and doing quick spin moves as they recover and dart out the front door.

When they're gone, Tilly turns on her heel, hitting me with her big blue eyes that have been the highlight of my dreams this past week. "Can it wait until later?"

I open my mouth to reply, and a loud flush echoes from the hallway loo between Tilly and me. A moment later, Booker's wife, Poppy, emerges, looking back and forth between us. "Sorry…just had to use the toilet."

"It's fine," Tilly says with a smile. She hooks her thumb toward the door. "I just saw your boys go out the front door in case you need to know."

She rolls her eyes and huffs. "Booker was supposed to be watching them." She moves towards the door but pauses briefly. "You know there's this really cute playhouse out in the woods behind the house. The kids aren't allowed back there alone yet because the little ones are too little, and then they throw fits if some get to go and not all. It's a disaster for everyone. Anyways…if you guys wanted some privacy, there's a path alongside the house that will take you right to it. Just go out the front door here to the left. You can't miss it."

"Thanks, but we're fine," Tilly states with a wave of the hand.

"No, we're not," I reply, firmly stepping closer to her.

Poppy's eyes widen. "Right. I'm just going to go make sure my children aren't trying to drive a car away again."

She hurries out the front door. My jaw is tight when Tilly looks at me with an angry glare and a twitch to her nose. I urge her again. "I really want to talk to you."

"Santino, now is not a good time." She looks away, her eyes warring with something.

"Why not?" I ask. "Presents and cake are done with. Everyone's just talking now. You really can't give me a few moments of your time? I'm that big of a monster to you?"

Her face looks hurt as she looks back at me. "I never called you a monster."

"Then please…just…come out back with me."

She exhales heavily, her eyes full of regret as she nods and turns on her heel to march out the front door without a glance back at me. I jog to catch up to her, shocked she can walk so quickly in those wedges she's wearing. My eyes can't help but drink in her arse and legs as she opens the gate to walk down the narrow path to exactly what Poppy described.

It's a storybook type of cottage surrounded by old trees and giant fallen leaves. There's a table outside, and it's obviously a well-loved area for the Harris kids.

Tilly stands in front of it and turns on her heel to face me.

"Should we go inside?" I suggest with a laugh, gesturing to the small front door.

"This is private enough," she snaps, her tone crisp as she crosses her arms over her chest.

I breathe out slowly and unbutton my jacket. "You're not going to make this easy on me, are you?"

"Why should I?" she barks, her eyes wide with fury. "You were an eejit to me last weekend. You let me get on that train and go home by myself at night. You didn't text or phone to see if I made it safely. You just let me walk out of your life without even a look back. Were you even bothered this week? Or was it just another week at the office laughing about how another two-month chump bites the dust?"

"Tilly," I reply with a heavy sigh. The ache in my body over how awful I was to her makes it difficult for me to stay upright.

"Answer me," she demands, stamping her foot and crunching the dry leaves beneath her.

My jaw clenches with frustration. "Of course I was bothered."

"Well, you don't look it," she scoffs, pointing at my suit. "You look perfect as usual. Perfect suit, perfect job, perfect family…even your stupid basil plant is probably still perfect."

"You're one to talk," I retort, jerking my head back. "You're obviously dressed to impress someone today, and I can't imagine it's Freya and Mac's baby. Is Belle's brother meeting you later?"

"Oh my God, jealous much?"

"Yes," I growl back, not even trying to conceal my anger. "I've never seen you wear heels before."

"Who cares what's on my feet?"

"I care," I exclaim, my body tensing with the ache to touch her now that she's right in front of me. "I care about everything pertaining to you, Tilly. And you have to know how sorry I am for last weekend. Thinking of you alone on that train fucking killed me. But I was a mess. I was terrified of losing you all while pushing you away. I have no excuse other than I'm a fucking arsehole."

"Facts," she snaps, her voice waffling as her eyes fill with tears. "You've been an arsehole, and I've been stupid. These past few weeks

I've shared all my scary, insecure bits and labeled myself the messed-up one while you got to sit there and be perfect with your secrets."

"I'm not perfect," I reply, my voice a whisper as the pain of my truth rises to the surface. I step closer to her and inhale deeply, willing myself to be brave like Nonno said. I'm a thirty-seven-year-old man who still needs my nonno's voice in my head for confidence. "My whole adult life I've been trying to portray myself in a certain way…a man who succeeds, who sets goals, who can take care of anything and anyone. I did this to prove to myself that I don't feel any shame. And I didn't feel it. Ever. Not even with any of the women I dated these past few years.

"But Tilly, the closer you and I became and the more I fell in love with you…the more I began to feel terrified that you knowing this truth about me could change how you looked at me. And I'm sorry, but I got caught up in this idea of perfection between us. A happy, carefree life. I loved that you thought I was perfect. It fed my soul. It made me feel alive and pure and worthy of a beautiful life with you."

"You are worthy, you arsehole!" she cries, her eyes red-rimmed. "How could you think you're not?"

"Because I'm not perfect and watching you leave me made me realise that all over again." My nostrils flare as I prepare to add the next bit. "I'm utterly terrified of telling you this truth because if you run from me again, I don't think I'll survive it."

"Santino, I don't want to run!" Tilly croaks, her voice garbled in her throat. "I've been miserable this week without you too. I've thrown myself into planning this baby shower because to sit down and think about what my life will look like without you is a pain that will break me…again."

She steps closer and cups my face in her hands. Her touch that I've been yearning for sends shockwaves through my entire body.

Her watery-blue eyes are laser-focused on mine when she says, "I know running has been a pattern of mine because accepting help makes me feel weak and incapable, but I've never felt stronger and more inspired than when I'm with you."

I inhale a cleansing breath, my trembling hands lifting to mirror her embrace as I begin to say what I came here to say, "Tilly, I want to tell you everything—"

"Just wait," she cuts me off, her eyes blinking rapidly. "Don't tell me now. Don't tell me under pressure or because you think I'm going to leave if you don't. I want you as you are today. And if whatever you're living with is something you want to keep in the dark, I will support you."

"Are you sure?" I ask, my brow furrowing as I search her face for any doubt.

"Yes, Sonny. I love you." She presses her lips to mine in a chaste kiss, then pulls back with a sniffle. "Unconditionally, I love you."

For a few glorious seconds, I let those words sink in and marinate in my soul. I let them spread their wings and get comfortable because they might just be the best words anyone has ever said to me.

Inhaling deeply, I slide my fingers into her hair and pull her lips to mine. She lets out a soft whimper before wrapping her arms tightly around my neck and yanking me close. We lose our footing, stumbling backwards as I catch our fall against the playhouse with one hand braced for support.

With her back pressed firmly against the wood, our lips part, breaths frenzied as our eyes rove over each other's faces before crashing into one another again. I grab tightly on her side, my hand skating down to grab her bottom as I cloak her body with mine, relishing in the feel of her touch once again.

I nip at her lower lip, forcing her mouth to open as I plunge my tongue against hers. She moans again, lifting her leg to my hip and causing my cock to thicken in my trousers. Her hands skate wildly through my hair, like she's going to rip it all out as we attack each other like two starving animals in the wilderness.

"Fuck me!" a voice booms from behind us, and we rip apart, turning to see Mac standing there looking…well…not well. "What the fuck are you two doing snogging out here by a wee playhouse? You could get arrested for this in public parks, you know!"

We fight to recover our breaths as we straighten ourselves out.

Tilly's voice is hoarse when she replies, "Did you need something, Mac?"

Mac continues to cringe at the sight of us. "Yes, but currently, I'm having a huge internal battle not to come tearing over there and kick the teeth out of Santino's face right now for snogging my wee sister at my wife's baby shower."

"Mac," Tilly warns.

"Aye, I know, I know. We're 'Team Santino.'" He growls an unimpressed noise, clearly forgetting all about our bromance status from before. He expels a loud huff. "I came to get you because the caterers are here to pick up their stuff, and no one knows where the punch bowls went. The wee hellion twins had something to do with it, if you ask me."

Tilly runs a hand through her tousled hair, picking out a sliver of wood that was lodged in there before begrudgingly detaching herself from my embrace. "I'm coming."

She moves to walk away from me, but I quickly fall into step beside her, combing my fingers through hers. I lost her once. I will not lose her again. She bites her lip and shoots me a smirk that says everything I need to hear. Meanwhile, Mac makes a puking noise. "You two need to get control of yourselves, or I really am going to be sick."

CHAPTER 39

Tilly

A LIST OF THINGS THAT ARE THE ABSOLUTE WORST AFTER YOU make up with your boyfriend and want to rip his clothes off:

1. Baby shower clean-up
2. Monstrous kids who won't get out of the bouncy castle for the nice men to take down their equipment
3. Mummies and Daddies who look at the bouncy castle as a free babysitter so don't seem bothered by said monstrous children
4. Professional footballers who should be in training but seem determined to drink every last drop of alcohol so none goes to waste
5. Friendly seniors who fancy a nice cup of tea after said baby shower
6. Overeager parents who linger for far too long nearly missing their flight home just because they can't stop talking to my boyfriend

Okay…that one wasn't so bad. In fact, it was quite nice.

After we tracked down the punch bowls from where little Teddy and Oliver had stashed them underneath some parked cars, I marched Santino over to my parents and introduced him as my boyfriend. Neither of them missed a beat as they stood up and cooed that they'd heard so much about him. My dad tried to score free legal advice, and my mum asked Santino what size vest he wore. She fancies herself quite the knitter, and it's said to be a cold winter in London this year. It was exactly what I would have expected.

And maybe even a little what I've always dreamed of.

When everyone finally clears out, I follow Santino back to his flat, and I swear the bastard is driving slower than Freya's parents. I know we need to be careful because it's nighttime, but we've been apart for over a week. I want Santino naked and in bed right bloody now.

As soon as we enter his flat, I grab him by the jacket and haul his lips to mine. This isn't going to be the type of sweet, touchy-feely makeup sex where we whisper how sorry we are and how much we missed each other. I'm not going to shed any tears as I imagine how awful my life would have been without him. This will be a desperate, frantic fuck that I need more than I need my next breath.

We're not even out of his entryway before I strip his jacket off him and struggle to get my heels off. I fumble with the buttons on his shirt as his large arms wrap around me to undo the zip on my back. The noise is an erotic precursor of much more to come. When the dress slips off my shoulders and pools down at my feet, he hums his approval as he takes in my black bra and knickers.

God, I've missed his noises. *But I didn't say it out loud, so it doesn't count as the touchy-feely kind of shagging.*

By the time we're both naked, I'm gripping his cock while also fretting about how far away the bedroom is. He seems to be on the same page because his next move involves cupping my arse and propping me on a small entryway table by the front door. I'm panting as I reach down and position his cock at my centre. As soon as it's where it belongs, he leans back and stares down as he grips my hips and thrusts hard into me, not even swiping my centre to see if I'm ready for him.

I'm always ready.

His eyes are rapt with fascination as he watches himself disappear inside me, his gaze shifting back and forth from my face to my breasts to where we connect. His thrusts are quick and unrelenting, his eyes roving and appreciative. I fucking love it. My cries of pleasure are loud as he pulls back over and over. I squeeze my legs around him and undulate my hips to meet his, my clitoris throbbing as he thumbs it in a small circular motion while rocking in and out of me.

When I pull him close to connect our mouths, my lips desperate to feel the chiseled scruff on his jaw, my nipples graze over his chest, and he breaks our kiss to tongue my puckered peaks. He drags his lips up my chest and along my collarbone before whispering against the hollow of my neck, "Resta con me per sempre." He thrusts hard inside me again, his breath laboured with need.

I grab his hair and force him to look at me with those half-hooded dark eyes of his. "What does that mean?" I ask, my eyes blinking back at him curiously.

His Adam's apple slides down his throat as he hits me with a heart-stopping look of vulnerability. "Stay with me forever."

With those words, my inner walls clench around his shaft, and my body throttles into climax, causing my head to fall against his chest as I hold on to him for support and try not to cry.

CHAPTER 40

Santino

"L ET'S SAY WE DIDN'T BREAK UP. WE JUST HAD AN EIGHT-DAY fight," Tilly says, her voice sweet in the darkness of my flat with only the blue hue of the city lights streaming in through the window.

My hand is teasing her damp hair, my body working to commit a muscle memory of how she feels lying against my chest.

After our quick shag, we showered, shagged again, got dressed for bed in my closet, shagged again, and now we're here…sexually spent and post-morteming our breakup like a proper couple.

"Can we make our fights shorter in the future?" I ask, reaching around to hug her close.

"Or…here's a wild idea…" She slides off my chest and lies on her belly, her feet kicking up behind her. "We just stop fighting full stop."

I laugh and roll on my side to face her, pressing a finger to her twitching nose. "You're a stubborn Scot, so there's no chance of that happening."

"Fair point." She giggles and looks so innocent at this moment.

The makeup of the day gone with her slender frame drowning in one of my white T-shirts. She's utterly perfect and having her back here with me is everything I wanted.

But not everything I need.

"Tilly."

"Yes?"

"I want to tell you what happened."

She frowns at me in the dim light. "I said you don't have to, Sonny."

"I know." I swallow the knot in my throat. "But lying here with you, being happy while having this on my shoulders…it taints it. I don't want to be with you and hide this part of me."

She nods slowly and cups my jaw in her hand, her thumb rubbing tenderly along my cheek. "Okay then. If you're sure."

I inhale deeply and roll over to sit up and prop my back on the headboard. The darkness of the room is comforting…like I can hide myself while forcing the words out.

My jaw is taut when I say, "My mother was raped when she was sixteen years old. And I'm the product of that rape."

Tilly inhales audibly, her lips parted as she processes that information. She reaches out to touch me. "Sonny, I'm so—"

"Please, don't give me your pity." My body tenses as I pull back and grip the blanket on my lap, wishing I had a shirt on right now because I feel naked in more ways than one. "Sympathy makes it all so much worse."

She lowers her hand and nods slowly. "Can I ask what happened?"

I dig deep in my soul for the courage that I thought would come easily when I found the woman I loved. I thought sharing this part of me would be cleansing and I'd feel seen for the first time in my life. I was wrong. The fact that I love her just makes it ten times harder.

I swallow a knot in my throat. "It was a person who my mum went to school with. It happened at a party, I guess. My family knew his family, but they denied it ever happening. My grandparents tried to go to the police, but it was a he said/she said situation, and there just wasn't a case. My family lived in a small village outside of Venice, and people talked. Zio Antonio was so angry over what happened, he came back from England and beat up the boy who did it. He was sixteen, so Antonio would have gone to prison for assaulting a minor, but the family didn't press charges…which only confirms the fact that they knew what their son did, and they didn't hold him accountable for it."

Tilly inhales sharply, and I force myself not to make eye contact with her, or I know I won't be able to finish.

"When they discovered a few weeks later that my mum was pregnant, they decided to leave Italy and start a new life away from all the whispers. Nonno said my mother was so terrified she couldn't even walk the streets alone in the middle of the day. So they joined my zio in the Cotswolds and hoped that a fresh start in a new country would help her.

"Nonno said they discussed options…abortion, adoption, even giving me to my uncle and aunt. My grandparents are pretty devout Catholics, but my grandfather said he would have supported my mother if she wanted to end the pregnancy. But my mother chose to keep me. She said there was never a doubt in her mind.

"I never knew anything about this when I was a child. My mother just said that my father wasn't a good man and we were better off without him. When I was really young, I used to look at footballers' faces on the telly and pray so hard that I belonged to one of them, and any minute now, they were going to come in and save me from my horrible mother.

"The older I got, the more I resented her for not telling me who he was. I thought I had a right to make my own opinion. It felt like she was keeping him from me, and I was angry with her every day for that. Then she married Bart, and I was a sullen teenager, jealous that little Angela got to grow up with two parents playing happy family. I felt like an outcast.

"I went to university in London and hoped that I could start a new life, but I couldn't seem to focus. I was still always so angry. I started failing all my courses, and was on academic probation. It was then I decided enough was enough…I was going to find my father.

"I came back to Bourton and demanded Nonno tell me his name since my mother wouldn't. I told him if he didn't tell me, I was going to quit school. Keep in mind, I was the first in my family to go to university, so when I said these words, they were like a dagger to Nonno's heart. They had saved every penny they earned at the shop to help pay for my education.

"That's when he sat me down and told me my father was a monster and a rapist who wasn't worth my time or attention. I felt like I'd been sucker punched. I felt dirty and wrong…like I had a monster's blood in my veins. Then Nonno started crying. My stoic, straight-faced grandfather wept right in front of me. He said I was destined for bigger things because when you begin your life in tragedy, you must end your life in fortune. And the best way to get back at the man who hurt my mother was to be better than him. Make something of myself. Be successful. Finish school. Don't let him win. He said my mother didn't let him win and neither should I."

I glance up and see tears falling freely down Tilly's face. She quickly blinks them away, trying her hardest to remain composed. My hands ache as I realise they have been clenched into tight fists the entire time.

I try to relax them and continue, "As horrible as it was to hear all of that, it fucking worked. I turned my life around, finished law school at the top of my class, and landed a job with Bethnal Green."

Tilly sniffs loudly, her voice garbled when she inquires, "Have you ever tried to find him?"

"That rapist?" I ask, my jaw clenching with anger, hating the taste of that word in my mouth, but knowing he doesn't deserve any other label. "No, and I never will. I spoke to my uncle about it, and he said even breaking the bastard's face didn't relieve the pain in his heart over what happened. And in many ways, I think going to find him would be a betrayal to my mother. She says her life is exactly how it was meant to be, and she has a son to remind her of that every day."

Tilly's chin wobbles with unconcealed emotion. "That is exactly what I would expect her to say."

I smile fondly and nod. "I thought finding a good job and being successful would be all I'd need to achieve in life to prove to myself that I'm more than where I came from." I swallow the knot in my throat. "Until you, Tilly."

"Me?" she croaks.

My heart thunders in my chest at her confused expression. "When I came to your flat that night, and you told me what had happened to you, it was the first time in my life that I cared about anyone other than myself. Before that moment, I'd never wanted anything long-term with a woman because I never wanted to be close enough to have to tell someone that I'm the spawn of a rapist."

"Santino—" Tilly says my name sadly, but I shake her off.

"But when you were in your situation, I realised I was capable of more in life. I could care for you and make a child's life better. I realise now that that was my white knight shit that you rightly called me out on. And I wasn't offering to help for the right reasons then. I was offering because I wanted to give a baby the father I never had. But that wasn't my responsibility. It was yours. Just like it was my mum's."

Tilly chokes back a sob and swipes haphazardly at her tears. "So, what does this all mean for us now?"

My face softens as I look at her and realise that her coming back into my life wasn't an accident. We may have started off on the wrong foot five years ago, but that past brought us here today when we're both changed and better and ready for a real life. It all happened for a reason.

I reach out and tuck a strand of hair behind her hear. She inhales sharply, waiting on bated breath for what I'm about to say next. "It means that I know now that I don't want a baby with you to save you. I want a baby with you because I love you."

"What?" she exclaims, her eyes wide, her voice a whisper. "You want a baby?"

"Yes."

"You said you weren't sure about kids."

"I lied."

"Santino, this is crazy." She sits up on her knees beside me and scrubs her hands over her face. "We just got back together, and you've unloaded a very heavy weight you've been carrying for a long time. How could you possibly be thinking about babies with me?"

"We just had an eight-day fight," I correct. Reaching out to hold her hand, I twine my fingers through hers, feeling a freedom in my heart that I've never experienced before. "And nothing in that fight diminished my feelings for you. Did what I just tell you change your feelings for me?"

"No," she gasps, looking horrified. Her eyes pin me with sincerity as she cups my face, forcing me to look into her eyes. "My God, Santino. Not even a little. How on earth could you ever think I would love you less after knowing that?"

Her question causes my body to unfurl a pain that I've buried deep inside me and desperately tried to ignore. A pain of not knowing how much of that monster actually lives inside me.

"I've struggled to shake this feeling of shame that I wasn't created from an act of love…that my existence is because of a traumatic experience for my mum by the hands of a monster." I lift my eyes to Tilly, a stinging in my nose as I add, "I know my family loves me, but they're obligated to love me. That's why after you left, I became determined to find a partner in life that could accept me knowing my full story. That felt like the only way I could ever forgive myself."

Tilly inhales sharply, her eyes welling with tears as she sighs. "Oh, Sonny."

I clear my throat. "Then when you and I got together again… and I…*fell in love with you*…" My voice trembles, and I have to take a deep breath in for strength. "The stakes suddenly became so much higher, and the idea that you could look at me with shame was a reality I was too terrified to face."

Our eyes hold each other for a second before Tilly throws herself against my chest, cinching her arms around my neck as she shakes with emotion and mumbles against my shoulder, "Santino, you've got it all wrong." She pulls back to look at me, and her tears cause my own to fall. Tears that I rarely shed. She swipes at my cheeks with her thumbs and adds, "I know what happened to your mum is awful, but don't forget that your existence is the product of countless love stories before that. Nonno and Nonna, their parents before that, and their parents before that. All those love stories paved the way for your wonderful existence. I'm sorry that happened to your mother, but I'm happy you're here, and nothing will ever change that."

Her words have an instant effect, and I grab her behind the neck and kiss her firmly, harshly, desperately. I want to feel the weight of her, the reality of her, the comfort of her. I want to commit this moment to memory as our lips dance together.

My mother has said similar words to me, Nonno, Nonna too... even Bart. They've all told me that my existence is important and special. But coming from the woman I love. Coming from Tilly Logan, someone I can see spending my whole life with...it's everything I've been searching for. She knows me now, body and soul, and I will do everything in my power to stay worthy of her.

I pull back, my breath shaky as I murmur against her lips, "You have no idea how much I needed to hear that, Tilly."

Her fingers comb through my hair as she presses her forehead against mine. "I'll say it to you every day. I'm amazed by you. You've carried this all on your own your whole adult life and if you think that story makes you any less perfect to me, you're dead wrong."

I hum with pleasure, feeling lighter, freer, and more at ease than I've ever felt. The corners of my mouth curl up as my eyes lift to hers. "I guess I'll have to come up with another way to screw up. Don't forget I'm quite jealous. If I see that Ronald bloke again, I'll probably give him a good thrashing just for looking at you."

"No, you won't." She giggles, and it sounds like a cross between a cry and a laugh. Her body trembles, and I hug her closely, relishing in the most wonderful feeling in the world. Her.

I kiss her forehead, my heart swelling as I add, "You know, if anyone is a white knight in this relationship, it's you."

She laughs into my chest. "I like the sound of that."

"Of course, you do." I tip her chin up to bring her lips to mine, dropping a featherlight kiss to her mouth before whispering, "You've saved me in ways you don't even understand, Trouble."

More tears slide down her cheeks as she replies, "I love you, Sonny."

"I love you too, Trouble."

CHAPTER 41

Tilly

I WAKE TO THE SOUND OF A FAINT BUZZING THAT FEELS LIKE IT'S been going off for ages. Squinting, I glance at the clock to see it's only six a.m. I set my alarm for six fifteen because today is my first day to work. The commute to Harrods Corporate will take me a solid hour, and I'll have to drive back to Mac and Freya's to get ready first. Luckily, my clothes are all pressed and ready to go, so I should be able to get to my new job well before my 9:30 a.m. introductory meeting.

Santino's mobile stops buzzing on the nightstand, and the screen flashes, saying he's missed two calls. I wonder who could be phoning him at this hour? My eyes are drawn to a piece of paper on Santino's empty pillow:

Went out to grab us sustenance because I have no food here, and I want you well-fed for your first day at work. I'll be back before you have to leave.

Love- Sonny

I smile and hold the note to my lips, inhaling it deeply like I can somehow get the essence of him off it. Yesterday was…a lot.

Everything that transpired between Santino and me makes that insane baby shower seem like child's play.

My God…what happened to his mother is awful. And watching a strong, virile man like Santino struggle with that truth, unsure if he'd ever find someone he could truly be open with about that had to be hard on him. And watching him last night as we talked about nothing and drifted off to sleep, I could sense a contentment in him that he's never had before. He's released a part of himself that held him captive for far too long. I count myself lucky to be the person to witness that change.

And then he just dropped all casually that he wants babies with me. Babies! My God. It feels like we've skipped several steps, but the fact that he's looking at a long-term future with me is exactly what I want with him. So, I guess…babies!

I can't wipe the smile off my face when Santino's mobile starts buzzing again. I roll over to see that it's his mother. I hate to answer his mobile, but she's phoned three times, so maybe it's important.

"Hello Carlotta, it's Tilly…sorry, Santino's just popped round to the shop and must have forgotten his mobile."

"Tilly?" Carlotta's voice is unsure. "You're with Santino?"

"Yes, I'm at his flat. Is everything okay?"

"Yes, everything is okay." She hesitates for a second. "He's not been taking my calls this week. I thought maybe trying him in the morning might work."

"Oh, I see." I swallow nervously. "Sorry about last weekend and just…everything. You must think I'm so rude."

"No," Carlotta rushes out. "I'm actually thrilled to discover you're there. Does this mean you two are…okay?"

"We're more than okay," I reply, inhaling deeply. "We had a big talk last night and sorted everything out."

"You did?" she asks, her voice unsure. "So he's talked to you?"

"Yes," I respond hesitantly, unsure if Santino even wants his mother to know I know, but I can't help myself right now. I began my relationship with Carlotta by being honest and not tiptoeing around difficult subjects, and strangely, I can tell she appreciated that about me. "Can I just say thank you for raising such a wonderful son?"

"Um…okay?" She laughs, sounding a bit put off.

My throat tightens. "When I met you, I felt strangely connected to you, and after talking with Santino, I think I know why."

"Why?" she asks breathlessly.

I steel myself to be brave to say this next bit. "I had someone take advantage of me about five years ago, and while I can't begin to understand what you have endured, I will tell you that I fully understand how impossible it would have been for you to give up Santino."

She inhales deeply, her breath trembling through the line as she replies, "It never even crossed my mind. He was something beautiful from something terrible, and I needed him to feel like that pain had a purpose."

My eyes well with tears as I clear my throat to push away my own personal reaction to those words that hit me right in the gut. "I really do love your son."

"And he loves you." She inhales deeply. "I am certain of that now, and that gives me great comfort."

Once we hang up, I exhale a breath I didn't realise I'd been holding. Santino's head suddenly pops around the corner, his eyes wide. "Was that…?"

"Your mother," I finish his sentence. "Sorry but she'd called several times, and I was worried there was an emergency."

"Everything is an emergency to an Italian mother." The bed dips as he sits down beside me and takes my hand in his. "I've been dodging her calls for days."

My eyes blink up at him. "Why?"

"I was nursing a broken heart." He winces slightly. "And my relationship with her is complicated. I know she's a victim, but so am I, in a sense. We both have very different journeys to take with this, and she sometimes loses sight of that and tries to force her strength onto me. She is amazing, but I process things differently."

"You're both amazing." I reach up to stroke his face, his eyes seeming brighter and clearer than I've ever seen them. "Do you feel better now after sharing it with me?"

"God yes," he replies with a laugh. "You know, I dated all those women searching for perfect love and expecting a perfect life to come after. But I don't want that anymore. I want real love with a real life. And I want that with you."

My eyes begin to mist. "I want the same."

CHAPTER 42

Santino

A Few Weeks Later

"Happy three-month anniversary," Tilly says, holding her coffee mug up to me in a cheers at an outdoor restaurant near Harrods' corporate office. "I'm your first official girlfriend that made it past the two-month chump mark. Are you feeling okay? Feet toasty warm still? Do you need a cuddle?"

"I need a lot more than a cuddle." I shoot her a dirty wink, and her cheeks flush.

She glances around nervously. "We're in public, Sonny."

I arch my brows. "It hasn't stopped us in the past."

"I was a wild party girl back then. I'm a properly employed adult now with responsibilities." She sips her coffee daintily. "And I've been crushing it at my new job, I'll have you know."

"I don't doubt that for a second," I drone, glancing down her body from across the table. "And I must say, your professional business attire makes meeting for lunch really fucking difficult." I sip my espresso for strength. "I'm sure all the men in your office have to hide from you all day long."

"What does that mean?" Tilly asks, her blue eyes wide and shocked. She glances down at her ensemble featuring a black pencil skirt, a cream blouse, and heels that I'm definitely going to want wrapped around my hips tonight when she comes over.

"It means you are a walking fantasy, and I think I should start dressing you for work from now on. It'll be baggy joggers and my dirty T-shirts so all the men can get a good whiff of me and kindly fuck off."

"Okay, you have turned into a complete caveman now. Are you happy?" She hits me with a scowl, but I can see gleeful mirth dancing in her eyes. "I half expect you to eat your lunch with your hands when the food arrives."

I respond with a growl, and she giggles shamelessly. *God, I love her.*

"Let's get back to our discussion," I state, setting my mug down.

"What discussion?"

"You moving in with me, of course."

She sighs. "Freya is still pregnant."

"And off bed rest. And you're working full-time and spending most nights at my flat as it is. What difference does it make?"

She chews her lip nervously and gets a serious look on her face. "I want to wait a bit longer."

"Why?" I ask, my brows furrowed in confusion.

Her eyes grow pensive. "Because this is my do-over with my brother. We really grew apart while I was getting sober, and I don't want them to think I'm slagging them off."

I exhale heavily. "Tilly, I understand that, but you eventually have to forgive yourself for things of the past and realise the brilliant person you are today. And we're still going to see Mac and Freya a lot. I've quite enjoyed those Friday night barbecues. We can make that a weekly thing if you like."

"You'd do that?"

"Of course, I would," I reply quickly. Christ, does this woman still not realise I'd do anything for her?

My heart thunders in my chest because I have these moments where I look at Tilly and think my entire life was just marking time until she came into it. I know that's insane and there's loads more to life beyond finding a partner, but with all my baggage, I had no idea how much resentment I was holding on to by not being open about my past. I even told Mac about what happened to my mother one night over a pint. He looked at me with such respect and compassion, I realised I'd been so foolish not to give people the benefit of the doubt all these years.

My past doesn't define me but denying it shackled me in ways I didn't realise. Now, I have peace with it, and I know what I want.

I want Tilly.

I expel a breath and reach out to hold her hand. "I'm not going to pressure you about this. I just want you to know that I'm ready when you are."

She smiles and shakes her head. "See? You're fucking perfect."

CHAPTER 43

Tilly

Six Weeks Later

"**Y**OU GUYS ARE DOING AN EXCELLENT JOB!" FREYA CALLS OUT from her seat on the sofa as Mac and Santino each carry the last of my boxes down the steps. "I'd love to help, but I'm in the middle of gestating a baby rhinoceros, so I've only got another forty weeks to go."

I laugh from the entryway as I hold Jasper in my arms to keep him from scampering out the open door. "Just hold out six more days until Christmas, Freya! Then I will win the due date bet!"

She groans dramatically. "You're an arsehole for picking Christmas. That'll have me well overdue by then, you cunt!"

Mac appears in the doorway. "Pay her no mind. Her language gets saucier with each passing day that wee one doesn't come a knocking."

"He's knocking!" she exclaims loudly. "He's knocking every single one of my organs and my bladder about every four minutes. Which reminds me...I need to use the toilet again. Can someone help me up?"

Mac rushes over to help Freya off the couch, and I school myself not to gawk at her. I didn't think she had any more room to grow a few months ago. Now, she's getting ready to pass her due date and fixing to burst. I fear every time she walks that she's going to tip over.

"Tomorrow, my belly will be so big, you'll have to wipe me."

"With pleasure, Cookie."

"Don't Cookie me," she snaps. "It's patronizing."

Santino comes back in from outside, closing the door quickly behind him and wrapping his arms around my waist for warmth. "What'd I miss?"

"Don't ask," I whisper, watching Freya waddle towards me in her floral muumuu with Mac holding her hand.

Freya lifts disgusted eyes to Santino. "Just look at him…wrapping his arms around her waif-thin waist like it's just a normal Saturday." Freya looks back at Mac. "Remember when you could do that to me? Because I don't. I've been pregnant for so long I'm elderly and have got dementia now."

Mac turns grave eyes to me. "Are you sure you have to move into Santino's flat today, Tilly? It seems like we could really use the help around here. I don't have much practise wiping lady parts. I'm more qualified to do other things down there."

"Don't make sex jokes when I look like this!" Freya cries. "You'll be lucky to ever see my vagina ever again after this baby rhino comes out."

Mac winces, looking like he doesn't even know how to put one foot in front of the other anymore, the poor lad. I feel awful, but I always planned to move out before the baby was born. The last thing Freya and Mac need is me nosing about the house when they're having a quarrel over whose turn it is to do a night feeding. They should have this time to themselves.

And I'm ready for a change. My job at Harrods is going wonderfully. It's quite a commute to work every day from east London, but I don't fancy myself moving west any time soon, and they actually let me work from home a few days a week, so it's really not that much of a bother.

Plus, Santino's been asking me to move in with him ever since we got back together. If I told him I was moving out of Freya and Mac's and into my own flat, he'd probably start another eight-day fight with me. And while we're very good at making up after a quarrel—not fighting is much more desirable. Furthermore, I'm quite certain he's "the one", so why bother taking things slow? I just turned thirty-three two weeks ago. I'm not exactly getting any younger.

Suddenly, there's a dribbling sound that tears my focus from Santino to Freya whose wide eyes snap to mine. "Did I just have a wee in the hallway?"

I glance down at the liquid dripping down her ankles. "I'm no expert, but don't you think that could have been your waters breaking?"

"Holy shit! Baby rhino is coming!" Freya exclaims, her head snapping to Mac. "Phone Belle…phone Allie…phone my mum. Phone your mum. Shit, we should have got another mobile!"

"You phone Belle. I'll phone everyone else once we're at the hospital!" I tell them and turn to Santino, who has a very strange look on his face. Maybe the waters breaking is a bit much for him. Blokes can be such babies.

I run down the hall and grab the hospital suitcase that has been packed for over a month now. I return to find Mac getting Freya into her coat that doesn't button and walking out the door.

"We'll be right behind you," I yell as they make their way to their car.

"After we drop Tilly's stuff off," Santino adds.

I frown up at him. "What do you mean?"

"Tilly, we can't park my car full of valuables in a hospital parking lot. Everything could get stolen."

I point at the car. "But Freya's having the baby."

"She'll barely be checked into the hospital before we're done."

I grumble my annoyance as we hop into Santino's car and he drives the opposite direction of the hospital. "You missed the turn to your flat," I say, pointing at the road we just whizzed by.

"Oh, we have to make a stop," he replies casually.

"What?"

"It'll be a quick stop."

"Santino! Freya is in labour."

"Are you helping Belle with the delivery?"

"No," I harumph and cross my arms over my chest. "But I want to be there the second that bairn is born. Jacob Fergus Logan will not go a day in his life without knowing who his auntie Tilly is."

"Auntie Trouble," Santino corrects.

I side-eye him and grow more and more frustrated the farther we get from his flat. "Santino, seriously, where are we going? I said I'd make calls!"

"You're going to like it."

"I'm going to like to see my nephew when he's born! We don't have time to be dawdling!"

"Jesus, you're bossy."

"Well, if you don't get me to that hospital before he's born, then you and I will be in another eight-day fight."

He frowns and shoots me a proper pout. "Too soon."

"Really? Too soon?" I roll my eyes. "I'm moving into your flat officially, and you still feel upset about our fight that happened ages ago?"

He shoots me a sexy smirk that has my mind going in a very different direction. I shake away that thought and ask him again, "Where are we going?"

"It's a new street art mural that just went up, and apparently, it's on a pay-by-the-day wall, so it will only be up for today. You're going to love it."

"Oh yes, I've seen those pay-by-the-day walls!" I reply, pulling my mobile up to scan through the photographs I've managed to grab. "That's such a cool idea, but it's always a shame they just paint over it to throw something new up."

"Capitalism," Santino huffs.

We park adjacent to the wall, and I rush out, wanting to get a look at this, take my photo, and get back in the car. As I round the corner, my jaw drops.

It's a stunning *Godfather* painting of Marlon Brando as Vito

Corleone with a famous quote beside his lifted finger that says "I'm gonna make her an offer she can't refuse."

"They got it wrong!" I call out over my shoulder, shaking my head in confusion. "They got the quote wrong! Can you believe that? I mean…first of all…it's a him. Vito's godson asks his godfather to help him get a movie part because this producer, a male, rejected him, and Vito says in the movie, 'I'm gonna make him an offer he can't refuse.' But the book said 'I'll make him an offer he can't refuse' so really, if you're going to do something, you should do it properly, you know? How could they screw this up? It's a cult classic! A quick Google would have—"

My voice trails off when I turn around to find Santino watching me with a knowing smile like he is enjoying my little outburst. "I didn't expect Mac and Freya to go into labour today of all days, but I'm afraid I've been planning this for a while, so baby Fergie will just have to share the spotlight."

"Spotlight?" I ask, my face twisting up in confusion.

He gets a peculiar look on his face, and suddenly, he drops down on one knee.

Twitching. My nose is twitching uncontrollably.

His voice is calm and collected when he says, "I commissioned this painting and told them to write it that way because I'm hoping to make you an offer you can't refuse."

My hands cover my mouth in shock as my belly swirls with butterflies. "Okay…um…you do realise this is kind of morbid because this offer concept in the books basically mean death threats. I mean, Vito's offer to the producer includes a horse head. You're not planning to give me a horse head, are you?" My voice ratchets up to a squeaky nervous pitch that I'm pretty sure only dogs can hear.

"No horse heads." With a laugh, Santino reaches into his pocket to pull out a blue velvet box. "Just this."

He opens it to reveal the most stunning, sparkly, round-cut diamond on a gold band I've ever seen. Though, in all honesty, I don't think I've ever seen a diamond I don't like.

"You gave me a replay on life in more ways than one, Trouble.

And I know everything seems to be happening fast between us, but it also feels right. And real. And important. I want a life with you. I want a family with you. I want you as a part of my every day, always." He pauses to pull the ring out of the box, and I blubber really inelegantly. He holds it up and asks, "Will you marry me?"

"Yes!" I cry, tears spilling out my eyes incessantly. "I could never refuse your offer!" I laugh and throw myself into his arms, nearly knocking both of us over in the process.

His chest vibrates with his own delicious amusement as he slips the ring on my finger and kisses me sweetly, passionately, and desperately all at the same time.

As far as second chances went, this one turned out to be not half bad.

CHAPTER 44

Santino

A Few Weeks Later

"**I**'M JUST GOING TO NIP UP TO THIS NEW RECRUIT'S FLAT TO drop off some paperwork, and I'll be right back," I say, stretching out across the centre console of my car to kiss Tilly on the lips.

She grabs my winter coat and holds me tight, tangling her tongue with mine before murmuring, "Well, hurry up because I'm absolutely starving."

I laugh and shake my head. "Why didn't you eat any lunch before we left?"

"Because we're going to sample wedding cakes, and I have a dress to fit into next month." She crosses her arms and starts to pout.

"You don't need to watch what you eat. Ever." I glance down at her body that is perfect in any capacity.

She rolls her eyes. "That's such a man thing to say."

"Well, it's the truth." I inspect Tilly's pensive face. "Are you doing alright? Planning a wedding in only two months is stressful. Plus, your job is keeping you very busy lately. We don't have to rush this."

"Santino," she cuts me off. "That opening next month at The Shard for our wedding reception was a sign that this is exactly what we should be doing! It's where you and I met again for the second time. It's going to be gorgeous! And look, if you want babies before you turn forty and lose all your good looks and get old man wrinkly balls, then a quick wedding is exactly what we need."

My shoulders shake with laughter. "I've got a few years before my balls start to drop, I suspect."

"Right, but if you want more than one baby, then we've got to get the train on the tracks."

I smile warmly over at her. "I think it's best we put in some extra training hours then so we're properly ready for our wedding night."

I lean in and try to kiss her, but she shoves me away, quite roughly actually. "Get your errand run so we can eat! Did you already forget I'm starving?"

I laugh and slip out of the vehicle to make my way up to Zander Williams' flat that the club booked for him. The American arrived here just two days ago, and I've had knots in my stomach ever since.

My light mood darkens the closer I get to his door. It'll be a relief when Tilly and I are married because then I can unload this burden that I've been carrying on my own for months now because of that bloody nondisclosure agreement. A wife can't testify against her husband in the court of law, so revealing this secret and getting some advice will feel like a huge weight has been lifted off my shoulders.

The secret being that Zander Williams may actually be a secret Harris Brother.

Bloody hell.

If only I had never signed that stupid NDA from Zander's mother. Then I would be none the wiser like everyone else. And I couldn't get the contract killed without raising red flags. It's out of my reach. And frankly, I didn't want to kill it. Zander will be a great addition to the team, and considering his mother still won't return any of my calls, it's safe to say I do not trust her.

Fucking hell, there's always drama in this job.

Regardless, today I have paperwork Zander has to sign for his flat leasing agreement. I decided to bring it over personally because I have a feeling that I'm going to look into this young player's eyes and know without a doubt that he's not Vaughn's son and that his mother got it wrong and that all will be right in the world again.

I knock on the door and prepare myself for clarity. For reasonable doubt. For anything that would make the rest of this football season not a living nightmare.

The door opens and a young, twenty-four-year-old who looks dangerously similar to Gareth Harris at that age stares back at me.

My voice is hoarse when I exhale. "Well fuck."

THE END

Preorder SWEEPER, a surprise Harris Brothers novel, coming soon! And if you haven't read Mac and Freya's full-length best friends to lovers story, click here!
https://geni.us/Blindsided

If you're already Mac & Freya fans…click here to read their bonus delivery scene and see Santino and Tilly announce their engagement!
https://bookhip.com/JLVDPAQ

And last but certainly not least, binge the entire Harris Brothers Series, all available in Kindle Unlimited.

Need a spoiler room to talk about all things Replay/Sweeper?
Join me in the Facebook group here!
www.facebook.com/groups/replayspoilerroom

MORE BOOKS BY
AMY DAWS

The London Lovers Series:

Becoming Us: Finley's Story Part 1

A Broken Us: Finley's Story Part 2

London Bound: Leslie's Story

Not the One: Reyna's Story

A London Lovers/Harris Brothers Crossover Novel:

Strength: Vi Harris & Hayden's Story

The Harris Brothers Series:

Challenge: Camden's Story

Endurance: Tanner's Story

Keeper: Booker's Story

Surrender & Dominate: Gareth's Duet

Payback: A Harris Brother Spin-off Standalone

Blindsided: A Harris Brother Spin-off Standalone

Replay: A Harris Brother Spin-off Standalone

The Wait With Me Series:

Wait With Me: A Tire Shop Rom-Com

Next in Line: A Bait Shop Rom-Com

One Moment Please: A Hospital Cafeteria Rom-Com

Take A Number: A Bakery Rom-Com

Pointe of Breaking: A College Dance Standalone by Amy Daws & Sarah J. Pepper

Chasing Hope: A Mother's *True* Story of Loss, Heartbreak, and the Miracle of Hope

For all retailer purchase links, visit:
www.amydawsauthor.com

ACKNOWLEDGEMENTS

Okay, going to get right down to it…every freaking book I write is painful. It takes me ages to get going, then once I do get going, I'm constantly questioning my characters and trying to figure out what their motivations are, their personalities, their quirks. All the things! And because I am a verbal processor, there are a number of people who are subject to the painful experience of writing for me…all of whom I am eternally grateful for and fully expect a restraining order to come through any day now.

Firstly, my PA, Julia: Thank you for the endless brainstorming, reading, and re-reading updates. I lean on you heavily for so much and I'm glad you have a strong back!

Beth, my Canadian critical eye. The words "I need more here" are synonymous with you. I so appreciate your patience and willingness to go back and forth with me until I truly find that "it" factor that I need for my characters big, emotional moments.

Jennifer! I love you! You are the bright light I need in the writing process. I love when we have the same thoughts and finish each other's sentences. You make the writing process fun and I value our friendship so much.

Jane Ashley Converse…you machine. You are that tough, critical beta that sees all. I value your feedback as a friend and as a fellow author. Thank you so much for having the patience to deal with me with every dang book!

Franci: Thank you for not making Freya be pregnant with a baby rhino! Haha. You have such a great eye for detail and as my final reader on the book, your input is so clutch.

My sister-in-law, Megan…our boozy brainstorms are my favourite. Thanks for being such a fun part of my process.

Laura Barnard, Teresa Cole, Lynsey Goddard, Chanah Dickson, and Jade Donaldson…my British and Scottish helpers: Thank you all so much for your valuable insights to make this book as proper as it can be. I know my Americanisms still sneak through, but I appreciate your attempt to beat it out of me! haha.

And to my editing, proofing, and formatting crew of Jenny Sims, Julia Griffis, Lydia Rella, and Stacey Blake...thank you for helping make my book shine.

Finally, to my hubby, my Lolo, and my angel babies in the sky...I am doing this dream job because of all you and I will never stop being grateful for that.

MORE ABOUT THE AUTHOR

Amy Daws is an Amazon Top 13 bestselling author of the Harris Brothers Series and is most known for her punny, footy-playing, British playboys. The Harris Brothers and her London Lovers Series fuel her passion for all things London. When Amy's not writing, she's watching Gilmore Girls or singing karaoke in the living room with her daughter while Daddy awkward-smiles from a distance.

For more of Amy's work, visit: www.amydawsauthor.com or check out the links below.

www.facebook.com/amydawsauthor
www.twitter.com/amydawsauthor
instagram.com/amydawsauthor

Made in the USA
Middletown, DE
27 September 2021